Advance praise for

Deception

"Kris Kennedy pens a vivid tale of romantic adventure and intrigue. The tension leaps off the page and grabs you by the throat—you won't be able to put it down."

—Julia London, *New York Times* bestselling author

"Adventure, passion, danger, and a romance that heats up history—Kris Kennedy's *Deception* will leave you breathless!"

ore, bestselling author

P tive medieval novels

"A daring romance. . . . The love story is both sensual and charming, with flirtatious and sizzling encounters. Kennedy has a way with words, and the witty banter between Jamie and Eva is a great pleasure to read. The history is absorbing and well-woven through this satisfying novel."

—*Publishers Weekly* (starred review)

"Kennedy's Middle Ages is an era of alpha heroes, strong-willed women, excitement, and treachery. The fast pace sets this tale apart from many others. Add to this marvelous characters, exciting escapades and plenty of passion, and you have a highly entertaining read!"

—*RT Book Reviews*

"Kennedy's book is filled with action and rogue knights. There are mercenaries, seductive women, and vivid pictures of a dark time in medieval Britain. . . . Sexy."

—*British Weekly*

"Where to begin with the compliments? . . . The plot is tightly written without a bit of drag anywhere. Every detail is relevant, every conversation is entertaining, every character is well fleshed—from the main characters down to the extras, bar patrons, and such. . . . *Defiant*'s a damned good book, y'all. Find it, read it, fall in love. Then you'll be pining for Kennedy's next one, just like me."

—*All About Romance* (Desert Isle Keeper)

"A nonstop read overflowing with action, to-die-for characters, and plot twists. . . . Lushly detailed. . . . *Defiant* is another of Kennedy's keepers."

—*The Season* (Top Pick)

"Spellbinding. . . . With wonderful characters and sharp, engaging dialogue, Kennedy brings the 13th century alive with a tale full of adventure and romance."

—*Night Owl Reviews* (Top Pick)

"Renowned for her talented writing and careful research, Kris Kennedy sets this amazing story in 1215 and quickly brings alive in vivid detail the tensions of this pre–Magna Carta time of civil war and shifting allegiances. Kennedy has written a passionate and enthralling romance. . . . This is a delicious and satisfying heartfelt read that I just could not put down. A magnificent medieval romance not to be missed!"

—*Fresh Fiction*

"Brimming with historical facts and fictional situations which cleverly entwine to create an enthralling medieval tale. Toss in an irresistible hero plus a lively heroine and the story will keep you totally immersed in every convincing detail."

—*Single Titles*

"I became a fan of Kris Kennedy's as soon as I read the first few sentences of *Defiant*. . . . I didn't want to put it down, and I definitely didn't want it to end."

—*The Good, The Bad, and The Unread*

The Irish Warrior

Winner of the Romance Writers of America Golden Heart Award

"This medieval romance has it all: tenderness, romance, danger, suspense, politics, sex, and a dash of fantasy. . . . The sex is hot and the suspense is breathtaking. This one is impossible to put down."

—*RT Book Reviews*

"Sexy and adventurous, intriguing and tender, *The Irish Warrior* is a page-turner full of high drama and hot, steamy romance!"

—Jill Barnett, *New York Times* bestselling author

"A sexy, taut medieval that'll leave you breathless and wanting more. . . . I devoured every delicious word."

—Roxanne St. Claire, *New York Times* bestselling author

"Medieval romance fans rejoice—Kris Kennedy captures the essence of old Ireland in this engaging, sexy adventure! The rich and imaginative story pulled me in from the start, and an irresistible hero kept me riveted till the end."

—Veronica Wolff, national bestselling author

Also by Kris Kennedy

Defiant

Available from Pocket Books

DECEPTION

Kris Kennedy

POCKET BOOKS
New York London Toronto Sydney New Delhi

Pocket Books
A Division of Simon & Schuster, Inc.
1230 Avenue of the Americas
New York, NY 10020

This book is a work of fiction. Names, characters, places, and incidents either are products of the author's imagination or are used fictitiously. Any resemblance to actual events or locales or persons, living or dead, is entirely coincidental.

First Pocket Books paperback edition August 2012

For information about special discounts for bulk purchases, please contact Simon & Schuster Special Sales at 1-866-506-1949 or business@simonandschuster.com.

The Simon & Schuster Speakers Bureau can bring authors to your live event. For more information or to book an event contact the Simon & Schuster Speakers Bureau at 1-866-248-3049 or visit our website at www.simonspeakers.com.

Designed by Jacquelynne Hudson

Manufactured in the United States of America

10 9 8 7 6 5 4 3 2 1

ISBN 978-1-4391-9591-8
ISBN 978-1-4391-9594-9 (ebook)

For my husband and son, again

Acknowledgments

Abby Zidle, the patient-est and trusting-est editor in the world.

Sylvia, for her generous assistance in helping me learn about silks. In the end, much of the information had to be left out, but that's a failing of my creativity, not her generosity or knowledge.

Noah Grant, who rocked the house on translations and a contact with a Spanish town regarding medieval ice storage.

Vanessa Kelly, friend, author, and critiquer of manuscripts at desperate eleventh hours. Lisa Chaplin and Debbie Macuzza, for beta reading at the drop of a hat. And Rachel Grant, for tireless plotting sessions.

To all the authors, editors, and publishers of the research books I used for this story: you may not know it, but we slept together. Repeatedly.

And finally, many thanks to Gabryyl, for suggesting the hero's name.

Commenda

The name of the [*commenda*] contract is virtually untranslatable, although such loose translations as "sleeping partnership" or "business venture" have sometimes been used . . . no aspect of commercial law has been the subject of so much heated controversy as the origin, legal character, and economic function as the commenda.

—Robert S. Lopez and Irving W. Raymond, *Medieval Trade in the Mediterranean World: Illustrative Documents*

Prologue

Trebizond, 1289

Flames roared. Fat blue claws tore through the walls, splitting them open, then igniting all the hapless things in the room: chests of silk and spices; a coffer filled with papers; the man sprawled, faceup, on the floor.

A few faraway shouts came from the doorway.

"Do you have the receipts?" one man called.

"I do."

"We're leaving him?" the first man shouted.

There was a pause. "He was marked for death. Stay and be burned if you will. For me, I ride to Cosimo."

A moment later, the sound of galloping hooves could barely be detected beneath the hot howling voice of the fire.

The man on the floor opened his eyes and stared into the blue inferno roaring around him.

This was the sort of thing that required vengeance.

He rolled to his feet as the first fiery beam fell.

Five years later, June 1294
Last Fells, England

So it had come to this, after all.

Sophia Darnly had known it would, eventually. It was as inevitable as spring flooding and salted meat in winter. She was tipping over into corruption and vice like a pitcher off the table.

It had only been a matter of time.

There was no shame in making a mistake. There was not even shame in committing the same manner of error a second time, by virtue of being "precipitous" or more inaccurately, "foolish"—they never named it "bold" or "ambitious," for she was a woman, and therefore occupied the same mental construct as all confusing, vaguely frightening notions, such as shipwrecks and comets in the sky and how one stocking always ended up missing in the wash.

No, none of these were the problem.

It was when one found oneself hurrying through the cobbled streets of the rich port town of Last Fells, en route to break into the offices of one of the most venerated moneychangers of all of England, to steal—*retrieve,* she reminded herself firmly—a ledger that could mean the demise of many a powerful man, and perhaps of *her*, it was *then* one began to suspect one was entirely cut out for a life of crime.

It was a sobering realization.

Additionally, as Sophia had been explicitly warned off, and as she was determined this matter would not cause any (more) deaths, that left trickery.

Fortunately, Sophia was very good at trickery.

Or had been.

She was diminished this far, then, to make use of corruption straight on.

It had only been a matter of time.

Your name is unfamiliar but the matters to which you allude are, unfortunately and unwisely, not, Tomas the moneychanger's terse missive had informed her. *I shall ignore the latter and address the former: my business is entirely by referral, Dame Silk, the only ones who make it through my doors are the ones who* can *make it through. Unless you are utterly unlike the tree from which you fell, and therefore full of surprises, it is difficult to imagine how that ever would occur,* it went on in blatant challenge. *My world is a dangerous one, and does not deal kindly with conspiracies. Return to your widowhood and your silk trade. Do not contact me again.*

Or perhaps it had not been a challenge, she reflected.

Never mind. She was here now.

But when neighbors informed you men had shown up at your door whilst you were away, bearing weapons and asking questions, questions that oughtn't be asked, you knew the time had come. When you found your silk warehouse burned to the ground, a threatening note nailed to the tree nearby, demanding the ledger or you would suffer the destruction of your livelihood, a note read through the ashen clouds of smoke still wafting off the warehouse, well, then you knew the time had come to arm yourself.

Thus, the ledger.

A sensible woman would face the truth. A practical woman might even see the benefits. Accept it as a way out from under the drawn-back trebuchet of her unwanted past. Simply give them the ledger.

Sophia had seen herself as *all* of these things. Sensible, reasonable, practical. Above all, law-abiding. She'd aimed at these things the way one aims an arrow.

Unfortunately, she was also angry.

The thought of her trade and livelihood being subsumed so completely, so swiftly, was terrifying. The realization that her will and efforts could be so cheaply commandeered was maddening.

These men who took, these men who plundered, these raptors in their finery, brigands in their brocades, they were worse than a pestilence. These men like her father.

She could be harvested like wheat, or she could pose *some* sort of defense.

Thus, the ledger.

They really shouldn't have pushed her so far.

Furthermore, two hardly counted as a conspiracy, she thought irritably. Tomas Moneychanger, of all men, should know that.

It took a minimum of three.

She gave her tunic another tug down and looked down the street. Time to make Tomas Moneychanger understand she was not a woman to be trifled with, nor ignored, nor set aside like a wooden spoon when the stirring was done.

He ought to have just agreed to meet with her the first three times she wrote.

One could almost say it was *his* fault it had come to this.

She stepped onto the bridge where his shop was located,

and as soon as the guard at its door came into view, she affected a noteworthy—nay, *pathetic*—limp.

When she was close enough, she stumbled directly into the guard, then pushed a stray lock of hair out of her eyes, and aimed a small, pained, apologetic smile up at him.

He stared a moment, blinking, then he slowly smiled back.

The first thing Kier saw was the curve of her neck.

Peering down from the window abovestairs, he could see little else. She stood with her back to the building, conversing quietly with the guard, but she'd lifted the heavy netted hair covering up to let in cool dawn air, revealing the pale curve of her neck.

This neck, it was a beautiful thing.

Surely, that should have been his warning. The trumpet call, the signal fire, letting him know his battle was coming. But it had been too long, too many submerged memories, and after all, it was only a *neck*.

Kier was upstairs when he'd first heard the voices, bent over an unlocked coffer, picking up ledgers for a swift perusal, then laying them back inside, hoping to find the ledger he wanted before Tomas Moneychanger came in, since he would not appreciate Kier going through his locked coffers.

Most moneychangers wouldn't. But then, Tomas was not most moneychangers. He was as close to a merchant prince as one could be without being either a merchant or a prince. What he was was a master with money. He knew who had it, who needed it, and how to make certain the two were united in terms very advantageous to himself. Kings, counts, princes, knights, and merchants, it was Tomas who invested in their risk and recouped large. It was an agreeable reciprocity.

Well, perhaps not quite reciprocal. But exceptionally agreeable.

Kier had no aversion to this. He had no interest in it either. He simply wanted what Tomas had: access and information.

Access to men who had capital to invest and who preferred to operate in the shadowy background. Men who liked to collect things: precious gems, the rarest silks, beautiful women, defaulted princes, and indebted kings. Men who claimed but the weakest fealty to their overlords, and satisfied their vows not with swords but with coin and the letters of credit that moved money from the burning sands of Palestine to the misty barrows of York.

It was an entire landscape, a veritable grammar structure that spoke a single language: power.

Indebted men were a highly lucrative business.

Kier should know.

He'd finished searching the coffer and carefully closed its curved lid, when he'd heard the voices, and lifted his head. It was too early for the hawkers, and even the waterboys could hardly be about yet.

Swiftly and on silent feet, he'd glided to the window, touched the back of his hand to the shutter, and peered down.

Tomas's guard was stationed beside the door, as he'd been when Kier arrived an hour ago. And beside him, the woman with the curving neck. All he could see was a slim, feminine hand draped in a light, rich-looking cloak, gesturing, and the knobbly nosed guard, grinning like a fool and starting to nod.

Whether she meant it or no, she was doing a fine job distracting the guard from his duties. And showing greater finesse than he, Kier admitted. He'd simply started a fight, and when the mayhem broke out, picked the lock and slipped inside.

". . . oh, aye, the Lark's Throat," the guard said in a portentous voice, clearly comfortable in his knowledge of the hell-hole of a tavern down the road. "A fine establishment, that . . ."

Fine if you were a pirate, Kier thought. He took one last glance at the top of the woman's head—she had a comely head, from what he could tell—then turned back inside. There was a ledger to find.

A few moments later, the silence grew loud. The voices had stopped. Relocking the last coffers—he had not found the ledger within any of them—curiosity drove him back to the window. Again, he angled the shutter open an inch and peered down.

The guard was gone. The woman remained. She was tipped forward, crouching before the keyhole and . . . thrusting a pin into it.

He stared.

Surely it was not possible that *two* people were attempting to break into Tomas Moneychanger's office in a single day? Surely not.

But then, he had not *attempted* it.

He must have shifted, for she tilted her head to peer up the side of the building. For a brief moment, her face was visible in the dawning light.

It was as if someone had punched him in the chest. He pulled back inside, stopped breathing, felt his bones crunching.

She.

His battle coming.

He pushed off the wall and went downstairs.

Three

Sophia stayed low as she hurried into the shadowy office, then pushed the door shut behind her.

The heat hit her first. In the summer, closed up all night, the room was like a hot grave, newly dug. She inhaled spirals of dust from the rushes.

In the back stretched a long table, and benches were pushed against the walls, bulky here and there with bags and packs. A door huddled in the back corner, as if trying to go undetected. Stairs to the upper floors.

A single, shuttered window split the back wall. Pale dawn light slithered through the slits, like dozens of narrowed gray eyes. Stripes fell across the edge of the table and the five huge coffers hunkering beneath it. A faint metallic odor hovered in the air, wavering like little wings: *coin.*

Pennies and halfpennies, deniers and soldi, gold florins, the coins of the empires: England, France, Italy, Florence.

She took a step toward the chests. They were huge and heavy with curved lids, banded in iron with large, ornate iron padlocks, two on each.

She arched her brows at the locks.

Two? *Two* iron padlocks apiece?

Hardly sufficient, she thought sternly. What sort of man

puts only two locks on his coffers when they held such riches?

The riches, of course, lay not only in the coin, but the objects within, most especially the Darnly ledger. In it lay a reckoning of the nefarious deeds her wealthy father had done with an untold number of other rich and powerful men.

But of course, the *ledger* told the numbers. In remarkably precise detail. Who had done what, for whom, and how much they had paid.

Its foul accounting lay in one of these coffers. The one with the triple iron banding. She recognized it immediately; it used to belong to her father.

She slowed her breath, creeped toward the coffers and kneeled in front of it, pin out.

It took no time at all to open the padlocks. To push aside the pouches of coins and gems that lay inside, to dig in and close her fingers around the familiar coin-stained ledger with all its dirty secrets. A moment more to shut and lock the coffer. To rise to her feet and turn to the door.

That's when she felt it.

Some energy, aimed at her like an arrow. Like opening a door to an oven, or lifting the last rock from a dam.

Trouble coming.

She froze.

"This was an extremely bad idea," said the trouble.

Four

The soft, dark words came from a few feet away. She turned slowly. Oh, *dark* was not precisely the word. *Dangerous,* that was more the thing.

Shadowed, difficult to see but for outlines.

Motionless. Sitting beside the table, hands crossed over his belly, boots kicked out, hair banded in a queue, sword hanging loosely from his side.

Powerful, intent, with a lean grace and restraint that did not so much create a sense of safety as a sense of being hunted by a predator willing to wait.

Smiling.

She backed up a step, her knees wobbling like cold jelly, ledger clutched to her chest, her fingers gripping her pin, a paltry weapon indeed.

"You, sirrah"—she aimed the pin at him—"who are you and what are you doing there, lurking in the shadows?"

"Are you certain that is the best way to begin this interview?"

It was a low, deep voice, somewhat like a wolf might sound, should wolves speak. Not at all the sort of sound she'd hoped for. She took a cautionary step back on her cold jelly legs, which put her buttocks against the wall.

"My apologies. I was startled."

Silence.

"I did not expect anyone. I thought . . . I thought I was early."

"You are."

"Yes. Of course." She looked around the shadowy room. "We're both early."

"Aye," he said in that lazy, predator rumble. "But I was here first."

She took a step back. That could be either threat or observation. He could be in the midst of a crime, or . . . she had no notion what else might explain his presence. Although sitting lounging on a bench was not precisely desperate criminal behavior.

"There is no use in robbing me, I have naught," she told him fiercely.

"My thanks for the caution."

Something small clicked inside her mind, the way the padlock on the coffer had clicked when she'd picked it open. Nothing was revealed, but a thin beam of some indefinable awareness shot through her.

She slid her bottom across the wall, inching toward the door, in case he turned desperately criminal.

"I had business with Tomas," she announced. Or rather, his coffers.

He inclined his head the smallest inch. "And I thought you came to steal."

"I do not *steal*." Stealing required one to take possession of things that were not rightfully one's own. She had no intention of ever doing such a terrible thing.

Tomas might see the matter differently, though. As might King Edward.

His eyes gleamed at her from the shadows. "I see. You only pick locks and beguile guardsmen."

She glanced at the door, then the coffers. "That . . . this all is aberrant. I generally do not go about picking locks."

"And yet, you do it so well," he said in lazy observation.

She felt his dark regard drift up over her shoulder, to the door, as if assessing how far she would have to run to reach it. "Do you intend to hurt me?" she whispered fiercely.

He paused. "Would you scream?"

"I would."

"Then nay."

Long legs stretched out of the darkness, crossed at the ankles. He seemed very at ease. This was not as reassuring as one would think, given the circumstances. "What has promoted your recent tumble into criminality?" he inquired.

"What has promoted yours?" she replied in a whisper.

"Who is to say I am a criminal?"

She snorted slightly, to communicate disbelief.

He smiled, a lash of white against the darkness of his shadowed face. "Or that 'tis recent?"

The small niggling in her mind scratched a little harder.

He pushed to his feet. "Now, lass, let's have this go easy."

And with that, the doorway to her memory was thrust fully open. The memories washed over her with such force she felt breathless. She actually, madly, took a step *toward* him, saying in a whisper, "Kier?"

But it was a ridiculous question.

There was only one Kier. Only one in the whole world. And he'd gently, surgically extracted her heart five years ago, laid it on the dust, and kicked it over a cliff, then flung himself off after, disappearing from her life as abruptly and dramatically as he'd come in, abandoning her to her criminal father and his criminal cohorts, leaving her behind, alone amid them all.

Five

Kier waited. The transformation occurred, almost precisely as he'd imagined it would.

First she recognized him.

Then all the blood left her face. Then it came rushing back, a miniature tide.

Then she attacked.

Swift as a cat, she came forward and slammed the heels of her hands into his chest so hard he stumbled backward.

The only difference between his imagination and reality was how hard she could hit these days.

"You!" she shouted in a whisper.

"Aye, 'tis I—"

She hit again. "You outlaw!"

He staggered back a step. "I—"

"You betrayed—"

"I—"

"You ruined—"

"Sophi—"

"You left!"

Her eyes were flashing in the darkened office as she pummeled him on the chest and arms. "Outlaw. Robber. Thief.

Bastard." She hissed the litany of whispered accusations, all true but the last. Unfortunately.

"Regards of the day to you as well," he said, righting himself. "Now be quiet."

He closed his hands around her upper arms and pulled her to him. The move was swift, firm, and contained a silent warning only a fool would miss.

Sophia Darnly had never been a fool, and so she stilled. But she also yanked her arms in close, her fists near her chin, and glared at him over the tops of them as if protecting herself. Which made sense.

He looked her over, as well as he could from this close, dark vantage point. He did not like how he'd immediately noticed how slim her arms were, nor how familiar the heat of her was. He did not like how stray wisps of hair lifted beside her slightly parted lips. He did not like how aware he was of the way each breath she took pressed her body into the silk of her gown.

She was staring back, her green eyes an amalgam of emotions: shock and confusion fired through them. But her body was certain; it was angry from the tips of her toes to the strands of dislodged auburn hair trembling beside her face. Her cheeks were flushed almost pink and her tunic lifted with swift, shallow breaths.

"You remember me," he said quietly.

"*Remember?*"

"Good," he murmured.

"Good!" she said, again in a shout, again in a whisper. "*Good?*" She argued very well in whispers. Nothing was lost as the volume went down. In fact, it all began fusing in her eyes. Great, liquid pools of fury skewering him.

He was very glad she did not know how to wield a sword.

"There is naught good in having known you, Kier, nor in being forced to recall you upon occasion, nor in you . . . in you . . ."

She stopped, but Kier presumed she could have gone on indefinitely, enumerating all the things that were not good about Kier. And she'd be correct in every one.

Neither of them spoke. For a ridiculous length of time, considering where they were and what they were doing, considering day was dawning and people were coming, they stood absolutely still for far too long, staring into each other's eyes.

Then Sophia tore free and stumbled away a few steps, ledger held tight to her chest. She stared at him through the hot shadows. "What are you doing here?"

A vast plain of explanation. He said simply, "Business."

"Of course." It was a cold, fierce whisper. "Wherever there are moneymen, so you will find Kier."

"I never claimed to be anything but what I was," he said quietly.

"No, you never did." She took a step away, closer to the door. "I do not know what misfortune has brought us together here, Kier, but 'tis sure to be as misshapen as ever your deeds have been. Go about your dastardly business and leave me to mine."

He took a step forward. "Unfortunately, Sophia, you have become my business."

Stray wisps of hair lifted beside her slightly parted lips. *"I?"*

"You."

"In what way?"

He nodded almost sadly toward the ledger. "Your father's, aye? The Darnly ledger?"

Her face paled. She took another step back. "What do you know of the ledger?"

He gave a soft laugh. What did he *know* of it? The ledger that documented all Judge Roger Darnly's foul deeds and the powerful men with whom he did them? The ledger rumored to contain the most damning details about the wealthiest members of England's noble and merchant classes? The ledger that would mean a man's life, if it was ever found in his possession? Or in hers.

"Lass, who in England does not know of it?" he asked softly. "Or rather, who among the guilty does not?"

"Do not call me lass," she said sharply. "What is your interest in the ledger?"

"One that doesn't concern you," he replied, mentally measuring the distance to the door. She would need five, perhaps six stumbled steps backward to reach its dubious safety. He could reach her in three.

Small spots of pink appeared on her newly pale cheeks. "As I am now holding the ledger, it very much concerns me."

"Sophia, truth, you do not wish to—"

"I very much wish to."

They stared at each other. He stepped forward and held out a hand. "I will take it now."

"No."

His eyes narrowed. "Sophia, I am asking politely—"

"Politely?"

"You do not wish me to begin insisting."

All that did was make her clutch the ledger tighter to her chest and take yet another step backward toward the door.

She was breathing heavily, her chest heaving, hair in glorious disarray all about her face.

"I will give you something you ask for, Kier, aye, when all the rivers in England turn to ice. I will give you a thing you desire when my conscience takes leave of my soul and swine take to the wing. I will give you a thing but to *ruin* you, as you so deftly ruined me."

He let the silence ensue for a moment.

"Then we have a problem, Sophia," he said softly. "I do not think you're going to like how I solve it."

For a moment the wisps of dark hair danced beside her mouth, her green eyes glittered at him; then she turned and bolted for the door.

Six

Sophia flung the door open, past caring if she had to plow through an armed guard to get away from the infinitely more dangerous man inside.

The guard was not there, but another man was. Sophia ran directly into him.

They staggered out into the cobbled street together. Waterboys and other early risers were out now, and every one of them turned to stare at the human explosion hurtling out of Tomas Moneychanger's office.

Sophia struggled to right herself and disentangle herself from the man. Nondescript, with a plain face, plain brown hair, and brown eyes, and of average height, he ought to have been a good deal less frightening than the armed guard she'd expected.

He chilled her like river ice.

His hands closed around her arms, pinching into her skin in a manner entirely unlike the way Kier had held her trapped inside. He looked down and smiled. "Sophia Darnly."

Coldness ripped through her.

"I am Remy the Black. You are a difficult woman to find."

She tried backing up but his grip tightened.

"Did you receive my message?"

She yanked on her arms, but his fingers bit in harder as his gaze dropped to the ledger pressed between their bodies. He smiled faintly.

"I see you did."

"It is not for you," she said in a violent whisper, then rammed her knee up.

He was prepared for such maneuvers and, dropping one of her arms, he twisted to the side, bringing his knees together. When he turned back, he was smiling. He also held a knife in his hand.

She jerked away, but cruel, hard fingers depressed her flesh. Then he glanced over her shoulder. His smile fled.

Kier was coming out the door.

His moment of surprise gave Sophia a bare breath to escape. She took it. She spun away so violently she tripped as she went and twirled down the street, but not before he ripped the ledger out of her arms. He tossed it onto the ground behind him and turned to face Kier, his sword out.

Kier's sword was already drawn and he never stopped walking, simply moved into range and started slicing, hard, violent cuts that drove her assailant back a step, then another.

Sophia skidded across the cobbles as the fight rent the morning air. Steel rang against steel followed by the rasping, bone-chilling slide away. Sunlight began slanting hazily over the rooftops to illuminate the swordplay below.

Shutters slammed open on the second and third floors as people poked their heads out of the windows, forming an audience for the early morning entertainments.

Sophia pulled herself to her knees, then to her feet. The attacker's face was fixed in a grimace as he fought but Kier was impassive, almost blank, as he pushed the man back, step by step, slashing and cutting. The people in the windows were shouting now, cheering and hissing. Someone called the hue and cry.

She started working her way toward Kier. Or rather, toward the ledger sitting just at the outer rim of their battle. She cared nothing for Kier. Nothing whatsoever. It was merely the sensible voice of reason that bid her stay nearer the buildings, nearer Kier, rather than dart forward to grab the ledger.

People were rushing out now from all the buildings along the bridge and the streets on either side, either heeding the hue and cry or excited by the prospect of mayhem so early in the morn.

"Cease, cease!" an elderly woman cried.

Tomas's delinquent sentry suddenly reappeared at the end of the bridge. Sophia's heart sank. He stared in astonishment at the battle, then ran forward, fumbling for his sword. It was caught in his tunic, but even so, he ran straight at Kier.

Kier spun and punched him square in the nose.

Sophia looked at the ledger, then her assailant. Her assailant looked at her, then the ledger. Then he took the opportunity of Kier's distraction to scoop up the ledger and take off running.

Sophia cried out.

Kier immediately spun and started after him, but the Watch, in a fit of cunningly poor timing and uncharacteristic alacrity, appeared at the bottom of the bridge, bearing pikes and blades.

Kier stopped short. Her assailant reached the bottom of the bridge a step before the Watch and whirled around the first corner he came to, into the warren of alleys that bisected the town.

A few of the Watch went after him, but most came directly toward Kier, who was standing in front of Tomas's wide-open front door with his sword out.

Kier backed up three swift steps and stood in front of Sophia, blocking her from view.

"Get out of here," he murmured. "And do not think to go after him."

She thought of nothing else.

Suddenly his hand came back. She felt the press of something soft and bulky into her palm, then his hand squeezed her fingers shut around it.

"Run."

Seven

It took quite a while for Kier to convince the Watch that he had not been breaking into Tomas Moneychanger's office (which he had), that there had not been a woman in attendance (which there had), and that Tomas Moneychanger's guard was not a reliable source of information in any event (which he most certainly was not).

Tomas's guard glared at Kier, but as the guard's version of the truth hinted at a certain dereliction of duty, he did not insist further.

Tomas Moneychanger appeared at that moment, striding up the hump of the bridge, his long tunic swaying around his ankles. He stopped short at the sight: his office door flung wide; the Watch arrayed; the townsfolk congregating in small, excited groups, as if an impromptu fair had erupted outside his office doors.

"What in God's name . . . ?" He scanned further, caught sight of Kier, and shook his head. "Of course. I should have known."

"Why should you think I had anything to do with it, old man?" Kier asked, crossing over.

They clasped hands warmly. "Because 'tis ever how the river runs with you," the moneychanger said, affection and scolding mingled in his tone. "Fast and furious and unpredictable."

Kier grinned. "Which is precisely why you keep stepping into it."

A smile crept across the old man's face. "You pay well."

But then, "old" was relative. Tomas was only a few years older than King Edward, and with a better chance of survival. He had warmth in winter, plentiful food year-round, and he scrupulously avoided armed combat. This generally tended one toward a longer life span. It was partly why Kier had abandoned the path of knighthood. That, and his disdain for self-approving chivalry.

Or chivalry in general.

The Watch quickly disbanded after that. The mess had, after all, originated on Tomas's doorstep, and he was now conversing with one of the accused. So they explained what had transpired, praised Kier for his sense of civic responsibility, and dispersed over the bridge, the backs of their bodies lit by the rising sun.

"Civic responsibility?" Tomas repeated, his voice deep with incredulity.

Kier shrugged. "I was simply standing here."

Tomas snorted, but, after glancing dubiously at his glowering guard, said only, "I presume you came to my offices at the break of dawn to hear my news?"

Kier grinned. "You have news."

Tomas's smile was restrained. "I have news. They have agreed: they wish to meet Lady Mistral's guide and factor, and hear your proposition. On the morrow, at the mayor's annual summer feast."

Kier grinned. "You are a broker of unparalleled talent."

Tomas made a dismissive sound. "I know. You will pay. Now regard, Kieran: I do but get you in the door. Everything after that is up to you. Convince them to hear your case and invest, or no. 'Tis entirely up to you."

Kier was grinning. The first step was always access. Now he had it. And from access flowed opportunity. "I owe you, old man."

The moneychanger shrugged. "I know. You will pay."

"Will I see you at the feast?"

"Fortunately, no. I have other things calling me away."

"Such as?"

"Sleep," the moneychanger said dourly.

Kier laughed. If the ledger were not so important, if Tomas were not so complicit in allowing some of the long-past deeds *recorded* in the ledger, Kier could almost feel bad for having broken into his coffers. Almost.

The lack of chivalric impulses was decidedly helpful in this way.

"Your lodgings?" Tomas inquired briskly. "I will have the invitation delivered there."

"The Spanish Lady, on the Rakke."

Tomas lifted his bushy gray eyebrows. "I know the place." He paused. "Your Lady Mistral lodges her factors expensively."

"She believes in the best for the best," Kier said modestly.

"And your lady? She will be joining us in England soon enough?"

Kier smiled. And so it began. First came the questions: *Who is she? How large a company did you say she owns? And you say she is unwed?*

"Unfortunately, Lady Mistral has been delayed," he said.

"For long?"

For however long as it took to make them come circling, curious and greedy, seeking to woo her, to buy her, to tear the flesh from the bones, the widow from her money.

That is when they would find Kier, waiting for them.

"Mayhap delayed indefinitely." He kept his tone light. "But not to fear; I am empowered to make all arrangements on her behalf."

Tomas nodded. Kier was about to turn away, then hesitated. "One last thing, Tomas. Do you know a man by the name of Remy?"

Tomas pursed his lips. "Why?"

"A passing curiosity."

Tomas looked at him flatly. "Kieran, I have done deals with you for many years now, and never have I seen you with a thing so tepid as 'passing curiosity.'"

He smiled faintly. "Perhaps 'tis more than passing."

"Well, tell me what you know."

"Very little. May go by Remy the Black. Pale man, dark hair, plain-looking. Forgettable."

"And yet, you have not forgotten."

They looked at each other. "No, I have not. I have business with him. He is skilled with a sword."

Tomas's canny gaze slid away, down the street, the direction the black-haired man had run. "Do I wish to know more?"

"I don't know, old man: Do you wish to know anything more?"

Tomas's gaze slid back. "I will see what I can find out for you."

"Again, I owe you."

"Again, you will pay."

Kier clasped his hand one last time and started to turn away, but Tomas's lean hand closed over his forearm and stayed him.

"I hope you have given this careful regard, Kieran," the moneychanger said in a low voice. "These men you hope to lure, the *commenda,* they are a world apart from all others."

"Ah, but careful regard would ruin everything," he said, keeping his tone light, even grinned, but it felt stretched.

Tomas's somber face didn't change. "You do not know these men."

Yes I do.

"They are investors, are they not?"

"They are dangerous. Their leader, Cosimo Endolte, even more so."

Kier shrugged. "As am I. As are you. As are we all, we merchants and tradesmen, are we not? The worst sort. Your counsel is appreciated, old man, but unnecessary. I have been wading though muddy rivers for some long time."

Tomas snorted. "My rouncy is older than you, boy. What I am saying is, if you go swimming here, 'twill be a deed done. No going back."

Well, that was rather the point, wasn't it?

"I do not wish to go back," he said quietly.

"And if you are seeking Cosimo Endolte himself," Tomas added in a dark warning, "then you are more mad than I thought. He is all but invisible, conducting his deals and seeing to his interests via a web of intermediaries and agents that would make a spider proud."

"What makes you think I'm seeking Cosimo Endolte?"

Tomas frowned. "Because I am fairly certain you are more mad than I thought."

Kier laughed.

Tomas scowled. "You are not being careful."

"I am always careful."

"You are never careful."

Kier slowly smiled. "I concede. I am not careful. I am *successful.*"

Tomas's canny gaze stayed steady on him. "I have to assume there was one such time you were not."

His gaze fell to the visible edge of the scar that ran the length of Kier's torso, twisting up the front of his collarbone, over the top of his shoulder, and down his back in a violent, puckered slash of pale white and pink, like a bleeding lightning strike.

Burning columns of oak did that when they fell on a person.

Kier felt his face harden, wood petrifying, stone forming. "I am the wrong man to make assumptions about," he said coldly.

Tomas gave a curt nod. "So be it."

"And you misjudge me if you think this is done without regard. It has long been in my mind, and I know precisely how the matter shall go, from alpha to omega."

Short, sweet, deadly.

"You cannot know such things," Tomas disagreed stubbornly.

Kier refrained from further argument. People won bets and games of chess; they did not win arguments. And here, there was no argument to be had.

Simply cold, hard vengeance about to begin.

Eight

Sophia was filled with so much anger it seemed to be propelling her down the streets, the wind in her sails, her rudder the name of the inn she'd overheard him say to Tomas. The Spanish Lady.

Sophia knew she'd exhausted her admittedly paltry array of options. Retrieving the ledger had been a stopgap at best, and a poor one indeed. And now she was without means, money, plans, or weapons.

But Kier, Kier *was* a weapon.

Oh, the decorations remained, but they lay atop the truth of him the way a sheath cloaked a sword. Handsome in an offhanded, unconscious manner, the way a wolf did not know it had jaws, but used them nonetheless. Charming in a brutally effective way, so much that the creases from his false smiles were carved alongside his wicked, lying mouth.

But the essential thing about Kier was that his waters ran deep. What you saw on the surface was what you saw when you looked into a mirror: you saw what you wished to see and, being pleased, thought you saw what mattered. But all you had seen is what Kier meant for you to see.

It made it easier for him to fool you.

What mattered to her now, though, was that Kier was lethal

at need and utterly determined, and whatever he set out to do he would do ruthlessly well.

Just now, he wanted the ledger.

Just now, Sophia needed "ruthlessly well."

Sooth, a confrontation had been too long in the waiting.

The trek to his lodgings led her down one of the most prosperous streets in all of prosperous Last Fells, the Rakke. It was intersected on either end by the High, a bustling avenue that wound its way down to the docks, and Goldsmith's Lane, which did not.

Deceit had treated him well.

But then, it had a way of doing that for the cold and calculating.

Her father, Roger Darnly, *Judge* Roger Darnly, had discovered that. The opportunities for malfeasance as a judge on the King's Bench were plentiful indeed, and he'd built a veritable kingdom comprising rich men who bought favors and verdicts, and poor men who could not.

It was inevitable that he should come to the attention of Cosimo Endolte and his *commenda,* a loose, shadowy association of wealthy businessmen and noblemen with an entirely new objective: to seek out opportunities in the increasingly profitable trade markets. They were neither bankers nor lenders, per se. They were investors. No longer would they simply respond to markets; they would *create* them.

This meant money. Mountains of it. Rivers of it. Coin and notes of exchange and other goods with commercial value flowed in and out of the *commenda*'s coffers like floodwaters through the Wash, always on the rise.

It also meant influence. All the *commenda* investors were powerful, respected members of their communities—Cosimo himself was one of the king's councilors—but that was an indirect influence. It depended partly on Edward's talking sessions, his parliaments. It depended on knights and barons and others whose interests diverged from the *commenda*'s. No, what Cosimo Endolte and his *commenda* required was a loyal man, someone whose interests aligned perfectly with theirs, who could direct that traffic. Someone both indebted *to* them and a beneficiary *of* them.

Judge Darnly served exceptionally well.

The two, Cosimo and Roger Darnly, had forged a miniature fiefdom of influence and corruption. Darnly was the forecastle, the guard tower of the *commenda*'s money. All suitors had to pass through the gates of his recommendation, and paid dearly for the privilege. Cosimo remained far in the background, never to be seen, his signature unpenned, any connections to his money vague and shifting and unprovable. Judge Darnly stood sentry, a respected king's justice.

As a father, he was less attentive, but had displayed sufficient care to ensure his daughter, Sophia, was never mentioned and rarely seen. He kept her in the dark background of his world. Few knew—or cared—that Darnly had a daughter.

Except one. Except Kier. For Kier was the bridge to the *commenda*.

Dark-eyed, dark-haired, that dark, slow smile, he was like a star that came down to shine in Sophia's dark world. Charming, handsome, and attentive, in the end it was Kier's confidence that drew her into his orbit. That and the way he looked at her. As if *she* were the star in *his* dark world.

But, as with everything in that world, it turned out to be a lie.

Kier's visits on behalf of Cosimo were frequent, brief, and marked by Sophia's fluttering belly and Kier's slow smiles sent from across the room. Soon, they were not sent from across a room, but from the other end of the table in the great hall, as Kier sat on one side of her father, Sophia the other.

He became her father's favorite, a family friend. Soon enough, the smiles were cast from across saddles on afternoon rides, and then from within the wedge of candlelight that lit a chess table at night. Soon, not even chess could keep them apart.

There they were, the young, up-and-coming lieutenant to Cosimo Endolte, and the old, powerful judge, spinning webs of money and corruption.

And there was Sophia, falling in love with a criminal.

Then the bridge had fallen. They'd reached across the chess table, taken things just a little too far, just far enough to break hearts. Soon after, her father left on a trip. "A *devoir*," he always called it, a duty, "a little task owing," he'd say. Kier left too.

Her father came back.

Kier did not.

The fall continued, albeit slowly. Soon, after Judge Darnly was accused openly of selling justice. It was a long year before the trial happened, but the verdict came swiftly on its heels: treason, and a traitor's death. King Edward was finally cracking his jaw on the hard nut of his corrupt officials.

During her last visit to his cold gaol cell, her father bid Sophia run. She was not only a pariah now, but soon, Cosimo would come for her. And the ledger.

"He may have it and choke on it," Sophia had whispered harshly, glancing over her shoulder at the guard.

"Then that will surely be your death." Her father's guttural, coughing whisper had bounced off the stone walls. "He knows you have seen the ledger. He will come for you. Go, girl, and never be found. Start your silk trade anew. There is a small town, Batten Downs. It will serve well. Go there."

That was the last time she saw him.

Sophia, stunned and frightened, did as he said, and ran. She also took the ledger.

The countryside was alight with excitement at the conviction of a judge. But even with the king's conviction of Judge Darnly, nothing connected him to the *commenda* or Cosimo Endolte.

Oh, there were rumors, a plethora of those, but no substantiation. No one who had benefited from *commenda* associations was willing to risk their profits; no one who'd suffered was willing to risk their lives.

Without testimony, there was no proof.

Except for the ledger.

Sophia marched down the prosperous Rakke with her head down, hands fisted at her sides, blown by a determination that made people step out of her way. She hardly noticed, intent on reaching the Spanish Lady before Kier did.

Indeed, it was long past time for a confrontation.

Midway down the block, separated from the surrounding buildings by enormous courtyards both east and west, sat the Spanish Lady. Her impressive stone frontage dominated the block, with a wide central building, easily the width of four shops. It rose four stories high as well, with two low-slung annexes spread out on either side, like wings.

All along the back, stairways laddered up to the inn's private apartments, crisscrossing the green hillside that ringed the village.

She stared up at the multitude of windows.

However was she to discover which was his?

Perhaps if she asked *very* nicely . . .

A rattle on the gates showed the courtyard was locked, so she went through the main door of the inn. She pushed open a silent, oiled door and stepped inside.

She blinked at the sudden darkness, but it wasn't too dark to see a burly, bearded fellow behind the counter, holding a tray of half-eaten food in his hand. He turned toward her.

His practiced gaze slid over her tunic and headdress, all now askew from her various exertions. She was dressed in fine-enough clothes, but they were mussed. And her hair had *strayed* from its constraints. Absent servants, mules, or even a maid, Sophia might easily be tossed back out on the streets.

His doubtful gaze came back up to hers. "Aye?"

It might have been that she hadn't eaten for a day, or perhaps it was due to her morning exertions, but when Innkeep looked at her, a platter of bread and cheese in his hand, she felt suddenly dizzy.

Her knees weakened. She put out a hand on the counter to steady herself.

A look of concern crossed his face. He stepped forward. "What has happened?"

She made a small laugh. "That, Master, would be a remarkably long tale. I await but the locusts." She straightened herself. "I am here for Sir Kier."

She might have laid a torch to him.

His face expanded, then he practically leaped out from behind the counter, platter discarded.

"My lady!" he cried, coming toward her.

My lady?

"Lady Mistral!"

She was speechless with surprise as he led her inside, then vaulted into the back room and reemerged with a cushion he insisted on laying upon a bench he then almost physically forced her to occupy. In quick succession, he offered bread, cheese, ale, wine, a beef broth, a chicken pasty, and his own supper, even now lying in the back room.

She sat back, astonished, and laughed when he finally unraveled to a stop before her. His bearded face was red with exertion.

"Master, never have I been afforded such a greeting."

He bowed. "'Tis your due, my lady. Sir Kier will be overjoyed to see you."

She doubted that. But who, exactly, was this Lady Mistral whom Kier would be "overjoyed" to see?

"After he reported your ship had been delayed, and all hopes were gone of your arrival, he was fair desolate that he must manage your many business endeavors alone. I'm sure of it."

Sophia tried to imagine Kier "desolate." She failed.

"And this your first visit in England. But now, here you are." He beamed at her. "He will be *most* pleased."

It started then, she realized later. The idea, the plan, it all began with that. At the moment, though, she was simply trying to imagine Kier "most pleased" to see her.

Again, it was beyond her.

She got to her feet. "Master, you have overcome me with your hospitality. Kier chose wisely when he chose the Spanish Lady. I will be sure to place this in my travel log."

He was a miniature sun, beaming at her.

"May I see the rooms?" she asked.

"Of course, my lady!" He thrust out his arm for her in a fit of gallantry, then wrenched it back and turned for the door. "The most luxurious in town," he said. "Befitting your station."

Her station.

Daughter of a criminal, on her way to persuade another criminal to take her in on further criminal acts.

"And your servants, my lady?" Innkeep inquired. "I could arrange . . ." His voice trailed off. "And your horses . . . ? Baggage?" he added hopefully.

"Everything, Master, absolutely everything, has been left behind," she told him softly.

He glanced at her and didn't say anything more.

They picked their way through the muddy courtyard to the wooden steps and climbed. At her side, profusions of scented flowers tumbled riotously down the hillside, sharp and lush with glossy green leaves. Butterflies flitted, and the sound of buzzing things purred amid the greenery.

It was all somewhat irritating, to have flowers scent the air and sweet bees buzz while her life was being upended.

They reached the top of the stairs and stepped onto an alcove that abutted the main door, like a small open-aired portico. Cool sea breezes raced up the hill.

The innkeep inserted a huge iron key into the lock and swung the door open. After many reassurances that she required nothing, absolutely nothing, he backed away.

"And, Master?" she called out softly.

He poked his head back in.

"Please, say nothing of my presence to Sir Kier. I wish to be a surprise."

He smiled, touched his fingers to his forehead, and backed out again.

She stood alone in the sudden, rocking silence, a ship that had suddenly docked. She felt pressed on from the inside, her skin tight and hot.

She wandered the room, and finally sat gingerly on the side of the bed, then lowered her hands to the mattress and touched the tight sheet.

Cotton. Soft woven cotton. How restful it would be to lay her head on it.

She moved her hands back to her lap and kept her head off the bed. She had a negotiation to conduct. It would not do to be curled up in his bed when she did so. Particularly not when she'd spent so many restless nights *dreaming* of being in Kier's bed. Of being in his heart, his thoughts, his . . . everything.

He, clearly, had had different dreams.

But this here . . . well, this was a murky matter. The expensive room, the use of his true name, the factor to a shipping widow? How much of it was true? For certes, very little.

Men were so terribly, tragically predictable. In defense, she must be anything but.

She became aware one hand was almost numb from still clutching the pouch Kier had shoved into her hand. She tugged open the laces and shook it out into her palm.

A tiny green gem tumbled out.

She pinched it between trembling fingers and lifted it up in front of her eyes. "God in Heaven," she whispered. It must be worth a thousand pounds.

And still, it was not enough. The men hunting her did not want money. They wanted the ledger.

She bent at the waist until her forehead rested on her knees. As if tipping over had released something, she felt tears press up against her eyes. Hot, stinging knives. How disquieting. And unusual. Everything seemed to want out today.

All she had to do was hold everything in and wait for Kier.

Nine

Kier shut the door to the apartments behind him. Darkness lay over everything, a wide palm of shadow. Through the windows, sea breezes nosed in.

The silence of the empty room spread out before him, and he stepped into its welcome stillness. Time to think, to reflect, to plan.

The list of potential ledger-hunters was long and unsavory. All rich, all well connected, most still engaged in a variety of shadowy deeds that would be exposed if the ones from the past were brought to light. Men with every reason to murder to stop the ledger from being revealed.

When its existence had first been discovered, during the Darnly trial, the king was so enraged he'd threatened to build gallows from York to Dover to punish the malefactors. But it had never been found, and in the subsequent years had slipped from the realm's consciousness, becoming a delicious rumor, more bark than bite. It still had teeth, but someone had to unleash it to do real damage. That meant finding it.

Kier had had his suspicions of where it was hiding, of course. Probing Tomas, who'd once held all Darnly's ill-got gains, confirmed them: Tomas had the ledger.

It seemed so simple at that point.

Then Sophia had showed up. Gone directly for the ledger.

And then, someone else.

He lit candles, then unbuckled his sword belt and dropped it onto the table, a clattering of leather and steel. He yanked off the leather strip binding his hair at the base of his neck and flung his surcoat onto the bed. He unlaced his tunic as he strode toward the cistern set in the far wall.

One beat, two. Breathing slowing, focus moving in, attention narrowing—

Female.

He stopped short.

A female was in his room.

He turned back to the table and began to slide his sword out of the belt now hanging precariously over the edge of the table.

From out of the shadows came her voice, "What are you conniving here, Kier?".

Something rushed through his body like beating wings. He inhaled slowly and turned to peer into the shadows.

She was sitting back in the darkness. Her eyes reflected the candlelight. He started toward her.

She lifted a blade in her hand. "That is far enough."

He appraised the blade. It was rather large. Vicious-looking.

Likewise, Sophia had the devil in her eye, the sort of glint that accompanied righteous anger or, God forbid, a *plan*. Sophia in possession of either of those was an unpredictable creature indeed.

It seemed wisest to placate. For now.

"What do you want, Sophia?" he asked quietly.

"An answer to my question."

"That is not what you want."

She nodded. He knew, because the gleam of her eyes bobbed up and down. "It will serve for a start."

"And if I refuse?"

"You do not want to try me this night, Kier."

He gave a low laugh. "Truly, now, lass, you cannot think—"

"Do. Not. Call me that," she said in a low voice. It shook slightly.

He watched the shadows of her face a moment more, then turned and finished his journey to the cistern at the far wall. Bending, he splashed cool water on his face, then straightened and dragged a linen rag over it. He turned back to the room.

"Let's do away with meaningless conversation, shall we?" he suggested. "How much do you want?"

She got to her feet and came into the main hall. He wished she had not. It was easier to deal with the shadow of Sophia than a well-lit one.

She was still wearing the sun-yellow tunic, but she'd loosened the laces crisscrossing up the curve of her waist. A silver girdle swung low, past her knees, its delicately wrought links shimmering.

She came to the opposite side of the table, leaned forward, and carefully set the emerald he'd given her in the center of the table. Then she lifted an eyebrow at him and passed on, pacing slowly through the room.

"You think I want your jewels, your money?" she asked, taking a slow, considering progress around the room, careful never to come near him. "You think I am like *you*, where every road I travel is a gutter, and every gutter flows down to a sea of coin?"

He sat down and watched her pause to examine a row of gilt-silver goblets sitting on a shelf in the wardrobe against the wall. She touched one and moved on.

"You think I care for naught but coin and its venomous pursuits?" She ran her fingers across a dark blue tapestry that fluttered as she drifted by. "You think I manhandle people, oppress and constrain them against their will, in pursuit of *money*? You think that of me?"

"Truth, Sophie, I think you mad."

She stopped short on the far side of the room.

"And I never mentioned money."

She turned to look at him. "What else should I want from one such as you?" The candlelight barely reached her where she stood. She was rimmed in faint light.

"I do not know, Sophia," he said quietly. "What do you want?"

She settled into a seat down at the end of the table and smiled at him. "The ledger, of course. And you"—she tilted the tip of the blade his direction—"have a plan to that end."

The sudden, inexplicable urge to smile almost overtook him. He shunted it aside and inquired coolly, "Do I?"

"Indeed. This." Without moving her arm, she flicked her wrist, moving the blade tip in a sweep around the room. "All this, here, is your plan. What is all this?"

"Rest assured, something dark and foul," he said, to please her.

The glint of her eyes moved as she examined the room. "All these riches and not a single servant," she mused.

"They are housed belowstairs, at the inn."

Her eyebrows lifted. "An extravagance."

"A worthwhile one. I cannot have people overhearing my foul plans." He smiled.

"Of course not." She smiled back.

And just for a moment, for the briefest hint of a heart-beat, he saw the dimple appear in her cheek. It was gone just as swiftly, a burst of a star pressed into a dark sky, then her mouth flattened again. But even flat, her mouth was a carnal thing: slightly crooked, lower lip more rounded than the top.

He had spent entire mealtimes feasting solely on her mouth in his mind.

"Perhaps I can assist."

Her voice broke through his reverie. He dragged his gaze away from her mouth. "Assis . . . ? Assist? Assist *me*?" He gave a bark of laughter. "You are not serious."

She waved the blade. "Does anything I am doing suggest I am in jest?"

"You most certainly cannot *assist*."

She leaned forward, her voice low, urgent, and coaxing. He did not want to hear her voice do such things as *coax*. "You are planning some manner of trickery, Kier. I know it the way I know you are breathing just now. You could help me. And I could help you."

"You could get killed," he replied flatly.

"I find myself already acquainted with that possibility."

"Perhaps if you did not steal into locked offices?" he suggested.

She narrowed her eyes at him. "Perhaps if *you* did not."

"Ah, but I was *successful*. At the least, I was not attacked on the way out."

She straightened sharply. "That was not my fault. You delayed me."

He laughed softly.

"And let us be clear, Kier," she added in a low voice. "You did not find the ledger. *I* did."

He leaned back and interlaced his fingers, considering her. "Now that is indeed a thing of note, Sophia. You went directly to the very coffer where the ledger was housed. The question is: *How?*"

She leaned forward, the yellow silk pressing atop the dark wood. "How badly do you wish to know?"

He shifted his gaze away, to the dark night outside the

window. Still, from the corner of his eye she glowed at him, yellow silk and burnished hair.

"Are you offering me something, Sophia?" he asked in a slow drawl, but his body was hardening, readying. For a battle, for trickery, for passion, it hardly mattered; Sophia was all those things. He was readying for *her*.

"I am offering you help, Kieran," she replied quietly, rounding his name as no one else did, as no one had for years—*Ciarán*—and in it he heard wild, sea-sprayed lands he'd not seen for half his life. He pushed it away with an almost physical shove.

"No." He shook his head. "Sophia, whether or not you once had some useful knowledge of the ledger, you do no longer."

"And thus, I am of no use to you," she said, her voice cold and brittle.

"None at all," he agreed, ignoring the way he had to force his mouth to form the words. It was like chewing sap.

They stared at each other down the length of the table.

"That is unfortunate, Kier, for I am not leaving." She made an impatient gesture. The blade tip swiped through the air. He watched its wild arc. She was getting careless. Angry. Reckless.

"Perhaps you should set down the blade, Sophia."

Unwisely, she narrowed her eyes at him. "No."

He pushed to his feet. She scrambled up too, so quickly she sent the bench skidding backward. He started down the length of the table. She skirted around the far end.

"We are finished here, Sophia," he announced, coming around after her.

"Kier, you have not considered—"

"I have considered everything. You are of no use to me." She slid up the length on the other side of the table, staying exactly opposite him. "You do not have the ledger. You have no money, no useful knowledge, and furthermore, you have been seen—"

"As have you."

He stopped short. "Pardon?"

"*I* have seen *you*."

He blinked at the veiled . . . *threat*? She was *threatening* him?

Her flushed cheeks reflected candlelight, but her fierce eyes did not waver. "I have seen *you*, Kier," she repeated softly, her breath coming fast. "How much do you think such knowledge would be worth to the men whom you betrayed? To the king?"

"You would not," he said slowly.

She nodded just as slowly. "I most certainly would."

They stared at each other across the table. He waited. And waited. Waited until her arm wavered, lowered the slightest inch. Then he leaped atop the table, grabbed hold of her wrist, and yanked the blade, with her arm attached, halfway across the table to him.

She lay there, chest across the polished tabletop, hair scattered in sprays of dark fire, their mouths inches apart.

"Ever were you my sinking ship, Sophia," he growled.

Her green eyes were fierce and bright. "And ever were you the rocks upon which we crashed."

A knock hammered at the door.

Ten

Kier slid into motion. "Into the back room," he ordered quietly, releasing her.

She glided to the bedchamber without question, turning and looking at him once before stepping into the darkness of the room. She shut the door behind her.

Kier strode to the front door and flung it open.

Four men stood there. Three were armed for battle. Gleaming swords hung at the ready and axes creaked ominously from their belts. They arrayed themselves like spokes on a broken wheel around the hub of a fourth man, a stocky, powerfully built man standing in their center.

"Dragus," he said quietly.

"Kier," the man cried, and thrust out his arms to pull him into a hearty embrace, clapping him on the back in greeting. But Kier knew the maneuver for what it was: a search for weapons, and a reminder of Dragus's power.

Dragus stepped back, his bearded face grinning. "How good to see you."

"I did not expect you." Kier glanced over his shoulder at the armed guards. "Or your companions."

Dragus laughed. "No, I presume not, as you neglected to

inform me where you were lodging. But word travels fast in our circles."

Kier brought his gaze back. "Does it? Why are you here?"

Dragus made a dismissive gesture. "I admit to a certain weakness for oversight, and find it useful to check in on my associates now and again. You are aware of my limitations, Kier. I confess to them all."

They stood a moment; then, as there were no other options beyond shutting the door in his face, Kier stepped back and said, "Come inside."

Dragus ducked his head beneath the low doorway, waving at his men-at-arms on the landing. "Wait here."

Kier directed him to the farthest point of the room, the end of the table beside the window, ostensibly to offer him the wine jug sitting there. But in truth, it was the farthest point from the bedchamber where Sophia lurked, and as such, the safest place he could put Dragus without suggesting they meet out on the landing with his guardsmen.

Silently, he poured Dragus a cup of wine and slid it over. Candlelight glinted off the buckles of Dragus's belt and the green gems inset on his sword hilt as he reached for the cup and took a sip. Dragus made a few compliments about the quality of the wine, which was, indeed, very good.

Then he said briskly, "You do not yet appear to be in possession of the Darnly ledger."

Kier shook his head. "No. Not yet."

Dragus gave a large, false smile. "Well, we could hardly expect anything so soon, could we?"

Kier lifted an eyebrow. "You are early. By several weeks."

"Two," Dragus agreed as his gaze floated over Kier's shoulder. He tapped the pads of his fingers, one by one, against the tabletop as he looked over the room and the wealth displayed on every silken surface and in every gilded edge. He brought his gaze back.

"Have you any scents to follow?"

"A few."

"Care to elaborate?"

"No." Kier paused. "Contrary to what one might expect, I do not run my fastest when chased by hounds."

Dragus waved his hand. "Of course, of course. Proceed in whatever manner seems best to you. That is why I have hired you, is it not?"

"We both know why you hired me," Kier replied evenly.

Dragus smiled. It was not pleasant. But then, one did not deal with Dragus for pleasantries. One dealt with him for the great sums of money available in consequence of such dealings.

"Never fear. I have no wish that you change tactics on account of me, Kier. I know you work best in secret, charming whomsoever crosses your path, with the whole thing ending poorly for them and richly for you." He smiled again.

Kier did not.

Dragus sipped. "Indeed, we worked quite well together once, did we not? We had a tight, lucrative little family: Cosimo and his *commenda,* you the piper, Judge Darnly the portal, and myself the sentry. You really oughtn't have turned on us. But trying to burn you alive . . ." He clucked his tongue. "It seemed excessive even to me, and you well know I tend toward excess."

Another hearty laugh came out of him, but his eyes never left Kier's.

"In the end, though, 'twas your *betrayal* that so angered Cosimo."

"Yes, I see that now," Kier said coldly.

"Do you? Well, well," Dragus murmured, almost consolingly. "It matters naught now, what you realize and what you do not. All those deeds are done."

Not all of them, Kier thought, and his blood started to pump hotter.

On occasion, separated sometimes by years, he experienced moments of such savage fury that it rose up within him like a wall of water, a wave through his body. It would crash over him, bidding large, hot, immediate things: attack, shatter, slash, destroy. Holding its force at bay was an act of will.

But it had been years now. He'd trained himself too well. No more waves, no more fury. Everything had been channeled in pursuit of this one end: revenge. Every thought, every emotion, every sinew and muscle was bent toward his purpose. He was a clepsydra, cold and merciless and methodical, relentlessly counting off the moments until his vengeance could be unleashed.

But just now, a ball of fire rolled through his veins, bidding him to close his fist around Dragus's lying throat. Close and squeeze.

He looked down and saw his hands tightening into fists around nothing, and knew it for what it was: the beginning. The unleashing.

What in God's name had untethered him now, after so many years, loosed such strong emotions at so inopportune a time?

Sophia. His storm at sea.

He loosened his hands and forced air through his nose, down his throat, into his lungs, tempering the burning wave, while Dragus angled his wine cup this way and that, watching glints of light bounce off the encrusted gemstones.

"Alas," Dragus murmured, tipping the cup to his bearded mouth, "I do not understand why I should have been targeted as well."

"Do you not?" Kier asked softly.

Dragus looked at him over the rim. "But what matters that anymore? For now we shall have our revenge, you and I, shall we not?"

Kier knew very well why Cosimo had got rid of Dragus; he

was both a braggart and a murderer. Either one alone might be tolerable, useful even, but together, the combination was too volatile to endure.

If only Cosimo had known he'd ousted an *attempted* murderer . . . ah well. It probably would not have made a difference.

Kier smiled and replied softly. "Yes, now we shall have our revenge." He got to his feet.

Dragus set down his wine and rose as well. "Please, do not let me detain you. I am certain you have other business to attend, a man of your talents." He waved his hand at the room and all its riches. "Other clients, perhaps, who do not know of your history . . ."

"You would not be interested in my business, Dragus. 'Tis legitimate."

Dragus laughed. "You? The piper who converts the unbelievers, then fleeces them for all they are worth? Legitimate?" He laughed again as they crossed the room. "The word is you have a richly prize in your sights, Kier. Lady Mistral, a great shipping widow, you serving as her guide and agent in all matters English."

Kier stopped short, midway across the room. "Who told you that?" he asked coldly.

A beefy, mottled hand waved off the question. "It matters naught. As we have said, word travels swiftly. She must be wealthy indeed, to afford such lodgings for her factor."

"I do not discuss clients."

"Of course not." Dragus stopped at the door. He smiled and reached for the handle. "You have two weeks, Kier. Bring me the ledger and you will become exceedingly rich. And remain among the living."

Eleven

Sophia stood in the bedchamber, ear to the door, her hand on the shelf of a nearby wardrobe, crushing sheaves of parchment underneath, trying to steady herself.

The innkeep bethought her Lady Mistral.

Should she step out into the room, why, this man would think her Lady Mistral too. This rough, sly man who *wanted her ledger.*

This rough, sly, *wealthy* man with whom Kier had arranged some deal to *deliver* her ledger.

She was breathing so fast her head spun. She gripped the shelf tighter, pressing her fingertips white, and stared into the wedge of light seeping into the darkened room.

So this was the moment of decision. Was she to follow Kier's command and leave? Was she to let him retrieve the ledger and hand it over to this brigand?

Was she so weak as to submit simply because Kier had told her no?

Absolutely not.

There was no Lady Mistral. She knew this without a doubt. The entire thing was a ruse, some trickery of Kier's.

But to what end?

The rough, sly man would leave in a moment, leaving Sophia precisely where she had been before he came in, with Kier kicking her out.

Or . . . she could ensure herself a place at this table of deception Kier was laying.

She straightened her body away from the door.

The time for legitimacy had ended, if indeed it had ever been to hand. What more proof did she require? She had been trained in lawlessness by Papa, seen corruption run through the strata of society like veins through a body. It most certainly ran through *her* blood.

Her life was as fated as the next; she realized that now. Attempts to circumvent it, to become something other, something better, were false. *Dieu le veut.*

No more skirting the edges. 'Twas time to dive in.

Her head was roaring as she swept up the sheaves of parchment she'd been crushing under her fingers. Then, like a whirlpool closing shut, everything quieted. She lifted the parchment to her nose and swung the door open.

"Why, Sir Kieran, you were correct," she said in a musing tone, keeping her head down as she stepped into the room. "Donatello indeed seems ready to strike a deal. He is to be in England soon—"

She lifted her head and stopped short.

The men stared at her, silent in shock.

She returned their looks, then she smiled and came into the room, saying softly, "Why, Kieran, you did not tell me I had guests."

SHE never took her eyes off the burly, bearded man, but she felt Kier staring, doing something she'd never seen him do before: hesitate.

It was the smallest pause, the narrowest window of hesitation, barely the length of a heartbeat. In it, he was no doubt debating how best to ruin her.

But the problem with debating was that it made one have to *decide,* and the problem with *deciding* to ruin someone was that it made one hesitate.

And during the hesitation, she, who was simply *hurtling* into ruin, glided past him into the room.

"And this must be Donatello," she said with a smile. "I have heard so much of you, but was not expecting you so soon."

The rough, sly man growled at her with a slash amid his beard that was no doubt some sort of smile. "My lady, I am sorry to disappoint, but I am not Donatello. God's blessing to you"—he bowed low—"I am Dragus of Last Fells, and most pleased to make your acquaintance."

She felt the darkness of Kier move in behind her and started to take a step away from it, but he put a hand on her arm. It closed like a circle of steel.

"My lady," he said in a smooth, tight voice. "Perhaps another time? Dragus is here on other business." He started to turn her away.

She turned sharply and almost stumbled.

Dragus's eyebrows shot up. "But I should like to hear more," he protested, glancing between her and Kier, his look close and examining. "Might you not stay a moment?"

She felt the iron circle of Kier's fingers slowly loosen and fall away.

Dragus immediately stepped forward. "I am honored to be among the first to welcome you to English shores, my lady." He reached for her hand and folded it into his like a feather crushed between rocks. "We have heard so much of you, but we were told you were delayed. Kier would not say. We did not know what to think."

She let him take her hand and lift it to his mouth. The beard was not silken soft. It was wiry and smelled of dinner. "Yes, Sir Kieran often has this effect on people. It is regrettable." She gently retrieved her hand and moved farther into the room, her face curved into a smile. "But I am desolate you were made uncomfortable, sir."

Dragus turned with her. "I was unable to be disappointed, as I was not aware you were coming, my lady." In the candlelight, his gaze dropped momentarily to trace the outline of the bodice of her gown. "But I am adequately recompensed in any event."

She reached the end of the table, Dragus a step behind. "I do not make my guests uncomfortable, and you are my guest while you are in my lodgings, modest though they may be." She waved disparagingly at the rich trappings of the room. "You need not hunker by this back table and drink the poor wine." She waved her hand at Kier without looking over. "Sir Kieran, bring the good wine."

Like a dark cloud, he seemed to rise up behind her, while Dragus grinned, first at Kier, then at her.

"My lady, we were just discussing—"

"I know what you were discussing," she said in a voice that sounded precisely like what he might expect from a wealthy, widowed merchant princess of the south: languid, warm, slightly carnal. "You were discussing *me*."

Dragus looked surprised, whether by her forthrightness or her accuracy. "That we were, my lady." Then he tossed a vaguely cunning look at Kier, and his bearded mouth broke into a grin. "I admit to curiosity on how so great a lady came to know dangerous Kier, though."

"Is he dangerous?" she asked, her voice rounded with innocent surprise. She turned to look at Kier. "I have not found him so formidable."

Dragus threw back his head and laughed. Kier's mouth was a slit of smile tightened around the teeth he was baring. Fury sheathed in flesh.

She kept her gaze on Kier as she said to Dragus, "I will tell you a story. Once, Kier had a thing I desired greatly, a small, middling thing, but although it was within his power to give it, he refused."

Their gazes held while Dragus murmured how unfair this was—what had she wanted, after all, perhaps a ruby to match her lips, or a florin to match her hair?—but whatever it was, it had been terribly ungallant of Kier to withhold it.

"Oh, do not worry over me," she said softly, their gazes still locked. "I took the thing anyway. I fear Kier has never forgiven me, so we continue to have dealings, he and I. Perhaps he is hoping to make it up. Perhaps he thinks, one day, he will get the better of *me*. But that will never, ever be."

Silence.

Kier's eyes were locked on hers. He looked rather like a large wolf, absolutely still, following its prey with his eyes, waiting for the perfect moment to pounce.

Then he stepped forward.

"Please forgive my lady, Dragus. The night is late, and she is exceptionally weary," he said, and this time, she could not escape the hand he closed around her arm like a band of steel.

Twelve

Kier locked the door after Dragus and turned back to the room. Sophia stood beside the table, her fingers lightly touching its surface, her lips parted, her yellow tunic like a shaft of sunlight in the candlelit room. He'd be able to see her from a thousand miles away.

"Happy?" he asked in a low voice.

She shook her head impatiently. "I am not happy, Kier. I am angry. And determined. That ledger is mine. I must have it back."

"Tell me why," he said quietly.

She rested her fingertips on the table, as if she were holding on, to not be blown away. "I received a message."

"What sort of message?"

"The sort that is delivered by men bearing weapons." Something uncomfortable jabbed inside his chest. "It made the matter clear: if I wish to continue in trade, and not be revealed as Sophia Darnly, daughter of a traitor, I am to deliver the ledger. I was not home when it arrived," she went on, and the sharpness receded. "But I received the message nonetheless. They know who I am, and they want the ledger."

"And?"

"And . . . I came to retrieve the ledger."

"For them?"

She shook her head. Her hair caught candlelight and shone, but her eyelids were lowered, so he could not see her eyes. "No, never for them."

Jésu, how he had once ached for her. Her body, her smile, her spirit. She was bold. Intrepid and clever, with the sort of cony-catching skills a merchant ought *not* have, but when one did have them, it made that merchant formidable indeed. Sophia could have attempted anything and been a success: merchant, trickster. Wife.

But that was all in the past. And now, her boldness might be the death of her.

"That was not wise, Sophia," he said quietly. "You should go home."

"I have no home. They burned it down."

"They burned it *down*—"

"And I have already attempted running and hiding," she interrupted firmly. "So, please, do not think to suggest that next. After Papa was hanged, I built my entire life in such a way. For years, no one knew who I was, not my clients, not even my husband knew I was Sophia Darnly, daughter of a traitor."

He fixed on the most trivial of matters. "Husband?"

She hesitated, then nodded. "I was once wed."

"Was?"

"His name was Richard. He died, a year past." She rubbed the fingers of one hand back and forth across the palm of the other, as if wiping off a smudge.

She was lying.

Or at least, not being entirely truthful. Something was amiss in her bright, averted eyes.

"But why did they come to *you*, Sophia?" he asked quietly. "All the rumors were that Tomas Moneychanger had your father's ledger in his keeping, the same way he had held all of your father's money for so many years."

Her chin tilted up. "Tomas Moneychanger did not have the ledger, until I gave it to him."

He blinked. "Until you . . . what?"

She sighed.

"For years after Papa's arrest, I held on to the ledger, locked up in a box. Almost forgotten, but not quite. Then one day I found my husband with it out on a table, staring down at it. He must have been looking for old records, and taken it from a chest I had always kept locked. I almost died of shame and fear. 'What are you doing?' I cried, and wrenched it out of his hands." She blew out a breath through her nostrils, still looking down at her hands. "I think I frightened a year off his life. The way he stared at me . . ." She shook her head. "Of course I explained then, about my father, the truth of who I was."

He felt a stab of something sharp in his chest. "What did he do?"

She gave a little shrug, looked away. "As he ever had done; very little. Months later, when next he left on a trip—'twas his last; he died on that journey, an attack by vagrants—I took the ledger to Tomas Moneychanger."

"Why then? Why not before?"

She shook her head. "I am not certain." Perhaps sensing the inadequacy of the reply, she shook her head again. "In truth, Kier, I don't know why. Just a feeling that it—*I*—wasn't safe anymore."

"Why not make use of it?" he demanded. The damage she could have wrought, the lives she could have ruined, the money she could have made . . .

"What use? What could one such as I have done, against men as powerful as they? I'd hidden, or so I thought. I was safe, or so I thought." She squeezed her fingers together and swung her gaze back to his. "I was frightened."

"Very wise of you. You ought to be frightened now."

She nodded. "Indeed, I am. But I will no longer make my decisions based upon that flimsy foundation."

He eyed her a moment, then pointed out quietly, "Frightened or no', you did not destroy it when you had the chance."

"No," she agreed softly. "I did not. Papa said without the ledger, I was as good as dead. But I think, somewhere inside, I hoped it might serve a purpose. That I might find the courage to make it so."

Kier had a very specific purpose in mind; bait was the best way to flush out your prey. But Sophia's purpose . . . ?

She shook her head. "Tomas Moneychanger used to manage all my father's ill-got gains. I thought this should be his burden as well. I stole into his office one night and saw my father's coffer—I recognized it well. So I laid a message atop the ledger, and a huge rock holding the whole thing down, right in the center of his desk."

Face downturned, she gave a little smile. He could only see the rounded tops of her cheekbones. "I have oft imagined his face when he came in that morning. My note said to place the ledger wherever he held the rest of Papa's ill-gotten gains."

His eyebrow arched up. "Your father had money?"

"Piles and piles of it." She ran her fingers down the side of her neck. "When I opened the coffer, the ledger was sitting atop a cache of gold and silver coins."

"You didn't take any of it."

She shook her head violently. "I do not want any of it. And in any event, it will not save me. These men do not want money, Kier. They want the ledger."

And you, he thought. *They want you.*

"And me." She echoed his thought aloud. She looked up and

swallowed. "Kier, I am caught betwixt Scylla and Charybdis, and I am sailing straight through. You cannot stop me. You can either help me or step out of my way."

Darts of energy seemed to come off her. In the candlelight, with her yellow bodice and auburn hair and green eyes, she fairly glowed at him.

Kier looked at the curving body he'd dreamed of for five years, five burned, broken years. There was nothing left of caring in him, naught of concern or tenderness. He was a husk, pecked clean of everything but revenge. But he was a risk taker at the bottom of his all but empty heart, and Sophia had ever been his greatest risk. Her dark green eyes reminded him of the sea caves of Italy, her breath of waves under a sailing ship. And she had been very, very good with Dragus. Kier could make use of very, very good.

She was in danger.

"Come here," he said quietly.

The air in the room felt skinned; sensitive, shudderingly responsive to anything that moved through it. As Sophia came toward him, the room *became* Sophia moving toward him: the rustle of her gown, the soft strike of her leather slippers on the floor, the darts of candlelight off the silken threads of her gown.

She stopped a foot away.

"Closer."

She lifted her chin and took a step closer.

He put his hands on her elbows and pulled her the rest of the way to him, then bent to put his mouth by her ear. "You are Lady Mistral, a shipping widow from the south of France."

Her breath guttered out in a broken, unsteady exhale.

His hands tightened on her arms. "I am your guide, your contact, and your entrée into the ranks of English money."

The side of her head brushed against his; she was nodding.

"You are in shipping," he went on, murmuring. "Luxury goods, but hoping to find clients among the wealthy English merchants. You are here in England, your first trip. Construct whatever romance you will about your life, but be sure it involves princes and kings and a great deal of money."

She kept nodding, her head tipped down, absorbing the information like water.

"You are about to become financially insolvent if you do not secure some lucrative deals with wealthy clients who wish to transport large shipments using Mistral Company ships or, perhaps, be purchased outright by an intrepid investor. In consequence of this pressing need for customers, you are not inclined to be overly curious about what is being shipped."

More nodding.

"Tomorrow, there is an engagement at the mayor's. We have been invited."

She nodded.

"Many wealthy men will be in attendance. We wish to acquire their interest, to make them begin thinking about the potential of Mistral Company, and then, to begin dreaming. Other invitations will flow in soon after. Wealthy men who want a closer look at the vulnerable widow of Mistral Company. One must be from Edgard d'Aumercy, Lord Noil. Do you understand?"

She tipped her face up slightly, met his eyes. "It seems simple enough. You have a false company, and you wish to make the man or men who hurt you invest in it, and suffer greatly by their acquaintance with you."

He smiled faintly. "That is an adequate understanding."

Stray strands of her hair tickled his chin and neck as the salty evening breeze drifted through the room.

"You are under my direction. You will do as I say, when I say it, for how long I say it."

Another nod.

"I am in earnest, Sophia."

"I am well aware of that, Kier."

Her eyes seemed guileless enough, her words sincere enough, if filled with anger. But Sophia *knowing* and Sophia *doing* could be vastly different matters. So he put his fingertips under her jaw and lifted it. A small gasp swept past her lips. Her bright eyes were very close to his.

"Listen well, Sophia. The past is gone. I am for retribution. This is vengeance. It involves money and very dangerous men. If they think for one moment you have misused them, they will circle you like the jackals they are. If *I* think you have misused me . . ." He let his breath linger by her ear, his words slide away into the air, then he held his body against hers like a second skin, and whispered, "I will destroy you."

He slid his palm up her waist to rest just below her breast, and felt her tremble from her shoulders down to the hips under his hands, the curving waist only an inch from his shaft, which was hardening even at this touch.

"So inform me now, *bella*, for after tonight, there will be no turning back. Is this too much for you?"

She exhaled a soft breath of air. His hand followed her body as her lungs compressed. "Nothing will ever be too much for me again, Kier. I cannot afford the luxury."

"Good," he said. "I am glad to hear it."

He dropped his hand and turned away, but Sophia reached out, touching his arm. He looked at it, then slid his gaze up to hers.

"Only an arrogance as massive as yours would think it could destroy me, Kier." She was shaking with anger. "I have already been destroyed. This is me, destroyed." She banged her chest with the heel of her hand, her voice shaking. "Perhaps you do not recall, but *I do*. Mayhap you do not remem—"

His hand flashed out and she stuttered to a stop as he cupped the nape of her neck and pulled her to him, up against his chest. He pressed his face against the side of her hot neck.

"I remember you."

The stunning, hot shock of it ripped through Sophia's body with such force that her knees almost buckled. She flung her head away, to the side, unintentionally presenting her neck to his mouth.

His lips lingered just above her skin as he breathed on her for one breath, two, three. Against her belly, she felt his manhood stir.

He dropped his hand and turned to the door.

"Now what?" she said, aghast to find her voice barely above a whisper.

He swung the door open. "Now, sleep."

"I have no bed."

"The bed is Mistral's." He shut the door after him.

EVENTUALLY, at some point late that night, Sophia lay down on the bed, occupying approximately ten inches of space at the edge of it, and occupied her sleepless hours with thought.

Kier had said "vengeance." He meant to lure men who had wronged him into investing large amounts of coin and gems into a company that did not exist, then make off with their money, leaving nothing in his wake but ruination. How like him.

But Sophia was not without plans of her own. And if Kier thought for even a moment that she could be toyed with, set aside, upended, or *destroyed,* he had a hard lesson coming his way.

Sophia was no longer a simple matter.

She rolled over and focused her mind on how to appear to be a merchant widow tottering on the edge of financial ruin.

She smiled at the ceiling beams as moonshine washed the room.

Why, that would not be difficult at all. Who better to play the part of a bankrupt merchant widow than a bankrupt merchant widow? It was almost as if God had arranged this for her.

Dieu le veut.

The important thing, Sophia decided sensibly, was to ensure she knew enough about the deception that was Mistral Company.

And to ensure a plethora of gowns.

So she thought about gowns and mayors and merchant widows, and did not, not for any *appreciable* length of time, think about Kier or his wrecked eyes or the way he'd sounded when he rasped in her ear that *he remembered her.*

Heat whisked in a sparkling whirl down her body. She did not think about the whirling either.

But thinking was a choice; dreaming was not. And she dreamed of him. Of his heat. Of his eyes. As she had every night for the last five years.

KIER stalked the darkened port town streets, safe in the steel blades covering his body and the impenetrable, chilling look he cast upon anyone who came near.

When he returned, the moon was setting, and its low light spread like a haze over the stairs and green hillside. He did not go inside the apartments, but threw his cape across a section of the planked portico outside and lay down.

Then he did as he did whenever the sun went down and the quiet came for him: he planned his revenge.

With Sophia.

He tried to ignore that last, but it would not be ignored. He threw his arm across his face to try and block it out. On ships or in tricks, women were naught but ruin. And in matters of the heart, the young, foolish, untamed heart, they were branding irons.

Fortunately, Kier had been burned straight through five years ago. And not even Sophia could touch him now. That was reassuring. He lowered his arm.

The dark tumble of greenery behind him was fragrant and still. Interlacing his fingers over his stomach, he stared up into the moonshine and ignored the fact that he could hear Sophia breathing through the bedchamber window that overlooked the portico.

Neither of them had spoken of what was to come. Of what would occur once they'd retrieved the ledger, both of them wanting it for their own purposes.

He knew Sophia would try to steal it.

Kier knew he would stop her.

Revenge was a dish that took time to assemble. One must have the most excellent ingredients, and Mistral Company was unsurpassed. A widow with a trove of riches and no one to watch over her. Just rich enough, just vulnerable enough. Just enough of everything to make the men who'd ruined him tip forward to get a closer look.

Then Kier would kick them in the back of the head and listen to their screams as they fell into the abyss he had devised, just for them.

If Sophia were in the way, she would go tumbling in with all the rest.

He threw his bent elbow over his eyes again and ignored everything.

But still, he dreamed.

Thirteen

Sophia awoke with two firm convictions: she needed to know more about Mistral Company, and she needed gowns. It was simply a matter of which should come first.

She stood in the great hall of the apartment, peering at the huge oaken coffers scattered about the room, then down at her body.

Account books, or gowns?

She went to find Kier.

"Kier," she called out softly as she pushed open the door that led to the small outdoor portico, where he had slept last night.

She stopped short. Her heart almost stopped beating.

He was half-dressed, wearing only breeches. His shirt was off and he was engaged in some sort of physical exertion that made her knees feel watery.

His body was stretched out low over the ground, like a plank. He held himself up on the balls of his feet and one hand. The other was tucked in the small of his back as he lowered himself on his hand, very slowly, until the tip of his nose touched the earth.

Then, just as slowly, he unbent his elbow and pushed his body back up again.

She made a gasping, breathy sort of sound.

Birds were plentiful amid the greenery of the old Roman

vineyard entangled on the hillside, and they sang riotously in the morning air. Sounds from the town and quay below floated up too, shouts announcing new wine, someone calling for additional rope, squawking chickens. Amid all this, the sound Sophia had made was such a *small* sound. Likely, Kier had not even noticed.

Without turning his head, he said, "What is it, Sophia?" He lowered his body down again.

She yanked her jaw shut. "I was . . . I thought to inquire . . ."

His hair, untethered, fell across his cheek as he turned to look up at her, one palm still overturned at the small of his back. He was covered in a magnificent sheen of sweat.

The perspiration covering her was not magnificent. It was hot and uncomfortable, but he, he looked like a Greek statue in the rain. His arms and back were contours of sculpted muscle. And his back . . . *Good God.*

She took a step back in horror. The valley of his spine and planes of his lower back were satiny smooth, but across his shoulder blade and like a brand over the ridge of his shoulder, an entire swath of flesh was burned, scarred, puckered, searing white, folding back on itself like jagged teeth marks.

"Sophia?" he said curtly.

She tore her gaze up. "I was . . . perhaps . . . wondering . . . I mean to say . . ." She was babbling. Had she ever babbled before? "Your back—"

He pushed up off his hands and leaped lightly to his feet, and yanked a tunic off the bench behind him. "You are here to discuss my back?"

She snapped her gaze away. "Of course not."

"Then, what?"

His rough-spun breeches hung loosely around his hips, draping down on one side, so she saw the flat bone of his hip. The drawstring dangled loosely before his . . .

"The books," she managed to say. She might have squeaked it.

He jammed the tunic down over his head, covering his chest and ridged stomach. She tore her gaze up. His sweat-damped head came out the top and the gaze he pinned on her was grim.

"What books?"

He hadn't pulled a blade over his face yet today, and it was rough with facial hair. His tousled hair fell against his jawline and neck in dark, damp spikes. His breath came slightly fast. He looked like a soldier coming hard out of battle, although perhaps that was due more to the merciless look in his eyes.

"What books, Sophia?" he asked slowly, in a tone of great patience.

"Mistral Company books," she explained weakly. "I think I should see them."

"No."

This pulled her attention from his merciless body and eyes. "But, Kier, I must."

"No."

"If I am to affect a pretense such as Mistral, surely I must know what to say."

He grabbed a linen rag off the bench. "I will be with you every step, Sophia. You will have no need to say much at all. That is my task; I am your factor. You are to appear handsome and rich and vulnerable."

"Yes, but—"

"No books."

He swiped over his head with the linen rag, then peered up at her from beneath. It made him look wild and rough-hewn and extremely dangerous.

"Anything else?"

She turned and went back inside. She would figure out the gowns herself.

Fourteen

Kier stood in the hall of the apartments, staring at the closed bedchamber door. It had been closed for hours. From inside came a faint but incessant silken rustling. She had been rustling for an extremely long time.

"You are aware we have an engagement?" he finally said, his tone one of grim warning.

"Oh?" came her muffled voice from inside. "With whom?"

He regarded the door dourly.

"Oh, yes!" her bright voice rang out. "With the men you are going to ruin. How silly of me."

He looked out the window for perhaps the thirtieth time. The sun was actually westering. *Westering.* Sunset poured down the streets of the town, arcing over the tall buildings and streaming between them like long yellow fingers. He closed his eyes, said a brief prayer, then opened them again.

The door was still shut.

Prayer: as ineffective as ever.

"I am coming in," he warned grimly, reaching for the handle.

The door was flung open. Sophia stood there, lit from the hot golden glow behind her. "Kier, you display an alarming lack of patience."

She turned back into the room.

He stared at the curve of her spine. Patience. Years of rebuilding his burned body and scarred mind, more years spent planning his revenge, moderating every impulse to hit and strike too soon, subverting every urge to maim and destroy, honing his patience to a steel-edged weapon, and she called him impatient.

He dropped his head and glared at her shoulder blades as he followed her into the room.

"What are we waiting on?" he asked shortly, looking about for some clue to indicate what task Sophia had spent the last five rustling hours engaged in.

She waved her hand at him and returned to the small table set against the wall. She lifted one hand slightly in the air and began tugging at something dangling from it. A thread.

"What is that?" he asked sternly, striding over and reaching for her hand. He held it up and examined it.

"You have a great deal to learn about women, Kier. That is my hand." She took it back.

He closed his fingers around her wrist. "What is the problem?" He peered harder. "'Tis not sewn properly."

"You are remarkably observant. I am hard at work on the matter."

He dropped her hand. "We are waiting on a sleeve?"

"We are waiting on a great shipping widow, Kier," she said patiently, "who must be assembled somewhat like a pear tart. Surely I would not travel without at least a few rich tunics to hand?"

He looked her over as she bent back to stitching. She wore a midnight blue surcoat that was slashed down the sides in dramatic fashion, revealing the pale rose chemise of the night before. Dark blue, fat silk ribbons crisscrossed up the sides of the thin outer tunic, tugging in her waist and creating a bold, formfitting design. The height of fashion.

He squinted at the ensemble. "What is that?"

She waved at the wall behind her, her attention on her unsewn sleeve. "There was a tapestry hanging there. It was finely stitched and well woven, but I must say, rather threadbare."

He glanced at the wall. It was bare. He looked back down. Her gown did have suspicious overtones of tapestry about it.

It was covered with pale, shimmering silver and multihued threads, like constellations against a dark blue sky. Out of context as it was, no one would think to identify the outlines as that of hart and hare and hunter, bounding through the woods in a merry chase. She wore the same silver girdle of yesterday, but it looked entirely different with this landscape as backdrop, joining in a low vee over her belly, draping in a long tail of silver past her knees. Her hair, caught in its silver netting, burned dark russet-gold in the sunset light pouring through the window. She looked like a midnight sky set aflame, gleaming and winking at him.

"I see," was all he said.

She looked up at him and found him staring. Pointedly. She lifted her brows. Pointedly.

He lifted his in reply. "Give it to me."

Her brow furrowed.

"The needle. Give me the needle."

She drew back, then turned her head slightly away to squint at him from an angle in complete silence. He'd rendered her speechless.

He must demand household items more often.

He waved his hand at the needle. "You have no maid and sleeves that need stitching. I will do it."

A smile edged up the corners of her mouth. "Kier. You stitch?"

"If it has to do with a woman and a gown, I do it."

"How amusing," she murmured. "And useful. For you."

He thrust out his hand. "The needle, Sophia."

She extended it. Squeezed between her slim fingerpads, it glinted in the sunlight. A long blue thread trailed from its eye.

He grabbed a bench, dragged it beside, and bent to his work.

The rose sleeve of her chemise lay over the back of her hand, draping as far as mid-finger. He fumbled with the needle for a while. It was slippery and narrow, difficult to get callused fingers around.

Finally, fixing it firmly between forefinger and thumb like a little silver splinter, he regarded her hand with grave misgivings. "Now?"

He felt her smile. "Just dig in."

"The sleeves hang halfway to your knees. What, precisely, requires stitching?"

She sighed. "The chemise, Kier, the undertunic. Not the tippets." She tipped down to peer into his eyes. "Have you never undressed a woman before?"

"Never one as talkative as you," he grumbled.

She straightened. "You are not undressing a talkative woman. You are stitching her up. An entirely different matter."

"That remains to be seen." He bent to the sleeve with grim determination. "How in God's name . . . ?" he muttered, poking at the folds.

"Tuck it so," she instructed, bending to see what he was doing.

"God's blood, I'm going to slay you," he grumbled, slowly piercing the folded fabric.

"It will be in pursuit of a worthy cause: fashion," she reflected.

"I shall display the bloody stump of your arm on the town walls," he muttered, pulling the thread through. It seemed to be inordinately long.

She nodded soberly. "A warning to all women: never let a man near your gowns."

He laughed, his eyes on the sleeve.

"Perhaps you can think of it as a battlefield wound," she suggested brightly. "My tunic sleeve has been grievously wounded."

"I am no soldier."

"Then view it more as the aftermath of a tavern brawl," she suggested brightly.

"What do you know of such things?" She shifted and he gave a sort of hiss. "Be still," he muttered. "I am in surgery here."

She stilled obediently. "My husband had a few."

"A few what?"

"Fights. He did not fare well."

"Then he ought not to have engaged in them."

"That is entirely what I suggested. But Richard, well, he was red-haired and left-handed and . . . he had a temper."

"A man with a temper ought to know how to fight."

The gruff retort brought her head down. He felt her peering at the top of his head with the sort of patient regard one used with children or dolts. "What a fascinating insight, Kier."

He cast his eyes up to hers. She nodded. "Truly fascinating."

He bent back to her sleeve.

"In any event, that was not his strength. He was an accountant at heart. Better with a stylus than a sword, but no merchant, in the end. The business faltered. In truth, I was greatly surprised that he ventured out on the missions for the silks at all. But he did it, once traveling as far as Trebizond to meet shipments directly."

Kier felt a surge of savage satisfaction that her husband had been gone for long periods of time. Which was ridiculous, as firstly, the man was dead, and secondly, Kier did not care.

"Do you miss him?" he asked for no earthly reason.

Her head tipped up, and the sunlight lit her chin as it beamed through the open window. "He was gone for a great deal of our marriage," she explained quietly. "Traveling south to source the silk, he would oft be gone for a year or more. I could not say I miss him, as he was so rarely there."

Good. Kier bent back to the sleeve. What a bastard he was, to be glad her husband had been unsatisfying in every way.

Her chest was moving in slow, silk-clad breaths. Some faint scent of flowers wafted to his nostrils, passing in from the outdoors, no doubt, but even so, it seemed to be flowing through Sophia, tinged with her.

For a few moments, they were quiet. Just the sounds of birds drifting in from the hillside and human voices drifting in through the front windows. It was quietly companionable. The room had an amber glow as the sun wended its way downward, burning against the threads of the tapestries, the silver in the wardrobe.

"I judge you err," she said quietly, "in not allowing me to examine the account ledgers of Mistral Company."

He grunted, his attention on the sleeve.

"Suppose I am posed a query?" she asked.

"Refer people to your factor."

"And if 'tis a matter related to the business?"

"Refer people to your factor."

"But should the query relate directly to a matter I, as owner, should know, what then?" she pressed.

He looked up. "Refer. People. To. Your. Factor."

She pursed her lips, then gave an elegant shrug. "So be it. I still say you are making a mistake."

"I have made many mistakes in my life," he agreed, tugging on the thread. "You will simply have to suffer through this one." He glanced up. "In silence, one hopes. Can you do that?"

She smiled brightly. "I do not know. You will have to ask my factor."

He grinned and bent back to his work, glad to have the distraction of conversation to take his mind off the slow press of needle through the delicate fabric, because it did, in some uncomfortable way, make him nervous. The gentle bend of her fingers falling away, her palm resting so trustingly in his.

It seemed to take forever.

When he was done, he lowered her hand to the table as if he were laying Venetian glass into a bowl, then sat back, cracked his spine, and felt the urge to wipe sweat from his brow.

She shook her hand, making the silk threads shimmer in the sunset, then bent to fuss with the hem of her tunic, revealing a shapely ankle.

She looked up. He ripped his gaze away.

"Do not be afraid, Kier."

"Afraid?" he grumbled. "I am hardly—"

"There is but one more."

He looked down at the other slender wrist awaiting him. He thrust out his hand grimly. "Needle."

"I do not have it."

"Pardon?"

Her face was completely composed. "You did not give me the needle."

His gaze snapped down. Turning slowly, he stared around him. "Where the devil—"

"Perhaps it fell," she suggested helpfully. "Somewhere on the floor."

It took five minutes of crawling about on his knees to locate the accursed needle. He found it directly beside her slipper. He looked up. "You knew that."

She smiled down at him. "Never."

It took another ten minutes to complete the job. By its end, he was sweating more than he had in the tourneys he'd participated in as a youth—always as an errant, lordless, fealty-free knight, entrance fee gained with stolen coin—back when he still had ambitions of rising above his origins and being a good man.

The irony of that did not escape him, a young man's attempt at nobility purchased with stolen coin, to earn his chivalry on the end of a bloody blade.

He'd been good, quite good, to the extent it mattered, which was naught. Kier knew he could never be good enough.

He never wanted to be.

He got to his feet and looked down at her grimly. "Have we finished addressing the needs of your gowns?"

She looked up, startled. "Why, yes."

He nodded and turned to the door.

"Oh, goodness, look at this!" she exclaimed softly behind him.

He flung the door open and stepped aside to let her through. "What?"

"I found another needle." She punched it through the leather strip on the table and smiled as she passed him by. "How silly of me to have forgotten."

Fifteen

"Which one is the mayor?" Sophia murmured.

They stood in the middle of the mayor's great hall. The room was overflowing with people. Wealthy merchants, wax candle sellers to wool exporters to shipbuilders, filled the hall from stairway to the screened passage to the kitchens in the back. Wax candles burned on iron spikes lodged in niches set into the walls. Huge oil lamps hung suspended from wooden beams overhead, burning bright, flickering off the gems and gowns of those attending.

"I do not yet see him," Kier replied quietly, belying the burn of tension that hummed inside him.

They both turned their heads at the same moment and looked at each other. Light flitted off the silken threads in her gown and shattered in the hot room. The midnight-blue surcoat, laces tugged tight, revealed feminine curves and the rose-colored chemise beneath. Her wrists were all but imprisoned; Kier had done his task well. The outer sleeves hung long and low, little more than sapphire ribbons cascading to her ankles. Her hair was caught up in a fashionable, complicated netting that looked woven with gold. A single length of blue silk danced off its lower edge like a small pennant. She looked like a star catching fire.

"You look fine," he said.

"As do you."

They turned back in unison to the room. "The task tonight is simple," he murmured. "Make them think the Mistral widow is someone of interest, of substance. Make them dream a little of the riches that might be theirs by virtue of association with her."

She nodded placidly. "Very good."

"Before we leave, they must be convinced 'tis worth their time and considerable money to consider investing. And they must begin to talk."

"Of course."

He looked down at her sternly. "And above all, do *not* speak about details of the business. Refer people to me."

She looked up with a pleasant, blank look. "Pardon?"

"Do not speak of business matters related to Mistral Company."

She gave another apologetic smile and tipped her head to the side. "Pardon?"

He narrowed his eyes. "I presume you are communicating something simple in an extremely complicated manner?"

"'Tis not complicated, Kier. As that is the twentieth time you have reiterated the prohibition on discussions involving business matters, I presume you must think me hard of hearing."

He snorted softly. "I think you hard of *listening,* when it suits."

She shook her head. "Our paths are conjoined for a brief, unfortunate period of time, Kier. In consequence of that. 'tis difficult to see how disrupting you would serve me."

"Yes, that is what one would *think*. . . ."

That made her laugh. It was a good sound, Sophia's laughter. Upon a time, she had laughed for him a great deal. "Be assured, Kier, I will not speak of *business matters*. Instead, I shall speak of . . ." She paused as if to ponder, then looked up at him brightly. "*Carnal* matters."

He stared. She smiled, as happy and cheerful as a spring bird, but mischief, deep, summertime mischief, shone in her eyes.

"Was that intended to shock me, Sophia?"

Slowly, her lips curved into a deep smile. "Did it?"

Just as slowly, he lifted one dark eyebrow. "What would you say?"

Her smile faltered slightly. "About what?"

His grew. "Carnal matters. What would you say about them?"

Her eyes widened, then streaks of reflected candlelight shot across the silken strands of her dress as she bent her head nearer to his. "Why, I think I would say . . . you will have to speak to my factor about that."

He laughed then, full and unreserved, and she tipped her head up to smile at him as she used to do when she saw him striding up the path to her father's place, ready to make her fall in love, she ready to be the fallen one, and he felt ensconced in a beam of light.

A surge of sound moved through the room. The world reasserted itself as the mayor entered the hall, making it rustle with the turning of silk and murmuring voices.

Sophia turned with the others. "He is here. 'Tis time."

"It is indeed." Her long fingers looked pale and slender against the dark blue silk. "No misgivings?" he said quietly. "You have this one last moment to back out."

God's bones, he was stalling for time. When had he ever done that?

Every night he'd had to leave Judge Darnly's, hoping for one last moment alone with Sophia.

Well, he'd had his one last moment. Five years ago. It was over now.

"I hardly see this as the moment to reverse course, Kier," she said, utterly unaware of his inner . . . whatever was occurring inwardly. "Firstly, I am ravenous," she went on, and he laughed. *That,* she'd always been able to do. Make him laugh, laugh at his jests. It was part of her deadly allure; Sophia knew how to laugh.

She turned to him. "Secondly, whatever should you do then?"

He affected a nonchalant shrug. "As ever I have done, Sophia. Improvise. Infuriate people. Get into a scuffle of some sort."

She shook her head, her eyes on him, no longer laughing. "Kier, I was sown for such things as this, to my eternal shame. I am not afraid. I am angry. What I worry about is being unsuccessful, and the only thing that will disrupt me is the presence of a glowering henchman."

He was nodding in agreement and approval, then stopped mid-nod. "Are you referring to me?"

Her warm, silk-rustling body shifted as she leaned in, rose up on her toes, and whispered in his ear. "You are the one who is afraid, Kier, and yes, I do refer to you." She dropped back to the ground. "Simply do not stand too close. I will manage the rest."

She turned, and her tunic belled out as if creating space for her, then she glided toward the mayor and the rich merchants surrounding him.

The mayor caught sight of her. His face brightened, his mouth moved, and the rest of the group turned, then moved toward her, hands out, like clams that saw their tide coming in.

Behind her, Kier smiled.

Sixteen

He was about to follow after when Tomas Moneychanger appeared at his side. "How goes the wooing?"

Kier turned in surprise, then inclined his head toward Sophia, who was now surrounded by a cluster of admirers. "They seem enamored."

"Then someone is doing his job," the moneychanger said.

Kier looked over, but Tomas continued staring across the sea of people. "I thought you were not going to be in attendance tonight."

"I could not sleep. And I was curious," Tomas admitted a moment later.

"About?"

"Lady Mistral." Tomas turned to him. "I made some inquiries into your Remy, the plain-faced, sword-wielding man."

"Is he mine now?"

The moneychanger shook his head. "No. He is Edgard d'Aumercy's. Lord Noil's."

Their eyes met. Kier nodded slowly. "I see."

"Do you?" Tomas's glittering, sharp regard stayed steady on him. "Some say Noil was—or is—Cosimo Endolte's creature. No one can prove the association, of course, but there is talk that Noil is one of the main *commenda* investors. Mayhap Cosimo's man entirely."

Kier looked away, over the sea of people.

"I hope this is pleasing news."

Kier rubbed his fingers over his jawline. He'd not expected such a swift intersection of his two pursuits—the ledger and Cosimo Endolte—but, of course, it was hardly incredible. The ledger was intimately tied to Cosimo, and Kier intended to use it to flush him out, to cut off all other avenues of escape but the one that led to Kier. And the question was not whether Noil was Cosimo's man—of course he was—the question was, had he delivered the ledger yet?

If so, it would mean finding some other way to flush Cosimo out of his lair, and *that* would severely hamper Kier's plans. Perhaps ruin them entirely.

But if Noil had his own designs, or if he delayed in sending the ledger onward, for even an instant, there was hope.

He settled on saying, "Somewhat," and looked over to find Tomas examining Sophia intently, across the room. He regarded the old man's fixed profile a moment, then said quietly, "Shall I introduce you?"

Tomas shook his head. "No."

Without another word, the moneychanger turned and kicked his tunic hem out of the way and strode off.

"WHAT the hell were you thinking?" Edgard d'Aumercy, Lord Noil, was all but shouting. He forced himself to lower his voice.

Remy the Black stood before his desk and stared back at him with those black, glittering eyes. "I was following orders."

D'Aumercy stared at him in impotent fury. Why must he be plagued by overzealous fools? Were there no *under*zealous fools?

"Cosimo wanted this to be a swift, quiet matter," Remy said.

"And so you burned down her goddamned warehouse? *And attacked her on a city street?*"

Remy's expression didn't change. "I was told she was docile. I could have roped her easily, but I was told to retrieve the ledger. I followed her from Batten Downs to Last Fells, and did as I was told. I retrieved the ledger."

Noil looked at him in disgust. "She does not seem so *docile* now, does she?"

Noil flung himself back in his seat and took a deep, calming breath. It was unwise to become openly angry or insulting toward Cosimo's lieutenant, Remy the Black. Remy was known to not only be brutal, but to enjoy it.

But then, disappointing Cosimo Endolte was an even more hazardous pastime.

And without that accursed silk merchant, Cosimo was going to be *exceedingly* disappointed.

D'Aumercy's inner-facing chamber was swathed in afternoon light. Summer usually occasioned a move to the north-facing office, but this year the north side was being expanded, with a high solar planned and a garderobe with running water outside the lord's chambers. The work could not be done without heavy stone, which could not be moved until summer, which could not happen during storms, and thus the work had been repeatedly stalled.

And thus, d'Aumercy sat sweating in oven heat as if he were some common bread baker, whilst around him the stones seemed to sweat and idiots gave him more bad news.

Remy glared with those tiny black eyes, then flung something across the table so hard it almost flew off the other side of the table. D'Aumercy closed his hands around it before it slid into his lap.

"The ledger," Remy announced.

A man of few words. And few wits.

D'Aumercy wished Cosimo would leave him to his own men and his own devices in settling this matter of the silk merchant, rather than putting Remy at his disposal, equally an offer of assistance and a declaration of ownership. Remy was Cosimo's, the silk merchant was Cosimo's, and in the end, Noil was Cosimo's too.

Cosimo was the head of the *commenda,* his vast resources the shining sun above the twisting and turning face of the thing, pulling their investments and business interests here or there. Cosimo had more money, more trading partners, more holds in more enterprises than anyone else in all of England, and as such, the *commenda* followed his lead. Noil followed his lead. Everyone with any sense followed his lead.

And thus, they were all on the hunt for some goddamned silk merchant. Whom Remy had lost.

But he *had* brought the ledger. . . .

Noil reached for the precious ledger and drew it to him. The thick wooden covers were unadorned save for an old Roman-style book lock, used to keep book covers closed.

D'Aumercy touched the metal briefly. Cold. "Cosimo wanted the woman as well," he said quietly, still eyeing the lock.

"What matters she?"

He looked up. "Witnesses always matter. They must be removed."

Remy shifted. "Someone got in my way."

"You are employed entirely in order to get people *out* of your way. Rather, out of Cosimo's way."

A muscle twitched on the man's plain face. "I was about to do so. Then the Watch came."

D'Aumercy slid his hand off the ledger. "Remy, my

instructions were to deliver the silk merchant and the ledger. It is a simple enough matter: You have brought the ledger. Now go find Sophia Silk."

Remy's eyes glittered at him a moment, then he turned and tromped out. D'Aumercy watched him, then slid his gaze back to the ledger.

Who ever would have thought it would come to this? The Darnly ledger, here, in his possession. It was said to contain the most damning details of the covert machinations and collusions of some of the wealthiest men in England.

Even now, years later, the ledger could still be used as a weapon. Edward was still king, as robust and hammer-handed as ever. Survivors could still be made to suffer, even if the perpetrators themselves had passed on. Entire family fortunes had been created as a result of deeds documented in that ledger. And, of course, what had once been given by powerful men could just as facilely be wrested away.

Judge Darnly had learned that, to his neck's misfortune.

But Noil cared nothing for the past nor the stretched necks of long-dead judges. What he cared for was coin, and if bringing Cosimo this ledger would redirect his attention to more pressing matters—namely, money—then so be it.

For the past year, it had been naught but a distraction to Cosimo, and therefore, to the *commenda*'s purposes. To Noil's purposes. Investments and collections had fallen off severely in the past couple of years; Cosimo seemed hardly interested anymore. It was as if he were shepherding his resources, honing his attention.

Then he'd sent a message: the Darnly ledger, *and* the Darnly daughter, had been found. The orders were swift and brutal: Bring Cosimo the ledger. And bring Sophia Darnly.

Noil was glad he had not been an associate of Cosimo's back then. *His* name would not be found among those pages.

Theirs was a more recent association, Noil taking over where the judge had once served: portal to the *commenda.*

And for years now, the ledger had almost been forgotten. The daughter too. The ledger had faded into the mists of time.

But now, the rumors were surfacing again.

D'Aumercy slid his hand off the ledger.

Ledger or no, Cosimo's dereliction of duties as financial hawk for the *commenda* must be rectified. They all suffered when Cosimo stopped hunting. He must be tempted again. And Noil was precisely the man to do so. All he required was a likely candidate.

Perhaps this shipping widow from the south, the one the mayor of Last Fells made mention of.

Noil looked out the window at the setting sun, pensive. A ray of orange light burned in, baking the cover of the fabled Darnly ledger and its black iron padlock.

No need to rush delivery of the ledger. Give Remy a day or so to bring in the girl as well. Which he would do, eventually.

It was impossible to imagine that a bankrupt silk merchant, all alone in the world, could thwart Cosimo Endolte, not once he decided he wanted her.

Seventeen

Sophia stood amid a crowd of admiring merchants.

"Lady Mistral, we are honored by your presence," the mayor said. A round, flushed fellow, bald but for the frizzed gray outcropping that encircled his head like a crown of thorns, he beamed at her.

She returned a curtsy. "And I by your gracious invitation, my lord mayor. I have been told that both the trade and the men of England are rare treats," she said, and the group gave an appreciative murmur.

"Your factor reports this is your first visit to our shores, my lady."

"Indeed, that is so."

"We are honored," a gray-haired, balding tallow merchant said, bowing. "With such markets as Venice and Florence closer to hand for you."

She tipped her wine cup a bit and said thoughtfully, "Mistral Company is a large and vital company, sirs, always seeking new clients. I—*It*"—she smiled at her own swift correction—"seems to have exhausted the merchants of Venice and Florence and Paris and Lucca. Several other provinces as well."

A silence fell over the corner containing the most prestigious men of western England.

"I do hope England is not so easily depleted."

A burst of laughter exploded. Several men cleared their throats, then one bold fellow sallied forth.

"Englishmen are never depleted, my lady."

She smiled. "That is good to know, for I have much business to conduct in my short time here."

The mayor puffed out his chest. "You are in for a rare treat, my lady. The summer fair of Last Fells runs in a fortnight. Perhaps you have seen the preparations already beginning?"

"You have your own Hot Fair here in England? How fascinating," she murmured.

"Last Fells wool hall is the largest in the western shires," volunteered one man. "I could show you—"

"I know a saddler who works the most finely wrought gems into his leatherwork, my lady," interrupted another. "You have never seen the like. Allow me to—"

"Iron smelt," an old, fat merchant said gruffly. He stood half a head shorter than Sophia and held his cup of wine like a weapon. "More lucrative than wool, if not as plentiful."

She smiled at him. "And you, sir, I suspect, are in iron smelt."

"Deeply so," he said, looking directly at her.

Sophia laughed, and the group joined in. Soon, a chorus of invitations rang out. "Lady Mistral, perhaps I could escort—"

"Allow me to offer my services for the fair—"

"We have a town home that might—"

"*I* shall escort Lady Mistral." The mayor spoke over them all. They subsided with a grumble.

Sophia smiled at the circle, holding out a hand as if to touch all theirs. "Already my travels to Last Fells seem to be worth the effort, with such merchants to hand. I hope we shall develop some mutually lucrative associations."

The group rumbled in approval.

"Aye, well, you ought to hope so. You'll need some recompense for traveling all this way north on such a summer as this," a reed-thin merchant observed. "Naught but brash heat and lashing storms, and promises more of the same to come."

"Ah, but I have always been an admirer of English boldness," she demurred softly. "In weather, battle, and bed."

The men were silent for a single, shocked moment, then the group burst into hearty laughter.

The conversation bounced forward for more minutes, but eventually, the mayor was able to extricate her from the horde and draw her aside.

He cleared his throat and wiped the thumb and forefinger of one hand together in a nervous way. "I took note you mentioned you are in England for only a short time, my lady?"

She picked at a thread on her sleeve. "That is so." She glanced over his head to the room. "If I do not find what I am seeking here, I must look elsewhere, must I not?"

"Yes, yes, of course. Your factor, Sir Kieran, well, my lady, he mentioned . . ." He saw her attention was wavering and cleared his throat. "Are you seeking clients?" he clarified bravely. "Or investors?"

She waved her hand, a merchant impatient at having to outline such distinctions. "Clients, investors, men who have large vision; I care not what you call them, my lord mayor, only what they can do for Mistral Company."

"How large, particularly?" the mayor asked, dropping his voice.

She looked over him then, as if for the first time he'd arrested her attention. "I am afraid I am in pursuit of the *extremely* large."

He nodded and bent closer. "I may have some . . . associations that would prove useful to one such as you. Pray, I do not suggest these channels lightly, but I only mention it . . . as my lady mentions *large* as à prime component in her considerations. . . ." He was wiping his forehead furiously now.

"My lord mayor," she said slowly, "*large* is the essential component."

His face flushed. "Well, now, my lady, the matter is, I have some knowledge . . . I have associates who have rather *large*-pursed interests, but they are also the sort who prefer to remain"—more stammering—"well, *anonymous,* to be blunt, my lady, if you know what I mean."

She laid a hand on his wrist, at which his nervous flutterings ceased abruptly, as in one who has fallen to the floor in a faint.

"My lord mayor, I know *precisely* what you mean." She removed her hand. He started breathing again. "Men of business who prefer to work outside the shine of public opinion suit me most well. And know this too: I should be deeply indebted to any man who assists me in this endeavor."

This necessitated another round of forehead wiping, but by its end, he was beaming at her.

"Well then, my lady, I do believe I know just the man. Tell me, my lady— Oh, Sir Kieran." He bent his head in the direction of Kier, who'd just appeared at her back. "Your steward and I were speaking earlier of this very matter, my lady." He beamed over her shoulder at Kier. "Lady Mistral has been explaining her requirements, Sir Kieran."

He turned and looked at her. "Has she?"

She smiled. "Indeed I have."

"Do you think that wise?" he inquired softly.

"Oh, yes, I do." She met his eye. "My lord mayor believes he may have the man to meet our requirements."

The mayor looked between them with a beaming smile. "Tell me, my lady, sir, as there will no doubt be *preliminary* questions . . . how many partners are you currently engaged in contractual obligations with?"

"None," she replied without hesitation, at the same moment Kier said, "Three."

They stared at each other for a long, silent second. Then Kier put his hand on her arm and bowed.

"If you will excuse us, my lord mayor?" he said tightly.

The mayor watched them as Kier steered her through the hall, taking their leave as they went, complaining of Lady Mistral's excessive weariness following long days of travel, all the way to the doors, and out into the night.

Eighteen

They arrived back at the inn just as the bells of Compline were ringing. Kier opened the door and stepped back to allow Sophia inside. He shut the door, turned. They looked at one another through a long silence.

She raised an eyebrow.

"Do not say a word," he warned.

She opened her mouth and he turned on his heel and went downstairs to check with Innkeep about messages. None had arrived, so he climbed the stairs again, slowly. He was not looking forward to what lay ahead. Sophia thwarted was not a pleasant notion, but thwarted she must be.

He had to cut her loose.

When he reached the top of the stairs, light poured out of the bedchamber window and open door. It fell across the cobbled portico in a grainy yellow swath. He unlocked the door and went inside.

She'd lit the room with candles.

An entire host of stubby—and expensive—beeswax candles warred against the darkness in iron holders and puddles of wax, like a sea of flame down the center of the enormous table in the center of the room. Anchored at the far end, head bent over a ledger, was Sophia.

He grabbed a flask of whisky out of the back bedchamber and thumped it onto the table. He uncorked it, threw back a hot swallow, then lowered his body to a bench beside the very expensive table he'd ensured graced Mistral's apartments, at which Sophia now sat, on an equally expensive chair.

"I am looking through your books," she explained, barely glancing up.

"I see."

She aimed a look at the pewter flask from beneath her downturned head, then slid her green eyes up to his. "I will not say I told you so."

He took another swallow of whisky. "I'm fairly certain that would be accounted as saying I told you so."

He saw the edge of a smile touch her lips. She bent back to the books.

She was still tightly laced in the midnight blue surcoat, but she'd untied the laces holding the sleeves of her chemise to her wrists, and pushed them up her forearms. She'd also removed the tight netting that bound her hair, then balled her hair in some loose, knotted array at the back of her head and shoved a stick through the contraption to hold it up. Loose sprays fell beside her face and curtained in front of the damned curve of her neck. Her skin gleamed in the heated night.

A peek under the table revealed a further immodest liberty: she'd removed her shoes. They sat beside her like sleeping puppies, one tumbled over the other. One slim foot perched on tiptoe, the other slung over it, resting on its heel. Pale white and pink toes were visible under the hem of her skirts.

She was bands of color, hot, earthy. Far too fervent and feminine to be in his bedchamber. Dressed. Looking through account ledgers.

He'd never let anyone look through the Mistral Company books before. But he required a moment to prepare himself—he took another swallow of the drink—and in any event, watching her was like watching fish swim through triangulated sunlight; it drew the attention.

Still squinting at the books, Sophia tipped to the side and reached into the folds of her skirts, and pulled out . . . a pair of spectacles.

He sat back in surprise. Spectacles were the domain of clerics and monks, although more men of trade were availing themselves of them these days. And women.

She pinched the spectacles between her thumb and forefinger, holding them in place on the bridge of her nose as she peered back down at the ledgers. He grinned.

She looked up sharply. Her eyes narrowed at him from behind the glassy rounds.

"Have you something to say?"

He shook his head, still grinning, and spun his finger around each of his eyes. He took his finger and pushed the invisible spectacles up the bridge of his nose, just as she had done.

Her eyebrows slowly arched up, one more than the other. Then, just as slowly, she lifted her hand and began tracing her own circles in the air, over the general direction of his chest. She made two circles, one inside the other, then mimed lifting a bow and releasing an arrow directly at the target she'd drawn over his heart.

His smile deepened. He shook his head slowly.

She bent to the books again, a faint smile on her face.

He didn't know how much time passed. The candles burned down a good deal, and the light of the moon was lower, that's all he knew for certain. Sophia barely looked up from the books but to shift occasionally into more comfortable positions. She flipped pages regularly, her finger running down the page. Every so often she made little sounds of satisfaction, and occasionally a few of dismay or impatience at some poorly recorded notation, perhaps. Small, feminine, whispery sounds.

He took another sip, then leaned forward toward the table, thinking the motion might draw her attention. It did not. He propped one elbow, then the other, on the table. She turned the page, her mouth moving in silent reckoning.

"Sophia," he whispered.

She put one slender finger over her lips, shushing him.

"Sophia," he said a little louder.

She turned the page.

He sat up straight. "Sophia," he said, quite loudly.

She jumped. "What?"

"I'm releasing you."

She frowned, making a furrow between her eyebrows. "You're . . . what?"

He got to his feet. "I no longer require your services."

"You no longer require . . ." She got up as well. "What are you saying?"

"Your attacker was employed by Edgard d'Aumercy, Lord Noil."

Her jaw dropped momentarily. "Why, Kier! You have learned who—"

He reached around her for one of the ledgers. "Noil serves Cosimo Endolte."

Her mouth was still open for speech, but she fell silent, then sank back into her seat. "Oh, no."

"At best, Noil is double-crossing Cosimo. At worst, it means Cosimo is hunting you down. The risk is too great. It has become too dangerous."

"*Become* too dangerous?" She gave a small, incredulous laugh. "Are you mad? That is precisely why I am here, because it has become too dangerous. Indeed, why I *ought* to be here."

"No." He reached for another ledger to stack it atop the first.

She scrambled back to her feet and put herself directly in front of him. Her hands were behind her on the table, her face very near to his. "Kier, you cannot deny me this."

"Sophia, I can."

He slid the ledger around her and turned to the coffer.

"Kier, you need me." He snorted softly. "Ask me anything. About Mistral Company. I have learned much in the hour past."

"Out of which port is the rock alum shipped?"

He tossed the question over his shoulder carelessly, neither thinking nor caring if she knew the answer. But of course she would not know it. The mention was buried, a single reference in the early pages of the ledger she'd been perusing, barely worthy of note and, indeed, hardly legible, scrawled immediately after he'd paid the bribe that would safeguard the ships in the formidable port of Kerasont, where the rock alum shipped from.

"Kerasont," she said firmly.

He paused.

"And I judge you paid the port official a hundred livres per annum for the privilege of doing so without incident."

He dropped the ledgers into the chest and turned. She was waiting, her head tipped to the side, eyebrow up.

"How many ships operate in the run between Genoa and Syria?" he demanded.

"Two *nefs*."

"Where are the contracts signed?"

"In Ayas, at the lodge of the Genoese."

His eyes narrowed. "What export do we ship from the Marche region?"

"From Fabriano?" Her eyes sparkled at him. "Paper. Very fine."

"Tin?"

"Venice."

"Wax?"

"Spain."

"Our Portuguese factor?"

She stopped, paused, then admitted, "I hope 'tis simply that I haven't reached that far yet, for I do not know his name."

A smile swept across his face before he could stop it. He quickly rescinded it, but not before she saw it.

Hope lighted her face, flushed her cheeks bright, made her eyes sparkle, and she smiled at him.

Sophia was beautiful when she was hopeful.

He looked away. "No."

She stepped toward him. "Kier, I *heard* those men. I saw them, saw how they acted, saw what they wanted, saw what alighted their faces. They do not want Mistral's friend or factor or guide. They want *me*."

"They will have to suffer the loss," he said curtly, striding back to the table.

"And what will you tell them then?" she pressed, following behind. "How will you tempt them then? How will you lure Cosimo from his lair? Oh, I know what you are doing," she said at his swift, silent look. "You want Cosimo. That was a simple row to tally, Kier. And I am telling you this: you will never be successful without me."

He reached for the last ledger on the table. She was standing in his path. He stepped to the side. She stepped with him. He stepped the other way. So did she.

They stared at each other.

"You underestimate me," she said softly.

That was most certainly true. He'd done it from the first moment he'd seen her, and his chest had expanded and his head had filled and his body had fired and he had told himself, *I can get through this unscathed.*

But he had not. And neither would she.

He reached around her for the ledger, grabbed it, and walked to the back of the room. "Perhaps you do not understand, Sophia. These are dangerous men."

She began to walk around the table toward him. "Perhaps *you* do not understand, Kier," she said quietly. "Danger lies fore *and* aft for me. I am in this, or I am in something other. But either way, I am in danger."

Her hair and its carnal disarray seemed lush, rich, reflecting the oil lamplight. She was illuminated like a red fox wraith moving through the darkened room. She kept coming, closer, closer, until she was barely a step away and it appeared she was going to walk straight through him. Almost in defense, he dropped into the chair behind him.

"This"—she pointed to the floorboards between them, her bare feet, his booted one—"this with you, this is my way through."

She leaned down and gripped her hands around the arms of his chair. "These men are plunderers, Kier. They take what they wish, when they wish, and care nothing that it is not theirs to take. I say no more. Not to me they will not. Do you hear me?" Her beautiful, fierce eyes met his.

"I hear you," he said quietly.

"And whether you like it or not, Irish," she murmured, her voice husky and low, "not only do I need *you,* but now, you need *me.*"

The tumble of loosened strands of hair fell down past her shoulders, curling brown-red ribbons past her deep blue surcoat. Her eyes, so close to his, caught the moonlight, which was quite a thing, her dark green eyes, glinting back candlelight at him.

"I should throw you out the window. Or tie you up," he muttered.

"Or let me in," she said, coming closer. "Will you deny me this chance?"

The whisky was doing its work, running hot through his blood. Her mouth was very close to his. "I am no knight, Sophia," he said slowly, looking at her lips.

"Does that mean no?"

"It means you should not be standing so close to me."

"Are you going to deny me?"

He took a length of her hair between two fingers. A tremble rustled the dark blue silk, and like that, his body grew hard for her. Her, standing before him, hips bent, curving like a canopy over the hot space between their bodies; he, seated, so close to the trembling silk of her.

"Do you know what I want to do to you, Sophia?" he murmured.

"Kiss me?" she whispered.

He brushed the back of his knuckle across her bottom lip, and when she parted her lips to gasp, he slid the knuckle just inside.

"I want to do more than kiss you."

Smoothly, he rolled down her lip and, pushing up in his chair, slid his tongue into the hot space between her lower lip and teeth.

Her breath came out in a low whimper. Knowing he was conducting fire and unwilling to stop, Kier pushed to his feet entirely, his mouth still on hers, and sucked her crooked, lush lip deep into his mouth.

A hot, whispered gasp burst from her. But she did not pull away, and it was as if, for the length of it, he'd been admitted into Heaven.

But that was foolish. Kier was never going to make it to Heaven.

He wrenched away, put his hands on her elbows, and backed her up far enough to step away. He did not look down at her—God knew he could only handle so much—and turned away.

He'd reached the door, was turning the handle, when her low voice reached out for him from behind.

"You left me."

That stopped him. A board or those words, either would have worked.

"You left me then, and you're leaving me now. Why?"

Hand on the door, he closed his eyes.

"Why did you leave me?"

He dropped his hand and looked back.

SOPHIA stared sightless at the planks between her feet, flushed and cold, furious with Kier, with herself, at the way her body shook with desire, at the way Kier could blow her over like the wind with one simple, ravenous, knee-buckling kiss.

It had always been thus. Always, always, always.

She wanted Kier the way the earth wanted rain. She ached for him, his body, his heart, and under it all like a bridge, she ached for him to be a good man.

But that was the rebel part of her, the childish part, the part that knew nothing of sense or reason or *history*.

Her body felt brittle, thin and rigid, like a sheet of ice, a pane of clear glass. The tap of a hammer might shatter her into a thousand bits.

"Why did you leave me?" she said again.

He stood by the door, silent and motionless, neither coming back nor leaving. He was not going to answer. He would never answer her. The rest of her life would be spent knowing she would never know.

Then he bent his head and she heard him take a long inhale. Then in his low voice, he said, almost sadly, "I did not want to leave, Sophia."

She nodded at the floor between her feet. "And yet, you did."

"There was a . . . a *devoir*," he said, using her father's term. It suddenly struck her that perhaps it hadn't been her father's term at all. Perhaps he had adopted it from someone else. Perhaps Kier.

"There *always* was some little task owing, some job to be done."

"Aye," he agreed quietly. "There always was."

And what did she expect? She knew her father, and she knew Kier. There was room for affection, passion, even for pleasantries and laughter, but these things were daub; they went between the things that mattered to men such as they.

"I didn't want to leave," he said again. Something in his voice made her look up in time to see his jaw clench, one swift tightening.

"Then why did you?"

"Sophia—" he began, sounding angry.

She flung up her hand. "Please, do not say it again, Kier. I know the lines well: there was a task to be done. But why did you go? You could have refused, yes? Or come back after?" She was horrified to hear her voice break. "You did not come back after."

His gaze was like a thread that bound her. "No, I could not refuse, Sophia, and nay, they did not mean for me to ever come back. And the task was *you*."

She started. "Me?"

"Your future. They were discussing it."

Her brow furrowed. "*My* future?"

"Your marriage, among other things."

This was horrifying, men she did not know discussing her and her . . . future. "*Who* was discussing it?"

"Your father. And Cosimo."

"You lie." She flung the words so fast she almost spoke over him.

His jaw flexed again, then he went still and terrible.

"My father would never expose me to Cosimo," she said loudly. "He bought a dying silkman's trade rather than see me wed to the wrong man, rather than expose me to any of his associates. Why, Papa was hanged as a traitor before I was even wed."

A frigid smile glazed up the corners of Kier's mouth. "Ah, well, mayhap that is because I told him I'd come back from the grave should he go through with his plan."

"Plan?"

The candlelight barely lit his face as he hesitated, there by the door. "Your father saw what was between us, Sophie."

"My father saw . . ." Her voice trailed off. "Saw you and me?"

"Aye."

She blew out a breath, sucked it back in. "I did not know he knew."

"He knew," he said grimly. "And he did not like it."

"And you abided by his wishes," she clarified bitterly. It wasn't precisely a question but it asked a thousand things.

He gave a shrug. "Your father and Cosimo made their case persuasively."

"Did they?"

"Aye."

"How much did they offer for you to never return?" She spat the words.

"Nothing."

She scraped her gaze up, not quite so far as his eyes. "Nothing?"

"No thing."

"And yet you did their bidding nevertheless."

"I do no man's bidding, Sophia." Something hard had entered his voice.

She threw her head up. "Then I do not understand."

"Nay, you do not," he agreed coldly. His words were cold, his eyes cold, his tone a winter plain of cold.

"And you do not explain."

He turned to the door, answer enough.

"Why not?" she almost shouted to his back.

"Because, lass," he said, and swung the door open. "I'm a black-hearted bastard and it does not serve me to tell you. Read whatever you wish of the account books, then sleep. With fortune, we will have a long day on the morrow."

Sophia stared after him, hardly noticing she'd gained her goal: he was not kicking her out.

She hardly noticed the low rumble of thunder from outside, far in the distance.

She certainly did not notice the way her hands were trembling.

She hardly noticed anything except the questions hurtling through her mind and the hot thwarted energy moving through her blood, of the way she'd wanted Kier to do more, much more, when he'd put his mouth over hers.

Five years of dreams could not be satisfied by that little thing.

It wasn't until much later, in the middle of the night, that she awoke and noticed the question: Why had he said, *Come back from the grave*?

KIER clattered down the stairs and barreled into the common room, which was now in the middle of closing. Innkeep, carrying a tray of tankards, stared at his headlong entry, and decided the rules could be bent for his most favored guest's steward. He pulled an ale and set it before Kier without a word.

For long minutes, Kier drank in silence, the innkeeper's bustling a comfortable background noise.

"Woman or horse?" Innkeep asked.

Kier laughed without looking up. "Woman."

Innkeep leaned his hefty belly against the side of the counter and nodded compassionately. "Trouble all around, and worth it."

That earned a grunt.

"For instance, your mistress, if I may say, sir. Fine lady, she."

He said nothing.

"It's what I told the messenger who just arrived for her."

Kier's head jerked up. "The what?"

Innkeep nodded toward the door. "The messenger who arrived for her. Just before you came in. Sent him up, I did. You must have missed him, coming through the back entrance as you did. Nobility, I'd venture, in keeping with her fineness," he called out, but Kier was already out the door, going to the stairs, taking them two at a time.

He stopped short midway up, a boot on the stair above him. Sophia was standing at the summit, staring down at him.

A strange, unfamiliar coldness trickled through his blood. "What happened?"

She lifted her hand. In it was a pale piece of parchment.

"We have been invited to Noil Keep."

They looked at one another. The hem of her tunic draped over the edge of the top step, dripping down like a multihued flood.

"You did it," he said quietly.

"We did it," she whispered back.

The faintest smile touched his lips.

She smiled too and for a moment, it was very bright in the dark night.

Nineteen

Sophia awoke clumsily in a murky dawn. She reached out her arms, blinked, tried moving her legs. They felt sluggish, trapped, as if something heavy was sitting on them.

She looked down.

Something heavy *was* sitting on them.

A lumpy mass of colors, pale and dark in the dim light. She sat up, her legs still trapped under the colorful weighted pile.

She scrubbed at her eyes, then reached out with a hand and touched the edge of the pile. Silk. Yards and yards of silk and fine-weave cotton and . . .

She sat up straight, tugging her feet out from under the expensive bundle.

"Kier, there is a great pile of something on the bed," she called out softly.

"You always were observant," came a disembodied voice. Kier, somewhere beyond the tapestry separating the rooms.

"You do not understand. I know silk, and this is silk. Expensive silk. A great deal of expensive silk, all . . ." She gestured. "Lumped together."

"My regrets for the lumping." The squeal of a door hinge bending back against the wetness of a humid day.

"Why is it here?"

"I believe they will all require some sort of adjusting. Sewing. Something of that sort."

"For whom?"

There was a brief pause. "Me, Sophia. They are all too short."

The squeal of hinges, and the door shut quietly against the dense morning air.

She grinned and got out of bed.

THEY reached Noil Keep late the next day. They rode under a beating sun, accompanied by two armed escorts and one large packhorse. All the hired servants were left behind in town; Kier wished for as few eyes and ears as possible.

The heat seemed to both rise up from the earth and hammer on them down from the heavens. They kept to the shadows wherever possible, guiding the horses under the eaves of the towering trees comprised by the chase. Birds and insects hovered in whatever cool spot they could find, and even the wind was desultory as it moved over the baked earth. They rode in still green shade and silence. Ominous storm clouds jostled on the horizon, huge, greenish ones, slowly rolling out of position and moving across the sky.

"We will beat it," Kier assured her.

She glanced at his profile, shadowed by facial hair and the wide-brimmed hat he wore. Clothed in naught but his tunic and tight-fitting breeches and boots, his weapons covered him more heavily than his clothes. Throughout their ride, with each rolling sway of the horse's rump, the deadly ensemble of Kier's weapons had creaked, iron, leather, and steel.

But Kier was a weapon himself, and in the time he'd been gone, he'd been fundamentally changed somehow. His strength had been tempered, like steel after fire and hammer. He'd always been strong, but he'd also been young. His strength had been mocking and arrogant. Loud.

This man was silent and hard. Hard in every way.

He took off his hat to rub at his head. His hair was tugged back into a queue at the nape of his neck and now, uncovered, it burned almost black in the sun. His face was tanned, and the roughness of new beard darkened it further. He squinted into the distance ahead, then turned to say something to one of the guards.

As he turned in the saddle, the soft fabric of his tunic was pulled tight to his stomach, revealing firm flatness. The tunic was unlaced as far as it could be, and Sophia had a view down past the base of his neck to the hollow of his tanned chest, covered with a light sheen of sweat, and the faint tangle of dark chest hair.

She ripped her gaze away.

"Sophia."

"What?" she said, too sharply. She could not see into his eyes, under the dark shadow of the hat he wore, but all he said was, "Ensure d'Aumercy sees this," and handed over two bound folios he'd tugged from his saddle bags.

"'Tis a recent shipping manifest and some account ledgers," he explained.

She perused it quickly—she had not read this one last night—flipping pages swiftly.

"It must be an accident that d'Aumercy sees it, of course," he murmured.

She nodded slowly, thinking, then said in a low, meditative tone, "I have just the thing."

And then he smiled at her, the slow Kier smile, his most formidable weapon. She found it a bit *crushing* in its power.

With no knowledge of his effect on her, he faced forward again and pointed. "We are here."

She wrenched her gaze away. They'd crested a rise in the land, and the forest fell away. Below was a long, browning stretch of sundried meadow and atop another rise of land, the keep of Edgard d'Aumercy, Lord Noil, right hand of Cosimo Endolte.

It rose four stories high above the sloping land below. Stout wooden walls surrounded its bailey on all sides, and a small village sprouted beside it like a mushroom, with brown and gray thatched roofs, and a slow-moving mill stood by the creek that ran through the middle of the valley floor.

The slitted windows along the walls and upper turrets spilled faint yellow light. Bright colors of people could be seen moving about in the bailey as a small group of riders entered under the gate. On the walls were guards, stationed at various points. Small shiny blobs of silver and copper red burned in the setting sun as men patrolled the battlement walls.

"Now, regard, Sophia," Kier's soft murmur came from her side. "Edgard d'Aumercy is a nobleman who is neither terribly noble nor terribly well-off. These things grate at him to no end."

She nodded. "Tell me, what does he appreciate in life?"

"Women. Wine. Horses. Hawks."

She nodded sagely. "A predictable man."

"A dangerous one. Do not be fooled. Do not . . . incite," he added, for lack of a better way to describe what Sophia had a way of doing.

She looked at him indignantly. "I do not *incite*."

"Be sure to make mention of the deep-water ports," he said, ignoring her indignation, looking instead at the castle. "And should you find some way to make mention of Philip, it would not go amiss."

"Philip?"

"Of France."

"King Philip of France," she clarified flatly.

He turned into the gaze she had aimed at the side of his head. "Aye. That's the one."

"In what manner should I invoke the king of France in our discussions?"

"He is a client of yours."

She narrowed her eyes suspiciously. "I missed that in your books."

"'Tis a recent development. Additionally, if you could find a way to keep Noil occupied, should I earn a moment to slip into his offices . . . ?"

Her squinting eyes flew open into bright, sparkling orbs. "The *ledger*," she exhaled. "Kier, you have found the ledger. The ledger is *here*."

He decided it was safest to return his gaze to the castle. Castles did not breathe or exhale or sparkle at him.

"Can you do it?" he inquired brusquely. "Keep Noil distracted?"

"Keep a man talking?" She made a dismissive sound. "With my mouth gagged. I shall simply encourage him to speak of himself. This entertains men *end*lessly."

Kier looked over, eyebrows raised. "You must find that quite useful."

"Exceedingly. Anything else?" she inquired. "Perhaps to have him dance for you?"

He snorted softly. "If you can make Edgard d'Aumercy dance, Sophia, I will give you a penny."

She sat absolutely still, then turned to him with the sort of slow grace he expected of a peacock. "Five," she said.

He turned to look at her. "Five?"

"Pennies. If I make him dance."

He laughed, and it was an easy, pleasing sound. Kier relaxed and enjoying himself was a lethal combination. "Done." His horse threw its head, ready to be off, and he reined it around smoothly. Masterful with everything except her heart. "Are we ready, lass?"

She gathered her reins. "I do but wait upon you. Let us go wreak your mayhem."

Kier grinned and followed her down the hill, first at a walk, then a gallop, as thunder rolled across the brightly burning world. The clouds were moving in.

Twenty

"Nothing?" Noil stared at Remy the Black, who shook his head.

"Nay. No sign of her anywhere."

Noil threw down the pen in his hand. "She is a woman, a small merchant, with no money and no family. How in God's name is she able to elude you?"

Remy the Black stared back at him with those black, glittering eyes.

"I do not have the time for this incompetency. I have other matters to attend." Noil waved his hand at the tabletop, which was covered with papers, then at the window. The guests for his hunt and saint's day feast were starting to arrive; he could hear the sounds from the bailey below. Merchants were coming, men—and one woman—who might just entice Cosimo to invest again. What cared he for a bankrupt silk merchant?

Remy's face never changed, his eyes just glittered a little harder. "What other matters?"

Noil pressed his fingertips carefully together. The audacity of Remy the Black, questioning him. "*Business* matters. You would not understand."

"Your business is that which Cosimo requires of you."

And there lay the crux of the matter, did it not?

Noil was weary of being Cosimo's hound, sent to manage his dirty tasks, from ensuring witnesses to sign contracts, to hunting down rebellious silk merchants. The lord of Noil had old, noble English blood. He was not some glorified varlet.

And yet . . . he was.

"I have a new investment for Cosimo," he said.

Remy looked at him derisively. "Cosimo has no interest in investments. He wants that." Remy nodded toward the ledger, sitting in the same place it had been the other night when he'd first delivered it. "Why is it still here?"

Noil covered the ledger protectively. "Because I do not trust anyone to deliver it but me, and I have my other business to attend at the moment. 'Tis safe in my keeping. Go find the silk merchant."

Remy's cold black eyes glittered at him a moment, then he turned for the door. "Deliver it sooner rather than later. King Edward will be moving soon; so must we."

King Edward?

For a moment, d'Aumercy was as stricken by the confusing nature of those words as he was by the fact that Remy the Black appeared to know more than he, Cosimo Endolte's right-hand man.

Sometimes, he was convinced Remy had been sent to him not as a guardsman cum gaoler, but as a goddamned *spy*.

D'Aumercy stared at the empty doorway for a long time, until a servant stepped into it, disrupting the wash of light spilling across his table. "My lord?"

He looked up. The servant's face was red from the effort of running up three circular twists in the stairs. Cradled in his arms was a small chest, the size of a baby, banded in iron, the sort that sat inside another larger coffer, additional protection for whatever lay within.

"Lady Mistral has arrived," the varlet announced, huffing his way into the chamber.

"What is that?" Noil demanded.

The servant set the chest on the end of the table with a bow. "There seemed to be some confusion regarding Lady Mistral's chests, but I am certain I was told to bring this here."

Noil reached out and tapped the iron flap that covered the keyhole. It flipped up and down with a small metal bang.

It was unlocked.

"Lady Mistral's?" he said, still looking at it.

"Aye, my lord."

He pulled the chest toward him as the servant left. He rose and creaked open the lid. In the chest's dark interior were two items. Account ledgers, or perhaps shipping manifests.

He smiled as he retook his seat and began reading. The account books of other people's business were always educational reading, particularly if the merchant did not know they were being read.

Noil flipped pages swiftly. The sailings and clients and profits of Mistral Company for the twelvemonth past were documented here, and documented well. He looked up at his man-at-arms, who stood outside his office door.

"Bring me Lady Mistral's factor," he ordered curtly. The mayor of Last Fells had said to deal with the factor, and as far as Noil was concerned, an Irishman was as good a place as any to begin a *coup*.

Twenty-one

Kier stood in the great hall of Noil Keep, peering up at a merchant who seemed to be in conversation with the wall on the far side of the room. Or mayhap it was a tapestry. Or a window. It was hard to tell at this distance.

The feasting had begun in d'Aumercy's hall, albeit mostly in liquid form. Noil had not yet shown himself, but all his guests had, and the drink was flowing freely.

Kier approved; drink made men careless.

"That one, he's from the Dale," said a merchant at his side, gesturing with his cup toward the man conversing with the wall. "Keep your lady away from him; he's as thick as the wood they fell in those parts."

A successful trader of wax candles, Aubry Warren had dragged his family out of some ditch on the borders of Gwynnyd. He was exceedingly rich, exceedingly jovial, and exceedingly shrewd.

Kier nodded his thanks. "I shall ensure Lady Mistral does not dash herself too miserably against his hard head."

Warren grinned. "You come to me for advice on where to aim your sights, and I shan't steer you wrong."

"I am obliged."

Warren eyed him as he would a thick cut of meat. "Mayhap you're already aimed, eh? Noil, aye? The *commenda*?"

Kier said nothing, in a diplomatic fashion.

Warren roared in laughter at having guessed so well and, lifting his hand, beckoned a few others to their side.

"Sir Kieran, my lords," he said as he introduced Kier around the group. "Factor and friend to Mistral Company." Their eyebrows rose as they exchanged glances. "An estimable competitor in the market, indeed, but do not be fooled by that young face; methinks he is not a man you wish to encounter in a dark alley."

"I cannot think of the steward I *do* wish to meet in a dark alley," replied one of the men, nodding to Kier. "I am eager to meet your lady, sir. We have heard much about her."

Warren beamed in the reflected glory of Mistral's agent. "Yes. She has charmed half of England, with the other half waiting in breathless anticipation. We have heard much of her." His voice dropped slightly. "And the situation she finds herself in."

Kier looked over. "Situation?"

Warren lowered his voice further. "Perhaps we can step to the side, the four of us, and I can clarify. Should the *commenda* not meet your expectations, that is."

Kier smiled, cup balanced on his palm, held gently between two fingers of his other hand. He was about to reply when a guard came up beside him, somewhat like a shadow, only armed.

"My lord desires your attendance, sir."

The exuberance in the circle of merchants diminished into silence. Kier lifted his eyebrows at the silent, disappointed men.

"Methinks my expectations are about to be met. My lords, sirs." He bowed and turned away.

HE was escorted to d'Aumercy's office chambers, searched for weapons he had already given over at the doorway, and allowed inside.

The soldiers shut the door after him, drowning out the revelry belowstairs.

"Ah, Sir Kieran. Good. Come in. Sit." D'Aumercy waved his hand toward the table, toward the empty chair. He poured a cup of wine from the flagon atop the table and handed it to Kier. "I was most gratified to have your lady accept my invitation to Noil Keep."

Kier took it and sat. "She was most gratified to receive it. And most impressed upon her arrival."

Noil waved dismissively. "She is new to England, and must be suitably attended and suitably impressed." He sat, his hands resting on the thick oak arms of his chair, and picked up his own cup. "I have heard she is most charming."

"Most."

"With a strong fleet of ships."

Kier inclined his head as he surveyed the room, memorizing the layout, where the coffers sat, what appeared locked and unlocked. The ledger might be here, or it might be in Noil's bedchamber. Or it might be gone entirely.

D'Aumercy had been watching him examine the room.

"And served by a most *assiduous* factor," he finished his compliments.

Kier looked back. "I serve. As do you."

Noil smiled tightly, as if he did not enjoy the thought. "Come," he said, leaning toward Kier in a conspiratorial fashion. "The mayor has already put your case forward."

Kier set down his cup. "Is there something you wish to ask, my lord?"

Noil gave a clipped nod. "I have investigated your lady. Mistral Company is a large shipper, primarily moving luxury goods, hoping to expand into wool. Upon a time it was rumored to have had capital in excess of thirty thousand *fiorino d'oro*. Mistral the man has died, and the widow inherited the reins of the company."

Kier suppressed a smile. It was so simple a thing to let people convince themselves. "You know a great deal, my lord."

"I make it my business to. Why is she looking to sell?"

"She is not, precisely. I am looking to buy. With sufficient investors, this may become possible. She is in trouble, trouble that will grow if she does not regain her clients. And far too many do not wish to do business with a shipper who has a woman at its head."

D'Aumercy nodded thoughtfully as he peered into the dark interior of his cup. He edged his eyes up. "You say she is foundering?"

"I say she is a sinking ship."

"And seeking buyers?"

"She is, shall we say, navigating without a compass."

A smile returned to d'Aumercy's face. "And you are her *stella polare.*"

Kier gave a seated bow. "I am fortunate enough to be called friend."

Noil laughed. "She does not choose her friends very well, does she?"

Kier smiled back, neither one pretending for a moment they were anything other than raptors.

"Here is where things stand," Kier said abruptly. "I have been given leave to seek out English merchants whom Lady Mistral will find most beneficial to meet, as clients, and perhaps more. The question is, my lord, are you going to be one of them? Or the *only* one?"

Noil threw himself back in his seat and stared at the rafter beams. A thin, tuneful melody of a flute and lute drifted up the stairs and under the door. The chorus played through, and they picked up the thread of another tune before Noil looked over at him.

"Why?" he asked. "Why now?"

"My lord?"

"You must understand my position, Sir Kieran. I am the portal to a vast sea of money. In that role, my recommendations carry weight. I must be diligent in my investigations. I must know, beyond a doubt, that whom and what I recommend is not only liable to be worth the risk, but is, in fact, a *genuine* risk." He swirled the wine in his cup again. "You can perhaps imagine how many charlatans I see, with naught but shells sitting atop peas. I am forced, unfortunately, to upend all the shells and ensure there is, in fact, a pea involved." He sat back and eyed Kier. "It is never a pleasant business when there is not."

"I can imagine," he said curtly. "Would you like to see the lady's ships?"

"I would like to see the lady," Noil said, getting to his feet. "I will question her myself."

Kier pushed to his feet. "She is delicate," he blurted out, thinking how absurd that sounded, to call Sophia *delicate. Mad,* perhaps, or *liable to drive a man to drink,* but she was not, under any circumstances, delicate.

Noil gave a thin smile. "Your concern is touching, but I do not bite." He pushed aside an account book that had been sitting beneath some papers as he got to his feet. The book was familiar.

Kier looked at it. He felt like grinning. Instead, he said coldly, "That is my lady's."

Noil followed his glance. "Why, it is indeed. Your lady had it directed here in error."

"And you looked in it."

"Of course I did. Why should I not? And 'twas illuminating reading. Your lady is rich in prospects and poor in execution."

"I have already told you that."

"I do not rely on the word of stewards, steward," d'Aumercy retorted coldly, and he started for the door. "I will meet with the lady myself, and ascertain what I must, in the manner I must. I hear she does not appear to be averse to the charms of men. Or their beds."

Kier felt the blood surge up inside him like a sea of fury. Noil had started around the table and, perhaps unwisely—no, most certainly unwisely—Kier stepped in front of him, blocking his path to the door.

The baron looked him up and down. "What the hell are you doing?"

"Ensuring your method of ascertaining is not to my lady's detriment."

Noil's face flushed a deep red. "You do wrong to trifle with me, man."

"And you do wrong to insult my lady."

Noil snarled, "Step aside, steward. You have no business in this matter anymore."

And then the oddest thing occurred, in a week of odd occurrences. Kier was overtaken by the urge to draw his sword and lay it against the throat of the only man in England who could take him to the object of his revenge.

Twenty-two

Sophia stared out the window of the chamber she'd been escorted to. It looked out over a brown meadow below. She could see nothing of the blue river they'd crossed during their approach.

Against the wall sat a high wardrobe, carved in intricate designs. The walls were whitewashed, painted with images of curling vines and leaves. Double straw-stuffed mattresses were piled on the bed, the floor was clean planks, and the whole place emitted the odor of wealth.

The last time Sophia had been in such a rich place, she'd been ten. Her father had been visiting a local baron who had a case coming before the King's Bench. High justice was expensive justice.

A soft rap came upon the door. A maidservant bobbed there, capped in linen like a little cork.

"Ma'am, I'm Elsperth, here to help with your gown." She bobbed again. "My lord sent me, you being without servants and all."

She opened the door wider, allowing the girl entry. How considerate. And convenient. She certainly couldn't have Kier come in and stitch her up for the evening as he had these last days. That would be ridiculous.

"I've the comeliest netting for your hair, my lady," the girl said, fussing around her head. "And a few ribbons for your wrists."

Elsperth outlined a variety of things she could and would do, and it all sounded quite complicated and handsome, requiring a skilled hand.

And the girl *was* quite skilled. She simply did not quite compare with Kier's stitching.

She did turn out to be quite *conversational*, though, a marked improvement over Kier.

She chatted volubly as she wrestled Sophia's hair into submission in a pile atop her head. Pins were inserted with confident vigor, Sophia suppressing all shrieks as Elsperth chattered on about the visitors they were having, how the festivities were to unveil themselves, how handsome Lady Mistral's steward was, begging her pardon, and how even Lord Edgard seemed impressed, impressed enough to bring the steward into his office only a little bit ago, attended by three guards, no less.

Sophia stilled, staring into the polished metal hand mirror she held.

"Three, you say?"

Elsperth nodded happily. "Not oft my lord does that, my lady, I assure you." She bent down in a conspiratorial whisper, "Doesn't like to lower himself to the *stewards*, you know."

"Ah, indeed." Sophia cleared her throat of the sudden knot that had formed there. "I have heard many things about Lord Noil. A great man, chivalrous beyond compare."

Elsperth's eyes flew up to hers. "You have, my lady?"

That was not encouraging, that the maid should be surprised to hear tales of her master's greatness were passing about the countryside.

"I mean simply that he is a calm, reasoned man." The maid's

fingers faltered in her devotion to a particular curl. Sophia pressed. "Even if he should be, say, *angry* with someone."

The maid's eyes flew up without hesitation. "I don't know about those tales, my lady."

Sophia met the girl's eyes in the handheld mirror. "Why? Is he not?"

"My lady," she asked in a low voice, one of a budding confidante. "Have you done something to anger my lord?" She looked exceedingly worried by this.

"No, not a'tall." She gave a little laugh. The maid seemed reassured and went back to piling hair. "But if someone had . . . ?"

"That would not be good, my lady."

Oh.

"Now tell me, my lady, do you prefer—"

"Either will do. Oh, Elsperth!" She got to her feet, turning and suddenly counting chests and coffers on her fingers. She whirled again, her face crumpled with concern. "How many chests were brought to my room?"

The girl pointed, clearly confused. "All those, my lady."

"Yes, yes, but one is missing. Missing! A most important one. Where do you think it has gone?" she asked in ominous tones, and looked at the door, suggesting the coffer may have snuck out by that route.

"My lady, I'm sure I don't know. I can—"

Sophia whirled back again. The maid froze.

"I made mention to one of the porters that that particular coffer carried things of the script, and was destined for an office. Think you he misunderstood, and took it to your lord's office?"

She dearly hoped he had, as she'd instructed him to do precisely that.

The maid looked exceptionally worried. "I am responsible for all your things whilst you are in our care, my lady. I can—"

Sophia moved briskly to the door. "Well, we cannot have

you suffering for someone else's incompetence, can we? Let us go retrieve it at once, and no one shall ever be the wiser."

The maid hurried after. "But, my lady, the meal is about to begin. If it has been taken to my lord's office . . . and if my lord is there . . ."

She looked positively sick at the thought.

"'Twill only take a moment," Sophia said comfortingly, already through the door. "I'm sure your master will be sympathetic to what is I hope undue concern over matters of coin. In any event, I'm certain he's already out on the hunt or something equally daring," Sophia said blithely. "He is no laggard to sit about in shadows when there are things to be hunted down under the sun."

The maid, apparently, could not disagree with this. Down they went, to the master's chambers.

Elsperth explained her lady's straits to the door warden while a cat swirled in and out of his booted ankles.

He eyed her suspiciously, but turned and pushed open the door.

Mouthing a brief, heartfelt prayer for forgiveness, Sophia stepped forward and tripped, pushing hard into the maidservant, who stumbled into the guardsman, who tripped over the cat, and all three tumbled face forward into the room.

Kier had just realized his ill-guided plan to put a sword against Noil's throat was a particularly bad plan, not because Noil was the man he needed to execute his trick, but because Kier had handed over all his weapons, when sounds came in from the outer chamber behind.

Both he and a red-faced Noil spun to the door.

The door flew wide open and through the opening tumbled an armed guard, a becapped maidservant, a cat, and . . . Sophia.

Noil stared.

Sophia floated in in the wake of the others, her hands out, as if that could prevent anyone from falling.

"Oh!" she exclaimed softly. "My deepest apologies. I was merely hoping to find—" Her gaze swept the room and when it fell on Noil, she flushed gracefully and executed a deep curtsy. "Oh, my lord Noil. I do beg your pardon. I was but seeking a coffer with a few folios that may have been brought here inadvertent—"

She stopped short and seemed to finally take second notice of the scene. Her factor in conference with Noil, in his office, a Mistral Company ledger lying atop the table.

A cold reserve settled over her face. "Have I interrupted something?"

Kier was overtaken by the urge to cheer. He stepped forward, murmuring, "My lady—"

D'Aumercy reached her first. "Lady Mistral, I am honored by your presence," he said, bowing low over her hand.

"And I by your gracious invitation, my lord," she murmured, appearing to regain her equanimity.

"Ignore this fussy gathering, and the worries of an old man. In perhaps excessive concern for your comfort, I asked Sir Kier to come and speak on how I might best make your stay here in England a welcoming one. Please take no offense."

She appeared to hesitate, then returned his smile. "You are hardly fussy, my lord." Her eyes sparkled at him. In fact, Kier could not recall ever seeing them so bright. "Nor is *old* a word I would use."

"You compliment me, my lady."

"Of course. As I hope you will do to me."

Noil laughed. "Come, my lady," he said, leading her to the door. "'Tis time for meetings to end and revelry to begin. Cook has prepared five courses, including roasted pheasant. I think you will enjoy our English fare."

He guided her out, leaving Kier to follow behind.

Twenty-three

Knights, retainers, lords from surrounding manors, a traveling minstrel show, and approximately forty-three dogs roamed Noil's great hall in between courses. It was just shy of being chaos. Competing voices, occasionally bursts of laughter, and the music from stringed instruments bounced off the stone walls and tapestries.

As such, it was both perfect and inadequate cover as Kier listened to d'Aumercy regale Sophia with tales of how he'd won the gleaming armor hung on the wall, which they stood back to admire. He explained how it was from some melee in his youth, and how he'd pulled it out of a puddle of blood or something fine and chivalric as that.

Kier grabbed a mug of ale from a passing servant and stepped closer, ignoring the people very interested in talking with him, intent on the ones who wanted nothing to do with him.

After a respectful pause over the youthful glories Noil had relayed, Sophia looked over and found Kier staring at her.

D'Aumercy followed her glance.

"Your factor is very interested in staying near you," he observed, then flipped out the edge of his tunic as he sat beside her on a bench.

"Oh, yes. Sir Kieran is like this, always watchful."

"He seems useful. For a hired man."

She inclined her head.

"And a very good watchdog."

"Yes, he is very good at many things."

"Is he, my lady?" There was an edge of sharpness to his tone.

"Oh, indeed, he is my everything man, no? He manages matters great and small, yet he cannot do everything for me, can he? And so, he fears. It is the way of men, is it not? Always desiring to scoop up the finest things, and keep others from doing the same."

He grinned. "That is so. You read us well. I for one am gratified to have a merchant of such stature come north to visit English shores."

She glowed a smile at him. "It is our southern way, my lord, to gratify our partners."

"And is that why you are here, my lady?" came his swift reply. "To seek partners?"

"A wise merchant is always seeking new partners, do you not agree, my lord Noil?"

Slowly, Noil smiled. "I do indeed. New partners breathe new life."

She looked languidly around the room, filled with rich men sweating in the summer heat and the press of bodies, her gaze skimming over Kier's without pause. She touched the tips of her fingers lightly to her neck as she turned back to Noil and returned his smile in equal measure.

"They do indeed."

He leaned closer and murmured something that Kier could not hear. Sophia smiled.

A few moments later, they rose together and made their way outside to the battlement walls.

"I desired but a moment alone with you, my lady."

The moon was just rising over the ramparts. Sophia leaned

over the battlement wall and peered out at the valley below. The gray walls with the fluttering red and blue Noil pennants presided over a land of brown grass, brown huts, and a muddy brown river. So it wasn't blue, after all.

Sophia turned back to Noil. "You wish to speak of my ships, no doubt."

He lifted the wine flagon he'd carried out with them and poured more in her cup. "I would not be averse to such a conversation, my lady. If it pleases you."

Glinting in the moonlight, his sharp eyes regarded her. The smile on his face was sincere, but not to be trusted. It was all in service of him. How many people had he fooled, though, with his title and his money and his associations? That is what these men did, rode over others like horses over turf.

All she need do was make him think Mistral Company a worthy investment. All she need do was be convincing enough that he would make a recommendation to Cosimo Endolte. She would not accomplish either of those by appearing too eager. Reluctance made people convince themselves, in their efforts to convince you.

Kier had taught her that much about trickery.

So, she would appear uncertain, vulnerable, sensual, and very, very rich.

And she would keep him occupied long enough for Kier to investigate his offices.

She lifted the wine cup in her hand and gave him a regal nod over its rim.

He moved into action immediately. "Managing Mistral Company after your husband's demise must have been burdensome indeed, my lady."

"Indeed, it is so." She took a large swallow of wine and leaned forward with a conspiratorial smile. "I used to have many associates and clients, but I will tell you, my English friend, that since my husband's passing, some are less eager to use Mistral Company these days. And so, my trade, it shrinks. Coldhearted Italians and Frenchmen." She sipped and eyed him over the lip of her cup. "One hopes Englishmen are not equally so."

"We are not," he assured her. "We have warm regard for clever women, and an appreciation for wise investments."

She smiled slowly and turned to look out over the valley below. The moon was so bright it lit the fields and small village in a silvery wash. She leaned her shoulder against the cool stone and looked at him.

"So, is this what you Englishmen do, then, my lord? Find ladies of trade and eat them up?" She smiled.

A wary silence ensued. An even more wary, brief laugh broke it. "I do business of many sorts, my lady."

"I'm certain you do," she drawled.

"I trow I am not opposed to picking up the jug that is already half full. I am sure your late husband was not either. You should have a difficult time finding a successful tradesman who is."

"Yes, 'tis so." She sighed. "I once tried." She tipped her wine cup from side to side, watching the dark liquid slosh.

"Aye, Sir Kieran has mentioned your recent . . . travails," he said carefully.

"Has he?" She slid her gaze over. "He is an ambitious man."

He gave a small bow. "As am I."

"Then I am surrounded by ambitious men," she mused, turning to look at the moon-littered valley. The browning grass of the meadow glowed silver. She leaned back against the merlon as a soft breeze curled up from below, up under the heavy knot of her hair. How had she come to be this, this false woman with a false name under false pretenses, attempting to navigate through this morass of false men to lead a simple life?

Noil shifted beside her. "You are fortunate, my lady, for in this, we all value the same thing."

"Me?" she asked, as if she couldn't be more bored.

He gave a low laugh. "Perhaps I could express myself in more certain terms."

She rolled her wine cup between her fingertips. "Perhaps you could."

"I may have investors who would be interested, my lady. In Mistral Company."

"Investors." She tipped slightly to one side and narrowed her eyes at him. "You mean to purchase me."

"Nay, my lady," he hurried to assure her. "Not a'tall. I merely suggest ways we may benefit one another. I have interests, I can—"

"What manner of interests?"

He rubbed his fingertips through his beard. "Rich ones. We have a group of like-minded men who invest in likely merchants and their trades."

She pushed away from the wall and said coldly, "I am not carrion, my lord."

He pitched his voice low and persuasive. "You misunderstand, my lady. Sir Kieran brought you to me for assistance. The *commenda* are powerful, with deep pouches and, when the need suits, utterly silent. And we have heard of your misfortunes, the investments that have failed, the clients who have fled. And I say to you, we are not so shortsighted as they."

She turned away to look out over the battlement wall. "Kier has spoken to me of this as well." She let the silence grow long. She waited, and waited, then, quietly, without looking over, she said, "How much help?"

The leather of his boots creaked as he stepped toward her. He set his hand overtop hers. It was slightly sweaty, and pressed down heavily.

"Are we speaking of price, my lady?"

He wanted her. He had assessed her and now he wanted her. Her work here was complete.

She pulled back. "I do not know," she murmured, pulling her hand away. She turned to the door, stumbling a step. "I find I am weary. The travel, and the storms . . ."

"Do not go yet, my lady," he said, his voice firm. He reached out and took hold of her hand, a hard grip.

The clang of spurs rang out on the battlement walls. The door behind them slammed against the castle wall as it was flung wide, and Kier stepped out with a woman in tow.

His wide palm was against the stone wall as he stepped through the doorway, dark brown against the gray stone. They stopped at the sight of Noil and Sophia, and the woman gave a startled squeak of surprise. Her leaf-green skirts swirled forward over Kier's boots. He put his arm around her waist to steady her.

The woman's face was flushed, her lips wet, her eyes dewy as she looked up in appreciation.

Perhaps it had not been to steady her.

What was he doing out here, *with a woman,* whilst he was supposed to be breaking into Noil's offices?

Kier apologized to them both in civil, if slightly inebriated, terms.

Sophia sniffed and took the arm Noil had extended to her. "Come, my lord. I find the evening air has become a bit close."

Noil sent Kier a triumphant look as they passed by. But Kier's eye held Sophia's, and it was not drunk whatsoever.

NOIL escorted her back onto the dais for the next course, and the next, and the next after that. There were approximately forty courses, or so it seemed to Sophia.

But perhaps that was because she was watching Kier navigate

the room in between each, stopping as he went, engaged by a hand on his arm or a word from someone. Generally laughter would follow soon after, and invariably a woman or three trailed in his wake, gliding in and out of Kier's range of vision like swans on parade.

Swans were vicious animals. Sophia did not like swans.

She scowled and plunged her hands with excessive vigor into the bowl of wash water a servant presented. Water splashed over the sides. The servant leaped back.

"Perhaps after the cheeses, I might show you my manuscript collection, my lady," Noil was saying. He glanced at the water drenching her sleeves and the edge of table linen. "Or perhaps you might rather rest. The games become distinctly less refined as the night progresses."

She fought off irritation and rested her chin on her forefinger, smiling, ignoring the water dribbling down her sleeve. "But this is fascinating. In what manner do Englishmen shed their refinement?"

"Naught you've not encountered elsewhere, my lady," he said. "Dicing, dancing, wh . . ." He trailed off, clearly uncertain how to proceed. "All manner of other thing."

She turned on her seat and aimed a deep, slow smile at him. "But I greatly enjoy dicing and dancing, my lord. And all manner of other thing."

Twenty-four

Kier was waiting in her room when Sophia was finally escorted back to it, hours later.

He sat silent and motionless as she pushed the door shut. She walked softly to the window and stood briefly in a spill of late moonlight, then turned to a small table, lit a candle, and began unpinning her hair.

He let her slide a few pins out, then a few more, until her hair began to fall down around her shoulders like russet rain. He did this simply for the pleasure of seeing her hair unbound. Then he slid his boot forward slightly, scraping it against the floor.

She stilled, her arms up, elbows out, frozen in place.

"You should take more care, Sophia."

She exhaled in a long stream. "Kier." She turned in her seat. "You frightened me."

"Good."

"What are you doing here?"

"Cautioning you."

The candle fluttered behind her, casting her face into shadows. "On what?"

"On bolting your doors when you return to your room. On

how you bait Noil. " Her fingers curled palely around the edge of the oak table. "He is a beast, Sophia. You should not dangle meat, then take it away."

"You said to make him desire me."

"I said to make him desire your *business*."

"Whatever he desires in me, it is making him talk."

He sat forward. "About what?"

She lifted a hand. It was pale in the moonlight. "About his desire to see the world. On a ship. One of mine. Or all of them. He asked about prices."

"Did he?" he said softly, smiling faintly.

She matched his quietness and his smile. "He did indeed."

He sat back. "That is a night's good work." She gave a little nod of acceptance of the compliment. "All of it. Noil, the account books in his office, the maid. The cat," he added.

She laughed softly. "The cat tossed herself into the mix, Kier. I can hardly take credit for her."

"Take credit."

She laughed again, then went back to her hair. He watched her begin the opening stages of undressing as they spoke quietly, unpinning her hair idly, as if she had not even thought he oughtn't be there.

"You should be equally careful, Kier. Showing up like that on the walls, when you were supposed to be searching Noil's office chamber." She shook her head. Another pin freed. He imagined its silky slide through her hair. "One would think you were jealous. That will not help a'tall."

"No," he agreed grimly. "It will not."

Glancing at him, she rose and took the few steps required to reach the rear of the small chamber, where a folding screen stood in the corner. She stepped behind it.

Without even a candle, she was nothing but a faint darker shape behind the paneling, shifting, bending over.

She was bending over.

He looked away. He should leave. Right now.

One silhouetted leg came up and she flicked her skirts away. The shapely curves of her arms began unlacing the dark ribbons crisscrossed around her black-clad calf.

He stared, helpless. He could not look away. He watched the shifting shadow that was Sophia-undressing-behind-a-screen, not wanting to say anything that might disrupt her from sharing her quiet thoughts. Nothing to stop her from almost undressing in front of him, from moving her silk-rustling body in the candlelight.

Soon enough, he'd go to his room, lie in the dark, and try to remember the sound of her body moving.

"You seemed to enjoy yourself tonight," she said, her voice slightly muffled from bending over.

He looked up blankly. "I did?"

"With the women tonight."

He searched his mind. There had been women tonight?

"On the ramparts," she clarified.

"Ahh. She was not a *woman*. She was a *device*, a stratagem, a . . . tactic."

Behind the screen, she stilled. "How unfortunate for her."

He shook his head. "She will not rue the loss of me, lass. She is enamored of whomever pays her the most attention. And that was surely not me."

She stepped out from behind the screen. Trails of dark brown-red curls unbent and laddered down beside her pale cheeks, and she lifted her head and smiled at him. It was the small sort of smile that you would miss were you not so very close, noticing how three small crescent moons deepened on the right side of her crooked mouth, and how her eyes truly *saw* him, and wanted him even so.

He felt as if he'd been slammed in the chest and pushed

back ten miles, the world rushing on, him standing still, smashed up against the image of her.

And then, finally, thank God, the anger appeared.

Old friend, he thought with a bitter smile, *where have you been?*

Empowered, he pushed to his feet. Wanting Sophia's body was acceptable, understandable, and inevitable.

Wanting *Sophia* was unendurable.

He reached for the door.

"He danced." Sophia's voice drifted out from behind him.

He stopped. "What?"

"D'Aumercy danced."

Twenty-five

Sophia stood in front of the small table. Snaking red ribbons were dark rivers across its oak top. The hammered design on the back of the silver brush glinted with moonlight.

"Did you not see?" she asked lightly, not looking over. Little rose vines pirouetted across the whitewashed walls in front of her. "D'Aumercy danced."

Behind her, his boots scuffed on the ground. He was coming back into the room. "I'm impressed."

She resisted the rebel smile pressing against her cheeks. No one could know this dastardly thing, not even her, this thing that made her no better than Kier, in the end.

She looked at him. A mistake. Everywhere was Kier. He was close, and tall, his tunic unlaced because of the heat. He wore boots and breeches and nothing else.

"He danced for you," he said quietly.

This time she didn't fight the smile, it came out full force. She nodded, and he smiled.

It was a slow Kier smile, the rare sort. It made her want to lean forward into him. It made her want to make him smile more. It made her feel as if she had expanded, and all the heat in the room was being absorbed into her skin, rather than pressing atop it.

She conceded to the sensation this far, to lean forward to whisper, *"Twice."*

He gave a low laugh as he tugged a leather pouch off his belt and laid it on the table in front of her. "You are very good at this, Sophia."

"I know," she whispered, feeling wild inside, like a storm breaking.

A faint smile touched his lips. As if he had the right, he slid his callused hand under the heavy weight of her hair and cupped the nape of her neck. Flexing his fingers, he pulled her to stand in front of him.

"Very, very good," he murmured, his Irish lilt in full force.

Long, fat, shivery ribbons unfurled in her belly as his thumb stroked down the heat of her neck.

Something about that, his low words, his lazy smile, the way he looked at her with approval, made something tall rise up within Sophia, a flag being raised, a fire being kindled. His fingers loosened, slipped around to the side of her neck, one finger at a time. His eyes drifted to her lips.

"Do you remember the last time, Sophia?"

Did she *remember*?

He'd come to her, in the dark, in a meadow, under the hawthorn tree. He'd come up behind her and put his lips on her neck, whispering words she could not understand, but she knew what they meant. And she went to him, pressed her back to him, let him slide one hard hand below her breast, cupping her. Then his other hand, sliding up beneath the light drape of her tunics, the light brush of his fingers tickling up her inner thigh, whispering wanton, wicked, wonderful things in her ear.

She'd almost died in his arms before her father had called for her.

She would *never* forget that moment, the way the sky above seemed to fill her with wide-open spaces and Kier. The way he'd made her feel as though she was his pennant being raised. For that is what Kier did; he raised her up, her hopes, her dreams, her passions.

Then dropped her back down to earth with a heart-shattering thud.

He leaned forward now, his mouth to her ear, and whispered, *"I remember."*

He dropped his hand and turned to the door.

It was shocking, the power of this subtle removal. On her chin were invisible stripes of heat where his fingers had lain. The back of her neck was branded by his searing touch.

Kier wanted her as much as she wanted him, there was no question of that. It had always been thus with them, the ever-kindled fires of desire. But if she wanted Kier the way the earth wants rain, he wanted her the way the wind wants something to sweep across.

She should let him walk out, say good night, and never reference the mad, restless dare of him again.

But she burned for him, her heart stretched in ache for him, every time she breathed.

And just now, she was humming with reckless energy, as she had not been since he'd left her five years ago. She might take flight upon the hum of it, float across the room on bumblebee wings.

"I remember too," she whispered to his back.

Twenty-six

He stopped, his hand on the door handle, and looked back at her. His eyes were a force, a power to be reckoned with.

"How well?" he said in a voice so low she almost didn't hear.

She inhaled. The breath lit her breasts with tingling fire. "Every night, I remember every moment."

She listened to him move across the room toward her, his slow, measured boot steps on the plank floors, the silvery cling of spurs as he drew near. The hard length of his body stilled a few paces away. He stepped behind her.

Her breath shot out but she didn't move. His finger hooked under the neckline of her tunic and dragged it to the side.

She exhaled hotly.

He bent his head, brought his lips to hover just above her bare shoulder, and he . . . breathed on her.

A ragged breath was torn from her lips and he'd not even touched her yet.

Softly he murmured, "Do you remember this?"

"I remember," she whispered.

He traced the air above her bare shoulder with his breath, so close she could almost feel his lips, *but not quite*, just breath on her skin, then, *oh Jésu*, along the arm he now bent to lift into the air. Breathing her in, exhaling his breath over her neck, her shoulder, her arm, his hard body so close, not touching, but burning her all the same.

Her body trembled. Freezing hot chills scraped down the front of her skin.

"I'm going to kiss you," he said.

She pressed her eyes closed and her head tipped back the smallest bit.

His lips touched her shoulder, maddening, breathtakingly light. She felt the hot swipe of his tongue and dropped her head forward the inch it had just fallen back, baring the back of her neck to him, baring herself.

He slid like a dancer over the bridge she'd made, his lips, his mouth, burning hotter now, moving faster, his mouth open, his tongue sliding across her sensitive skin, so she shivered in the dark heat. She could feel wisps of her hair under his mouth, but he did not brush them aside; he kissed them, those fire touches of lip and tongue, working across her shoulders and neck like across a battlefield.

"Hold on to the bedpost," he whispered, low and carnal. She did. Lifted her arm, heavy as hot wax off a candle, folded her fingers around the wooden post, and held on.

"Now I'm going to touch you," he said in her ear, and he cupped the side of her ribs, not where she'd expected him to lay his assault on her. His fingers folded over her ribs, his thumbs behind her back, and then he slid down her sides, over the tunic and her ribs and belly to her hips in a slow, sliding embrace. His hands, still moving down, swept off her hips like they were taking flight.

His body was the range, the mountain behind her. Without pause, he pushed his hands up the front of her belly now, his open palms across her heavy breasts, over the taut, almost painful nipples, laid his mouth to the side of her neck, and sucked.

She gave a shuddering cry and let her head fall back into his mouth, her body pressed forward into his hands.

He made another bold swipe down her body, and this time, when he came away, he'd unlaced the ties on the sides of her gown. He tugged them again, until they hung in loose streamers beside her body.

"I can do more," he rasped.

She quivered, desperate for his next slow assault. But he did nothing, just stood motionless, all restrained power and heat, his wicked hands hanging at his side.

She felt veined with silver and gold, alive and trembling, like a taut drum skin, resonating with the lightest touch of his fingers.

"Aye, Sophia?"

She whispered some wordless sound.

His dark voice came by her ear. "Say aye. *Aye*," he whispered, a husky, dark syllable that went on and on, rasping over the unspoken possibilities she suddenly, desperately wanted.

She felt his knee bumping the back of hers. He wanted, he was primed and ready, he was simply waiting. For her.

She let her head fall back to his shoulder. "Aye," she whispered.

She might have lit him on fire.

He gripped her hips and pushed, a hard, powerful push against her buttocks, just to feel her, hard, to make her *know*, then he swiftly pushed the outer tunic off her shoulders, so it puddled around her feet in a sea of shimmering green.

Then, before she could right herself, before she could retract her consent, he stepped in front of her and kissed her.

He pulled her up against his long, powerful body and dove deep into the recesses of her mouth, coaxing her to come closer, to open further, to return his fire. His hands skipped down her body, and everywhere he touched, he ignited. His hands glanced off her ribs, leaving fire in his wake. He caressed her waist, making her burn. He slid his hands down her hips, ever down, a lowering flame, the flame that bids, *Come down further, further yet, stretch out your hand and you will see what fire truly is.* He boldly cupped her bottom, lifted her on his palms, and the shock of searing heat scalded her. She cried out. He *burned* her. Branded her.

Then he lowered himself before her body, holding her face into his kiss, until he sat on the chest at the base of the bed, his kiss leaving her lips, going lower, lower, until he was kissing her belly through the gown. With firm confidence, he folded his hand overtop hers, making her keep her hands wrapped around the bedpost, while he moved his other hand down beneath her skirts.

"Kier," she whispered.

"Sophia." He cupped his palm around her cool, trembling knee, and began sliding it up. Her knee bent and bobbed against him. *Sweet Sophia, so close.*

Eyes locked on his, she reached down to cup his face, her hair falling over his hands and face, and Kier descended into a place carnal and incendiary.

His thumb touched her damp curls first. Her body jolted, her hands clenching around the bedpost. He pulled away and carved a hot path up her sweaty skin with his mouth and closed his hungry mouth around her breast and suckled at the same moment he pushed a finger up into her.

She flung her head back, crying out.

"Aye, just like that," he said thickly, his tongue now on her navel. He pressed his thumb into her slippery folds, swirling up against her, and his finger pushed inside, slow and sure.

"Oh, please, oh, Kier," she was whispering. Her hands were still on the post, gripping it, as she moved to the slow, rhythmic pressure he built, designed to make her howl his name and gasp sweet nothings that spoke of how she ached for him, how he was more to her than a partner in this crime, how his touch was more than arousing, it was fated.

He kept up his slow, restrained strokes until her hips started pushing against his chest of their own accord. Her head tipped back, her breath nothing now but little whispered gasps of his name and *please.*

He increased his pressure, the depth of his stroke, the push of the fingers and the slide of his thumb, until her hands were clenching even tighter around the bedpost and her head was tossing, her hair falling in marvelous disarray around him. Her breath started coming in arhythmic little gasps, and she moaned, an uneven, unsteady, upending sort of sound.

"Look at me," he ordered in a rasp.

She tipped her head down to him, and in the dark silken cavern made by her hair, her eyes met his.

"I remember you."

She erupted in a wild, shuddering mess and collapsed onto his lap, a perfect tumble of messy kisses and whispers of his name.

Twenty-seven

Sophia had no idea how long it was before she came to her wits. A moment, an hour. All she knew was it was still dark and his hands were still on her, gently stroking, his mouth pressing soft kisses to the side of her damp head.

Kier was kissing the side of her head.

Good and merciful God, what had she done?

She ripped away, gasping and dizzy.

Reeling like a drunk person, she stumbled across the room, feeling her way to the window, ignoring Kier sitting in dark silhouette where he'd turned her traitor to herself, coaxed her to entwine her fingers in his hair.

She leaned against the window, but there was no relief here. The summer heat lowered over the fields and earth like a fog, and everything that had occurred had still occurred.

She stared down at her hands planted on the sill, her head down, her body still, *still* gasping for air. It was a very fine line to tread, this one she walked, between her fated past and the choices she made in the present. Much of the past could be attributed to youth and the poor lessons learned there, not what she truly *was.* Not what she intended to be.

But it was all a mist of lies. She was *this.* Cony-catcher,

Kier's doxy, doing his bidding at the merest suggestion, wanting him like earth does rain.

If Kier, with his masterful kisses and slow seductive focus, could upend her, that meant she was . . . stoppable.

As good as dead.

She straightened. "It appears—" She stopped, shocked at how hoarse she sounded. As if she hadn't spoken for weeks.

So, he has even changed the passage of my time.

She jerked away from the window and came back into the room. Kier was sitting where she'd left him, not looking at her. He was leaning forward, looking down at his hands.

He was magnificent ruination. His sculpted body was exposed in swipes of skin: dark chest hair where his tunic fell apart, the strong column of his neck, boots still on but breeches unlaced, his hair in disarray from her fingers.

She grabbed his hand angrily and dragged him to his feet. Then she took a large step back.

"That is *all*," she said fiercely, her voice thick.

His gleaming eyes were hard in the moonlight. "No, it isn't." He walked to the door, then paused and looked over his shoulder. "Bar it after me."

As if that would protect her now.

Twenty-eight

Kier launched himself down to Noil's office to begin his search. It was ridiculously simple to break in; there was a single lock and no guard. When a man felt safe, he was usually at his most vulnerable.

As had always been the case for him with Sophia.

He picked locks and flung open coffer lids, keeping one ear trained, listening for any thin ribbon of sound that would indicate someone else was awake and afoot.

But likely, other than the drunkards, only he and Sophia were astir.

Sophia. Even the name conjured images of her mouth. Her crooked, mischievous, generous mouth.

He'd thought a kiss might rectify the accursed *animal* wanting. Take a taste, sate the appetite, particularly when she so clearly wanted it too. She was not a virgin, not a child, not a whore; she was a grown, willing woman and there was nothing off-limits about Sophia except their history.

But both history and the present day crossed the borders of his heart.

He ran his fingers through his hair and spun on his heel. That's when he saw it.

Sitting on a side table under the window, carelessly laid, was the Darnly ledger.

Swiftly he flipped it open. His focus narrowed and deepened, as if he were falling down a hole, as he examined the dark scrawling lines of carefully penned words detailing deeds done that never ought to have been done. And as he read, he went slower, and then slower yet.

He'd expected details. He'd not expected this *level* of detail. It was staggering.

It covered what he'd expected: agreements made, payments done, and in what form—coin, gem, position, influence. But these sorts of things could still be denied by the perpetrators, albeit at some battering to their reputation and perhaps the loss of some royal preferences.

But the details here were damning.

There was no way to explain away the "coincidences" this ledger described.

A sudden, sharp reduction in one's coffers might be claimed as an unreported robbery, or an endowment to some far-off monastery. A sudden increase, perhaps an inheritance from some heretofore undisclosed uncle in Toulouse. Or Edinburgh. Or Palestine; the farther away, the better.

But the resultant and perfectly timed appearance of *commenda* investors on the company rolls as shareholders? A daughter's unexpected wedding into the nobility? A son's investiture with sinecures, one after the other, following a deposit into some bishop's account? Very particular votes in Edward's parliament?

That sort of thing was much more difficult to explain away.

And it did not stop there. In case anyone should still have the bollocks to try to deny their culpability, here too were identifying notations about the meetings themselves. Dates, times, traveling arrangements, jewelry worn, mistresses and guardsmen who'd been in the entourage—people who could, of course, be questioned.

Eventually, someone would break.

There were tightly scribed lines containing the details of what had driven people: the bankruptcies, the ill-gotten gains and ill-gotten sons, the simple and complicated greed. And overriding it all, the massive, resounding errors of judgment in trade and family life that encouraged one to dally with Roger Darnley, judge and gateway to the *commenda*. The sort of missteps that would destroy lives if they were ever discovered.

It was as if someone had sat in the shadows at the back of hundreds of private, personal conversations and written everything down.

It was a collection of some of the most damning details on the middle gentry and high nobility of western England.

And it was all written in Sophia's hand.

All but the most recent entries. Those were in Richard the Scribe's hand.

Sharp-edged and slanting as only a left-handed man's writing did, Kier would recognize it anywhere: Richard had once been Cosimo's bookkeeper.

And Sophia's husband.

Twenty-nine

Sophia awoke to the sound of pounding at her bedchamber door.

She flung herself out of bed, disoriented, her fingers cold and trembling, chemise hem tickling around her ankles. A steamy gray dawn illuminated the room. The air lay thick and sullen.

She tiptoed to the door and whispered, "Who is it?"

"Lucifer. Open the door."

Exhaling in annoyance and relief, she lifted the bar and swung the door open. Kier stood there, head down as he shoved his sword into its sheath. He looked up briefly, then backed her inside, already speaking.

"We're leaving."

"But why? There is a hunt—"

He beckoned to a pair of servants who hovered in the background. They tromped in, each grabbed a side of one of her chests, and lumbered out the door with it.

She stared after them in amazement.

Outside, across the landing, servants bustled by on various errands, bearing candle nubs and sheets and chamber pots, and a guest in a tunic went by, holding a hand to bleary eyes, descending the stairs.

Kier pushed the door shut.

"What is happening?" she demanded. "Why are we leaving? I have men to convince—"

"They are convinced. We leave."

She gave a clipped nod. "Very good, then. But must you be so precipitous?"

"Aye." His gaze flicked down her chemise. "How long will it take to ready yourself?"

She crossed her arms over her chest, feeling very exposed, with Kier's gaze touching her in all the places his hands had last night. "Rather longer than usual, as the servants have just absconded with my gowns."

He narrowed his eyes. "Why did you not say something?"

She narrowed hers back. "Why did not *you*?"

For a long moment he stared at her, then he flung the door open. "Be ready within the hour."

IN the steel and iron shadows of the stormy morning, Kier escorted Sophia out Noil's front door, with news of pressing business. She returned all kisses of the peace as they stood at the doorway, then leaned to d'Aumercy and murmured, "I have thought a great deal about the matters we discussed yesternight."

He grinned.

"I would be interested in meeting your investors." She tugged her hood over her head and smiled. "But I should not accept anything less than twenty thousand, you know."

Kier flung a cape over her head, took her arm, and they stepped out into the whipping winds.

THE storm was not toying with them; it meant business. It held off for most of the day, only to build by truly terrifying degrees, threatening and rumbling.

They rode hard for Last Fells. Before midday, clouds were mounted on the horizon like angry horses about to be loosed, mottled gray and rumbling.

By noon, the winds had picked up in a moaning sort of way. Behind Kier and Sophia, the guards hunkered in their saddles as small branches bounced past them, touching the earth in little hops, like children skipping to the fair.

"I am forced to comment on a certain lack of flexibility in your planning, Kier," she observed loudly, to be heard over the winds. "Might we not have delayed our departure until the storm had passed?"

"No," he replied curtly and pulled his hood farther up his head. With the growth of his beard and his cape and mud-splattered boots, he looked as menacing and lethal as any ruffian.

She glared at him. "Why not?"

He turned and gave her a long, wordless, utterly impassive look. He might have been staring at a wall. Then he faced forward again.

How was one to make sense of a look like that?

They were within a mile of Last Fells when evening turned to twilight and the storm finally broke. It started with fat, pelting raindrops that raised puffs of dust as they slammed into the earth.

"Come," he called, kicking his horse into a gallop. She was fast on his heels.

By the time they galloped into the courtyard at the Spanish Lady, the rains were sheeting down. They ran into the inn with water streaming off their clothes.

The common room was crowded and stinking of bodies and smoke and food; the storm had channeled all the guests back to the Spanish Lady's hospitality, and they were drinking and eating heartily.

Kier and Sophia found the bustling innkeep shouting at a serving boy covered in ale, apparently recently spilled. He turned to them, wiping his hands on his apron.

"Any messages?" Kier said curtly.

"Nay, sir. Not since you left. My lady." He bowed to Sophia.

Kier tuned to survey the common room with a suspicious eye. "We need food upstairs."

"Very good, sir. "

"And drink."

"Very good, sir. I've a nice brick of cheese, and some bread from this morning, and . . ."

Kier looked at him with a sort of terrifying blank regard. Innkeep's voice trailed off.

"Send it up. All of it."

Innkeep paled and nodded.

Kier all but swung Sophia out the door and up the stairs to their apartments.

SHE looked around the room, debating where to wring out her chemise skirts, for she surely was not going to *undress* to dry them, not with Kier standing there. And as he did not appear to be leaving, she would have to make do.

Nothing presented itself except the chamber pot, so she stood beside it and began carefully wringing.

Behind her, Kier tossed shutters closed and flipped latches down. When a knock came on the door, he ripped it open and all but grabbed the tray of food and drink out of the startled servant's hands. Coming back in, he set down the tray, scooped up one of the mugs of ale, and downed a significant portion of it.

She watched the entire spectacle, then turned back to wringing the parts of her gown that could be wrung with a sniff.

"I must say, I do not see it," she said airily.

She heard him set his mug on the table. "See what?"

"Your charm. You have lost it entirely. I am not impressed. Neither," she added significantly, "was Noil. Nor our innkeeper, for that matter."

Kier did not seem to share her compunctions about disrobing. He strode to the bed and began unbuckling his belt.

"I am not here to impress Noil," he said curtly. "And certainly not our innkeeper."

"Indeed, *I* am to impress Noil. Which you assisted with approximately not a'tall. My point is simply that should you occasionally use phrases such as 'Good morning' or 'God's grace to you, sir' or 'please' or even 'thank you,' you might find people more disposed to do as you will them."

"People do as I will them oft enough, Sophia." He tossed his sword belt, blades attached, onto the mattress.

Her face flushed. Surely he could not be alluding to last night, could he? It was entirely possible. And undiscussable. And unrepeatable. She ignored any possible allusions and sniffed again.

"I am merely saying that a well-timed 'please' might serve even *your* nefarious ends," she said, giving her skirts a tighter squeeze. The silk would be all but ruined.

"I do not say 'please.'"

She looked over her shoulder at him. "You have never once said 'please' or 'my thanks'?"

He pulled the tunic up and over his head, then balled it in his fist.

The heat started in her belly, spreading out in ripples. Naked. Kier's chest was bare.

"To the contrary, Sophia, I have oft given thanks."

"But not please?"

"Nay."

"That is foolish."

He looked directly at her. "As is lying to me."

She stared. "Against my much better judgment, I have ne'er lied to you," she said coldly.

He looked at her for a long time. Long enough to cause . . . not fear, quite, but *something* to shiver along her spine. Then he tossed the wet tunic onto the bed, reached into his pack, and took something out. He turned to her with it in hand.

Bound in dark leather, cracked along the edges, it was a ledger.

"Kier!" she cried excitedly, reaching for it. "You found it."

"I did."

The flatness of his voice wrested the smile from her face, replacing it with a cold knot of unease. She lowered her hand. "What is it?"

"Do you know what is in here?"

She felt heat race up her cheeks. "I do."

He took a step closer. "Names. Dates. Deeds."

"I know that. Terrible things were done."

"Aye. And 'tis your hand that records them all."

Thirty

Sophia drew in a breath, then nodded and lowered herself to a bench behind her.

"You are correct. That is my hand. I documented all those deeds."

"At your father's behest?"

She shook her head. "No. He did not know about it for many years."

"That is impossible."

She gave a small, bitter smile. "What is impossible, Kier? I know how to scribe. I know how to listen. I know how to detest."

"How?"

"I sat in the background, outside the chamber door, whenever his associates arrived, and I wrote everything down. Everything they said, everything they agreed to, every coin they exchanged, every promise they sold. I wrote it all down."

"Why?"

She felt his gaze on her, but didn't look up. "Because I hated what they were doing." Her voice vibrated a moment, then steadied. "I could not stop it, but I could document it. These men who wished to be in shadows? They would be shined upon."

"To what end?"

She shrugged a shoulder. "I wished to . . ." She swept her hand out, then lowered it carefully back to her lap. "I wished one day to stop them."

"Did the things in the ledger help convict your father?"

She looked at the damp chemise pasted thinly over her knees. "No. There was evidence enough without it. But the rumors had begun about the Darnly ledger. People thought my father kept it as a blade to hold to Cosimo's throat should the need arise. But it was not my father's deed; it was mine. And they will never stop hunting me."

Silence filled the room, while outside the storm crashed against the shutters. A blue-white streak of lightning slashed the air outside, and illuminated the room in an eerie light. A moment later, thunder crashed. Kier did not move.

For a moment she thought they were done. She felt washed through but strangely taut. In a thousand years, she could not have predicted her secret would have been unburdened this way, in a confession to the outlaw she'd loved. And what Kier would do with the knowledge, she couldn't say. The next few moments with him were mirrors of their past; fraught with intensity and entirely unpredictable.

She looked up and swallowed down a raw, dry throat.

His gaze followed her swallow. "And that is when you came upon me," he said slowly. "In Tomas's office. Came to me aft, showed up on my doorstep, wanting into my schemes." His voice was low, slow, full of unsaid things.

Her heart skipped a beat, hurrying onward, pounding harder, faster. Why, such timing *might* look suspicious. If . . . if . . .

"Tell me about your husband."

She shook her head, confused. "My husband? Why?"

"Because I asked."

She bent her head, trying to gather her spinning thoughts. Why should Kier care about her husband?

She took a deep breath. "As I said, I moved to Batten Downs soon after Papa was hanged. Richard moved there himself sometime later."

"How much later?"

She cast her mind back, thinking. "A few weeks, a month mayhap? It was soon after. He always spoke of how serendipitous it was. Two outsiders, alone in the town. We became close."

She paused, remembering what had substituted for closeness with Richard.

"He offered marriage out of pity, I am sure, for he was not a man in need of a wife with no dowry and an almost bankrupt trade. It had been hit hard. Moving and establishing myself anew, dealing only with those clients who had never seen me before, this all took a toll. And as a woman alone, no husband . . ." She shook her head. "Richard stepped forward, offered for me. Not many would have. He was kind to do so."

And distant, and never to home, and slightly, ever so slightly, violent.

"He was not being kind." Kier's voice was dark.

She glanced up. "I do not know what you mean."

"He was not kind."

She squinted at him. "You did not know my husband, Kier."

Silence.

"You did not know my husband," she said again, insisting. When there was still no reply, only his inscrutable regard, she got slowly to her feet. "Kier?"

"I knew your husband."

"How—"

"He was Cosimo's bookkeeper."

Her jaw fell. "Impossible."

"Richard the Scribe. Left-handed Richard, 'better with a stylus than a sword,'" he said, tossing her words back at her.

Coldness started like a sheet of water, flowing down the front of her, freezing her.

"No. Richard was a . . . a simple man. He was—"

"The *commenda*'s clerk."

"No."

"Cosimo's bookkeeper."

"No! That is impossible. I ran. No one could have found me. I took up a new name, a new—"

"*I delivered money to him,* Sophia," he insisted, pressing deeper into these awful truths. "I took his signature upon my receipts. I know his hand. He managed Cosimo's money. Until he disappeared. Vanished. Soon after your father's death."

She said, "No," but it was faint, because they both knew it was "yes."

"And in the ledger, your husband's hand has recorded entries—"

"*What?*"

"—showing he received money."

"Money?"

"Large amounts. Excessively large."

She looked down at her hands. They were shaking. "How large?"

"Thousands."

Chills were everywhere on her; his hands were hot against her wet gown. "That is impossible, Kier. We never had that sort of coin. Always, we struggled, and—"

"*Someone* had that sort of coin, Sophia. And your husband received it all."

For some reason, her heart thundered inside her chest. Ignorance was not enough to explain it. This felt more like the wavy object visible just below the surface of a stream; if you looked closely enough, you'd realize what it was, and known you could have seen it all along.

"Received it from whom?" she whispered.

"An envoy for the king of France."

It was like a punch in the belly. She lost her breath. "I do not know the king of France," was the idiocy that left her lips.

"Your husband did." Dark eyes held hers, the darkness of Kier and his cunning, Kier who knew things. "And King Edward has just declared war on him."

Thirty-one

Sophia felt the blood drain from her face. She stepped back. He let her go. She touched her fingers to her lips. Everything was cold.

"Merciful God," she whispered, turning away, hand pressed to her forehead. "I do not understand." She wiped a shaking hand over her mouth, turning to the wall to think, to think.

Her husband had been in league with Cosimo Endolte and the *commenda*? No. Absolutely not. That was her *father*, not her husband. It was impossible.

And yet . . . not.

There was nothing specific, of course. Her husband had been a simple man, a clerk at heart, who . . . moved to the same town as Sophia only a few weeks after she.

Who sought her out from the first moment there.

Who proposed a union within months.

Who never seemed to care much for her, one way or the other.

Who sourced the silk, going so far as Trebizond to establish contacts, and yet did not know much of the trade nor seem to care in the least how much money it made.

Who had found the ledger. And had not seemed appalled or frightened by it.

And her father . . . her father had been the one to suggest she flee to Batten Downs. Where Richard had found her.

There was nothing there, nothing to grasp hold of, but . . . there was something there. Her dead husband, her dead father, Cosimo Endolte. It was all some horrifying web of . . . of what?

Her mind couldn't focus. It skipped over implications and ramifications like a skidding stone. Why? To what end?

She rubbed her hands down her rain-drenched sleeves to ward off a sudden chill. "I do not understand."

"Do you not?"

Oh, she did not like how he said that *at all.* She turned around.

Kier was standing where she'd left him, in the center of the room, tunic off, damp breeches clinging to his thighs, jagged locks of hair pressed against his neck, watching her, completely motionless. As he generally was when he thought danger was nigh.

"Kier, you cannot think I *knew* something about this?"

"Why not?"

She reached out, reflexively, then dropped her hand at what she saw on his face: suspicion. Why did she feel so . . . bereft?

His dark eyes were cold, like glittering darts. "You are saying you have no knowledge of your husband's involvement with the *commenda*? His receipt of monies?"

"Of course not. How could you think so?"

"Because your father was a corrupt judge who dealt with the *commenda*. Because your husband was their clerk. 'Tis all very convenient, with you in the center of it all."

She swallowed.

"They were up to mischief, there at the end, your father and your husband. Whether in service of Cosimo or outside his knowledge, I do not know. Yet. And now, they are both dead."

She was shaking hard.

"And I am asking what you know."

She got to her feet. "You are suspicious of *me*?" After all that Kier had done, after all that he was, after all that had been, he thought to accuse *her* of unscrupulous things? "You accuse *me* of dastardly deeds, Kier?"

"I do not accuse. I asked you what you know." His voice was still low, still in control, and somehow, this calmness of his infuriated her more than anything else.

She lifted her chin. "Naught."

His eyes searched her face. "And yet you are very angry about it."

"Oh, but that is what you do, Kier," she said in a low, furious voice, anger making her reckless. "Everyone you come across at some point or another finds himself wishing to *murder* you." She pointed at the wicked, white puckered scar that cut across the planes of his shoulder. "A reward for angering some powerful man, no doubt."

A twisted smile touched his mouth. "No doubt."

"I hope it satisfied," she whispered wickedly.

"I would not know, Sophia. You might, though: What *did* your father say of the matter?"

She froze. Her jaw fell. "What did you say?"

His hard eyes locked on hers. "I said: I do not know whether trying to burn me alive satisfied or not. What did your father say when I did not return?"

Her head felt submerged in oil; her thoughts were thick, sluggish, hard to form.

"He said . . ." She swallowed. "He said you'd left me . . . us. That I was to forget you. That you had tried above your station and failed, and good riddance to the Irish trash you were."

The terrifying smile stayed in place, etched in his icy regard. "Well, then," he said softly. "I suppose it satisfied."

Chills, freezing, pricking, stabbing chills, clawed down her chest and arms. Her jaw felt frozen and thick; it was difficult to move it to form words. "Are you saying my father—"

"Tried to murder me."

"Burned down—"

"The building."

"With you—"

"Inside." He finished all her terrible sentences, completing the unspoken truths of her life.

"How?" she whispered. *"Why?"*

The terrible smile was etched across the ice of his regard. "Just as he said, Sophia: I overstepped."

Her head spun. The revelations were coming too fast, but they all followed naturally, one after the other, like rocks falling off a cliff. Once you pushed, you could only hope to get out of the way before you were crushed.

It was too terrible to imagine, that her father would have left Kier there, burning alive. "I cannot believe my father—" She exhaled.

"Oh, he was not alone in it."

Her gaze flew up. The awful coldness of Kier's eyes was waiting. "He and Dragus did the deed. On Cosimo's orders."

"Dragus?" Her head felt pressured and hot, filling up. "The man with whom you are *partnered*?"

The cold smile on his face twisted. "He is not my partner, Sophia."

"And my father knew him. . . ."

"We all knew one another, Sophia, for as long as any of us lasted, which was never long. We were Cosimo's regiment, his legion, his horde."

Horror moved like floes of ice, sliding down her body. "This is not true," she stammered. "My father would never murder— My father *loved* you. *I* loved you!" She fisted her hands and stepped forward to smash them against his chest. "You . . . *lie.*"

"Not to you." His fingers tightened on her wrists. "And rarely to others. I mislead, I encourage people to misunderstand, but most commonly, I simply allow them to hope, which clouds their reason, such that they believe whatever they desire is just around the bend, and I will take them to it."

Her. He'd done all those things to her, led her all those places.

"I hate you," she lied in a whisper.

His eyes were terrible, hard, granite things, reflecting candlelight but no life. "You think I do not know that?"

She wanted to lean forward, put her hands on her knees, and breathe, just breathe. His scar was in the edge of her vision, dragged across the muscles of his body like the echo of some evil white whip, but she couldn't drag her gaze away from his piercing eyes.

She shoved her hands against the wall of his chest. Her eyes felt hot, her chest tight and pressured. Good God, if he didn't release her, she would explode. She shoved against him again, harder. He didn't move.

"Churl," she whispered hoarsely. "Brigand. Devil."

The thin sliver of that anti-smile slashed itself across his mouth. "Just the sort of trash your father dealt with."

For some ungodly, unfathomable reason, *this* was the thing that made hot tears well up in her eyes.

"You were *never* like them," she said fiercely, defending him. Or rather, her image of him, that youthful, shining image of a dark-eyed rogue with a heart of gold.

Stupid, stupid, stupid girl.

She shoved again, harder. He didn't move. She wanted to cry. She wanted to strike him, hit him, bite him. Demand he not be what he was.

He wrapped his hands around the low part of her back and pulled her up against him. His hard body was on hers, dark, wet hair falling down beside his cheekbones.

"I am exactly like them, Sophia," he said hoarsely. "Curse you for wishing me to be something other. Your father was right: I take what I want and I walk away."

And then, being himself in every way, he didn't hesitate, simply bent his head, put his mouth over hers, and undid her.

You never could trust criminals.

He took possession with a hot, ferocious kiss. From the first, his kiss was unbridled, hard and insistent, demanding, forcing her mouth open, lashing her with his tongue, kindling fires of desire that burned everywhere, her cheeks, her breasts, her belly, between her thighs. He was not asking permission, not with his words or his mouth, or the hands boldly roaming down her body, touching, pushing her up to the wall.

And she was not resisting. Not when she stood up on her toes, not when she pressed her body up against his, not when she met every lash of his tongue with one of her own until their teeth clicked together, ceding to every demand he made with his lips and hands.

Tightening his hold, he lifted her and planted her up against the wall behind them, then stepped between her thighs, her skirts dragged up on his legs. Then, watching her, he lowered her body against the length of his erection, her legs dangling on either side of his hips.

It was all raw desire now, fierce and taking. He had her up against the wall so her head was above him, and she tipped her face down, wet hair falling around them as she kissed him, her hands on his stubbled jaw, his neck, his hair, anything to be touching him. His chest was naked and hot against the front of her. Their harsh breathing was the only sound in the room as she pushed her hips forward, into the muscled wall of his body. He gripped her tightly and lowered her down the length of his shaft again in a slow, hard, wicked slide. A thick, undulating pulse of heat shuddered through her. He shifted his hips and made her do it again. She wrenched her mouth free, flinging her head back with a sharp cry.

Immediately, he cupped her head and pulled her face down to his. Bodies still pressed together, his hair wet and curling beside his neck, he whispered, "Do not turn on me, Sophia. It will not go well for you."

Then he lowered her to the ground, and even though he did it gently, even though he held her palm until she steadied herself, even *so*, he still turned and walked away in the end.

She stumbled backward, reeling. Her body thundered and roared. She spun around, then turned again. Rain lashed against the building, whipping winds and darkness. She wiped her hand against her forehead, trying to still her hammering head.

Kier was not a good man; he was a dangerous, ruthless, focused man, with no room for affection that did not serve a purpose. She knew it. He knew it. They had just had an almost violent kiss about it.

So why, deep inside, down the long well of her, in the dark, quiet place where she was perfectly capable of separating what she *wished* to be true from what she *knew* to be true, why, *why* did she still believe in him?

It was madness.

It was time to face that. Past time. Time to admit the "long well" of her had no bottom, and was utterly unreliable. Her love for Kier would go on and on, no matter what he did.

She could not trust him, and so, she could not trust herself.

It was time to leave.

Thirty-two

Kier didn't go far. And he didn't do much.

He went down to the common room and drank an ale he very much needed and thought thoughts he very much did not need.

Sophia was the keeper of the ledger that the most powerful, corrupt men in England were now chasing in the sort of frenzy that marked dogs after their tails. He almost laughed aloud.

He sobered immediately.

Why had she done such a thing? Such a mad, wonderful, stupid thing.

He kept seeing her standing there, wet, bedraggled, and beautiful, her fingers trembling before her makeshift gown, desperate, and trying to hide it. On ships or in schemes, women were, as ever, ruination. And they had a way of looking desperate and needful when the thing they needed was the very thing that would destroy you.

He raised his mug and realized it was empty already. He lifted his finger to order another. He must have looked morose, for Innkeep brought it at once, slid it directly under his downturned nose. He stood there, apron hovering just before Kier's downcast regard.

"Woman or horse?"

Kier lifted his head an inch. "What if I said a horse this time around?"

The innkeeper rubbed his chin. "Well, seeing as you're even more churned up than last time, I don't see how we can downgrade the matter to that of a horse."

Kier smiled. "You are a wise man."

The innkeeper nodded. "She's confounded you?"

"Mightily."

"Well, they're a powerful dialectic, women are."

Kier leaned back against the stool and examined his confidant. "I do not know your name, Innkeep."

"Stefan."

Kier inclined his head, then waved his hand toward the room. "And the Spanish lady?"

Stefan grinned. "My wife."

Kier lifted his cup in toast. "To your wife. And to being acquainted with the confounding dialectic that is Woman."

Stefan hesitated, then turned and grabbed a mug off the shelf behind him. He filled it halfway and smashed it against Kier's, held aloft midway across the counter. They drank deeply.

Wiping his mouth, Stefan eyed him a moment. The room was stuffy and hot, for even in the storms, often the close air did not relent. Heat stayed like a stain on the land and people. Stefan drank again, then said abruptly, "Would you have an interest in something cold, sir?"

Kier looked up. "I could be convinced to do bodily harm for something cold."

He held up a finger, disappeared into the back, and came back a moment later with a wooden mug. Inside were hundreds of tiny, glittering chips of ice, sitting in a little puddle of cold water.

"Good God, man," Kier said reverently, taking it. "How?"

"The caves." Stefan pointed down at the floor. A proud smile lit his face, as if he had built the caves. "They run all through the rocks beneath the coast here, for miles. Smugglers like them, but so do I. They're excellent storage, and they're ever blessed cool."

Kier lifted the mug, poured. Freezing cold water slid into his hot mouth and down his throat. "*Ifreann na Fola,*" he exhaled, dipping his hand into the mug. He scooped up ice chips and held them against his neck. They melted between his fingers, dripped down the collar of his tunic. It was like cold rain.

Stefan the Innkeeper went back to cleaning up the common room while Kier drank the ice chips. After a moment, Kier glanced over his shoulder. "My apologies for my gruffness earlier," he said. "I was . . . churned up."

Stefan waved his hand, dismissing it. "The antithesis that is Woman. You've God's whole world"—he held out a palm to indicate everything in God's creation—"and then you've Woman." He lifted his other hand and met Kier's eyes in placid resignation. "We've simply to find a way through. Some days, that's all you can do."

"Some days," Kier muttered. He was growing maudlin, here in the empty taproom, peering into a mug of ice chips and commiserating with an innkeeper.

He went upstairs, feeling his boots hit each step slightly askew. More trouble due Sophia, he thought dourly. When had he last imbibed so much?

She might be lying. That was the dangerous part.

She was not lying. He knew it in his gut.

That was the dangerous part.

For if Sophia truly did not know anything of what was afoot, if she was ignorant and simply running scared, then she truly was doomed. And even he might not be able to protect her.

Thirty-three

It was the middle of the night. Sophia crouched in the shadows of the portico outside their apartments as the rains lashed down, and crept toward the steep wooden stairs.

The thick bound edges of the ledger pressed into the underside of her arm and ribs, but that didn't make her loosen her hold. The reverse, in fact; she pressed it tighter, as if this blunt edge of pain was a reminder of what lay ahead, if she did not stop being a foolish, stupid, gullible woman, and follow through with what she needed to do.

Escape with the ledger.

A sudden sound, small beneath the rain, made her scurry backward and crouch in the deepest part of the shadows of the portico, deep in the greenery. Its leafy ceiling and walls enclosed her.

She stared in amazement as three burly men climbed the stairs. She dared not breathe, stayed absolutely motionless, as they clomped past her and knocked on the door.

Kier did not open it.

They kicked it open and went inside.

She inhaled sharply. Her mind raced. She looked to the

stairway. *Now, go now,* the sensible, reasonable part of her brain counseled sternly.

Her feet didn't move.

Foolish feet. Move.

Voices drifted out, men's voices, low, low and harsh.

". . . business with Noil? Dragus . . . displeased to hear it. Mightily."

Then came a thud, like fist against bone. A faint male grunt, responding to the impact.

Kier.

Her knees jerked straight. Her feet stepped forward. Her hand was reaching for the door. Her body was going rogue, rebelling against her brain, which was shouting *Run, run, run.*

Again came the sickening crunch of fist on bone.

She flung the door open and plunged into the darkened room, dropping the ledger onto the floor.

Three huge, burly, bearded men turned, saw a woman standing there, and froze. This lasted approximately three seconds.

Two of the men held Kier between their arms, slumped, his dark head down, knees bent at an unsteady angle, as one might after having received a hard punch in the gut.

"Knaves," she said in a cold, regal, unafraid voice. "Who are you?"

Kier flung his head up, a fierce look on his face. His mouth had a seepage of blood coming from it.

"Get out," he growled thickly, around the blood.

The largest adapted first, unfisting his meaty hand and taking a step toward Sophia. "Woman, get back—"

"You misjudge and overstep," she intoned in a cold, powerful voice. "I am Lady Mistral, and you are in my abode."

The brute stopped, caught between confusion and, perhaps, the desire to hit Kier again, a sentiment with which she *did* have some sympathy. He executed a clumsy bow instead. "My lady, we did not know—"

"Of course you did not. Else you would not be committing assault upon my factor and friend."

He threw a disgusted look over his shoulder and made a motion with his hand. The men dropped Kier in a heap between their boots.

The brute looked back at her. "My lady, we were but inquiring as to Sir Kier's recent travels. He had some business with my master that went untended as a result."

Kier towered back to his feet as Sophia replied coldly, "You may inform any who ask that all Sir Kier's recent travels have been in service of Mistral Company, as guide and friend."

The sergeant stood uncertainly, his elbows out, one fist shoved into the other palm, as if he had to forcibly restrain himself from punching something.

"My lady—"

"You may also inform your master I find myself uncharmed by how he conducts his business."

"My lady," he grated, half bowing. "'Twas but a misunderstanding. We thought—"

"I know what you thought," she interrupted coldly. "You thought you could do as you please because it pleases you. Tell your master that should he find himself overcome with the desire to conduct any further *inquiries,* he will be met with the might of Mistral Company."

She lifted an arm and pointed to the door, the long sleeve of her surcoat sweeping low like a wing. "Leave, ere the Watch arrives."

Implying the Watch was on its way. Which it was not.

The burly leader glowered at Kier, then turned on his heel and clomped out the door, into the storm. The others trundled out after him, weapons and spurs clinking, leather creaking.

Sophia was certain she watched them with cold, haughty regard the entire way, but somehow, when she looked down, she saw she was slumped against the wall, her heart hammering, and her knees about to buckle.

Thirty-four

Kier stood out on the landing, watching the brigands descend into the muddy courtyard below. He stood under the slanting rain and low rumbles of thunder, motionless.

Then he turned and looked in the open doorway at her.

He looked like sin. His hair was dripping dark and wet over his face. His clothes were molded to his form, tunic slack and pressed to his body, breeches tight, black boots gleaming, as were the dark eyes he pinned on her.

"Where were you going, Sophia?"

It was quietly said. Quiet and low. So quiet and low it made a shiver run through her body, chest to belly.

He advanced a step. "Where were you going with the ledger?"

"Kier, stop," she said in a low, warning tone.

He kicked the door shut behind him.

"Oh, Saint Jude." Her breasts pricked with hard shivers. She backed up, stumbling over a bench at the foot of the bed. She pushed it out of her way with her boot.

"Kier, stop," she said firmly, but the resolve in her words was belied by the way she was backing up, one hand out behind her, feeling for obstacles as she went.

"Where were you going with the ledger?" His eyes never left hers as he shoved the bench out of his way. "To Cosimo? Or had you others in mind? Surely you could have offered me right of first refusal, could you not, now?"

"Merde," she whispered. His Irish was getting stronger as his emotions ratcheted up. Jagged chills raked across her chest. She backed up again and the back of her knees hit the bed. She dropped down onto it.

"Kier, no, you must see—"

"See what? Perhaps you were evening the score, aye? I left you, now you leave me?"

She began scooting backward toward the center of the bed. "No, 'tisn't—"

He closed his fingers around her ankle and began dragging her back to him.

"Oh, Jésu," she whispered, feeling tears smash up on her shores. She struggled, for naught. He pulled her slowly, bundling the sheets beneath her, until she was below his towering body.

His eyes were like fury, his face like stone.

"You erred," he rasped.

She stifled a scream, kicked hard into him, and launched herself off the bed and took off running for the door. She made it two steps before his arm closed around her waist, stopping her like an iron bar.

"Kier," she exhaled, not so much afraid as . . . shivery. She'd never seen him so angry. Always, Kier was in reserve, cool like sunlight sparkling atop a very deep, dark pool of fire and fury. But now, it was unleashing. On her.

She twisted free and backed up until she hit the wall. He was right with her, his body a wall of muscle.

He planted a palm on the wall on either side of her head.

"Kier, you do not understand. I must—"

He slammed the heel of his hand into the wall beside her head. She jumped. *"What?"* he demanded in a rasp. "*What* must you do?"

Trembling, she tipped her face up to the ceiling and opened her mouth to breathe.

For a moment they were motionless; then, hands still planted on the wall beside her, he lowered his rain-soaked head before her.

She released a shuddery breath and said in a voice so low she almost couldn't hear it herself, "I must find a way through. And you are not that way."

Droplets of water skated down the slick, jagged-edged locks of his hair and trembled at the ends, tiny, shivery bulbs. Then they dripped off Kier onto her gown, penny-sized dimples, darkening the silk. A few dripped into the hollow between her breasts. The splash of coolness shocked her hot, dry skin.

She forced herself to exhale slowly. Staying calm was of the utmost importance, because some people, some *fools,* might construe what she'd been about to do as a betrayal of sorts. That was ridiculous, of course, but there it was, deep inside her, the hard dusty kernel of truth that she'd been about to betray Kier.

How she despised this part of herself, the part that turned toward Kier as a flower did to the sun.

His head was still bent before her. "To you, Kier, this is a thing of money," she said softly. "'Twas ever that for you. How much will that man recompense you if you bring him the ledger? But if you do not earn this money, you will find some other. That is your way. There is *always* a way through for one such as you. You have fortune, Kier, you always have," she said, with a bitter sort of admiration.

A ripple shuddered across the muscles of his broad shoulders, but his head stayed bent. He was listening.

"Kier," she whispered. She touched his jaw with her fingertips. "I am sorry."

His hand came up and took hold of hers, gently but inexorably, and lowered it away from his face, down between their bodies, his head still bent, his breath an unsteady rhythm.

"Sophia," his dark voice said, "why do you think I let you into this madness?"

She swallowed. "Because I forced your hand. Because, mayhap, you decided you had a use for me—"

"Because without me you are a dead woman." It was hard and hoarse. "You are not so much a fool as to think Cosimo Endolte would honor any agreement you mistakenly believe you have, are you? The moment you hand over that ledger, Sophia, you, who have held and seen and *created* its contents, you are *dead*."

Her mind struggled to attend all his words, but it had snagged on the unstated, underlying foundation that supported everything else he was saying.

He'd brought her in to . . . protect her?

"You cannot give this back to him," he said.

"I was not going to."

His head tipped up. Even his eyes were dark in the dark room. "What were you going to do?"

She shook her head, feeling tears press.

There was no use in hiding her purpose anymore. "I am taking it to the king."

Kier said nothing.

"War is coming," she whispered. "The king must know whom he cannot trust, and who has done deals in the past to the detriment of his kingdo—"

"The king already *knows*."

"Mayhap, but absent proof, he could do nothing. If I give him the proof, he will never let them go. Edward is not a forgiving king."

"No, he is an impoverished one. Allowing you should even gain an audience, what do you think Edward will do when presented with proof of the intrigues of his greatest and richest subjects, whilst he totters on the brink of war?"

She shivered and shook her head.

"He will not destroy them, Sophia. He *needs* them. But you? The person who documented the deeds, the only living witness to those corruptions?" His fingers tightened around her wrist, then he dropped it and planted his palm on the wall again, as if he couldn't bear to keep on touching her. "Edward may destroy *you*, Sophia. But not Cosimo. And Cosimo must be destroyed."

"And who is going to do that?" she demanded. "Who is going to destroy Cosimo Endolte, councilor to the king, all but a prince in his own lands? He owns half of southern England, and what he does not own, he leases out. He has bands of armed men who prey upon the countryside on his behalf, ensuring no one dare cross him. If not the king, then who? Who?"

He lifted his head and looked at her. "Me."

She gave a short, wild laugh. "You are mad."

"Nevertheless, Sophia, do you think yourself safer with me or without?"

She gave a laughing sort of gasp. "Kier, you *are* the danger. When I was younger, that tempted me."

Something swept across his hard face and was gone again, as quickly as the lightning that suddenly broke within the storm outside. "And now?"

It excites me, it enlivens me, it sustains me. I was dead before and after you, and I can no more stop the power of you than I can extinguish the sun.

"It frightens me," she said aloud.

The full force of his gaze locked on hers. "Sophia, should you walk out of this room, you truly *will* have reason to be frightened, for you will be out from under my protection."

"Kier," she said quietly, almost smiling from the sadness of it all, "we are past all that. I cannot *be* protected."

The strong column of his throat worked. Dark and low and fierce, he said, "*I* protect you."

His voice was a dark, low-pitched rasp, hardly audible, but in it, she heard things she didn't understand, unfathomable, confusing things, things not of Kier and his black heart, but of *her* heart: desperation. Devotion.

She stared into his eyes. "But . . . *why?*"

She meant *Why now, why not before, why did you leave, why are you here, why are you still capable of hurting me so?*

She almost felt like crying. "You cannot even protect yourself, Kier." She touched the scar that ripped over his shoulder.

"I was protecting you." It was a rasp of sound, a shred, a ragged strand of a masculine growl.

"Me? But, I thought . . . my father. The building . . ." Something terrible formed in her mind, a thought, a fear. "What happened?"

"I asked to marry you."

If she thought she'd been kicked off the cliff when Kier disappeared all those years ago, it was naught compared to the spinning, falling sensation now. Everything in her felt like it was tripping, slipping, falling, everything outside her seemed to be rushing by; all except Kier, who stood before her, his hands on her, slowing her down.

"Marry me?" she whispered.

"I suggested it. But your father had other plans for you."

"Plans?"

"Other than an Irish dog."

Tears welled up. "Oh, Jésu," she breathed. "I did not know."

"You were not supposed to."

"You wanted . . ."

"To marry you." He dragged one of his hands away from the wall and *almost* cupped her face. Instead, he curled his fingers around the air just beside her cheek. "Sophia, you are either with me now, or you are gone forever: Everything that has gone before is over now. *Now*, you must choose."

She knew criminals, knew the travails and tricks and terrible futures. But she looked into Kier's dark, tormented eyes, and threw her lot in with the criminals, tipped her face to the side, into his touch.

"*Mo chuisle*," he rasped, and threaded his fingers deep into the dark thick mane of her hair, dragged her up on her toes.

"You will stay close to me," he said, his mouth against the side of her neck, licking, kissing, nibbling. With one hand he started extracting pins and ribbons from her hair.

"Yes, close."

"You will follow my lead."

Madness. "Of course."

"You do what I say, when I say, how I say." His mouth was on her neck, moving down with hot, dark Kier kisses.

"Aye, I will, I will, just as you say," she whispered, and other foolish things like that.

His hands were on her waist. "You will have no contact with Cosimo Endolte. When he is lured in, you are out."

"Of course."

"I will not stop this time," he vowed hoarsely, tugging at the ribbons that laced up the sides of her gown.

She pulled more of the pins from her damp, knotted hair. "I do not want you to stop."

More ribbons broke free, but not enough. Kier decided he'd waited long enough and simply wrenched the gown over her head as a bolt of lightning rent the darkness. Thunder rumbled behind. She pulled the last pin and her hair fell in burnished curls over his hands as she pressed her body to his.

He felt like he was holding flame.

"You are so beautiful," he said against her mouth. He wrapped his arms around her waist and lifted her, and she curled her hands around his shoulders as he walked them to the bed. The room was charged with their passion and the storm. Mouths locked, hot and wet, as they fumbled together with his belt and her clothes as he went.

He dropped her onto the bed, tearing at his tunic and breeches and boots, flinging everything behind him in a storm of clothes, his eyes never leaving hers. She propped herself up on her elbows, her long body stretched out on the ivory sheets, her hair a dark curtain.

He kneeled on the bed, pushing his knee between hers. She reached for him, but he only ran a fingertip down the length of her body, starting between her breasts, down her belly, over to her hip, like water flowing off. Shifting, he bent and ran his mouth sideways up the shivering length of her in reverse, belly to breast. He did it again, and this time caught her nipple in his teeth as he went. Her breath caught, then gusted out, a hot, breathy, feminine thing in the storm-soaked room. Her body, still propped up by her elbows, arched to him.

Unintentionally seductive, her lids were slightly lowered, her head tipped back as she watched him, her chin pushing forward, just a little, on each exhale. It was fire-breathing erotic.

"Why did you stop?" she asked, sounding a little worried. "Do not stop."

He ran his fingertip down the length of her. "Slow is not stopping, lass. And do not tell me what to do." Then he bent and flicked the dark nub with his tongue, drawing it to a tight peak, sucking hard. The breath exploded out of her, and he leaned down on his forearm and whispered, "See, *mo chuisle?* Slow is not . . . stopping."

"Kier," she whispered, reaching for him. *"Please."*

"Please what?" He caught her wrists together and pressed them to the pillow above her head. He laid his other arm down the length of her and swiftly, without warning, pushed a thick finger inside, a single, swift stroke.

Her hips bucked in the air, her head tossed back into the sheets, her mouth open. She was wet, pulsing hot.

He bent to her ear. "Please . . . that?"

She gasped something indecipherable. It might have been his name. It might have been a sum of some sort. It was unintelligible, a rasping, gasping whisper.

"Shall I do it again, Sophie?"

Sophia's head was spinning, his touch a thick, tempting pressure teasing her, but it was his low masculine rumble that almost sent her tumbling over the edge.

"Yes," she almost pleaded. "Again."

"Where?"

"There." Her voice was ragged and broken.

He bent his finger, pressing with tortured slowness through her hot folds, until he reached the swirling apex of her, long, sweet, circular strokes, soft and fast, making thin ribbons of fire snap through her body. Her hips lifted, pressing into his touch.

"There?" he whispered.

She cried out in wasted, wet whimpers. Not truly words, just vibrations of passion and desire slipping from her lips.

"I want you to make that sound again, Sophie," he growled in her ear, then kissed her, and he made her make that sound, over and over again.

Whatever she'd imagined Kier had meant when he said

"not stopping," Sophia had never thought it would mean Kier unleashed. But that is what happened. Before, in every kiss, in every touch, in every smile, no matter how harsh or angry or aggressive his words, Kier's touch had always been gentle. His touch had always been . . . restrained.

No more. Lifted up on his palms, his sculpted body stretched out above hers, he simply took her apart. He was unbridled, bold and confident, a pioneer of her body, hard and insistent, conquering her, demanding something she'd never known she possessed. But then, it had always been a thing he awakened, the part of her roused by his call.

He kept his hard, magnificent eyes on her, using his mouth and hands to push her ever further, to make her arch her back and toss her head, to bend her knees, to lift her hips to him, seeking just a touch of him, to whimper when the thick curved length of his manhood slid silkily across her belly. He moved it away again.

"That is not fair," she whispered.

He gave a low chuckle, then his hard thigh finally pushed between hers, the hair of his legs scraping against her inner thighs as he slid a knee up and simply pushed her legs apart. Propping himself on his palm, his dark hair fell forward as he wrapped his callused hand around the thickness of his erection, guiding it forward. Hot, thick, hard, velvet, slowly pushing past her folds, gliding over the wetness.

She pressed her head back into the pillows, waiting, trembling, charged at waiting.

She felt the silky, hard, rounded tip of him pushing in.

Kier, inside her.

And then, she did cry, just a little, as one does when the long-held dream comes true.

With a muffled curse, he pushed up inside her fully, a single, slow, hard thrust.

She tossed her head back into the sheets and wept a low moan, her eyes shut. "Kier," she whispered brokenly.

"I am here," he rasped. "Do you not feel me?"

She nodded, her eyes still shut and full of tears.

"Look at me," he ordered in a rasp.

She opened her eyes and his gaze was on her, his eyes full of dark desire and something she dared not name, and the tears almost spilled over. The fullness of him inside her, his gaze upon her—it was wicked and perfect and hot and made her shiver from the inside out.

"Do you know how long I have wanted you?" he said in his dark voice.

She was dreaming. Her skin was alight with bright sparks, her interior glowing. "How long have you wanted me?" she whispered.

"From the moment I saw you, I said, *'She will be mine.'*"

Now she was being held. And the holding broke, and a tear slipped down her cheek as he moved inside her. She lifted her hips and met his thrust.

"I thought I must have been wrong." His shadow voice drifted through the lightning and thunder and rain, down to her ears.

She put a hand on the back of his head. "I have always been yours, Kier, even when you were gone."

He muttered something harsh and Irish, but his hand was gentle, his movements were smooth, as he slid himself inside her, high and deep, touching shiver spots, then pulling out, over and again, in and out, his breath by her ear, her lips on hers every so often, tasting a kiss, the tip of her tongue, her swollen lips.

They danced together in this primal rhythm for a long time, slow and steady. She sought nothing more than the sight of him, watching his head toss or his jaw tighten as a surge of slow-moving pleasure moved through his body, knowing it was caused by her. But the wave was building, and slowly he increased their pace, guiding her always a little faster, a little deeper, with her legs spread a little wider, until they were a frantic tangle of hammering bodies.

Her body was an ocean of hot, swelling ripples. She bent her knees and pushed up on her heels, meeting him at the crest of each plunge. He leaned his head back, his eyes closed, arms taut beside her as he held himself up and surged into her.

Harder and faster, deeper each time, pounding into her with a relentless rhythm that dizzied her so she did not know which way was up, did not know any direction but Kier. She needed more, and more, and gripped his shoulders with her nails and bent a heel up onto his back, and hung off of him.

"Aye, lass," he growled in her ear.

He pumped harder, and she urged him on with her whispers. He cupped her bottom with one palm, his other arm planted to hold them up. Their kisses were fierce, sudden and swift in the darkness, as the storm raged outside, so the air was filled with whispers and the click of teeth and sharp, heady cries, with thunder and lightning and Kier taking possession of her.

Something broke inside her, something fragile and weak, the thing that had sufficed for binding these last five years, holding her life together like knotted bandages. Tight spirals whipcorded through her body, snapping in unraveling threads down her back and legs. Her body suddenly clenched, jerked hard.

He knew it. He didn't stop the rolling motion of his hips, but he stretched out over her, his chest to her breasts, his hard stomach against her belly. "Aye, lass," came his low urging. "That is what I want. I want to feel you."

That sent her over the edge. Her head jerked backward and her body exploded in thudding tremors that undulated along his shaft, and he lost himself too. Hard, hot spasms of orgasm surged through him. He propped himself on his elbows and their bodies hammered together in hot, wild thrusts. She was calling his name, crying, and he was coming alive inside her.

Neither knew how long they lay there, lit by streaks of lightning and a candle and the sheen of sweat on their entwined bodies, Kier still deep inside her, kissing her sweat-damped head, her still shuddering body. She felt taken, and filled, and loved, and yet . . . this was Kier.

When he finally pulled out and fell onto the mattress, the storm had passed. The candle had guttered down to its iron base, its flame growing tall and thin, then fat in turns, as drafts eddied through the room.

They simply lay, breathing.

Sophia floated in a netherland of still thudding pleasure, both her body and her heart, and fear of what was to come.

"Kier," she whispered, once.

He pulled her into his side, his arms heavy and strong around her. "I am here," he murmured tiredly, and kissed her for so long, so gently, she forgot how perilous everything around them was. Forgetting was enough for now. Kier was enough.

For now.

Thirty-five

Dragus strode into his hall after a hard ride, during which he'd been caught in a wicked storm, to find his guards, shamefaced, shuffling their booted feet on his tiled floor.

This did not bode for a satisfactory outcome to the night's endeavors.

Slapping his gloves into a palm, he brushed by them and went inside, saying over his shoulder, "What is it?"

"Kier was without a ledger or account roll of any sort, sir," his captain, Arnauld, reported.

"I presumed as much," he snapped, dropping to a chair's rich red velvet cushion. "Else I should have it in my keeping. Did you inquire as to why he was dancing attendance upon Edgard d'Aumercy, Lord Noil?"

Our mutual enemy, he thought but did not say. Surely the rumor of Kier visiting Noil was an error. Kier would not be, *could* not be . . . playing him.

Could he?

Dragus sat back, wet cloak still pinned to his shoulders. He kicked his muddy boots out toward the dark fireplace and waved off an approaching servant.

The notion of trickery was chilling, but so far out of the

realm of possibility as to be unthinkable. Kier had been absent too long from the rapine body of the *commenda* to have any knowledge of its current machinations.

In any event, Kier was too impulsive and reckless to track and then upset such a long-standing villainy as this, one birthed when Kier was still . . . well, when he was still dead.

And what a source of occupational disgrace *that* had been, Dragus thought with a flicker of self-reproach. Next time, he would make sure the entire flaming building collapsed on its victim before he rode away.

Not that Kier would ever know who'd done the deed. Sooth, who could tell him now? Everyone thought Kier—*de Grey*, back then—was already dead.

And as a result of those five long, almost-dead years, Kier was not the threat he had once been. He was ignorant of the things afoot now, and without a network. Alone, he could do nothing. He *knew* nothing. He had no notion what information was penned in that sought-after ledger; he thought it capable of nothing more than extortion.

Dragus smiled faintly at the gaping black maw of the fireplace. That ignorance was Dragus's net of safety.

For even if Kier recovered the ledger, even if he attempted to use it himself, he would overlook the truly vital information therein, thinking it at worst inconsequential, at best, meaningless.

Kier, double-dealing? Possible. Nay, *probable.*

Kier, successful? Never.

He simply wasn't capable of attaining such heights of trickery. He was a useful pawn, nothing more. No, he'd been a burn victim from the day his black Irish soul was born. A scab to staunch a wound, then to be plucked off at will by men like Cosimo Endolte.

And Dragus.

"He *was* attending Lord Noil, sir," Arnauld said, interrupting Dragus's thoughts less by his words than the harsh scrape of his boot against the expensive tiled floor.

Dragus's gaze slid to the offending boot. Arnauld stilled.

"He and the lady were indeed at Noil Keep, sir," the soldier repeated. "Per the lady's report. They were there for business. *Her* business."

Dragus looked up. "The lady said that?"

"Aye, sir."

"Lady Mistral stepped out to assist Sir Kier during your . . . interrogation?"

Arnauld, bulbous-nosed, thick-headed, but eminently useful, nodded. "Aye, sir. She seemed affronted. Called for the Watch."

"Did she now?" Dragus lowered his gaze to the mud-splattered buckles of his spurs. "And she said they were at Noil Keep solely in the interest of Mistral Company?"

"Aye, sir."

He pushed a clump of mud hardening on one boot with the toe of the other, considering this development. Edgard d'Aumercy was showing an interest in this Mistral of Kier's?

Which meant *Cosimo* was interested in this Mistral of Kier's.

What was Kier up to?

A tinge of excitement lifted his spirits slightly. He got to his feet, throwing off his cloak. "That is all," he said to his retainers. "Leave me."

The guards exchanged nervous looks, then hurried out of the room.

Dragus stopped in front of the window to look out at the lightning breaking overtop the wet tiled roofs of Last Fells. 'Twas time to find out more about Lady Mistral.

Thirty-six

Sophia awoke in darkness and silence. The storm had passed. The heat had not. A sheet was tangled around her legs.

She pushed up on her elbows at the edge of the bed and dangled her head off the side, and let the heavy tail of hair hang down. Warm air wended its way over her neck. Her legs were caught in the close sheet, too hot. She kicked at them, pushing the sheet off.

That's when she saw his boots on the floor.

She lifted her head slowly. He was sitting, slouched back on the bench beside the door. His tunic was off. His eyes were on her, and his breeches were slung low over his hips, his waistband loosened, his hand, carelessly, slid inside.

She pushed up on her elbows, shoving hair away from her face. "Kier."

"Sophia."

Why did the simple sound of her name spoken in his dark voice make her shiver? She took a breath. "What is amiss?"

It took him a long time to reply. She felt her heart thud against the front of her chest five, six times.

"Naught." Low, dangerous.

She looked down at his hand, his strong, flat wrist and forearm, tanned, slid beneath the waistband of his pale white breeches.

She looked up to his shadowed face. "What are you doing?"

"I am watching you."

Dangerous shivers raked down her body. She inhaled, hotly and slowly, and lowered her forehead to the bed.

"Why did you come back, Sophia?"

"Back?"

"With the ledger."

"You were in danger."

"I am always in danger."

She inhaled; his musky male scent was faint on the warm tangled sheets. "I know."

Silence.

"I am hot," she whispered.

His head roared. His body fired. He wrapped his hand around the burgeoning thickness of himself.

"Lift your chemise."

Fire roared between Sophia's thighs.

She did as Kier bid, not because he wanted it, but because she did. She reached back and pinched the light tunic between her fingers and pulled it to the side, revealing by degrees the back of her calves, then her knees, then her thighs.

"The rest," he rasped.

She pulled it off entirely. Kier felt his body fire, as if whipped. The low curve of her spine rode to the rounded perfection of her buttocks, and he dragged his gaze back to hers.

"Come here."

And she did. She slipped off the bed, padded to him, stopped a pace away.

Reaching out, he trailed the tips of his fingers down her

belly, the only thing he could reach from where he sat. He did not move forward.

A breath was torn from her lips, ragged and laden.

He did it again.

She stepped closer. This time his hand skimmed over the delicate vee where the bones of her collar joined, etched the ridges of her breastbone, and glided down the crevasse between her breasts.

She exhaled weakly and took another step closer, so she stood between his knees. Kier slowly dragged his feet across the floor until they met behind her, forming a circle. She was inside.

This time his hand swept up, starting at her knee, the back of his knuckle forging a slender, fiery path up her thigh, across her gently rounded abdomen, over the dip of her belly button. His hand turned and now his wide, hard palm rose on her body, and her head fell backward as he wrapped his long fingers around her waist and entangled them in her long, russet curls. His other hand joined the first, until he held her encircled by his hands on her waist, his feet on the floor, and she finally stepped forward fully into his arms.

Their touch was explosive. Kier growled indecipherable words into her hair as he pulled her onto his lap. His hands roamed shamelessly over the dips and curves of her body until every move of hers was a response to his, her body like hot silver, arching and curving on his lap.

She trailed her hands up his hard, beautiful, scarred body. She leaned down and kissed him, his scar. "I am so sorry," she whispered brokenly, her lips lighting against his numb skin.

He was frozen, her fingers on his scar as she spoke it. He never spoke of it, touched it only to wash. But Sophia was touching it. Licking it. Speaking about it.

It was like burning him again.

She lifted her fierce, startling green eyes to his. "We will never be as they," she vowed, and he let it be.

He pulled her up and kissed her. It was a kiss that went on and on, in great, adoring attention, his hands never leaving her face, his mouth never leaving her lips. Sophia wanted more, begged him for more with tiny whimpers, tried to move his hands across her body, slid her hips farther up his thighs, but he did not give her anything but the kiss. The needless, life-affirming kiss.

It might have lasted an hour, this kiss. It felt like half her life. The better half. The half that had not yet been lived, beyond the dormant dark inside her, and this kiss was kicking down the rocks that had barred the way

She might have cried, silently. He might have held her until the sun rose, his arms around her, murmuring in her ear. She might have been ruined. But she didn't pay it any mind, for Kier held on and did not let go.

Then, lifting her up, he entered her in a single, hard, deep thrust.

Her head dropped back and she cried out in a long and low moan. Then she dragged her head back up and, looking at him, she took over, lowering herself onto him, slowly, farther, until his shaft was buried inside her. Her breath caught in a sharp cry.

"Dammit, Sophie," he growled, leaning forward to press his lips to any skin he could get. He lifted his hips, surging up into her, lifting her toes off the ground.

Her mouth was on his, her hands on his, her thighs parted for him as he slid up almost desperately into the pulsing wetness of her, to take possession of her, to feel her, to make her feel him, because what else lay in wait in this dark world but the brightness of Sophia? She watched him each time she lowered her body onto his, each time she let him enter her, her hands on his shoulders, her hair falling down around them like a dark fire curtain, looking into his eyes, and in that moment, he felt as though he was Sophia, was not only in her but of her and knowing every fiber of her, and that was enough.

They made love all night, slow and sweet, hard and fast, making up for all the times they had missed. And it was enough.

For now.

Thirty-seven

"The ledger is gone?"

Cosimo Endolte's soft query chilled Edgard d'Aumercy's blood more than he liked to admit. But the only way through the morass was directness. Cosimo had little patience for ineptitude, and none at all for deceit.

Not that it should matter, Noil thought with a stab of irritation. *I ought not be imposed upon by such matters.*

Noil was the one of old English nobility, even if they'd been reduced to all but destitution for a few generations now. It was a noble destitution. And Noil was en route to recovering the family fortunes, by just the sort of association that Cosimo Endolte provided.

But even so, one should never forget that Noil was the noble one, the one of old English blood. Cosimo was little more than an upstart Frenchman with some mingled Italian blood for poor measure and an eye for troubled businesses that was, really, quite staggering.

But none of that meant that Noil should be treated like a *hound.*

"It is gone," Noil explained again, simply. "The ledger was taken."

Cosimo stood by the window in his office chamber, staring out across meadows of baking wheat.

"I bethought this a simple enough task. A woman and a ledger." He turned to look at Noil, casting the near side of his face into shadow. It was like a wall painted black. "A woman. And a ledger."

The repetition, the pause, was unnerving.

Beside him, Remy shifted. "I *had* the ledger, sir."

Cosimo's eyes slid toward his chief lieutenant. "And do no longer."

"I gave it to him." Remy snapped his head in Noil's direction.

D'Aumercy gave him a black look.

Cosimo stepped back into the cooler shadows of the room. He looked at Noil. "Your counsel on how to proceed?" he said in a clipped tone as he crossed to his long oaken table that dominated the center of the room.

D'Aumercy cleared his throat. "There were forty men at the saint's day feast, Cosimo. Southcote, Essex, Pourte. None are the savory sort. Any might have taken the ledger."

Cosimo's sharp gaze flashed to him. "Aye, and you hosted them."

"On matters pertaining to *your* business," d'Aumercy shot back. He truly was growing weary of dancing to the tune of this man. "They have long been your partners, Cosimo. And they need to be questioned."

Cosimo slid behind the table. Seated, he steepled his tapered fingers and rested his chin lightly upon them.

"So let me understand. Your counsel is that I institute a small-scale inquisition upon the leading members of the English merchant community and local officials. An approach that requires explaining, or otherwise revealing, that we seek an account ledger misappropriated by unknown parties, a ledger that may well have materially damaging information about *them* within?"

He cocked his head to the side like a dog who has heard a curious sound. "Pray, Noil, how does that serve me?"

Remy seemed to enjoy this line of questioning. The slit of his mouth lifted in a flat grin.

D'Aumercy shook his head. "Cosimo, I see no other course of action."

"Of course you do not." Cosimo sat back, his fingers still interlaced, and looked to Remy. "Find me my silk merchant," he ordered softly.

Remy nodded and turned for the door. Noil watched him go. *Stupid ox.* He waited until Cosimo and he were left, then stepped forward. "And in other matters . . ."

Cosimo snapped his gaze up. "*Other* matters? What *other matter* do you wish to interest me in just now, Noil?"

D'Aumercy tamped down on his familiar irritation. "I have found a likely investment opportunity. I believe it offers the potential for great riches."

"What is it?" Cosimo was already shuffling through the papers on his desk.

"A certain Lady Mistral."

Cosimo made a dismissive sound and picked up a stylus.

"A shipping widow, recently up from southern France," d'Aumercy persisted. "She is seeking investors and clients for her company, which seems to be foundering on the shores of widowhood. I recommend the *commenda* explore her further, as investors. Perhaps even majority investors. Owners."

Cosimo had looked up with faint interest at the mention of "shipping," but as Noil continued, his face clouded back into anger. He slammed his pen on the table.

"What *use* have I for your Lady Mistral, for *any* shipper, without first having something to *put* on their *goddamned* ships?" He slammed his fist on the table next. "And that means first *retrieving* what is on board Sophia Silk's goddamned *ship!*"

Noil stepped away, shocked at the explosion from his heretofore composed, if vaguely chilling, business partner.

And what shipment was he referring to?

Cosimo's slanted jaw tightened as he regained his composure and retook his seat. He pushed back his oiled locks of hair with the heel of his hand, then picked up the pen. He looked at it a moment; it had been smashed by his fist. He calmly picked up another.

"In any event," he went on quietly, as if the explosion had never occurred, "I already have a shipper. He is discreet and experienced, the sort of discretion ten years of service breeds. I have no need of your Lady Mistral."

He dipped the scraped tip of his pen into a container of ink and ignored Noil until he finally turned and left the shadowed room.

Truly, Noil was nearing the end of his rope with this strange, chilling Frenchman.

Thirty-eight

Kier was looking through the ledger in the dim morning light when Sophia awoke. The darkness shifted as she sat up, wiping hair off her face. He could barely discern her eyes, just a glint of reflected candlelight; she was a darker smudge within the shadows of the room. But he felt their gazes meet. He felt her smile at him.

"Good day to you, sir," she said in a throaty morning murmur.

His chest felt wide open, filled with cool air. The sort of thing one did not dream of was the sort of thing one could never have, such as Sophia awakening in his bed, smiling at him.

"Good day to you, lass," was all he said.

"What are you doing?"

"Choosing."

She was quiet a moment, then said, "I am coming. I will help." Her shadow arm reached down and retrieved a tunic.

He turned pages softly as she dressed, washed in the cistern, taking care of morning rituals. Then she padded up behind him.

Without looking around, he reached his hand over his shoulder. Her fingers slid into his. Her breath was slow and steady.

He allowed himself this much, then, to forget the things to

come, simply inhale the warm scent of her coming to stand behind him, feel her chest expand with each breath.

One pale arm draped down over his shoulder, in front of his chest, and a slim finger pointed at one of the names.

"Start with him."

He leaned in to read the name and details. "I do not know that name. Why him?"

"He must have come after you. But I recall him," she said, still looking at the page. "Bagly. A shipper. A smuggler, for the right price. He and Father spoke many times. He might be amenable to securing luxury goods one might not find readily available, the sort that a Mistral ship could access."

"We will pay the man a visit." He tipped his head back and met her eyes, which were now pools of dawn light sheen. "Anyone else?"

The candle burned down as she looked through the pages of her own penned words.

"Oh, yes, him," she whispered, pointing again.

"Tell me."

"He was the queen's man."

He looked over his shoulder. "The queen?"

She nodded, still looking at the book. "The old queen. Eleanor. You know she made out well, acquiring richly estates indebted to Jewish lenders, the moment they looked ready to topple. It helped to be previously informed of such vulnerabilities. The *commenda* did that for her. Here, you can see the mention of the estates . . ."

She pointed again, her fingernail below the dark lines with the name of estates that had been bankrupted years before, whose owners still petitioned the Crown for redress, for the return of family estates that had been bought out from under them by, among others, the previous Queen of England. "There are more, here." She flipped pages.

Kier sat back with a low whistle. "Edward will not be happy to see his beloved Eleanor's name here."

She smiled. "No, he will not."

"Anyone else?"

She looked over his shoulder again, and he rose, giving her the seat. She took it, hardly looking at him, her gaze on the tightly scrawled lines of years past. The candle burned for a while, then she whispered, "And here, see? This man? He is another. He came to Papa's oft. He is wealthy and powerful and circumspect. He tolerates neither mismanagement nor mistakes, and yet practices a great deal of both himself. Additionally, his trade would never survive such rumors."

"What trade has he?"

She looked up at him. "The Church is his trade. He is a bishop. And a very dirty one is he."

Kier nodded. "Then let us have at him."

THROUGHOUT the weeks that followed, they went through the ledgers from the beginning, selecting their targets. They aimed for those men who would be vulnerable, either by their guilt from past deeds or their associations with other guilty men today.

They never threatened anyone nor even intimated they had the ledger—they simply knew a *tremendous* number of details, tossed out carelessly, details that could make people stop breathing. Lady Mistral, flitting butterfly that she was, could never recall where, precisely, she'd heard the tantalizing tidbits, but was certain it had been at least two other gatherings. Perhaps three.

They did not need to commit extortion, and had no desire to. They simply raised its specter everywhere they went.

They went to feasts and dinners and visited dignitaries, they met with merchants who needed shipping and shippers who needed merchants, and throughout it all, they spread rumors about the lie: Mistral's widow was a rich but fast-sinking ship. Open to many—nay, almost *any*—deal that could alleviate her current straits.

This made them exceptionally popular. Once in, they began the rumors.

"Do you have any suppliers who deal in camel dung?"

Kier and Sophia exchanged a long, silent look, then turned in unison back to Oliver the spice merchant, who was sitting on a stool in his hot, bustling little shop in front of them.

Kier sat just beside Sophia in his role as the attentive assistant, prepared to facilitate and document any agreements that might be concluded. Oliver was one of the largest spice merchants in Last Fells, and this was one of their most important meetings. If Oliver revoked his associations with Cosimo, rejected the investments of the other *commenda* investors, others would follow.

And yet, Oliver, for all he ran a company worth a hundred pounds annually, was more a rag doll than a bear of commerce. He beamed at them, wiped his shining, bald head with a linen, and asked questions with a childlike enthusiasm. Such as this one, about the camel dung.

Sophia smiled at Oliver and leaned forward to reply. Kier clamped his jaw shut. He was going to have to allow her to speak at *some* point, after all. It may as well be now.

He was ready for anything to go wrong, but there was no way to exclude her. Oliver specifically and precisely mentioned his ardent desire to meet the effervescent Lady Mistral. So here they sat, Kier with his mouth shut tight, Sophia with hers wide open.

How had it come to this?

Sophia beamed back at Oliver. "Cinnamon dust! But, of course, we have shipped such goods before, Master. I am sure we know men who might serve. Sir Kieran, do we not have knowledge of a supplier of *terre de cannelle* we could recommend to Master Oliver?"

Kier nodded gravely. "I will send a name and letter of referral later in the day."

Oliver beamed some more as he took another swipe at his shiny dome. Trickles of sweat ran down his temples and embarked into the forest of his incongruously bushy black beard.

"And Sir Kieran?" She waved her hand in his general direction. "Credit our indulgent friend Oliver a discount on his first transport using Mistral ships." She smiled at Oliver. He smiled at her.

Kier murmured, "Of course, my lady."

She glanced over her shoulder at him. "A larger one than whatever you are currently thinking, please."

Oliver's face shone at her.

"Of course." Slower coming was, "My lady."

Oliver shuffled forward as much as one could on a stool, his face sweaty and bright.

"And mummy, my lady? Have you any suppliers to recommend?"

Kier leaned forward to interject, "None at present."

Oliver's face fell. "What a tragedy. I have many customers requesting it, ready to pay the highest rates. Physicians most especially."

"Yes, it has great pharmacologic effects."

"And is quite aromatic."

Sophia decided not to inquire what manner of aroma it possessed, as the look on Kier's face was information enough. She leaned forward in an interested pose. "Master Spiceman, have you heard the rumors that *momie* can bring back the life force if it is not long gone?"

He looked horrified. "My lady! That is a falsehood." He

looked at Kier sternly, as if he were the perpetrator of such lies. "That is but a rumor, one that borders on heresy."

"Ah well." She sat back with a wave of her hand. "Rumors abound in our businesses, do they not, Master?"

He nodded gravely. "Indeed they do. I have known some passing strange ones indeed."

She brightened. "Tell me one, Master."

He looked startled.

"You must know of ever so many, and I am struggling to understand much of my late husband's trade, and of England. It is always good to speak directly to the experts in their trade."

He preened. "Well, now, let us see . . ." He leaned forward conspiratorially, his face glowing in warm regard, somewhat like a bed of coals. "I have strong suspicions that sugar, in any of its forms, is not a medicine a'tall, except perhaps to make people smile."

She smiled herself. "But indeed, Master, that is a medicine on some days, is it not?"

He laughed. "'Tis at that, my lady, 'tis at that," he said, still laughing heartily.

"I have heard a rumor of late"—she pressed on while he was enjoying himself—"one that concerns me greatly. Perhaps you can help me navigate your English merchant world."

He blinked at her. "Rumors?"

"Yes. Of the Darnly ledger."

"Oh, that." He nodded emphatically. "The rumors are everywhere."

"Think you there is any truth to them?"

He pressed his lips together. "I cannot speak to the ledger itself, as to whether its existence is real or no. But as to what it is supposed to contain . . ." He leaned forward with prurient glee. "If it records half of what it is supposed to, then it contains but a small portion of what it ought."

He wiggled his eyebrows, pleased by the intrigue.

Sophia nodded. "How fascinating." She touched the shot-silk cord attaching her heavy purse to her wrist. "And yet, I am sure this *commenda* does legitimate business as well?"

"Oh, aye, indeed," Oliver agreed comfortably. "In fact, I myself have a few investors."

"You do?" Sophia leaned forward with wide eyes. "But, Master, people are abandoning this Cosimo like a shipwreck."

He blinked again. "They are?"

"Oh yes," she said with a sage nod. "Everyone I have spoken with is nervous indeed. I should not like to be the only merchant left in the coming financial maelstrom with Cosimo Endolte."

Oliver's face paled. "Maelstrom?"

She sighed sadly. "Your English world of trade is even more complicated than we make things in France. But as a visitor here, I cannot venture into those waters, even for legitimate business. I cannot afford to anger your king."

"The king?"

She nodded happily. "But you are a kind man, to indulge me in this gossip." She rose, sweeping out her skirts in an array of eye-catching silk. "Master Oliver, it has been a pleasure. We shall meet again, I hope."

He toppled into a clumsy bow. "By God, I hope so, my lady."

They left Oliver amid fervent parting sentiments regarding the merits of Mistral Company's proprietress and her hearty largesse, and embarked out into the road.

"I think he will go to Cosimo," she murmured.

Kier agreed.

"But I feel bad," she said as he escorted her out, arm out like an open gate, making room for her to pass. They stepped out into the hot street. Sun beamed down on their heads.

"Allowing these merchants to think something will be coming their way that shan't."

"Perhaps if you stopped offering such wonders as camel dung," he suggested, taking her by the elbow to direct her around a flock of chickens pecking in the straw and dirt.

She nodded. "We must ensure that poor man receives cinnamon dust."

"Have you any?"

She blinked. "Of course not."

"Neither do I."

She waved her hands. "But we cannot keep making deals and promises that we cannot honor."

"*I* am not doing that."

She frowned and rested her fingers on his arm, stopping him. "We must ensure these men engaging in deals with Mistral have some . . . some recourse to the things they are so hoping for."

She allowed him to move her across the cobbled streets, a small touch on her arm enough to shift her. "Sophia, here is my suggestion: refer people to *me* to negotiate any deals. Your task is to charm people, not set terms that will ruin me."

"Ruin you?"

He nodded, his dark hair gleaming in the bright sunlight. "Already I have been approached by a number of merchants who, after speaking with you, find Lady Mistral to be one of the most *gen*erous ladies on the seven *seas*."

He said it effusively, as they no doubt had, and she laughed. "I based my promises upon what I found in your books, Kier. What seemed possible for Mistral to deliver."

"*Possible* diverges widely from *financially viable*, Sophia. And those men know it."

She stopped short. Much of her went up: her chin, her hands, her eyebrows. She stared at him for a long moment, then everything about her fell like a tapestry coming down, and she said in an astonished murmur, *"Mistral is real."*

He closed his eyes, then opened them to look down into her bright green eyes. "Aye, Sophia."

"Real?"

"Real."

"You have a shipping company."

"I have a shipping company."

"A genuine shipping company."

"Genuine," he agreed.

"Named Mistral Company."

He laughed. "Named Mistral Company."

"Kier." She dropped her voice. "As a rule, I believe approximately a tenth of what you say. For certes, I did not think Mistral Company was real."

"The company is real, Sophia. The ships are real. And I do not lie to you."

"Never?"

He shook his head. *Yet.*

"You mislead, misguide, and prop up false hope." She repeated his litany of sins.

He nodded, his hand still on her arm.

She narrowed her eyes at him. "And there are actual ships?"

Wordlessly, he stretched his arm out and pointed down the hill. She turned.

The street was raucous with people and loads of laundry, loud with merchant cries and dense with the scent of pasties being cooked, of damp hay and leather. Past all them, down the hill, off the quay, anchored off shore, were the huge merchant ships.

"Which?" she asked softly.

"Green sails."

Some ships had oars poking out of their sides like branches

off a fat-coned tree trunk. But his did not. One of the fleet of Mistral Company ships, she was clinker-built, a sleek, fast ship, with hull speeds approaching thirteen knots, should the need arise. On her, Kier could outrun almost anything.

It bobbed alongside five or so others, looking very adventurous in its green sails, his ship, with its ever-green, emerald green, Sophia's-eyes green sails.

"What stunning sails," she murmured.

"Expensive," was all he said.

"Mistral is real," she whispered, turning to him, as if he did not know this truth. She said it again, more loudly, more excitedly. "*Mistral is real.*"

People turned to look at them.

He put his hand on her elbow and propelled them to the side of the road. "As everyone in town already thinks that, you may want to be less *loud* in your astonishment."

She turned again to look at the ship, excitement rising off her. "Why Mistral?" she asked swiftly. "Why that name?"

"The mistral is a wind," he replied, looking at her profile, her rounded cheekbones. She was still smiling down at the ship, as if it were a child she was proud of. The sun was bright on her face. "In the south of France. A fierce, cold wind that blows down from the Alps. The trees of Provence are bent forever in the direction it bids them go. It changes weather in Africa and foments storms in the sea. It destroys crops, makes children restive and women weep."

She turned to look at him.

"And after," he murmured, "the air is so clear it is like unto silver. So clean, 'tis as if you breathe iridescence. You can drink its clarity. The smallest details of a flower are so keenly wrought, 'tis as if the flower is inside you, and a man can see forever, if that is what he wants."

The bustling crowds around them, bumping into their

unmoving bodies, the cacophony of voices all around, the donkeys and chickens and dogs—neither of them noticed any of it.

"Was that what you wanted?" she asked quietly.

Upon a time, what he'd wanted was her. Nothing but her. Then came the revenge.

Right now, what he wanted was to pull her to him, to make her smile, to forget the hell of the world and lay her down on their bed, but he resisted all those urges, and told her the truth instead.

"I wanted to come back to England and destroy the men who tried to kill me."

He did not say the rest of it though. That part of him that had wanted *her*, from the moment he'd been aware she was alive in the world. For within the depths of his despair, in the desert of those five years filled with physical pain and fury and dark plans of vengeance, in the center of it all, like a campfire, had been Sophia. He'd warmed his hands over the memory of her, burned hot for the want of her, ached to come to her, to take her, *knowing* it could never be. Knowing that was for the best, as he would only ruin her.

But now, here she was. Sophia had come to him.

Just as he had been coming for Sophia his entire life.

She watched him, her eyes washed colorless by the sun. She looked down at the ships, then back to him.

"And that is what you are going to do," she whispered. "Wreak your vengeance."

"That is what *we* are going to do," he corrected.

"God save our souls," she whispered.

"God save theirs."

Thirty-nine

The message from Dragus arrived after the sun had set, requesting a meeting. Dragus met him at the door to his office and waved him inside. The usual array of guards stood outside the door, and two were inside. That did not bode well.

Dragus pointed. "Have a seat."

Kier did. Dragus sat across from him and considered him for a long minute. "You have not brought me the ledger."

"No. I have not."

"I paid you very well for you to bring me the ledger."

"You *offered* to pay me well," Kier interrupted. "You have not, in fact, paid me anything."

Dragus eyed him, then sat back and folded his fingers across his stomach. "Very well," he said slowly. "Are you going to deliver the ledger to me?"

"Possibly."

For a moment, nothing moved but candle flames guttering. Then Dragus smiled. "I see. I thought you too simple to do me some trickery here," he said softly.

"Did you?" Kier said absently, his attention on the burly guards standing behind Dragus, in especial the left-flanking guardsman, he of the tremendous wart, tremendous glaive, and the tremendous inability to back off.

"I have a solution in mind," Dragus said.

"I did not know we had a problem."

"We have a problem. Tell me about your Lady Mistral."

Kier shifted his gaze away from the guards. "Why?"

"Because I have been investigating. Because you have been showing her off to d'Aumercy."

Kier affected a casual shrug. "She is a wealthy merchant, new to England, seeking investors."

"How fitting. I am seeking something to invest in."

"Why?"

"Why am I interested in Mistral's widow? Is not everyone curious about your comely, distressed merchant princess? The one you are dragging before the noses of England's wealthiest merchants, hoping someone will follow the scent." Dragus smiled. "I do not believe she is what you say she is."

Kier kept carefully still. "Nay?"

"No. But she is a useful herring. Just the sort Cosimo Endolte might sniff after. With just the sort of ships he might wish to load his next shipment onto."

Kier nodded slowly.

"I did not think you knew anything about the shipments," Dragus mused, massaging his fingers through his beard. "Clearly, I underestimated you. Cosimo always vowed you were the best he'd ever had. How we all enjoyed hearing that." He smiled, and his eyes glittered with menace. "But now, Kier, our interests are aligned."

"That is an unpleasant thought."

Dragus laughed. "Ours is a world of reciprocity, Kier."

He returned a chilling smile. "Is it? Odd, that is not how I recall it. I suppose the fire burned it from my mind."

"Ah, yes. The fire." Dragus emitted a small smile, like a puff of smoke. "The fabled fire at Trebizond. De Grey, Cosimo's favored lieutenant, with all his Irish wit, dead inside. So sad."

Kier's skin tightened, felt parched, like the long plain of a desert.

"How much do you usually charge for brokering these sorts of investments, Kier? For Lady Mistral?"

"I did not find her for the likes of you."

Dragus laughed. "The likes of me," he echoed, then made a sudden motion with his hand. The guards against the walls launched forward. Kier was already scrambling out of his seat but they grabbed him. Twisting his arm behind his back, they held him as Dragus came forward and pushed his face into Kier's.

"*You* are the likes of me, Kier," he hissed. "Get me on Mistral's ship when Cosimo comes, and I will let you live. Refuse and you die. See how the scales thus balance?"

"Mistral is not yours," Kier said in a low voice.

"She is now." Dragus flicked his fingers at his men, and left the room while they beat the hell out of Kier.

Forty

Sophia perched on the edge of the cushioned bench beside the window and stared down at the moonlit-strewn street below. No one was about, not since the message had come for Kier several hours ago. Not since he had left on its heels, telling her to bolt the door.

She rose, as she had a hundred times before, paced the room, and returned to the window, as she had a hundred times already.

Moon, mud, straw, puddles. Nothing else.

The outer stairway creaked.

She flew to the door, fumbled with the lock, and wrenched the door open.

Kier was halfway up the stairs. He flung his head up with a fierce look.

One side of his face looked bluish, and his mouth was shadowed in a funny, lumpy way. As if it were swollen. And his hand . . . Her heart skipped a beat. His hand was cupped to his side, as if covering a wound.

"I suppose the view from above is satisfactory?" he growled.

She almost tumbled down the stairs and hooked one of his muscled arms over her shoulders.

"Sit." She pointed him to the bed the moment they were

inside and crouched before him, reaching for the hand that cupped his stomach. "Let me see. Are you bleeding?"

"No." He moved his hand. She yanked up the tunic, eyeing his flat stomach and ribs. She touched them gently and he didn't recoil. "Just a punch," he muttered. "A great many of them. Hard ones."

She prodded some more, but everything seemed intact.

She hurried to the basin of water that sat by the window. "I suppose this was necessary?"

"Aye, well, I probably wouldn't have insisted if he hadn't." He touched his jaw gingerly, then gave a low hiss and shook his hand. A spray of blood flicked across the room, feathered gore.

She snorted softly as she looked for any strips of linen or cotton. Nothing. "You were sitting quietly, minding your own affairs, I presume." She carried the basin to the bed stand.

He sat down suddenly on the bed.

She flung her arms out to prevent him from toppling over. But he was not tipping over, he was reaching for the edge of the sheet, buried under the edge of the mattress, and yanking it up. Then he removed a knife from one of the many compartments covering his body and started slicing through the sheet on the bed, making linen strips.

He sat on the bench at the base of the bed and handed over a strip of linen. She kneeled and dabbed it in the water, and began wiping away the blood on his lip.

"Are you going to tell me who they are?"

He stiffened at the first swipe and grabbed the linen. "They are part of the plan."

She gave a soft, incredulous laugh. "The plan."

"The plan."

He bent over the basin and, jaw fixed, began scrubbing at his cheek, then his mouth. The water turned pink. He was being excessively rough with something she knew had the ability to deliver great pleasure, and it was impossible to sit by and allow it.

She reached out and laid her fingers atop his. He jerked his head up.

"Let me," she said softly.

"I will do it."

"You are going to pull more skin off, and then you'll bleed all night, and be dead by morn, and you'll never get your revenge."

Their eyes held. His eyes lightened from their dark dangerousness to a small degree, and he released the linen. She took over, dabbing, inspecting, and murmuring all the while about how it awful it looked, and how large the scar would be, to make him feel better.

"Sophia," he finally said.

She looked up.

"Do not patronize me."

"I am not," she protested. "It looks truly . . . splendid."

He grunted. She went back to dabbing.

"You are correct; they are not deep wounds. It seems as though they were simply enjoying themselves, not out for true injury."

"Aye," he grunted. "Likely that's due to the fact that they think I'll serve their purposes."

"And will you?" she asked, reaching out to gently wipe a trickle of blood off his neck by his ear.

"Will I what?" he almost growled. The air brushed over her wrist as she pulled her hand out of the pocket of warmth between his surprisingly soft hair and not surprisingly strong neck.

"Serve their purposes," she said quietly.

"I told you, lass. They are part of the plan."

"*This* was part of your plan?"

He gave a sigh and leaned back on his palms. "Sophie, fights are *always* part of the plan."

His gaze was penetrating and unwavering even though one eye was going decidedly puffy.

"How sacrificial of you," she murmured. "Your eye is blackening."

He gave a muted curse and sat forward.

She dabbed again. "Or rather, *greening*."

His one good eye regarded her dismally. "Are you done, then?"

"No."

She finished wiping his eye and lip, then straightened. "Have you any unguent?"

"Aye. In the hall." He jerked his head toward the room beyond.

"And willow bark?"

He did not, but Stefan the Innkeep did, and was happy to give it over when Sophia showed up at his doorway, insisting to know how troublemakers had come into his courtyard and thus up to her apartments.

Stefan was horrified, vowing increased security, and not only provided willow bark and cobwebs for the wound, but sent his son running for the midwife, who sent along a leech, which reduced the swelling of Kier's eye within minutes.

Innkeep eyed his cheek soberly, though. The blood had stopped for the moment, but it was a deep gash, just over the cheekbone. "That'll need stitching."

Sophia looked at it too. "I know." She cleared her throat. "And a bath, perhaps, Master?"

He vowed to send one up. "First in the morning will be good enough," she said softly, eyeing Kier. He appeared to need sleep more than anything.

After Innkeep and his son and leeches were gone, the room

fell quiet again. Kier stood by the window, peering down into the lamplit streets below. She cleared her throat.

"Have you anything to drink?"

He didn't turn from the window. "I'll stitch myself up, Sophie. I've done it oft enough. You needn't trouble yourself."

A brief perusal of the hall revealed precisely what she was looking for: a flask.

She came back into the bedchamber, smiling. "I knew you would have the means to every depravity I might think of," she said cheerily as she dragged the bench over to sit before him.

He looked over his shoulder, eyeing her doubtfully. "Aye, a particular talent of mine, depravity." Then he saw the flask.

She uncorked it and passed it to him. "Drink."

He did; then, without warning, she poured half the flask down his cheek, over the wound. He jumped as it burned, sawing into the cut.

"Dammit, Sophia," he growled, ripping the flask from her hands. He glared at her, then took another swig. "Jésu," he added vehemently. "You're to warn a man before you do something to his body."

"I am about to stick a needle into you," she said curtly, eyeing the cut. "It shouldn't take more than three or four." The needle glinted in the candle glow.

"I cannot imagine anyone better than a silk woman to stitch up my face," he said cheerfully.

She looked at him. "Drink again."

Her fingers pushed his face to the side, and she began her work, absolutely silent. He ignored the snapping pinch of the needle pushing through his skin, and the glint as it pulled through the other side and drew near his eye. He focused on the far wall.

"I think you should be more careful," she said. She dragged the needle through.

"Aye."

"I think you should stop angering people quite so much."

"Aye."

"I furthermore think we need to find you new associates." Jab, scalding sawing, pinching push. She was quick and efficient.

"Aye." He agreed, and it was also the only word he could say just now.

She seemed to notice the repetition of his replies, for as she lifted her hand again, she said casually, "I think you should say 'please' more often."

He almost laughed.

Two more quick, vicious stitches and she was done. Thank God. He had endured hundreds of stitches in his life, and had hated every one.

She sat back and eyed his cheekbone. Then, giving a private nod of approval for her own handiwork, she poured another river of whisky down the side of his face, *again* without warning.

He hissed and grabbed her wrist, lifting her away. He glared at her. She sat back on her heels and wiped her hands over her cheeks.

"Well, Kier, you have made it through another one."

He stared at her a moment, then fell back onto the bed and stared up at the smoke-blackened rafters. "I'm racked with good fortune."

"What I mean is, it does not look as if it will fester, require another leeching, or make you die or anything such as that." He gave a soft groan. "He was either not very good, or you were exceptionally good."

"I venture we both know the answer to that."

She rolled her eyes. "At the least you are a cooperative patient," she allowed, washing her hands in the basin. She looked down at him. "And you look perfectly awful."

"Aye, well, here's to looking like God's own sin," he said, lifting the flask still clasped in his hand. He downed a large swallow. His bleary eyes traveled over her gown. It was splattered with blood. "You look quite fine." He looked back up and said slowly, "Even if you are a traitor's daughter."

She shook her head and turned toward the door. "You will need a bath."

"I need you to come here and sit with me."

She hesitated at the door, looked at his clothes, then came back, saying, "So be it. But not with those clothes on."

He gave a faint smile as she pulled him to his feet. "I'm sorry to disappoint, but I'm no good entertainment tonight, lass."

She snorted. "You are mad if you think I desire you right now," she muttered as she bent to begin unlacing his hose.

"Aye, you do," he said lazily, taking over for her with his hose.

She flushed, because he was right. She wanted him every time, any time, and a battered Kier still lit her fires in a way not even fire could do. But she wasn't *mad* like he, and had some self-control.

"I am not mad like you," she informed him. "I practice self-control."

"Is that what you call it?"

His head was bent to finish unlacing, and he pushed down the hose to his knees, revealing hard-packed thighs. They looked at each other, then he closed his eyes and dropped back onto the bed. She took over.

Off came his boots and tunic and when he lay unclothed on the bed, the skin of his hard stomach and the tops of his thighs glowing pale, the rest of him darkened with tan and hair and power, when he lay stretched like some magnificent injured beast on the bed, she kneeled down beside him and washed his wounds.

With cool water, she wiped his brow and his battered hands and hot neck, and as she did, she told him stories. Stories of her small life—the difficulty in ensuring the silks were properly packed for transport so moisture could not attack; how she eschewed the more vivid colors on silk, as the deeper the hue, the more rough the fabric; the excitement of gaining a new client as a result of a recommendation—matters that surely could not entertain or even interest someone as well traveled and hard spun as Kier. But he did not stop her, so she kept talking, until finally he reached up and pulled her down beside him.

They lay together, looking up at the rafter beams in an easy quiet. The power of his arm, gently resting over her shoulders, was good. His breathing, rhythmic, deep, and relaxed, was good. His body, being so close to hers, was good.

This was very bad.

"You must be a fine silk woman," he murmured.

She nestled more comfortably into the crook of his arm. "Some say."

"You love them."

"I love everything about them. The feel of the silk, the trade, the negotiations. I even find pleasure in managing the books. There is something satisfying there too." She smiled. "Rather simple of me, finding pleasure in such small things."

"'Tisn't simple at all," he said quietly. "Some men cannot do it throughout the whole of their lives."

The moon had risen. It washed in low, flooding the room with its silvery sheen. Some items cast back the moonglow—the etchings on her combs, the rivets on Kier's sword belt on the bench. The gems she'd worn in her hair today still rested on the table, gnarled lumps of black, although the yellow pouch had a ghostly illumination. The bed was a sea of dark motionless waves, with her lying in the middle, with Kier, not sinking.

His quiet voice rumbled out of the darkness beside her.

"My father was a pirate."

Forty-one

"Your father was a pirate," she echoed, surprised her voice was so quiet and steady when she felt so stunned.

The darkness of him nodded. "Plagued the Spanish coast for a while, then came north to wreck his wife's homeland, Ireland."

"His wife. Your mother."

"Aye. My mam." He folded his hands on his belly and looked up at the ceiling. "He was a wastrel and worse than a rogue. Killed a score of men, likely women too, although I didn't see that. Highwayman of the seas."

She rolled over, leaned toward him on her elbow, and waited.

"He took me with him when I was old enough."

"What is old enough to sail with a pirate crew?"

"Nine."

"You were nine."

He tipped his head down to look at her. "It took a month before I killed a man."

She nodded, allowing him to have killed a man at nine. Here, tonight, there was space for that.

"He came over the railing. We were anchored off the shore, and I was up with the night watch, a joke, for they never meant for me to do them any good. The others were up front, and he came over the side, off a rowboat we never none of us saw. I had a man's sword in my hand, which I ought never have had, not by any stretch, and I started swinging like the mad thing I was. I remember pissing myself. I could have hit anyone, but it happened to be him. Sliced him right in two." His voice was blank and even. "He split like a lemon."

He unlaced his fingers, lifted them in the shadowed air and looked at them.

"Blood is slippery, but thick." His low voice was like music in the room; it reached every edge. "Sticky. It painted the wood grain of the deck. Red lines, like on a palm." He turned his hands in the air, then dropped them. "A score of men had already been killed there, in that very spot, but I knew which lines were his. That, I had done."

"You were nine," she reminded him quietly, protecting him from himself.

He looked over, a faint smile on his face. "I'm not hanging on to the thing, Sophie. 'Tis simply a thing that was."

She nodded. Fine. *A thing that was.* That was how he understood things: they were receded in the past, unchangeable. Untouchable.

"I marked out from under his thumb as soon as I was able," he went on in his low, quiet way. "Came to England, toured the fairs, practicing shell games and cony-catching all the way from Chester to London. I had a lot to learn, but at thirteen, that happens quickly, else you die. I grew adept. But then, I'd had a good tutor. I amassed a goodly sum, and stuck it in a coffer I stole from a tallow merchant. Over a hundred pounds."

"A hundred pounds?" She pushed up on her elbow to peer down at him. The simple, overwhelming joy she found in his hot, resting body lying beside her was sinful, surely. "You safeguarded a hundred pounds? As a child?"

"I was no child," he said, in that voice that sounded so close and yet so hollow.

She let that be a moment, then said, "Kier, that is a staggering sum. What were you planning to do with it?"

Kier looked up at the blackened rafter beams on the ceiling. "Och, I had grand plans. I purchased myself a horse and some armor, a sword, and accounted myself a knight. I already had the spurs."

"I remember your gold spurs," she said, sounding almost wistful. "That first night you supped with Papa and me."

"Aye. I recall the night."

That had been the night he'd set out to catch Sophia's eye. The night a gaze had been as good as a touch, the night Sophia had smiled at his jests and lighted fires he'd not known were banked inside him. She'd awakened a yearning not even the fiercest battle had done for life, nor the glint of gold spilling out of a smashed-open coffer had done for money. He wanted Sophia, from that moment on, as nothing else, ever.

"The way you dressed and spoke, I bethought you a knight," she said quietly.

"That was the point," he said.

"But you did not win those spurs."

"I did not."

He felt her thinking about this. "However did you get them, then?"

"However do you think, Sophia? I stole them." Why did his voice feel thick in his throat? "Me, the Irish knight errant. I traveled south and east, to France and the Empire, spent time in and circling the Levant, hired myself out on raiding parties and those endless petty feuds the French and Germans host so well. Plunder was everywhere; fighting, well, that was already in my blood, as was the desire for ready coin. It was most ready, in those days. 'Twas not difficult, being the false knight, which is a fitting thing, for what we did down there was neither gallant nor chivalrous. But it was god-awful profitable."

A two-tiered breath came from her, as if she'd inhaled, then had to catch her breath to finish the task. "Did you kill many men?"

He shook his head. "Not so many. But neither did I save very many."

"And yet, you stopped."

"And yet, I stopped."

"Why?"

He exhaled. From outside, in the warm night, came the faint scent of honeysuckle. "Truth to tell, lass, I find I do not like killing people. That, I suppose, is not in my blood. A failing of the pirate code."

"Mayhap you are not a pirate, in your heart."

It sounded rather like a suggestion. He gave a soft laugh through his nostrils, and said only, "Mayhap not."

A long silence enveloped the room, but it was of them, in them, it was theirs. Kier knew he owned this silence of Sophia's. It was a terrible burden.

But he was not letting her go a second time.

He curved his arm around her back. "Close your eyes, lass. I will tell you a story."

Sophia closed her eyes and listened to his words, rough and quiet, sometimes making her laugh, and sometimes making her want to cry, as he wove a tale of heartbreak that seemed, in some strange way, to mirror their own.

". . . And after defeating the knight Morholt, Tristan dragged his sorry arse back to Ireland, the fair and irritable Isolde in tow, for his uncle the king to wed. But that is not at all how the thing turned out to be. For simple things are never simple, and like the surface of a lake, you can go down and down, and down some more, until you're drowning in the thing . . ."

She fell asleep to the sound of Kier's earthen voice recounting ancient tragedies, as she wove her own with him, she was sure.

But then, she'd been wrong before. So very wrong.

TOMAS Moneychanger looked placidly across the table at Remy the Black's plain, angry face.

"You say you've had no contact at all with Judge Darnly's daughter?" Remy pressed, apparently indifferent to the fact that he'd barged into Tomas's late at night, and was now demanding answers to questions that were none of his business. "Despite her being seen coming out of your offices a fortnight past?"

Tomas sat back and rubbed his bony index finger against his beard. "Do you refer to the morning of the sword fight?"

Remy nodded.

"Well, Sergeant, you are correct, in that some reported a woman had been seen, but I saw none when I arrived. Whereas," he added, "I did see a man with a sword running away."

Remy glowered. "Then what of *any* silk merchant, by any name?"

Tomas pressed his fingertips together. "I shall endeavor to be clear. I have not had any dealings with Sophia Darnly in the last five years, nor have I had any dealings with *any* silk merchants, be they from Lucca or the infinitesimally small town of Batten Downs."

Remy's face adopted a faintly animated look: he scowled. "I am not a fool, Moneychanger." Tomas thought that was debatable. "Sophia Darnly came to your offices once; she might come again. Her father knew you."

Tomas reached for a small pot of ink that sat near the center of the table and drew it nearer. "Whereas I would think that is precisely why she would *never* come to me. Not if she were wise," he added. "Ours was a union that did not end well."

Remy's eyes glittered. His face remained unchanged, like a stone. One wondered if he actually understood what was being said, or simply reported it back to his master, like a pirate bird with a script.

"Judge Roger Darnly was ever the rogue," Tomas explained, not knowing if it would clarify or confuse. "He could not be trusted with a wooden spoon. When he was hanged, defendants everywhere breathed a sigh of relief. One assumes the poison ran through to his daughter. If Cosimo has loaned her money, all I can say is that he may never see it again."

"What matters money?"

Tomas did not show the slightest surprise at such a statement. "I am forced to suggest you take your charms to one of the other moneylenders of Last Fells," he said. Anything to get the man out of here.

"If you have been less than honest with me, Moneychanger, Cosimo will be mightily displeased."

Tomas dipped his pen in the inkpot placidly. "I am not in the habit of taking the advice of lackeys. If your master wishes to speak with me, I am not difficult to locate. You may go."

Remy left without a word.

Tomas dipped his pen point back into the inkpot and finished reviewing the contracts that needed to be completed before signatures were affixed the following day.

He had not lied. Not precisely.

At least, Tomas could not be *certain* the red-haired woman he'd seen with Kier outside his office, and then again at the mayor's, was Sophia Silk of Batten Downs, formerly Sophia Darnly, daughter of the notorious and exceedingly wealthy judicial brigand Roger Darnly.

But if Sophia was in league with Kier, she was either

entirely mad or soon to be entirely dead, for Kier was up to some mischief. Tomas knew it. If it was not outright nefarious, it bordered on disrepute the way Wales bordered England: dangerously so. Tomas did not know what it was, nor did he wish to know.

Not knowing was how he made it through, how he threaded the webs of secrecy and intrigue that large amounts of money carried with it like an odor. Not knowing, not caring, and never, ever getting involved.

He bent back to the contracts, reviewing the tightly penned lines with exacting care. This was what he did best and what he did most, and he'd done it so long he didn't even notice his hand was shaking as he did it.

Forty-two

The days passed in a blur of a few essential things for Sophia: the stirring of rumors; hot, stormy weather; Kier.

The rumors disturbed the rich community of Last Fells and its surrounding countryside like a rock dropped into a pond. The murmurs were like ripples, reaching beyond the town, into the countryside, into London: *The rumors are leaking out. The ledger has been found.*

"How much could you bring me?" asked Bagly the shipper. He was sitting back in his seat, at his offices above the docks of Last Fells, eyeing Sophia with a mixture of interest and suspicion. A very good response, based on the proposal she had just made.

Sophia pursed her lips, then turned to look up at Kier, who stood beside her shoulder like a guard. "Sir Kieran? How much spice can we bring Master Bagly?"

"How much can he take?"

Bagly smiled. Sophia smiled. In the office chamber, bare of almost all ornamentation—it was a place of business, for rough men—her green silk tunic was like a beacon of opulence and promise.

"How much can you take, Master Bagly?" she inquired.

He sat forward. "A great deal. So, I bring you the wool."

"And we bring you the spices." She smiled. "It is a pleasing solution, is it not? So well matched to our clients' needs. One could hardly say we are even in competition, if we join in such a way. Your clients wish for luxury goods from far-off places, which we, of course, can get, and will provide to you, at almost no cost, in exchange for some of your very good untaxed English wool. For which we will pay handsomely, do not misunderstand. It is simply the *customs,* you see, the *taxes,* that become so troublesome."

Bagly nodded. Taxes were a trouble, make no mistake.

"We are simply exchanging necessary things. And we will do so at sea, out from under the watchful eyes of men who would wish to skim some of the profits, but do none of the hard work themselves. Then I will arrive at my destination port with wool that, for all intents and purposes, has had its custom paid.

"But truly," she went on, smiling, "what does any other duchy care if England gets her penny? And you, Master, you will return to England laden with luxury goods at very little cost to yourself. Think how happy our clients will be," she suggested warmly, as if they were discussing charitable giving rather than smuggling operations.

Bagly nodded thoughtfully, then glanced at the emerald sitting on his table where Sophia had carefully laid it an hour past, when their negotiations began.

Then he lifted his gaze to a point on the wall, computing the profits to be had from this venture. Smuggling out contraband wool to a single, known customer, avoiding the danger of delivery, and receiving in return both money and luxury goods he could sell at a significant profit. *Significant.*

Sophia rustled. "This also solves a little problem I have had, Master, as I firmly do not wish to break the laws of any land I am currently in. But if I am not *in* the land, well . . ."

He nodded, clearly not listening.

"So, if we are agreed—"

"Agreed," he said swiftly.

"Then there is only one other, trifling matter," she said hesitantly. "At least, I hope 'tis trifling."

"Trifling, my lady?"

"Yes. It is most difficult to discuss."

Bagly's brow furrowed. She looked uncomfortable and waved her hand, which brought Kier forward a step. "My lady is concerned about the ledger," he said bluntly.

Bagly stared. "The *ledger*?"

"Aye. The Darnly ledger. Your name—"

Bagly's face, previously furrowed, went slack.

Sophia lifted her fingers. "Allow me, Sir Kier. Master Bagly, were you aware that your name is being bandied about as one mentioned in this . . . *missing ledger* of the late Judge Darnly?"

Bagly was on his feet. "No! It is a lie."

"Is it?" She smiled in relief. "That is most reassuring. Then that business along the Kentish coast, with the caves, and the movement of slaves . . . ?"

His face was a blister of red. Kier stepped forward. "Christ's mercy," Bagly snarled. "Where in God's holy name did you hear about that?"

She turned to Kier serenely. "Darnly. Was that not the name of the ledger?"

Kier gave a silent nod, his eye on the irate merchant.

"You have seen the ledger?" Bagly wheezed. He was clutching his chest.

She waved her hand. "One need not *see* the ledger; one hears of it, almost incessantly these days, does one not? It seems to be in the ether. I cannot recall precisely where the Kentish business was first mentioned. 'Twas not by any *one* person; I believe I heard it twice or thrice of late," she explained.

In fact, it was twice, both times she'd mentioned it herself in the preceding two days.

Bagly wiped his grizzled cheeks with the palm of a beefy but shaking hand.

"But if this is not true, merely rumors . . . ?" Sophia allowed.

He whipped his gaze to her. "Yes. Of course. Rumors."

She nodded and got to her feet. "Well, then, one can hardly control rumors, can one?"

"No, no," he muttered.

"And yet . . ."

He snapped his gaze back. "And yet?"

"And yet, you still engage in business with this Cosimo Endolte, yes? The one whose deeds this Darnly ledger deals with?"

He hesitated. "Yes."

She nodded. "As we have agreed, one can hardly control rumors. It is an unstoppable threat. But one can control how one is perceived in response to the threat." She picked up the emerald off the table.

"Your meaning?" he asked, watching her pocket the gem with wild eyes. It, along with her astonishing business proposition, bearing almost no costs and untold riches to gain, was about to walk out of his office.

"Meaning I am glad to hear 'tis a rumor, this Kentish matter. But still, I cannot see my way to do business with someone who associates with this Cosimo."

"But, my lady," he protested. "No one need know of our association!"

She swept up her skirts as she went to the door, Kier at her side. "I cannot take the risk that you would be investigated as a result of the ledger. That would lead to an investigation of your deeds, and that would lead, eventually, to me. You will have to choose, Master Bagly."

Lady Mistral was the first merchant to bring the issue of "deciding" to Bagly's attention, but she was hardly the last.

By week's end, three of his customers had threatened to abandon him, and two in fact had.

It was happening all up and down the southeastern coast, in ports and towns, people who'd thought their pasts already buried scurrying to pile on enough dirt to cover their tracks.

Kier and Sophia wafted through the middle of it, dangling lucrative business ventures, expressing her concern at the stability of the English merchantry, with war on the horizon and this missing ledger.

In her wake, Sophia left staring faces and terror.

Within weeks, the merchants started fleeing Cosimo like fleas off a dying body.

Forty-three

The summer was pitiless and pushing, hot sweltering heat that spent itself in occasional storms of ravaging abandon, before it cleared to brick-red heat again. There were dim memories of winters that once had been, and might be again, but it was a romance, a lay, a fantasy. Nothing was real.

Nothing but Kier. Kier's hard forearm under her fingers as he led her from merchant to tradesman to local official. Kier with men in close circles, turning to her, always turning to her, his eyes dark, his smile faint and aimed at her. Kier's body beside hers at night, turning toward her.

The offers started rolling in. Suggestions for contractual agreements. Attempts to retain Mistral to find ships to engage in various privateering endeavors—this was of particular popularity, with the recent hostilities between King Edward and the French king. Edward had been humiliated; his barons were furious. Ready for war. The entire countryside was starting to mobilize. The merchants were cashing in.

And the offers kept rolling in.

But still no word from Cosimo.

"ARE you out of your mind?" Bagly all but shouted. "A shipment, you say? On one of *my* ships?"

Cosimo was weary of this sort of thing, getting shouted at by his partners, his investors, the men he required to execute his business. And now, his most important associate, the shipper and smuggler Bagly.

"I assure you, there have been no misdeeds," Cosimo said. They stared at each other. "That will affect you," he added, because otherwise, it looked as if he was outright lying.

Bagly wiped a sheen of sweat off his mottled forehead, a sheen not due to worry, but the heat. A veteran of the seas for over twenty years, Bagly was hardened from being buffeted by rough seas, rough storms, and rough seamen.

Now a businessman, he was still a practical man—meaning he was unopposed to smuggling—which had made him a rich man. He did not find the need to investigate his existing clients' transports exceptionally well, as long as he was being paid exceptionally well, and he was not intimidated by powerful lords. Which was precisely why Cosimo had secured his services.

It was the reason he was so difficult to herd back into the fold now.

"Sir, I can no longer take the risk." Bagly shook his head. "The king is capering about impressing ships for his ventures against the French. If his attention turns toward *my* ships, as a result of my dealings with *you*?" He shook his head. "I cannot risk it."

Cosimo touched his stomach lightly with his fingertips, a light touch against the small point of fire that was alighting there. "I am your largest client."

"My largest, aye, sir. But not my only." He met Cosimo's gaze. "'Tisn't to be, sir."

He left Cosimo standing alone on the quay, staring after him, a muscle in his jaw ticking.

That was how the morning unfolded. The evening hours did not go any more satisfactorily.

By the time he arrived back at his manor house, two groups of people were waiting for him. Unhappy groups. One was represented by a bishop with a great deal of wealth and extremely loose morals. The other group comprised the aldermen of two powerful port towns.

He saw the aldermen first; God could wait.

They were dressed in clothes of merriment, tunics embroidered with silken thread, gems affixed in various places, jaunty caps on some of their heads, but their sober faces met Cosimo's. Money was not a merry thing.

He looked across the table at their fat faces and knew what their pompous, muddled minds were thinking. He resisted the urge to get back up and walk out. But as this was his home, that would be ridiculous. Having them escorted out was an equally poor decision. These were powerful men upon whom he relied. For the next week or so.

"Are they true, these rumors?" one asked without preamble.

Cosimo fought the urge to pick up his stylus and stab him in the eye. Instead, he picked up a fig, chewed it, and swallowed before answering.

"To which rumors are you referring?"

They scowled, almost as one. How swiftly these self-serving men closed ranks. For years, Cosimo had been most pleasing to them, he and his money, his investments, his contacts. Now? Now he was a murrain. They could hardly get away fast enough.

"The rumors of a ledger documenting various . . . deals," one stammered.

"Yes," he said curtly. "All true."

The second sat forward and asked in a low, urgent voice, "But why did you *keep* such a book, man?"

"I did not. Roger Darnly did."

Everyone knew Roger Darnly, first a rising star in Edward's reformation, then a traitor and a hanged man. His downfall had wreaked havoc far and wide, after the depths of his machinations were known.

But the depths were *not* known. Not yet. And these men knew it. The ledger was still on the loose.

"But ere you think to peer down on me from your lofty perch," Cosimo said coldly, "regard the fact that *your* names are featured prominently within."

Down the table, in a line, their self-righteous faces flushed like a flooding river valley.

"You think we do not know that?" the spokesman snapped. "That is why we have come."

"You do poorly to bring your complaints to me, when you voiced none at the outset, when you were the beneficiaries of such dealings, Masters. Do not think to ram me onto the shoals which you now see looming, ere your ships suffer. I am not yet without power, and you do poorly to threaten me." Cosimo got to his feet. "I think we are done here."

They rose and were herded out by Cosmo's guards like the fat ducks they were.

"You must recover that ledger, sir," their leader insisted as they went. "There must be no more *incidents*. It affects us all."

As if Cosimo cared for the effect of anything on these self-satisfied, unvisionary men.

And of course there would be more *incidents*. One more. One more very large shipment that, whether he desired it or no, was sitting on the goddamned silk merchant's ship, somewhere, in some port on the eastern coast of England.

The meeting with the bishop went much the same.

It was dark by the time Cosimo was alone again. He sat at the dais table, the hall lit only by a few torches on the walls and a few candles on the table before him. Barely had he lifted a cup of wine to his lips when another servant scraped up to him.

The man's thin face was startled white. "Sir, 'tis . . . 'tis . . ."

"Who!" he shouted, slamming his fist on the table. Candle flames shuddered. "Who dares show now to disturb my peace?"

"The earl de Sandwich."

Cosimo closed his mouth, then his eyes. God's wounds. Ralph de Sandwich, coming to see him. Once Master of the Wardrobe, Keeper of the Seal and Chief Justice, he had always been one of the king's favored councilors and convincers, a powerful, aggressive man oft sent to assure people they did in fact desire to bend to the king's will. Even papal legates bent before him. As Constable of the Tower, de Sandwich held an especial menace.

Cosimo opened his eyes and he waved the man in.

Grim-faced, Ralph de Sandwich came down into the bowels of the hall and drew up beside the dais table. "Our sire extends a query, Master Moneyman."

No niceties, no preambles. Cosimo sat back tiredly. "How may I serve the Crown today?"

"The rumors of improprieties circulating the realm do the Crown no service," he said in a voice neutral and cold. "The matter with France requires all the royal attention, yet the king finds himself accosted daily by men on this matter of a ledger kept by Roger Darnly, lately of this world, hung for treason against the realm. Always does the king find *you* mentioned within these conversations.

"As you know, long has the king sought this ledger. It has come to his attention also that the evildoer Roger Darnly placed lies about the late lady queen in said ledger, base untruths that nonetheless must never be seen. The king commands you recover and destroy the ledger, ere you end up as the keeper of the ledger once did. Our lord king is rampant on punishing treason these days. He is assured you will see the value in this course of action, and the opportunity being given you thereby."

The opportunity to stay alive.

Silently they regarded each other. Cosimo nodded.

Ralph de Sandwich turned on his heel and left without another word.

Cosimo wiped his forehead with the heels of his palms for long minutes after he'd left. *Treason. Pressing need. Loyal councilors.*

What a fool the king had become.

He inhaled hard and pushed to his feet. What he needed to find was a way out of England, for himself and his most precious cargo. Which he first needed to locate.

When he looked up, he saw Noil awaiting audience.

He sat back in his chair. "What do you want, Edgard?"

"They are fleeing the sinking ship like rats," he said quietly, stepping into the room.

"I know that. What do you want?"

"Have you thought any more about the Mistral shipping investment?"

Cosimo opened his eyes. "Tell me about her."

Forty-four

The morning sun rose like a vein of blood. Kier watched it flow across the horizon in a thin crimson line, then its hot orange head pushed up, scalding the sky.

It would be another brutal day.

Both doors of the apartments were flung wide and had been so all night, coaxing the shy breezes to slip through the rooms in the dark hours. It had done little to alleviate the dense, cloying heat.

He stepped inside the north-facing bedchamber where Sophia was. It lay in dimness, slightly less close than the rest of the world.

Sophia lay belly down on the bed, sheets knotted in a heap beside her. Every so often she whimpered, turning her sweaty head to the opposite side, resting her cheek on her forearms.

Kier stood beside the bed, listening to the faraway sounds of the day beginning outside. Few would move unless they had to, few would do more than breathe today.

She'd knotted her hair at the back of her head, but long tendrils fell in crinkled auburn tails all around her, sticky ribbons. A thin shift clung to her thighs. A sheen of sweat covered her arms and the backs of her calves. She shifted restlessly and flung her head to the other side.

He went downstairs to talk to Stefan the Innkeep. When he came back up, he had a large bowl in hand, covered with a soft towel. He carried it into the bedchamber.

SOPHIA tossed her head again, half drugged by a night of shallow, interrupted sleep and oppressive heat into an exhausted half-slumberous state. Heat felt like it lay atop her, pressing down, skimming off motivation and energy and leaving behind sweat. She felt slick. She was limp from it, and there would be no respite. Only in her mind.

She wanted stone walls and riverbeds. She wanted an ice cave. She whimpered and tossed her head to the other side, bent her knee, and dragged it up. She wanted to lie atop the Thames in January, a frosty rime on her skin. She wanted . . .

Something utterly, impossibly, wonderfully cold slid across the back of her hot, sweaty neck.

It yanked her from her drugged heat exhaustion. She gasped and pushed up on her elbows. Kier sat on the bed beside her, a rag in his hand. Beside him was a bucket, filled with the coldness.

"Ice."

"How?" she rasped, her whisper hoarse.

"Caves," was all he said. It was enough. "Lie down."

She no longer cared. Kier was a god. So be it; she was a heretic, already burning at the stake. She flung herself back onto the hot bed.

He slid his hand with the dripping perfection down the middle of her back, over her chemise, down the line of her spine. His hand hesitated at the rise of her buttocks. The ice was melting, wetting her tunic, soaking into her thirsty skin, and as he laid his hand just at the edge of her bottom, she almost cried. She wanted, oh, very desperately, to arch for him, to move into his confident touch. Instead, she just shivered and might have moaned.

She heard him shift beside the bed, then a low murmur, by her ear: "Push up."

She was under his command now. She pushed up on her elbows and she heard him reach for something, then both hands came around to her front and he cupped her breasts with a handful of ice.

She flung her head back and his mouth was by her ear, licking, and she was turning to him, kissing his mouth sideways, and his hands circled her breasts, pushing the icy shards in circles over her nipples, cupping her breasts with his hot hands, and the ice melted down between his touch, until she was pushed up on both her palms, her back arched from him, him kneeling up beside her, making her moan with cold. Their mouths were hot and messy on each other, and she was somehow whispering, "Please, oh please," and all she knew was he must not, not ever, stop.

One hand left her for a moment and she writhed for more touch, but he'd only been reaching for more ice—it must be in a bowl—and then he slid it down her spine again, but this time, he kept sliding up over her buttocks, and she lifted to him.

"Aye," he whispered, his tongue hot on her ear, his hand on her breast doing wicked, knowledgeable things, the hand down her back now beneath her tunic hem and sliding between her thighs, which she was spreading for him, and he slid the ice between her thighs.

She cried out, a single, hot gasping cry, and he was on the bed, straddling her, his hips resting lightly on her risen buttocks. He started sliding the ice across her hot folds, and the sensation of burning desire and hot skin and ice and a skillful hand made her suddenly explode inside in small, quite perfect little ripples that he knew. He knew. She heard him mutter a curse, then lean to her ear.

"You are the most beautiful thing in the world," he rasped in her ear, raggedly, broken. "I will never earn you."

No, he had not said that. She'd misheard, because he said it so tightly against her ear, because her body was shuddering with the opposing sensations he was crafting, fire and ice, his hands, pushing her into every bend her body wished to do, until she was on her hands and knees, him kneeling behind her, her head hanging down, hair swinging, knotted, gasping, sweaty, Kier's. She felt his erection pressing at her buttocks, between her thighs, and whatever he wanted right now, he would have.

He shoved his knee between her thighs, forcing them apart, pushing up her tunic, ripping it in two, and then, dear God, he was pouring cold ice water all over her back, down her spine, between her legs, and she was crying out, her body bucking, her head tossed back, her nipples hot and hard, her skin shivering, and she was in the perfect space of Kier's body and devotion.

He stretched out over her, his body hard and long and a bare hot inch away, and all she wanted was for him to lie atop her, crush her beneath his sweaty heat. He cupped both her breasts in his and forced her to rise on her knees, her back up against his chest, her head tipped back on his shoulder.

"Don't," she whispered.

He froze.

"Don't . . . ever . . . stop," she gasped, and shoved her hips into him.

He growled something entirely indecipherable this time and slid a hand down her belly, across the torn ragged fabric of her tunic. She was an instrument for Kier's work, keening and swaying, tossing her head, as he slid his fingers between her hot thighs and circled through her wet folds, his fingers pushing, nudging, rolling; then, he leaned them both forward, and he shoved them up inside her.

She broke into a sob, panting, and leaned entirely on him now. "More," she demanded in a whisper as he rocked her body with swift, shuddering tugs and plunges.

He would have. He would have taken her right then. He had a hand fisted around himself, guiding him forward. His other hand was on her back, pushing her down, positioning them, her head tossing, her hips pushing up to him. He could feel the pulsing tight heat of her close around the tip of him, and she gave a low, long moan.

He closed his eyes and dropped his head back, focusing on entering her, hard and slow and deep.

A fierce pounding erupted at the door.

His head was spinning so hard it took another pounding to break through his consciousness. Sophia froze on the bed, and turned her head over her shoulder with a stunned, startled expression.

They stared at each other.

Someone spoke softly through the door. "A message, my lady. Reported as urgent. Both of them."

"Both?" she whispered over her shoulder to Kier. "Who?" she called out, aware her voice sounded as uneven as cobblestones.

"Tomas Moneychanger, my lady. And Lord Noil."

She whispered a happy exclamation.

Kier uttered every curse he could think of in a long stream of vile, guttural, if muttered, curses.

Sophia turned her head and looked over her shoulder at him. "Kier," she scolded in a whisper.

"I know," he muttered. He lifted his voice just enough to be heard outside the door. "A moment."

Then, unable to resist, he leaned forward and kissed the center of her arched, sweaty back. He pushed her down on the bed, pressed his thighs to the back of hers, his cock to her bottom, and said in her ear, "I am not done with you."

She turned her head slightly, toward him. "Neither am I done with you."

He licked her ear, then pushed up off the bed. Yanking on a pair of breeches, he pulled open the door a crack. A freckle-faced messenger stood at attention on the landing, two clutched letters in what appeared to be a crushing grip.

"For your lady, sir," he piped loudly, in several octaves, looking hard over Kier's shoulder.

Kier gently extracted the missives and handed him three pennies. "Well done."

The boy stared down at the coins, then jerked his head up, but Kier was already shutting the door.

In the murky, dusted sunlight, he read them aloud for Sophia.

From Tomas Moneychanger, a simply curt, blunt message, much like the man: *I do not know what you are up to, but Cosimo Endolte is coming to Last Fells.*

And from d'Aumercy, equally curt: *He wishes to meet your Lady Mistral.*

Kier looked up. Sophia, belly down on the bed, grinned at him.

"We did it," he said.

She started to push off the bed, and he tossed the missives aside. They fluttered to the ground. "Do not move," he said, striding back to the bed.

"But I thought—"

"Not an inch."

"But I—"

"Not a single inch," he ordered as he crawled back onto the bed and finished what he had begun. And Sophia did not move more than an inch, just as he said.

STEFAN the Innkeeper did not like the manner of the man standing before him, this plain, nondescript, chilling man.

"No silk merchants," Stefan said curtly, folding a palm

overtop his youngest serving boy's head as he rushed by. "Slow down, Roger."

The plain brown man took another long look around the common room. "And no women in residence, either? Women alone?"

Even if Lady Mistral had been there alone, Stefan would have said nothing to this one. But as she was not alone, being always attended by her devoted and good-natured factor, he could say with a perfectly clear conscience, "None at all. Now if you please, I have other matters to attend."

The man gave the smallest bow, but then he said, in that same strange, calm, forgettable voice, "None with red hair? Or perhaps brownish red?"

Stefan frowned. "As you are not lodging with me, I shall now ask you to leave the Spanish Lady, ere I find myself fined for providing service to those who do not lodge within."

A faint smile crossed the man's face. He turned and left.

Stefan would be sure to mention it to Lady Mistral's factor when he came back in, this cunning man who knew what Lady Mistral looked like but not who she was.

LATE that night, after Sophia was deep in sleep, Kier composed a message.

It contained all the proper flourishes of language and obsequiousness, but in the end, it was a simple message, suggesting a meeting between Lady Mistral's factor and Cosimo Endolte, at the mayor's abode, to coincide with the start of the annual summer fair of Last Fells.

Kier tossed down his pen and stared at the parchment. The ink was dark, and around the rim of each letter it had spread a little distance, like a faint black halo.

Five years of planning and Cosimo was finally coming out. Cosimo the cautious, Cosimo the wealthy, Cosimo the cutthroat, the extortionist, the murderer was finally tipping forward to get a closer look.

Satisfaction did not describe it.

He glanced at the other note, from Tomas Moneychanger, at the part he'd not read aloud. It reported Tomas had received a nondescript, black-haired visitor who'd asked a great many questions about the woman outside the moneychanger's office the morning of the sword fight.

As I distinctly recall you insisting on there was no woman present, I informed him he was in error. My trust in your powers of recollection will no doubt delight you.

Kier smiled faintly. His smile faded as he glanced to the bed. Sophia was tumbled amid the pillows, her slim arm flung out, fingers curled. She was his as much as his breath. As much as his heart. That was why this was about to get exceedingly difficult.

Perhaps she could simply be deflected.

He called for the messenger to deliver the missive to Noil, who would ensure it reached Cosimo.

He said nothing to Sophia.

Forty-five

"Delayed?"

Sophia looked at Kier, who was readying himself to go out after informing her their previously arranged engagement with the mayor, to show Lady Mistral the glories of the annual fair, had been abruptly postponed.

The sun never truly dawned that day. It was blotted out by the rising storm clouds that sat at the far horizon, glowering greenishly at the earth. It was a strange respite, neither here nor there; one gained relief from the sun but not the heat, and when the storm came, it would bring only mucky roads and overflowing rivers.

Last Fells paid the weather no mind. Fair or foul, it was not as powerful as the business interests that propelled the town into its annual summer fair. A fortnight of frenzied feasting and dancing, drinking and debauching, and most especially, buying and selling, was commencing today, and a quarter of the population of southern England was in Last Fells to partake.

Kier nodded as he wrapped his belt around the plane of his stomach. "Aye, lass, delayed. And just as well. The day is wicked hot, and not made for wading through crowds. I will be back soon enough."

He gave his belt one last tug and slid his gaze up, traveling up her body on its way to her eyes. "I will bathe you when I return."

He may have meant it as a promise, or an entreaty, or perhaps a bribe, but despite flushing, Sophia felt angry. He was leaving her. Again.

"And you will not say where you are going?" she pressed, following him to the door.

He flashed a smile. "To ruin them, Sophia."

Which, of course, was no answer at all. Which was, of course, exactly what he wanted.

One could almost begin to suspect Kier of something.

Sometime after he left, after Sophia had grown tired of waiting but knew there was only more waiting ahead, a servant announced a visitor.

She opened the door to a man in a bright blue tunic, a messenger in the mayor's household. Coming, she presumed, to suggest a new time the mayor could make good on his promise to escort her to the fair.

"My lady," he said, bending into a bow. "My lord mayor wishes to suggest Sir Kieran bring the company books of the last annum's draws to their meeting, if it pleases you," he added hurriedly, clearly uncomfortable and unsure if it was entirely proper to be asking the owner of the company to supply her account ledgers. "My lady," he added in another fit of discomfort.

"The mayor's meeting . . . with my factor, Sir Kieran," she repeated.

"Indeed. My lady." Another nervous bow.

Kier was meeting the mayor. Without her.

Which, of course, was outside her concern. Mistral Company was, after all, Kier's matter. If he wished to meet with the mayor, planned or unplanned, to begin, conclude, or otherwise fashion any matter related to Mistral Company, and to leave her out of it entirely, well, surely it was none of her affair.

But . . .why? Had she not proven herself capable of Kier's grade of mischief? A skillful player in their impious mystery play? To mistrust her now was rather . . . insulting.

Had she thought it through, she would have realized being left out of Kier's machinations was the best possible thing. She might have even realized how far she had fallen, to be seeking his good opinion of her trickery.

But there was time for none of these things as she walked to the far end of the room, flung open one of the coffer lids, and snatched out the ledger under discussion.

"I have it here," she announced brightly. "Unfortunately, Sir Kieran has already left for your master's. But I shall bring it myself."

It would be satisfying to watch Kier's face fall when she entered the room. To hear how he might try to explain. To perhaps throw something at him. Something hard.

She and the messenger pushed their way through the heaving crowds to the mayor's abode, then Sophia was escorted to the second-floor landing. The mayor's private offices were on the floor above. His steward went up to announce her.

Which is why she was standing on the landing, peering out the window, when Cosimo Endolte arrived in Last Fells.

She knew at once the man riding a chestnut horse down the center of the High was someone of import. Someone feared and respected.

A score of armed riders rode in escort for their nexus, a tall, handsome man in clothes that flashed with expensive threads and a bejeweled saddle that cost more than some villages. Behind them came a line of heavily laden wagons creaking through the muck of the streets, and perhaps thirty servants, making their way through the busy streets of Last Fells.

And then came the murmurs of the crowd as it moved aside to allow them by.

Cosimo Endolte.

The heat of the burgeoning day had no power to stop the cold that swept through Sophia. Excited cold, fearful cold, glad-she-never-had-to-be-near-the-man cold. All the men in ruin and flames due to him, all the women weeping in back rooms, all the monies funneled down his deep, insatiable throat, destroying anyone who stepped into his path, destroying everyone she'd ever loved: Papa, Kier. Murderer, destroyer, king's man . . . stopping at the gates to the mayor's courtyard.

He threw his reins to an attendant, said something to the others, then, in large, confident strides, alighted up the stairs to the main keep.

Sophia froze.

A flurry of activity came from below, then she heard voices, muffled, alternately lifted to her ear, then swept away, drowned out by the sounds of the courtyard and bustling streets beyond.

". . . with the mayor . . . crowds . . . Lady Mistral. . . . Is that so?"

He'd mentioned her.

Her heart began to hammer.

There was a murmur of excited responses as servants scurried about.

"Of course, sir, of course. Come, upstairs, let me just—Ralph, see to Master Endolte's horses. Oh, sir, await me. Sir? If you wait—"

Boot steps were rounding the bend in the stairwell.

Sophia stepped backward. Her boot scraped against stone, loud in the small space. She looked around. A small alcove, deep in the shadows, storage for candles and linens and women who wanted to hide.

"Sir? Just a moment." The steward was puffing up the stairs, far behind Cosimo, who'd apparently charged on ahead. "The steward will announce you, sir, and take you up, if you will just . . ."

Kier. Cosimo was going to the mayor's office. Kier was inside.

Hard boots were coming around the final bend.

". . . office chamber at the top. Sir? If you will just wait a moment . . ."

Sophia's heart hammered. If Cosimo Endolte went into that room, what were the chances he would recognize Kier?

But certainty was not a thing to be computed; it simply was.

Cosimo would know Kier in a heartbeat.

On the other hand, Cosimo *might* have heard tales of Roger Darnly's daughter's red hair, but then again, he might not have. In any event, her hair had darkened considerably over the years. Eyes of green were not sinfully uncommon either, and they too were dark enough. Hardly a thing of note.

But Kier and Cosimo had *history.*

A history full of deeds between two men who knew not only how to read a man, but how to see inside his heart. Conycatcher skills.

A long and lucrative history. Then a short, betraying history, followed by a deadly one.

Even the coldest of hearts recalled the person he had tried to murder.

It would take a heartbeat, mayhap two, before Cosimo recognized Kier. Perhaps as long as three, but when the moment of recognition came, five years' hard planning would come crashing down atop Kier's head.

Then he would be dragged off like the outlaw he was, hanged, taken down while still alive, cut into quarters, and dragged by galloping horses until his body split apart.

That is what happened to traitors.

Sophia swallowed the hot stream of bile that raced up her

throat. And then, Cosimo would remain at liberty, unpunished, unchecked.

Her body started shaking. It was a slight thing. Her head, though, seemed to expand, and a whooshing sound rolled through it. Mayhap it was her blood pounding; she could not be sure.

He had come around the twist in the stairs. She could see the side of his face, lit by torches.

Her rebel feet stepped out of the shadows and stood in the center of the landing, in the daylight.

He would see her. And then he would recognize her. Or not.

If he did, it was all over. But if he recognized Kier, her heart would contract into a puckered, shriveled shell.

Cosimo stepped out of the stairwell. He lifted his head and his hawklike eyes pinned her. He stopped short.

"Who are you?" he demanded.

"God's greeting, sir. I am Lady Mistral."

Forty-six

Tall, lean, dark-haired, he did not have a knight's hard physique, nor a merchant's pale softness. He was simply . . . there. Cultured, reaching out with long tapered fingers to take her hand in his.

"My lady," he murmured. He took her hand and kissed it. She stared down at his mouth on her skin. He straightened with a smile. "I have heard much of you, my lady."

"And I, you, sir."

"But I did not ever think to meet you in a passageway landing," he said, smiling faintly.

"Ah, but surprises are the spice that enlivens the meal, is that not true?"

"It most certainly is," he said, his tone and regard one of mounting interest.

"Shall we walk?" she asked. "The air of the house is close."

His eyebrows went up. He glanced at the open window that overlooked the town. "No more so than the town itself, I daresay. There is a fair unveiling today, my lady. The Hot Fair of Last Fells."

"So I have been told. And yet I wait, and do not see it."

"I find it impossible to believe you have been abandoned."

She gave a delicate shrug. "Englishmen. They are cold even during their own Hot Fair."

He laughed. "I would offer myself, except—"

"I would accept."

He started, then gave a soft, warm laugh. "You do me an honor, my lady. But . . . I see no servants? And the mayor . . ." He gestured toward the stairs that led upstairs, to the office where Kier was.

She smiled. "Meets inside. But I do not suffer waiting on the timelines of fussy officials very well. A failing, assuredly, but one I claim wholeheartedly."

He glanced at the stairs. "Surprises are spice," he murmured.

She laughed softly. "Just so, sir. And truly"—she lowered her voice—"do we find us in need of a *mayor*?"

He laughed fully, bowed, and extended an arm. "I most certainly do not require a mayor, my lady. Come, let me show you the fair."

She hurried them out before the mayor could be alerted to Cosimo's presence. It was a bit tricky when it came to the servants, but not whatsoever with Cosimo, almost as if he'd come only for her, and had no wish to see the mayor at all.

The focus of his regard, his utter attention to her, the every direction of her every glance, to the exclusion of his men, the mayor, all passersby and merchants, these things could have been complimentary. Stimulating. Flattering.

Sickening.

They strolled through the cloudlike heat of town, heavy with humidity. A train of Cosimo's servants billowed out behind them like a haze.

"You have traveled far to be here, my lady."

"That I have."

"We have heard much about you, here in England."

"Have you?" She eyed him, then touched the rounded bottom of a copper kettle hanging off a vendor's stall as they went slowly by.

"We have indeed. I should like to know more yet."

People were everywhere, good-naturedly jostling and shouting. Criers were out with news of the realm and of newly tapped wine casks, offering samples, inducing people to come inside. Music came from every corner as musicians played and walked, played and sat. A man and his son were doing acrobatics down another street, walking on their hands while the crowd shouted and cheered.

He guided her to a small bridge that crossed a stream, and stopped them there. Sophia leaned back against the stone wall, positioning herself carefully just this far from him, and just this close.

"What more would you like to know, sir?" she asked.

"How a woman has succeeded in a difficult business such as yours."

She nodded. "I have a small but strong fleet of ships. They carry goods from many places. Genoa, Alexandria. I have clients who move tin and some who move rock salt and some who move . . ." She smiled. "Let us just say 'many other things.'"

That earned an appreciative smile.

"I am the carrier of spices for a count's family in Venice, you may know."

Cosimo gave a gracious smile. "Those ports are closely guarded, and the Venetians are warrior-merchants. You have carved out difficult territory."

She hesitated, then leaned forward with a conspiratorial smile. "Very true, unless you know a certain man."

He leaned forward with her. "What certain man?"

She straightened. "The certain man whom I know. And who knows me, well enough to allow in my ships when others must wait, and helps me avoid being examined too closely when it is inconvenient. We have already established, I think, that waiting is not a thing I do very well."

"No, it is not," he drawled. "I find myself enchanted by your impatience."

"If you like, I should say Mistral Company has friends in many places."

"I do like," he murmured.

"'Tis costly at first, to secure these friendships," she admitted. "But it is all recouped, you see."

"I do."

She turned to look over the wall of the bridge at the small brook that wound below. "One must be a very valued . . . partner. A very profitable one."

"And yet, I am told you have lost partners of late."

She sighed. "That is true, sir. Not all wish to deal with a woman."

"How unchivalrous of them."

"Is it not? That is precisely what I told them."

He laughed.

"But nonetheless, they spurn me." She glanced over. "But I am told you too are in the business of losing customers recently."

He looked at her sharply, wariness back in his gaze. Good. She had every intention of keeping him unbalanced, uncertain, unsure of himself. And of her. Was she a rich fool, a grieving widow, or a hard-hammered merchant princess?

"You must forgive me," she went on, averting her gaze to look out over the town, "but the name of Cosimo Endolte is much on the tongues of England merchantmen these days, and not favorably so. Something about"—she looked directly at him—"a ledger?"

The sharp edges of his face tightened.

"Many people are speaking of it."

"Many people are fools."

A dark gray cloud rose off the horizon, blotting out the sky above his head. It was most unsettling, how alike Kier and this man were in how they drew their map of the world. She could almost hear Kier saying these exact words.

But then, they'd moved in the same sphere for so very long. They were, in many ways, the very same.

She gave her head a little shake as if tossing off an irritant, a fly. "That is sharply true, sir. I find far too many men tiresome and distinctly un-bold in their thinking."

"Do you?" The measure of interest in his voice notched up.

She regarded the bustling town below. "Too many men do not appreciate the things that are rare. They all show interest in the very same things the others want."

"What I am interested in, my lady, is beauty and money."

She lifted an eyebrow in a knowing way. "And when the beauty is *with* the money"—she stirred her index finger through the air—"that is the very best of all, no?"

He gave a low, appreciative laugh. "The very best."

She allowed the corner of her mouth to lift. "Perhaps you find something you desire in Mistral Company?"

The leather of his boots creaked as he stepped up beside her. "I am fairly certain I do."

Ignoring the coldness that came with his nearness, Sophia put her hand on the stone wall and tipped her head to the side. "But what I meant, sir, was perhaps you have something you wish to transport on Mistral's little fleet of ships?"

He laid his hand very near hers on the wall. "Must the two be exclusive?"

She paused, then lifted her lashes to peer at him. "Not to the wise man."

"If I may speak boldly?"

She angled her body toward his slightly, communicating interest deeper than her words. "I should expect—and desire—nothing other."

"Perhaps we can be of some assistance to one another, my lady."

He was a powerful man. Power emanated from him like a scent. A young man, missing a home and full of need, could so easily be enticed, captivated by the allure of a man such as Cosimo. His coin, his confidence, the promises of what might be, if only you did his bidding. You might become anything.

Or, you might be burned alive in an inferno if you did not.

"How much assistance?" she asked flatly.

"How much do you require, my lady?"

Her chest felt empty of air. She forced herself to look him in the eye. "Rather, let us ask: How much do *you* require, sir?"

For a moment, he stared at her in astonishment, maybe even anger. Then he suddenly threw back his head and burst out in a laugh. "Yes," he murmured. He looked down at her. "My lady, may I suggest an alliance?"

And *then* she turned to him fully, smiling. "You may suggest anything you like, sir."

"I have some goods I might be interested in using Mistral Company for."

"How much, when do you wish to move them, and to where?" She smiled.

A slow smile touched his lips too, admiring and assessing. "There has been an unfortunate delay in my most recent shipment, a small but most valuable cargo. My troubles stem from a recalcitrant merchant. I shall manage the matter. Then, perhaps, we can engage in business that will benefit us both?"

She let her smile become as admiring as his. "Perhaps you have some questions for Mistral Company."

For the next half hour, he posed a series of incisive questions, everything from weights to customs to duties, to whom she knew in which French ports, and piracy and how much she paid—and was willing to pay—in bribes, and most of all, how much she needed to know, precisely, about what was being transported onto her ships.

She looked into his hawk eyes. "Very little, sir. My interest lies in profit. And pleasure. In various orders, depending on the profit. And the pleasure."

He laughed again, and his cold, white teeth gleamed at her like hard little moons.

Forty-seven

Sophia shut the door to the apartments, shaking from her shoulders to the tips of her fingers, burning with a strange fire that not even the slanting rains could quench. She was soaking wet, shivering, and lighted up from within.

She had done it.

Kier would be here. Soon, he would come.

Shivers ran down her chest, came up her belly. She walked to the window to look out. The door behind her opened.

She turned.

He just stood in the doorway, watching her silently. He looked . . . not angry, not furious, simply . . . dangerous.

"I had no choice," she announced.

He closed the door quietly. "Not so."

She opened her mouth to inhale. "You are correct. 'Twas a choice to circumvent his design, and I would do so again. Kier, he was coming, up the stairs, into the room . . . he was going to walk into the room where you were."

He started across the room. "I said no contact with Cosimo."

"I know. But, regard—"

"You must do as I say."

"I will do as you say. I simply . . . he was coming." Her breath was unsteady. "I had to stop him."

He stood before her. "You did more than stop him."

"He showed interest. I needed to press him."

He grew still as a mountain, the gleam of his eyes fixed on hers in the dark room. "How much interest?"

"A great deal. He has a small but valuable shipment he would like to use Mistral ships for."

Something rippled through his body. "He said that?"

She nodded.

"When?"

"I do not—"

"Where?"

"He was unable to say. It has been delayed."

His look grew sharp. "Delayed?"

It was infinitely preferable to have Kier focus on her news, not her actions, so she didn't pay attention to his abruptness. "Some mishap in delivery, it seems. But when it arrives, he wishes to put it on our—your ship."

Something flickered in his eyes, that was all.

"Is this a satisfactory outcome?" she asked quietly, but her skin was tingling.

Had she paused, for even a moment, she might have reflected on Kier's abruptness, so unlike his typical slow, confident, conquering way. But one could hardly focus on such things when the object of one's desire had stepped so close his body skimmed hers, when he was murmuring in his dark voice.

"I am impressed with what you accomplished, lass"—his hot hand brushed up her waist—"but it does not change the matter: you did not do as I said."

"I needed to stop him."

"No." He ran the back of his hand down the front of her body. "You needed to do as I say."

A hot rush ran through her. "I will," she whispered.

His gaze raked over her face. "Will you?" he murmured. Then he lowered his head and danced his lips over hers, light and breathtaking and infinitely sensual.

"Turn around," he murmured above her lips.

She did.

Hands on her shoulders, he raked his fingers through her long dark hair until it fell loose and unbound to her hips.

"Take off your dress," he murmured against the back of her neck.

Heat hammered between their bodies. She tugged at the laces that held the outer tunic. With each gentle tug, the material tightened around her breasts. Behind her, Kier leaned down, ran his lips over her shoulder, sending shivers down her body like hot rivers. Then he tugged her tunic up and over her head. She stood in the tighter, longer blue kirtle, which fell to her ankles.

He tugged that off in seconds.

And she stood then, unclothed, her back to him. Shivers cascaded down her shoulders to her shins, and she waited, knowing he was watching her. His fingers spread through her hair, from skull to the ends tangled in his hands. Then he pushed her hair over one shoulder, so it cascaded over her breast and down her belly. Another long moment of nothing but knowing he was watching her standing naked before him. Her nipples tightened into nubs. Then the long stroke of his thick finger came, from the nape of her neck to the curve in her back above her buttocks.

"Put your hands on the wall."

Hot, heavy, hard desire pulsed through her. She did as he said. Encasing her hips in his hands, he stepped up behind her. The length of his hardness strained against her back. Then he crouched, laid his open hands on the backs of her legs, dragged them hotly up her body, up her calves, over her thighs, hard over the curve of her bottom, his fingers splaying out as he slid up her back, to her neck.

Violent, hard pulses of want moved through her, spreading out, a lake of desire.

He rose, bent his head over her shoulder.

Her skin shivered hot, her body pulsed with the goodness of his touch, from the want of him. From his want of her. There was nothing but this moment of heat and desire and hard, good wanting. Heat flooded her; the undulating center of her body began to ache in rolling waves, demanding to be satisfied.

He bent and kissed her neck.

She whimpered and leaned her head to the side, into the kisses he was running down her, his mouth hot with sensual commands. She almost thought she heard him whisper through her hair, *"Trust. Trust me."*

He pushed his knee between her legs.

"Open for me."

She leaned her forehead against the wall and bent her knee, let him have his way.

"Good." His growl of praise sent another wash of wetness through her. He swept up her inner thigh with his hand and stood between her legs. His hardness strained against his breeches as he rocked his erection against her bare skin, rubbing into her wetness.

"Get on the bed," he commanded softly.

She walked over and started to lie down, but he took her hips from behind. "Kneel," he murmured thickly.

Her breath shot out in a rush. She did as he bid, panting and breathless, her head dropped between her arms. He placed his palms on the bed beside hers, muscular arms stretched out on either side, and kneeled behind her. His body was pure sculpted heat. His chest curved over her back, his lips nibbling on her ear, the front of his muscular thighs were solid against the back of hers.

He leaned back on his heels, just behind her. One hand was on her bottom, the other resting lightly on the small of her back. His fingers danced between her thighs, pushing in from behind. One long finger nuzzled into her slippery wet folds and stroked, back to front, ending with its wicked, tempting flutter against the hard nub at the crest of her. Her head dropped forward. He did it again, harder. She threw back her head and arched her back. She knew he was looking at her kneeling naked before him, looking at her while he did what he was doing. Her breath came out in a long, shuddering gasp.

Placing one hand firmly on each of her hips, Kier guided her backward as he moved forward. They met in a single, slow, rocking thrust. She shifted on her knees, moved slightly to the side, and then, *"Oh."* He did not have long.

How many years had he dreamed of her? But not even his reckless imagination was as perfect as this. Because never in his imagination had it occurred to him that what would move him most was Sophia's utter trust in him, her willingness to be so vulnerable before him.

His hand closed around her hip and he rose up behind her. With a single, sure move, he sheathed himself inside her, thrusting deeply. Her body shuddered.

"Oh, Kier." The breathy moan shuddered out of her.

He rocked into her slowly for the longest time, holding himself in check. He stared at the ceiling and clenched his jaw, trying not to notice the way her soft bottom bounced against his groin, the way she threw her head back and gasped with each deeper penetration, the way her curving hips felt locked beneath his palms. Little whimpers began skidding out of her. She started to move faster, became more frenzied in her movements. Her back and arms, muscles taut, grew slick with sweat. She threw her head to the side and dropped down to her elbows, her buttocks pressed up higher, open for deeper penetration. Kier adjusted himself on his knees and pulled harder on her hips, back into him. Her hair was dark silk on the bed, sprayed across her forearms and her hands.

"Oh, please," she whispered. "Oh, please, please."

He leaned over her sweaty back, still pumping, and dragged the hair away from her ear. "Is this good, Sophia?"

She made some incomprehensible gasping reply. Her hands clutched into fists on the sheets and her body started clenching and rippling around the length of him. "Oh," was her single, soft, whispered cry.

"Marry me," he rasped against the back of her neck.

Sophia's eyes flew open.

For a moment she was motionless, then tears began spilling onto the bed, but he could not see from behind her, and she had no time to attend them, for her body shuddered over the edge.

She threw her head and cried his name as he thrust into her. Their bodies slammed together as he barreled straight into a violent, staggering orgasm, spilling himself inside her, trying to make her trust him, to feel for him what he felt for her, even though he knew it might destroy her in the end, to love him.

THEY talked for hours, through the rise of the moon. They did not speak of what Kier had said in the throes of passion. Sophia did not trust she'd heard right, and Kier did not repeat it. Best to forget.

"Kier, what would you have done, if Cosimo had seen you?"

He looked up at the ceiling.

She was quiet too, then said, "You have some contrivance in mind, some sort of plan."

"Some sort," he murmured.

"And you will not tell me?"

He turned his head on the pillow and shook his head, meeting her gaze. "No."

Looking into his eyes so close as akin to touching warm steel; powerful, only hinting at its danger. But inside, in the long, deep well, she thought mayhap if Kier kept on as he seemed to be now, if—while inscrutable and mysterious and infuriating—he had changed, then mayhap, one day, she might just give herself her heart's desire and fall in love with Kier again.

Though it was, of course, impossible to do it *again*, for she'd never fallen out the first time, fool that she was.

And she entirely overlooked the fact that Kier had never said he'd changed, nor even that he wished to.

After that, they did not talk of Cosimo, or the crimes that had been committed, or the things that had almost destroyed them or the people they wished to destroy in turn.

They talked, instead, of smaller things, the silk threads Sophia hoped for in her next shipment, the sights Kier had seen in his travels.

He told her about the red rocks of southern France and the gushing, frothing rivers that cut through the treacherous mountain passes of the Alps.

He described trekking through the murky wet forests of the Holy Roman Empire, and the bone-shivering wolf howls of France, and the first time he'd seen the astonishing blue of the Côte d'Azur.

He spoke of the floating world of Venice, bustling with merchants and spices and festivals, and the brown, angry camels of Egypt, and the towering arches that built the ancient Pharos of Alexandria, a lighthouse taller than any other on earth, casting its bright light across the dangerous waters, a magnificence, a marvel that had to be seen to be believed.

She pushed herself up on her elbows. "Oh, I should like to see it," she exhaled, her eyes bright. "Someday, I should like that very much. Have you been there many times?"

Kier touched the back of her sweaty head. "Many, many times."

She settled back into the crook of his arm, and he bent it, pulling her in closer. "I have only been to the places I could run to."

"That will change," he murmured.

"Tell me of other places you have been."

So he did. They built a world apart that night. Separate and singular, it was crafted of breath and hopes, at once tremulous and indestructible, for it did not exist.

But, just before she fell asleep, Kier said sleepily, "Sophia, if these men were interested in you for some reason other than the ledger, what would it be?"

She considered this, her tired brain searching. "I have no money, no name, no family but a disgraced father already hanged for treason. I do not know why they should want me for anything a'tall."

He rolled his head toward her. "And yet they do."

"And yet they do," she echoed.

KIER'S murmured words rang against her, not allowing her to sleep.

She looked over at him. He had no such troubles.

She slid out of bed and tiptoed across the room to where the Darnly ledger lay open. Taking the nighttime candle stuck on an iron spike, she tilted it to the side and lit three others, surrounding the ledger with little sentries of light.

Then she settled down into the cushioned chair, took out her spectacles, and began to read.

Forty-eight

When Kier awoke, contrary to his plans for a slow-moving, lust-driven *dawn* awakening, it was rather more unpleasantly done, entirely free of lust, by a hard poke against his chest, and it appeared to be in fact *pre*-dawn. Not by a great deal, but still . . .

He snapped his hand up and closed it tight around the offending object. When the object squeaked, he pulled down on it and opened his eyes.

Sophia's face was an inch away.

"You'd best have an exceptionally good reason for poking me in the ribs."

"Look at this."

He rolled to sit. She pushed the ledger into his hands and held a candle just above the page. Her slender finger directed his attention to the spidery lines.

"Read. What does that say? In Richard's hand."

He looked closely. *"La Welyfare, BDS, arv Lt Fls, laden, est mid-Sts Paul and Peters."*

"Why is my shipment listed in here?" she demanded.

He looked at her.

"*La Welyfare,* that is the ship we often use."

"The name of many ships," he pointed out. But his heart began to beat faster.

"*BDS*, that is my company. Batten Down Silks."

He looked at the ledger again. The trailing ends of her hair pooled on the page. She grabbed them and pulled them aside. They stared at the last entry of the ledger.

She looked at him. "Why is *my* shipment listed in Cosimo's book of foul deeds? It has all my ship's information."

He looked up slowly. "They didn't want the ledger, Sophia: they wanted this information. They want your shipment."

She leaned close. *"What is in my shipment?"*

They looked back at the book. The entry was clear, if not adhering to any particular method of recording manifests, but as this was a book of "foul deeds," that didn't matter: "*La Weylfare*, home port Bristol, to arrive in Last Fells, laden with goods, estimated arrival between Saint Paul and Saint Peter's days."

That was *now*.

Her shipment was sitting there, waiting.

Richard had never sent word that a shipment was arriving,

Looking through glowing aura from the candle she still held aloft, Sophia looked at Kier.

"What have they done to my silks?"

He rolled to his feet. "Wait here."

"Wait here? You *are* mad."

"I thought we spoke about you doing as I say." He reached for a soft chamois shirt lying on a shelf in the wardrobe and yanked it over his head. "I'm fairly certain you gave your word."

She looked at him as one would a leaky roof. "But, Kier, this is my *life*. My trade. You cannot think . . ."

Her voice trailed off as he pulled out a mail shirt, its gray-metal links undulating in the candlelight. She stared at the armor. He yanked it down over his head, shaking his head as it came out. He looked directly at her.

"It may indeed be your life, Sophia, if you do not heed me."

Sophia was still staring at the armor. "What are you going to do, Kier?"

He paused for the length of a heartbeat. "I'm going to make them pay."

Hose were attached to his belt with swift competence. He flung on a tunic, then buckled on a much heavier sword belt than the one he usually wore. It had elaborate, beautiful stitching across it and loops for any number of weapons, which he began filling at once, reaching into the back of a wardrobe like it was a kitchen pot. Various sizes and shapes of knives and—dear God, was that an ax?—came out, and Kier slid them into the belt with the skill and ease that comes only from long practice.

He shoved on his boots, snatched up his cape, then reached out to cup her face and give her one swift kiss. "Stay here."

He strode to the door. Outside was dark and drizzling. "Lock this behind me."

"Kier—"

He flung the hood on his cloak up over his head. His eyes were hard glints within the dark folds. "Wait here. Or you will be sorry."

He shut the door behind him.

SHE stood in the middle of the room, silent, for a long time. The sounds of the night were soft but clear: the occasional laugh or shout from a window, the creaking wood of rocking ships, the patter of raindrops.

She grabbed her cape, then stalked to the door and flung it open. Kier had left his two guards on station and they snapped to attention, then examined her from under their dark-green cloaks, the leather-wrapped hilts of their swords poking out, getting splattered in the rain.

"You are here to protect me?"

They exchanged a look, then nodded mutely.

"Well, then, you will want to know I am leaving now."

"Leaving?" echoed one in consternation.

"But, my lady—" began the other. "We have instructions—"

"I am sure you do. I am leaving. I presume that means we are *all* leaving." She started down the stairs. "In which direction did Sir Kieran go?"

Silence followed her down the stairs. The guards did not. She stopped and looked back. "You may tell me now, or I will wander the streets until dawn, which, I presume, means we shall *all* wander the streets until dawn. I warn you, though, I expect to grow exceedingly unhappy. And hungry."

While a hungry, unhappy woman was no doubt an alarming proposition, still they hesitated.

Sophia sighed. "You do comprehend who pays your wages?"

Now, of course, *Kier* paid their wages. But they did not know that. So far as they knew, Mistral did. And that brought them down the stairs, quick on her heels. Money won the day. How predictable.

She would have to remind herself more often that people bethought her Lady Mistral. And Kier, why . . . Kier was merely her factor.

She smiled grimly. Deception had its benefits, after all.

Forty-nine

She found Kier easily enough. He was standing near a small, lantern-lit hut along the quay, asking questions of a port official, learning which ship was hers.

She followed in the darkness, the guards a few steps behind her, her hood pulled forward to shield her face and deflect the spitting rain.

The master of the quay had told Kier it had been bobbing there, sail furled, for two days, with no word from its mistress, although word had been sent some days ago.

But, of course, Sophia had not been at her burned-out warehouse, so she'd never received the message.

She waited until Kier hired a small skiff and paid extra to dismiss the services of the surprised oarsman who usually rowed people out to their waiting ships. Kier stepped down into the boat and tossed off the thick rope that held it to the dock.

Then she stepped forward. "Good evening."

Kier stilled, then blew out a breath and turned.

She stood just above him, her cloaked figure getting drenched in the rain. He inhaled slowly. "Well?"

"Well," she repeated calmly, and stepped down into the boat. It rocked back and forth, and little waves splashed up.

Kier looked up at his two guards, standing sheepishly on the quay. For a long moment, his absolute silence delivered its message. In unison, their wet faces flushed as sullen raindrops fell onto their hooded heads.

"Sir, what were we to do?" one said almost plaintively.

Indeed, what were they supposed to have done? he thought. Short of physically restraining her, how were they to stop her when she'd made her intentions clear? Sophia was unstoppable without ropes.

He ought to have left rope.

The waters of the little cove were beginning to churn with activity. All around, boats were rowing men to the huge carracks and stern-ruddered cogs, where they clambered on board. Sails were unfurling, men were shouting to one another.

He looked at her. She looked back, her hands folded neatly on her lap. "This is my ship, Kier. Not yours. And I wish to know why people are hunting it like a roe deer."

"Return to the apartments," he said to the guards. "I have her now."

The guards clattered off and he began rowing, his eyes never leaving hers. "You will be sorry."

She looked over his shoulder to face the sea and the bobbing, tall-masted, dark mass of ships. "I am sorry about so many things, Kier. What matters one more?"

They reached the ship without further incident. A few seamen had been left behind on guard duty, as well as one huge, gray-muzzled dog, which rose to its feet, growling as they came up the ladder and climbed onto the deck.

The seamen leaped to their feet. In the darkness, the steely blades they each extracted were bright flashes.

Kier put his palm on his own sword.

Sophia crouched down, extended her hand, and called softly, "Come, Lo."

The dog's tail started wagging. He scrabbled over to her, tongue out, claws clicking on the damp planks. He reached her side and licked her with abandon, tail thumping.

The sailors relaxed, and one swept off his head covering and bowed to her. "We did not know what to expect. The master dead, and you not showing up."

She smiled and rose, the tips of her fingers still touching Lo's huge shoulders. "I am here now. You have done well," she said, looking around the deck. There should be another dog. "And where is Behold?"

A faint pause, then one of them said solemnly, "He passed."

"We gave 'im a proper burial," the other piped in, dagger back in his belt. "Right over the side, into the deep blue, like the proper seaman he was, aye, that we did."

She smiled sadly. "I thank you for tending him so well." She glanced down the ship. "The cargo is below?"

The other looked concerned. "Aye, but, Mistress, we can't offload now. The tide's ebbing too fast, and no one's to hand."

She felt Kier, standing behind, his hand still on his blade, but silent. "You are correct, Roger. We will not be offloading. I wish only to inspect."

He looked slightly uneasy. "Right, and no one's been down there since 'twas first loaded, per the master's instructions, all those months ago."

"And right you were. A year or a day, the master's orders must be followed. But he has passed, and I am here now, and I will go belowdecks and inspect my shipment."

They brought her a lantern. Kier nodded toward the far end of the ship. The outline of a hatch was easily visible amidships, a square within the weathered floorboards.

"Down we go," he said quietly, lifting it.

The hinges squeaked. He held the door in its upright position, gesturing to her. "I will go first."

She grabbed the rusted iron handle in one hand; the entombed darkness exhaled onto her dirty dark air like pitch, which Kier was climbing down into.

Taking hold of her mind and the sudden merry images of horror dancing through it, she held on to the sides of the narrow ladder and went clumsily down. She lowered the door after her, over her head, to ensure the seamen did not witness . . . whatever might be witnessed.

It was quite as if one had agreed to be buried.

The ship creaked, much as a casket would. Wooden planks groaned, stretched and pulled by the rolling tide. She stood absolutely still, holding on to the ladder with one hand and the lantern with the other.

She forcibly uncurled her fingers and pushed open the tiny squealing door of the lantern. A dark shape reached forward—Kier's arm—and he lit the wick of the candle within. It flamed into a tiny, bright light. She squeaked the door shut and held it aloft.

The air was close and damp, smelling of wet wood and salty air, of musty tarps and damp iron, of rat droppings. The back of the hold was filled halfway to the ceiling, a bulky mountain of canvas-covered goods. Her shipment of silks and whatever else so many men were risking so much on.

She crept forward, lantern in the air. Her silks would be in tightly wrapped bales, double-wrapped in canvas and covered in tinplate, then sacked, the silk within wound into skeins. *BD Silks* was burned on the sacks, with a fat looping *S*, her seal. There wouldn't be many.

There were, it seemed, hundreds.

Kier was moving down the hold, tossing back the heavy canvas tarps covering the sacks as he strode deeper into the belly of the ship. Sophia followed, holding the lantern up, so high the muscles in her arm began to burn, as she tried to examine the cargo by the tiny beams of candlelight.

It was silent but for creaking wood and the occasional splash of water or shout from a man on some other ship.

"Hold the lantern higher," Kier said quietly.

With trembling fingers, she pinched the little door and swung it open to throw out more light. Kier put his hand into his tunic and drew out another candle. He lit it, then crouched down on the balls of his feet and lifted the last tarp, and lowered the candle above it.

"They wanted this, Sophie." His voice was flat and grim.

"What do you mean?"

"Have you ever heard of gunnes?"

Fifty

They looked at the long, graceful things. Kier let his body roll backward to sit on the bundled, canvas-covered sacks. Sophie stood with the lantern held high, staring into the swaying shadows.

"Gunnes," she whispered. "'Tis but a . . . but a tube."

"Not a tube, Sophie. A weapon."

She stared down at the strange, slender things, unable to believe a weapon could be fashioned from such a thin, hollow thing. "What manner of weapon? Do you strike with it?"

"No. It . . . flames."

"It bursts into flames?" The rocking ship made her feel ill.

He shook his head. "You touch a hot poker to it, and it *delivers* flames. Or rather, it projects whatever you put inside this tube." He tapped it. "Propels them like spitting seeds."

"What sorts of things?"

He shrugged. "What sorts of things do men put in trebuchets?"

Sophia shuddered. Men put awful things in trebuchets. Canvas sacks covered in burning pitch, the heads of one's slain comrades, decaying pigs' heads, after their bodies had been rendered into fat to burn out the tunnels dug under the besieged castle.

"This is smaller, of course." Kier's voice was thoughtful and quiet. The creak of the ship almost drowned it out. "But with saltpeter, 'Chinese snow,' it propels objects far and fast. Much farther, much faster than a trebuchet. The force . . ." He shook his head.

"How far?" she whispered, bending her knees to crouch beside him.

"Hundreds of yards."

"Impossible."

"So fast you cannot follow it with your eye. Aside from the noise, you might have no notion anything had occurred. Until the people start falling down, dead, hundreds of yards away."

She stared in horror at the little thing. She reached out to touch it, then retracted her hand. "What do they call them?"

"Fire drug. Hand cannon. Chinese arrows. Fire lance."

"Fire lance," she repeated softly. "How many are there?"

His face was all shadows with a few candled highlights: cheekbones, nose, chin. He got to his feet and, striding up and down between the rows and piles of items, he climbed up onto the mountainous bundles and started flinging back canvas coverings.

There were hundreds of them.

She got to her feet. The bobbing of the ship was very gentle, but Sophia was shaking from chin to knees.

Kier's face, grim-set, peered down at the weapons before him, muttering to himself, "But how?"

"How what?" she asked weakly.

"How do they ignite it?"

"You said fire ignites it," she said between almost chattering teeth.

"Yes, but I mean the propellant," he replied absently. "It must be saltpeter. But from where?"

Standing atop the mountain of bundles and packs, he

stared down at the long line of gunnes with a sort of fatalistic regard. He didn't seem upset or nervous. "Edward will not be happy about this."

"Edward?"

"Aye, Sophie. The king of England." Dark, lantern-lit eyes regarded her. "He has just declared war on France."

She stared down at the sleek, dark little tubes of death. "You think these are meant for France?"

"What do you think, Sophia? If 'twas coming in for Edward's good, why hide it?" Kier's voice was contemplative. "I see now how they did it. Your father bought the silk business with this in mind. He wanted you to wed Richard."

She put out a hand to steady herself. The only thing nearby were the piles of gunnes, and even in her shock, she felt the irony that *they* should support her. Kier kept on.

"Your father and your husband, they double-crossed Cosimo. The gunnes were Cosimo's idea, but your father and then your husband transacted the purchases, prepared them for shipment. He traveled to the southern markets, found the vendors, secured the gunnes and transported them back, over stormy seas and mountain passes. It would have taken years."

Sweat slid in cold trickles between her breasts. It *had* taken years. And she had suspected nothing.

"My husband bought these," she whispered, pointing at them.

Kier nodded, appearing merely thoughtful at this unraveling of facts, not horrified, as Sophia was. "Of course. That is why he wed you. Your father set him up in this."

She took a sharp step back, away from the awful things being said. She bent her knees, pressed her fingers to the hull of the ship, to steady herself.

"That seems the most likely," he murmured, crouching down beside her, an arm slung over her shoulders, but his face forward as he relentlessly, dispassionately pushed into the web of deceit and dread that was her life. "These gunnes were Cosimo's grand plan, but your father and your husband did all the work for him. Then they got greedy. And when your father was hanged out of the picture, Richard came to finish the matter."

Her father had suggested Batten Downs.

"Then Richard very inconveniently died."

She covered her mouth in horror. "You think Cosimo . . . ?"

"Found your husband and murdered him? No. I think Remy did, on orders from Cosimo. I think Remy was supposed to convince Richard to tell where the shipment was coming in. And when he did not, he was killed. Do you not see?"

She did see. She saw it all. Her life had been a puppet show, and the only one who'd even attempted to cut her free had been the cony-catcher Kier, who was now engaged in an act of vengeance that threatened the safety of England.

She sank down to a crouch, head spinning, fingers freezing, heart smashing against her ribs. Ruination. It stalked her like a beast.

"This is my ship, Kier," she whispered. "It will be my neck. Just like my father."

"No," he said grimly as he got to his feet. "Not yours."

His face was shifting through light and darkness in the lantern flame that danced like madness on the softly rolling ship. He held out his hand to help her rise.

"Did I not say you would be sorry if you came?"

Fifty-one

He hurried her up the ladder, across the creaking, swaying ship. He had her bid her seamen good-bye as normally as possible, and instruct them to treat Kier as they would her, following his every order.

Then Kier helped her forward, down to the wherry, and rowed them back to shore, all without a word.

The danger was mounting like storm clouds. Cosimo was ready to deal, prepared to transfer everything onto Mistral's ships.

'Twas time to get Sophia out of the way.

How could he ever have thought it would come to anything other?

Fool. He'd already tried deflection. But Sophia could not be deflected.

His heart grew a skin of steel. He felt it covering him as they rowed across the hard little waves in the cove, as he walked her through the silently dawning streets of Last Fells. Slick fibers stretching in a cold weave across what had been a beating heart. But his was a heart that beat only during Sophia. Not before and surely not after.

He escorted her through the wakening town, stiffly, she leaning into his hands as if she were reeling, through the streets they'd walked so many times, she on his arm, smiling at him, suggesting to him, permeating him.

He helped her up the wooden steps to their apartments, and it felt like a death march. Up the stairs with the abandoned vineyard, fluttering with tumbling glossy green vines and birds and the scent of burning honeysuckle.

He unlocked the door. They went inside. The sun was rising, already hot and hard against the windows, the walls.

Sophia sat down on the bed, hands in her lap, face haggard, her eyes wide and staring.

This was beyond her, as he knew it would be. He'd always known. He *wanted* it to be. Sophia was beyond this dirty world of his.

Time to be as awful as Sophia knew he could be.

SOPHIA'S mind was on a march. Thought after thought lined up in orderly fashion and hammered its boot heels against her heart.

If Kier had not known precisely what was on that ship, neither had he been surprised.

Kier was not trying to make Cosimo buy into a company that did not exist in order to leave him penniless and ruined. He was trying to . . . steal their shipment of weapons and leave them all ruined. *All of England.*

She felt like the ship was still rocking beneath her feet. She understood now. She was almost certain she understood.

The hollow echoing thoughts banged against Sophia's skull as Kier went into the bedchamber.

What had she *done*? Joining Kier, trusting him, relaxing into him, as if nothing were amiss, as if nothing were at risk, like the utter, ridiculous, impetuous, intrepid fool she *always* was whenever it came to Kier.

But there was much to doubt, much to fear, and Kier was

at the center of it all. It was *deceitful* of him to make her believe otherwise. To make her live otherwise.

Her bones were like rocks, her skin stiff and scraped like unoiled parchment. She could hardly breathe.

Kier strode back into the room, boots hard on the plank floors. He carried a small coffer in his arms like an infant.

"What is that?" she asked stiffly.

"A great deal of coin and gemstones." He tapped the corner. "Take what you want. Then leave."

"What?" she asked stupidly. Stupid and thickheaded, unable to think.

He was looking at her, just as he ever had, dark hair falling, legs planted, but his eyes were empty. Cold. The way she'd seem him look at men he did not like and did not trust and did not want anything to do with.

"Let me clarify, Sophia: I am done with you. 'Tis time for you to leave."

"But, you told me . . . you said . . . you asked me to—" She stopped, unable to finish.

You asked me to marry you.

But he knew. The coldness of his smile told her he knew what she was about to say. She did not need his terrible, horrible words to prove it to her.

"Sophia, surely you know this much: I say what I must, do what I must, and in that way, I achieve my ends. Women are to be managed, that is all. 'Twas the first lesson I learned." He smiled. "After never to trust anyone."

She started shaking her head, an involuntary rejection of his words.

"I tried to tell you," he said.

Horror welled up inside her, thick, choking wads of it, rancid honey.

"You said you never lied to me," she whispered.

The angles of his handsome face angled into a smile. "I lied."

She backed up, away from the awfulness of Kier. He tapped the corner of the chest again. The gems and coins inside jiggled, winking red and blue and gold in the firelight.

"Yours." His voice was cold. Chilling, in fact. His eyes were steel.

"For what?"

"Services rendered." His gaze slid down her body, but there was nothing in his cold eyes now but a tiny red gleam from the fire. His gaze came back to hers. "I have had better. But not much."

She jerked, all the breath punched from her lungs.

"I particularly liked the ice."

She flung her head up, recoiling as if he'd slapped her. She pressed her arm over her stomach, as much protection from his words as to combat the nausea roiling up inside her.

He tapped the corner of the chest again. "Look inside; whatever you want is yours. They will support a wise woman for a very long time. Forever and then some. Take what you want and go."

Even as she stood there, horror turned to stone-cold fury. She stared down into the box of jewels, plucked out a length of pearls, then flung it at his face.

"Take what I *want*?"

The pearls struck his cheek. He didn't move. She reached in again and closed her fingers around a handful of gold coins and threw them across the room. They spiraled and tumbled as they flew through the air, glinting merrily as they struck Kier in the chest and fell to the floor. She began reaching in blindly now, launching handfuls of gems and coins at him.

"Take what I want? Of *this*? This . . . *trash*? You think I want *this*? *You think I want this?*"

Some of the items struck him in the torso, but most scattered wildly throughout the room; in the rushes, across the table, onto the wardrobe shelves, so the room was like a beach of shipwrecked gems, glittering red and blue and green and gold after a storm.

Kier didn't move.

When her arm finally fell, when she stopped throwing, he quietly repeated what he'd been saying all along.

"Take what you want. Then leave. I am done with you."

And he walked out on her for the last time.

Fifty-two

Sophia stood in the center of the room, reeling. She was halfway between screaming and crying. She did not know which way to turn.

Kier was precisely who she thought him to be?

It was . . . unthinkable. It was the one thing she'd counted on, that she could doubt Kier.

And in doubting him, she had actually started to believe in him. To think he was something else, something more, something different.

Now, there was no doubt.

He was just as she'd thought.

God's truth, she'd been a fool. To trust Kier for a *second*. For the length of an inhale. For as long as it took to blink. She'd had a plan, and then she'd seen Kier and—

She'd had a *plan*.

The thought strengthened her sufficiently for her to straighten away from the wall. The plan was still viable. She'd allowed herself to be distracted, to be convinced the king would not take kindly to proof of past associations of corruption when he needed money from those very same men. Which might be true.

But now, she had more than a ledger. She had a shipload of weapons.

If anyone believed her. If she could even make it through the door. Edward was not in the habit of hearing petitioners with outrageous claims against his subjects.

She'd allowed the sorcerer Kier to put a glamour over her, make her think it was *he* who could—who *would*—stop such men as these.

But, of course, Kier was *one* of them. He did not change things; he simply lifted them to their next natural level.

She started across the room, hardly noticing the way she had to hobble after having stood so long in one place. The bottoms of her feet felt debrided, her spine creaking and unwilling to unbend, resisting every move she made to walk away. Her fingers felt cold.

She bypassed the coffer, picked up the ledger, then stopped at the desk to scribble a swift note.

I am the rocks now. You had best sail away.

Then she opened the ledger and flipped through until she found the page she wanted. She ripped it out, crumpled it in her fist, and dropped it beside the note. And on top, she laid the emerald Kier had folded into her palm, when he thought such things could keep her safe. Then she crunched across the gemstones and scattered gold coins on her way to walk out on Kier.

As he'd all but begged her to.

Her hand was on the door, when a knock hammered against it. She leaped backward, heart thick and in her throat.

The knock came again. "My lady?"

It was Cosimo Endolte.

She clutched the ledger tighter, bound now in a velvet satchel, and stared. She opened her mouth and inhaled silently.

"My lady? I thought I heard you inside?"

"Enter," she whispered.

He swung the door open and stood in the doorway, cool and calm in his rich clothes. The sun was rising and had touched the hillside behind him, an almost ethereal golden glow. The gemstones stitched into his belt winked at her. His gaze lifted over her shoulder and swept the room, then he smiled at her. "I received your message, my lady."

"My message," she echoed weakly.

"With the bill of lading for signatures, as well as instructions for loading my goods onto your ship."

She exhaled. *Kier.* Kier had sent it, telling Cosimo to load his goods . . . those *gunnes* . . . onto Mistral's ship.

Her fingers tightened around the satchel. It drew his eye. Forcing herself to smile, she affected the same calmness he was exuding, and turned back to the room, and carelessly set the satchel on the table.

"But of course," she said, turning back. "The contracts."

"Rather than sending a reply via messenger, and desiring to see you again sooner rather than later, I took the liberty of coming directly in response. I hope I do not overstep." He bowed.

"Not at all, sir," she said as freezing cold shakiness swept through her. *Think, think.*

"I am glad. You seem to be . . ." His gaze moved to the overturned coffer, the jewels pouring out of it, strewn across the floor and the linen sheets. "Without servants. Were you going somewhere, my lady? Have I interrupted your plans?"

"Not at all." She forced a laugh to accompany the words that were not precisely a lie. One could hardly call her intention a *plan.* More a reckless leap off a cliff with a breaking heart.

The despair of it all made it hard to think clearly.

"Again, I am glad to hear it." And again, his gaze swept

over the bejeweled chaos of the room. "In England, we have adopted the custom of storing our valuables in wardrobes or coffers. I am charmed by your southern approach."

She found another false laugh inside somewhere, and when it emerged, it sounded absolutely natural. She was as shocked by this as anything. It helped her resist the almost overwhelming urge to bolt and run. Running would do nothing, for while Cosimo said "charmed," what she saw in his eye was the same thing she'd seen yesterday: the predatory self-interest of an animal closing in for its kill.

She had to get away without alerting him to give chase.

She waved her hand airily. "I, too, make use of coffers, Master Cosimo. I simply also made use of the wrong factor."

Cosimo's eyes drifted up. "Did you?"

She met his eye. "I did."

"I am sorry to hear it. We have all had the experience. Perhaps I can be of assistance?"

"You are kind. That will not be necessary, although I fear we must delay our meeting of signatures. In truth, I am en route to see the king," she finished on a faintly triumphant note. He would not stand in her way now.

Although she did not know where the king was precisely. He might be a hundred miles away. Not that she'd implied he was close to hand, but she hardly looked ready to set out on an itineration to track down a king.

Cosimo did not seem overcome with despair by the news. In fact, his eyebrows rose, then he smiled warmly. "Why, my lady, our interests are again aligned."

"They are?" she said weakly.

"A fortunate happenstance. I, too, have an audience with the king, this very morning."

He bent into a bow and swept out a hand, prepared to be her gallant escort.

She stared at him, almost shaking on the threshold of panic. Then a thought occurred that swept the shakiness away. Why, this was not tragedy—this was unlooked-for hope.

She'd had no way to gain an audience with the king nor his greater officials, nothing but to claim herself Sophia Darnly, which was as liable to get her imprisoned as it was an audience.

But with Cosimo Endolte as her escort, she was assured entry. Then, at the proper moment, she would ensure she had a little aside with the king or one of his officials.

She lifted her chin and returned a smile at least equally warm. "Master Cosimo, it is as if we are of one mind." She laid her fingers in the upturned hand he still had extended between them. "One might almost say 'twas a fated thing."

He closed his fingers gently around hers as he straightened and led her out the door.

"One almost might."

Fifty-three

Kier stared at the note and crumpled parchment. He unballed the parchment and flattened it with his palm.

It was a leaf from the ledger, with Kier's name penned in bold black ink, a citation of his first visit to Roger Darnly, all those years ago.

Very good, Sophia, he thought, a silent cheer.

And yet . . . something was wrong.

He'd been prepared for the emptiness in his heart. Prepared for the silence in her wake. Prepared for the hollowness and rage in his heart. He was, after all, a vessel of revenge and nothing more.

Upon a time, that had been enough.

He was even prepared for it not being enough.

What he was *un*prepared for, though, was the unsettling sense that something in his plan had just gone terribly awry.

He turned and went to find Stefan the Innkeep.

The common room was crowded. People had decided they'd had enough of hunkering down under the storms, and were out for a night of revelry.

"She left with a lordly soul," Stefan said hurriedly, standing with a tray in the center of the bustling room. "Cosimo Endolte."

Kier felt his body harden from the boots up.

"Aye. He's the rights to the old Bishop's Palace, by the west gate," Stefan assured him. "For years now, it's been his, though he's hardly ever there. Right up above the cliffs, it is."

Kier stood motionless in the middle of the crowded room, amid all the sounds of voices and laughter and plates clattering, getting bumped as people made their way by him in the crowded room, Stefan asking him insistently if there was anything he could do to help, but everything of Kier was focused inward.

His heart was still steel, wrought and hammered, impenetrable.

His mission was still clear: revenge.

His mind was still focused, his attention still unwavering.

It was his priorities that had shifted.

Sophia had asked about his plan. It had always involved revealing himself to his old nemesis. It was unavoidable. No man would load a shipment such as this onto a ship without meeting and assessing the owner or agent. Thus the meeting at the mayor's.

But now, Cosimo *had* the owner. Lady Mistral. What he did not have was his shipment of gunnes.

Cosimo needed that shipment.

Kier needed that shipment.

He needed a way to propel Cosimo into necessary actions and lure his attention off of Sophia.

A factor was not necessary here. An old adversary was.

For years, Kier had prepared for this day of confrontation. He'd planned out every detail with loving, focused, rageful attention. He *craved* this meeting, the way one craved drink or women, could almost taste the beginning of the end.

He'd never expected it to take place at Cosimo's hidden lair.

There was no worse place in the world for it.

It would put him inside Cosimo's stone walls. Inside the ring of Cosimo's guards. At Cosimo's mercy.

As Sophia was right now.

Accursed woman. Why could she not march off to the king in rebellious defiance, get trussed up and imprisoned for the short period until Kier could get her out again? For the Tower of England was the one place in England where Sophia Darnly would be safe.

"There's time to catch them, sir," Stefan the Innkeep said. "They left but a moment ago."

Kier turned and ran for the stables.

Stripping Cosimo's power away too soon would only frighten him, perhaps into untenable actions. He had to be persuaded, coaxed, made to believe he was still the leader of the pack.

Alternately, neither could he be given too much control. Vanity such as his must be managed; he must be impressed. You had to accomplish the thing they never could have dreamed of, then hand it over to them, make it due them. Cosimo could always be impressed.

Kier dismounted at the outer walls, then sent in the message: *I am standing at your gate. I have a proposition.*

Fifty-four

Cosimo escorted Sophia in the comfort of a padded saddle, an awning held over her head, as they crossed town to the stone keep that guarded the northwestern corner of Last Fells.

The awning was a complicating nicety. The winds were rising rapidly, ripping at the cloth covering like teeth. Two hardworking servants battled it back as best they could.

Clearly Cosimo was not often in attendance in his palace in Last Fells. The road was almost empty of shops and people. Typically princes and kings and bishops brought wealth. But occasionally, should they be absent, they brought the reverse. Now, hovels rose up on the streets beside, tipping forward on weak legs to peer at the novelty of a passerby. The barefooted inhabitants stared sullenly, hair whipping, as they rode past, awning splayed into strips, cackling as it snapped in the winds.

The draw creaked as it was lowered, and thirty feet of cobwebs broke off as it crashed down, bending and snapping like silvery bones.

The draw hit the earth with a resounding thud. It reverberated through Sophia's body like a hammer strike. Her teeth clattered together. Clenching her jaw did not stop it, cessation of the vibrations did not stop it; a small, steady shake stayed in her body.

Inside, the place was in an uproar. Iron-banded coffers squelched heavily into the mud at the base of the keep stairs, ready to be lifted onto wagons. The doors to the stables were thrown open, and although it was barely midday, the wide swath of yellow light did much to illuminate the gloomy bailey as horses were led out, being hitched to wagons or saddled by grim, helmed men.

Servants hustled in and out of the main keep and outbuildings, arms laden with packs and small chests holding accoutrements of the household. One young varlet lost his fisted hold on a bulky canvas sack. It fell to the ground and a cluster of pale wax candles rolled out onto the muddy cobbles. He was roundly cuffed by an older servant, and the two hurriedly wiped and repacked, then hurried away into the gloom.

Sophia stood back as Cosimo was accosted by both servants and messengers from the moment his boot touched the stairs to the keep.

He moved swiftly into the great hall and turned her with a skillful sweep of his fingers to sit her on a cushioned seat before a trough fire that ran down the center of the room and, despite the hot summer, was needful here in this cold castle.

Then he climbed onto the dais and stood behind his great oaken table to field the barrage of questions from servants and reports from messengers and a chilling array of well-armed men who all came and left with the same name on their tongues and in their disappointing reports: Sophia Darnly.

Cosimo tossed her an apologetic smile during a lull. "I shall have to beg your forgiveness, my lady. My recalcitrant merchant. Rebellious, more's the like. You may remember we spoke of her? You must know the sort."

She sat very straight in her seat on the main floor of the

hall, her fingertips resting carefully on her knees. "Yes," she breathed. "Yes, I do."

Cosimo smiled at her. She smiled back.

He frowned at a pair of mailed guardsmen who still stood there, helms in hand, after their instructions had been given. "Well, what are you standing there for? Do as I bid: ensure she is not still lurking in Batten Downs."

Her body was enveloped in a single cold chill. She'd become an icicle, smiling at winter.

He sat back, looking at her, his chin on his fingertips. "Tell me, my lady, how do you manage them?"

"Manage whom?"

"Independent-minded merchants who do not know their place."

She inhaled a thin breath. "I do not do business with them."

He burst out in laughter. "Just so." He leaned back in his seat and kicked one leg out. The table was bare of linen cloth, and she could see the grimy bottom of his boot beneath it. He ran his hand once through his hair, a strangely human motion of weariness and worry. "Unfortunately, my lady, I was not so wise as you. I find my shipment is not quite ready to load."

"Is it not?"

He shook his head. "It has been unavoidably detained."

"How unavoidably?" She forced herself to speak above a whisper.

He smiled, perhaps to reassure her. "Do not concern yourself, my lady. I will bring her to heel, and repercussions will be had."

"Repercussions?" Her voice was a windswept, high-pitched thing.

"Oh, yes, indeed. She has caused me far more trouble than she is worth. Hair like yours, I am told," he added carelessly, sitting forward and touching a handful of papers on the table. "Do not fear, though, my lady. It does not concern you."

He smiled at her but she was saved the necessity of replying when his door warden came hurrying into the room. "Sir?"

Cosmo jerked his gaze over. "God's blood, what is it?"

"A visitor."

A queer smile touched Cosimo's face. "Ah, good. He is here."

Sophia did not know how her blood could run any more coldly than it already was, and yet it seemed to crystallize into shards of ice at that. "Who is here?" she whispered.

"An old friend," Cosimo said softly.

A dark, caped figure stepped up behind the servant, backlit by torches. Kier stepped into the fire-lit hall.

Fifty-five

Cosimo looked entirely unperturbed by the sudden resurrection of the man he'd tried to murder. "De Grey," he said softly. "I should have known fire would not be enough for you."

Kier came down the steps. "Aye, you should have."

Sophia shot to her feet, but Cosimo only sat back more comfortably in his seat and rested the ankle of one boot upon the opposite knee. "I did not believe it at first."

"Believe what?"

"Believe Dragus."

Kier laughed.

Cosimo shook his head slowly as Kier moved through the shadows of the hall, coming closer. "I still do not believe it." He was quiet a moment, then said softly, as if to himself, "You always were my best." He turned to Sophia, perhaps just recalling her presence. "You should leave, my lady."

Without waiting to see what she did, he turned back to Kier. Sophia sat, absolutely quietly, and watched Kier make his way through a hall smoky with tallow candles and a sputtering trough fire.

Cosimo nodded to Kier. "How can I help you?"

"Oh, no, I am here to help *you,* you rotting piece of dung."

Sophia rose again with a shocked gasp, but Cosimo laughed. It was a buoyant, almost delighted sound, light and merry. "I always said you were my best, Grey." He laughed again. "For certes, you always had the biggest bollocks."

A clatter of boot heels sounded on the stone stairs behind Kier as additional guards ran up. Kier never looked away from Cosimo. "Tell them to leave."

Sophia's breath lodged in her throat. *Kier was mad.* Obviously, the wisest thing was to have him dragged to some dark, dank cavern with chains, perhaps snakes, certainly rats, and be done with it. But Cosimo was never obvious, and she was suddenly certain Kier was banking on precisely that.

Cosimo glanced to his guards, then back to Kier. "You are unarmed?"

Kier nodded. "I am."

"Go," Cosimo ordered his men, his eyes never leaving Kier's. He waved Kier forward, and Kier stepped up onto the dais. Sophia held her breath as he passed within inches of her.

He didn't so much as look her way.

He yanked out a short bench and lowered himself onto it, a leg on either side. Cosimo sat back and smiled at him.

Neither of them looked at Sophia.

"How have you been?" Cosimo said.

Kier smiled. "Since you tried to burn me alive?"

"Yes, since then." Cosimo sat forward in earnest. "Grey, what did you expect? You turned on me, tried to destroy me."

"I *threatened* to destroy you." Kier let his gaze travel down the rich embroidery and silk threads that adorned Cosimo's tunic. "You do not appear destroyed."

"You turned on us all. Over a *woman.*"

"Aye," Kier agreed with cold, slow mockery. "Turned on all my thieving brothers."

Cosimo shrugged. "The decision was as simple as awakening in the morn, Grey: you could no longer be trusted."

"My name is Kier."

Cosimo squinted at him. "Kier? What in God's name is that?"

"In God's name, 'tis Irish. 'The dark one.'"

"Ah." A smile cracked Cosimo's face. "No longer are you some complicated melding of light and dark? That is good to hear; your tortured soul was always so difficult to watch. But now, matters are simplified. You are simply the darkness."

Kier smiled back. "Simply the Irish."

For a moment, the room was silent but for the low, intermittent, thin crackle of the damp wood. Cosimo's smile faded.

"What do you want? Why are you here?"

"You have erred."

"So I see."

"I do not mean the attempt. I mean your utter failure."

"I said, I see."

"I am going to ruin you."

Fear rippled across Cosimo's face in whitening shades. "I ask again, what do you want from me?"

"My life back."

"I do not have it in my keeping."

"How unfortunate for you. For I"— Kier dropped his voice to a whisper—"very much have yours in mine."

In a single move, he got to his feet, shoved Cosimo's head back, and held a dagger against his naked throat.

This is where one could say he'd stepped out past the end of the plank. If Cosimo had no curiosity, if he had not been pressed hard enough to the wall by now, if he truly wanted Kier dead, then dead he would be.

Silence descended. Their breath was like wind in the empty stone chamber. The lines of Cosimo's aristocratic face were harsh, ravines cut by the unbending, brutal firmness of resolve that had made him a leader of truly awful men.

"I thought you were unarmed," he choked.

"I lied."

Cosimo's brutal eyes glittered hollowly at Kier. "So, this is how it shall end? How unlike you, such a banal approach to something so satisfying as revenge."

Kier's hand shook. His fingers were slippery on the hilt of the dagger. The urge to do it, to press down and draw the blade back, to slice open and loose the force from this malevolent facsimile of a human life, was almost crushing. It was a roof falling slowly down upon him, the pressure of it: *Do it.*

"I ask again." Cosimo managed to emit the sound from his bent-back throat. "What do you want?"

"Your money."

"We can talk," wheezed Cosimo.

"I have a proposition."

"I am listening."

Kier released him with a shove. Cosimo's chair squealed backward and he lurched to his feet, rubbing his throat, glowering at Kier, but not calling for his guards.

"What is your goddamned proposition?"

Fifty-six

Kier stood at the edge of the dais, calming his breath. "You are in trouble."

Cosimo laughed like the cawing of a crow, harsh and loud in the echoing room. "As are *you*, *Kier*."

"Do you wish to attempt it, please, try. If you dare. But I have discovered something: fire has a way of burning through fear. Who would have guessed *that*? But there it is; I am mad. So, have you fearful things to say or do, please, say or do them, and get it over with." He rested an elbow on the table and leaned forward. "Otherwise, shut up and listen."

Cosimo stilled.

Kier said softly, "I can bring what you need."

"Why would you do that?"

Kier leaned back and crossed his arms over his chest, an insouciant smile lighting up his face. "Because you are going to pay me half of the profits off your latest . . . shipment."

The slow emphasis on *shipment* made Cosimo go still. "What do you know about my shipment?" he said in an ominously quiet voice.

Kier smiled. It was not the hot Kier smile, nor the dangerous Kier smile; it was a frightening one Sophia had never seen before.

"What do you think?" he said, just as quietly.

Cosimo lurched forward in his seat. *"What do you know of it?"*

Kier leaned forward an equal amount, smiling into Cosimo's eyes. "I know what it is."

Cosimo jerked as if struck by a whip, then went still.

Kier sat back. "So, do we deal, or do I leave you and your 'shipment' to sink here in England?"

Cosimo remained silent.

Kier sighed. "Consider what you pay me that which would have been Richard's portion."

Cosimo's gaze lifted slowly. *"Richard?"*

"Aye."

"That traitor?"

Kier looked amused. "What did you do to make him turn?"

His face flushed. "Nothing. I did nothing. He betrayed me, and—"

The silence hung a moment. "And?"

Cosimo swallowed, his jaw tight, but he said only, "And he commandeered my shipment. I do not know where it is."

Kier burst out laughing, then got to his feet. "I will find it for you."

Sophia looked at him standing there, so coldly confident, smiling faintly, his eyes glowing with reflected candlelight. It was so difficult to tell with Kier, whether he was a self-serving, coldhearted bastard or if he was the banked coals buried deep in the ashes, waiting to burst forth. She had gone through such extremes in her regard of him, her opinions, her desire for his ultimate demise, that she felt stretched upon the rack of her heart.

Cosimo got to his feet. "You would be able to find me this ship?"

Kier smiled. "Of course."

Sophia closed her eyes.

"For fifty thousand. French."

Cosimo's face transformed. It was as if this amount did not insult, or frighten, or outrage him, but *honored* him. His lips peeled back in a smile like a skull. His white teeth grinned at Kier. "You always were the best." His voice was filled with fierce, possessive satisfaction. "I pay well for the best. But I require it swiftly; can you do that?"

"I have already made inquiries." Kier glanced around the room, with its half-packed chests and feel of departure. "You appear to be embarking on a journey."

"A few last items, then I am gone from England forever."

Kier smiled. "A wise plan, as so many people are hunting for you."

Cosimo gave a wan smile in return. "Remy the Black will manage them. Just find me the ship. I can have the money delivered in the morning."

Kier nodded. The torches guttered as a draft blasted through the hall. "With luck, my news and your money ought to pass each other along the way."

Cosimo nodded. "It will be done."

Kier took one last sweeping glance around the room. "My horse needs to be fed and watered."

Cosimo snapped his head toward his guards and servants huddled in the doorway. Instructions were conveyed both to stable and kitchen staff to feed horse and man.

"Until morning, then, Piper," Cosimo said, with a mocking bow, as the doors were opened again. At once, a messenger came hurrying in. Cosimo turned to him.

As if released from a rope, Kier's dark eyes snapped to Sophia. It was a physical thing, this look. A steel thread, binding them. At once, he disengaged.

She looked away too, shaken as if he'd ravished her. Her breath came shallow and halting.

He came across the dais, away from the men now blocking the stairs on the near side. His spurs jangled softly as he came. His body, hard and hot, passed close enough for her to touch as he went by.

He didn't so much as look her way. But he brushed a finger against her stomach.

"Get him to sign the contracts."

Then he hopped to the floor and, without a word or look, strode out of the room.

Fifty-seven

The contracts were signed with no fanfare or even a great deal of attention. Cosimo's steward served as witness. Both were distracted.

Cosimo seemed to have no notion that Sophia had overseen or overheard anything; he made no reference to the meeting she'd been witness to. She said merely, "You seem to have found someone who can locate your recalcitrant debtor," to which he muttered, "He will find her."

There was a strange, distant, exultant energy about him now. He was both preoccupied—staring across the room, needing prompts to reengage in their conversation—and highly attentive. Sophia was the recipient of too many appreciative looks, murmured innuendoes, and dainties from the kitchen to "tempt your appetite and brighten your pale cheeks," he avowed with a chivalric intensity that was disturbing.

It was the fervor of a tourney champion with one last joust to go and the certainty he could never be unseated.

Such distraction, of course, served a purpose.

"And what quantity shall we say, sir?" she inquired at one point, midway through.

He looked over blankly. "Quantity?"

"The shipment."

He blinked.

"Is it dry goods, sir?" she inquired gently. "Liquid?"

"Dry. Silk."

"Have you a notion of amounts?"

He stared ahead.

"I shall proceed thusly," she suggested gently, so as not to pull him from his reverie. In fact, she attempted to lull him deeper into it, lowering her voice, deepening it as she wrote out the bill of lading, the contract for shipment, the formalized agreement of the terms of the shipment, reading it softly aloud as she went.

"In the name of God, so be it. Done at the Bishop's Palace in Last Fells, I, Cosimo Endolte, do transmit to Mistral Company, in the name of God and of salvation, on her flagship, by the ship captained by the agent of Mistral's choosing, fifty sacks of silk. . . ." She looked up. "Shall I proceed?"

"Yes," he mused, not looking over.

She did, and while he was staring across the room, she wrote in smooth, swift script: *oak-banded, double-wrapped canvas, tinplated silk goods; miscellaneous sundries within.* So there would be no way for him to deny what was his.

And if this all went wrong, what was hers. She did not fool herself; the thing on the altar was Batten Down Silks. Was Sophia.

She pushed the contract in front of Cosimo and, lowering her shaking hand to her lap, she continued with the negotiations.

A few moments later, he signed both copies without so much as looking at them. They arranged for the money to be sent to Tomas Moneychanger, in care of her factor.

Fifty-eight

Sophia paced her bedchamber, staring at the door, debating how risky it would be to tie her bedsheets together and lower herself down the tower wall.

The door suddenly swung open, and Kier strode into the room.

It was sinful, the flood of relief and joy that crashed through her.

"What the *hell* are you doing here?" he demanded, coming toward her.

Shock dropped her jaw. "What am I—? *What am I doing here?*" She lifted her hands to pummel him as she had in Tomas's office.

He grabbed them as he had then and said, almost angrily, "I thought I could at least rely on you to be reckless and bold as is your wont, and go to King Edward."

"Go to King Ed—" Her words dropped off. "You *relied* on me to go to King Edward?"

His gaze fired with a dark light and he pulled her roughly to his chest, lowering his mouth to hers.

"Are you hurt?" he said, even as his lips touched hers. "Have you been hurt in any way?"

"No, of course not."

His hands slid over her face, his eyes searching. "Not in any way?" he pressed. "He suspects nothing?"

"Not of *me*," she retorted in a low whisper. "What are you *doing* here, Kier? What madness is this, of revealing yourself?"

He pushed her face from side to side with his thumb, a soldier's assessment of health. She batted his hand away. "You need to leave." He dropped his hand from her face. "Now. Do you have the signed contracts?"

Her head was whirling. "I do, but—"

"Come."

"Kier, stop—"

"You're leaving."

"Leaving?"

He was already peering out into the corridor outside her chambers, then tugging her down its shadowy length. "There have been wagons and shipments leaving all night; you will be on one of them."

"Be on one of them?" she whispered as she crept with him, keeping close to the walls.

"The kitchen is sending out a delivery to the ships within the hour; you will be a part of it. I have arranged it with the porters."

"How?"

"Money, Sophia. Come."

They hurried down stairways, past dark, stale, empty rooms, held back in whatever dark corner was closest when servants came near, carrying heaps of goods, continuing through the night to pack up the household for an early morning move.

He pushed open the creaking door on the ground floor, which opened in to the bailey. He looked out, then drew her into the warm starry night. "Come," he whispered.

Servants and retainers were scattered across the dark courtyards as they hurried along, Kier whispering instructions as they went. The household was in flux, and that meant controlled chaos, and that meant disrupted schedules, disgruntled men, and drink when the longer shifts ended. Small fires for cooking burned here and there throughout the bailey, as Cosimo's guardsmen and hired soldiers camped outside for the night, and three pigs were herded, squealing, through the center.

They were safe in part *because* there were so many people. What were two more, cloaked and quiet amid the scurrying?

Kier pulled up in front of the kitchens. Even at this hour, fires burned inside as the staff prepared food to take on their sea journey. Or rather, for their lord to take, for it was unlikely that Cosimo would bring his entire household as he fled the realm, and even less likely he would have informed them they were all going to be out of employ come the morn.

They drew up outside the kitchens. The windows of the building were brightly lit. Two wagons stood there, half filled with sacks and chests containing food and kitchen utensils. A horse stood harnessed to each one, tails whisking, hooves cocked sleepily. From inside came the sounds of people calling and metal banging.

Without a word, Kier pulled her to him and kissed her. She pushed him away.

He pulled her back to him.

"Now what?" she asked, trembling.

"Now, you trust."

She dropped her head with a little laugh. "Kier, how can I ever trust you?"

His palms slid across her cheeks. "Not *me, you*. Trust yourself, Sophia. All you need to do now is the thing you think is right." His eyes never left hers. "Now, get in the wagon."

She looked at it. "That would require me to trust you."

He reached in and lifted a blanket. "Get in."

Behind them, a member of the kitchen staff suddenly appeared from belowground, climbing up out from a hidden cellar, hauling up a sack behind him. They stared as his fat face appeared out of the ground, but he seemed even more startled. He shouted in alarm, then wiped his hand over his face, apologizing.

"My lady, sir," he said hurriedly, his face red from exertion. He bent into a bow, midway up the earthen stairs, then he climbed out with a puff. "My apologies. I'm simply . . ." He turned to the sack and strained on it, heaving hard, but it would not budge over the lip of the cellar trap. He might be there for minutes. Finally, Kier reached out and pulled it up for him.

"My thanks, sir," the servant grunted appreciatively as he kicked the trapdoor shut behind him. "The cellars are a mighty task for an old man on a warm night."

Kier looked at him, then down into the hole he'd climbed out of.

They watched as he dragged the sack into the kitchen, then Kier turned at once to Sophia. "Get in."

"Kier, I cannot."

More footsteps sounded outside the door, then the clink of armor. They held their breaths, staring at each other. The steps hurried by, murmured voices of two servants dissipating into the cold ether of the castle air.

"We have no time, Sophie." His voice was a notch above silence, his dark, patient regard a feather brush against her heart.

She clutched the contract that was still in her hand, and slapped it into his.

"Go now," he said, pushing her toward the wagon.

She closed her hands around his arm, stopping him. "And what will Cosimo say when Mistral has disappeared?"

"I care not what he says. He will be on Mistral's ship come a day; he has no choice. All his gunnes will be on it."

"But not if I leave before then. If anything appears wrong, if Lady Mistral goes a-missing before the gunnes are loaded, before he is inexorably committed, he will balk, will he not? Run. Escape."

His eyes hardened.

"You know I am correct on this," she said swiftly, quietly. "I will claim myself indisposed. Ill." Behind them someone in the kitchen dropped something heavy. It crashed to the ground. A muttered curse followed swiftly. "I will tell him I am unable to attend him to the ship. I will send him on ahead, tell him to send back a litter."

He hesitated. She saw the hesitation, not Kier's way, by the bunching of his muscles. His jaw flexed, once. "And the moment he leaves . . ."

"I run."

He hesitated, then gave a clipped nod. "Remember everything I have told you," he said quietly.

"I will."

"Everything," he insisted.

"Kier, you are worrying."

He cast her a dour look. "Aye, 'tis unfathomable, is it not?"

The urge to touch his cheek was strong. She settled for looking directly into his eyes "I recall everything you've ever said to me, Kier. Tristan and Isolde, the reason you risked the fire, the lighthouse of Alexandria. I forget none of it."

He smiled faintly. "The lighthouse. I knew it would entice you."

"I wanted to see it someday."

"You will."

She smiled sadly. "When?"

"When you marry me."

Her jaw dropped. "Kier, you are mad," she whispered fiercely, glancing around. "I am not going to *marry* you."

"Aye, you are," he said placidly.

Deep in her belly, there was a hot, swirling whoosh through her. "I would have to be *mad* to marry you," she assured him. Assured herself.

He lifted his eyebrows. "Is that so? Why?"

"Why?"

"Aye. Why?"

"Why, because"—she looked at him helplessly—"because we . . . and you . . . why, you are . . . *Kier*," she finished in a faint, stern, inadequate reprimand.

"Ah. I see."

How could she be standing here arguing about *marriage* in the middle of their enemy's encampment? And yet, this was the part of Kier that drew her like a moth to a flame. His calm confidence, the way he knew what he was going to do and did it with staggering efficiency, the way he . . . trusted himself.

He glanced around, saw no one, and stepped so close she felt the heat of his breath, of his body, of his intentions. "Well, I'm sorry to relay, lass, you'll not have a choice." He stroked his hand down her back. "You're going to marry me."

She gave a soft laugh. He backed up and shoved something into her hand. The emerald.

He began drifting into the shadows of the towering gray keep.

She looked at the gem, at him. "But—"

"In case of need."

She stared at him in horror. "In case of *need*?"

"The ownership papers are with Tomas Moneychanger."

"Ownership—"

"Of Mistral Company."

"No! You—"

"Trust, Sophie."

She swallowed. "But not you?"

"No. Just yourself." Another step back and he was almost one with the shadows. "I promise: I will show you the Pharos of Alexandria."

Then they heard Cosimo's voice.

Fifty-nine

"My lady?" Cosimo called.

They both knew the moment for what it was. Kier could draw his sword and fight for her, perhaps even get her as far as the door, before they were both cut down. Or at least Kier would be cut down—perhaps she could maintain the mummery a little longer. Pretend she'd been abducted, ravished.

But even if the impossible happened, and they made it out entirely, if they escaped and ran, it would not be over. Cosimo would not be captured. He would be loose, weapons in hand, and they would be running. Forever.

Kier said he could stop him.

So, the choice was this, then. And it was hers.

Kier was watching her even as Cosimo turned toward her, ready to do as she silently bid.

She stepped backward, toward the keep, toward Cosimo.

The rest was in Kier's look, a brief, forever look.

Trust yourself.

Kier, dangerous, aching, scarred Kier, was precisely who she thought him to be.

Unlike anyone else.

So she gave him a chance to be that.

It was as sudden as dropping a rock into a lake; one moment the lake was still, the next, its vast surface was covered in liquid ripples. It was a very conscious thing, not at all a matter of "sensing" this or "feeling" it. She simply decided she would trust him. Trust herself.

And, that being settled, action was required.

She turned slowly and laid her fingertips on Cosimo's arm. With the other she pressed back the hair that had been pulled loose from the netting by the winds and Kier's hands.

"I thought I needed air. But the storm draws near. Come inside with me."

AT dawn, Kier sent word to Cosimo: *The ship is anchored off Last Fells. La Welyfare.*

And to Dragus, he sent another, equally simple message: *Cosimo will be on Mistral's flagship by nightfall. Green sails. La Sophia.*

In theory, all he had to do now was wait.

SOPHIA spent the night pacing her room and staring out the window. She dozed for perhaps an hour, maybe half of another, then was up again, just after dawn, in time to see the messenger come clattering under the gates.

Sixty

In the morning, Cosimo stood in the great hall, Kier's missive in hand, laughing.

"Last Fells. *Last Fells!* Richard the Scribe, that wily beast, hid the shipment directly under my nose. And I never would have known were it not for Kier."

It wasn't often the household saw him doing something as unfettered as outright, nay, joyfully laughing. Everyone stared in shock, most especially d'Aumercy, newly and unexpectedly arrived that morning.

"Do you *see*?" Cosimo cried, exultant. "Do you see why I always favored him? Without fail, Grey was always my best. Even if he is Irish."

He grinned and gave the parchment a little shake. Its upward edge fluttered like a pennant, then dropped, limp again. "This, *this* is why 'twas such a difficult decision to have him put to the torch."

He looked around, gleeful as a child. Seeing the room staring at him, motionless and dumbfounded, his face fell.

"Come, come, *move*. The wagons must be loaded. Mistral's ships lie near; the goods come off the Darnly ship, go onto the Mistral ship. Quickly now, by nightfall we must be embarked and in readiness. We sail with the tide."

He gave swift instructions to his men on moving the shipment from *La Welyfare* to the Mistral ship, and they hurried from the keep.

"Sail with the tide?" D'Aumercy repeated, rather stupidly, since the evidence of a hasty departure was all around him. Chests, wagons, goods rolled in linens and packed in coffers, servants in chaotic disarray.

Cosimo laughed. "Aye. I am leaving damp England to the Englishmen, Noil; it holds little good for me anymore."

D'Aumercy stared. This abrupt cessation of everything lucrative they'd been engaged in for years now was so baffling he could not immediately comprehend it. "But our investments," he said. "The *commenda*."

"Will continue without me. Or not. I am past caring."

"But, you cannot."

Cosimo glanced at him in amusement and said nothing.

"What of, what of . . . Lady Mistral?" D'Aumercy pounced on their most recent venture with alacrity.

Cosimo slowed his pace, and smiled a slow smile. "I have plans for her."

D'Aumercy stared at Cosimo, at his dreams of regaining his fortunes all slipping away, then he turned and strode from the room.

He almost stumbled over Sophia, who was standing in the shadows outside.

"My lady," he said with a sweeping bow and a distracted smile. She was not foremost on Noil's mind today.

"My lord," she said in a low voice. All traces of coquetry and southern accent were gone. "You do not know your associate so well as you imagine."

He gave a bitter laugh. "I am certain I do not know him a'tall." He looked at her closely. "You are leaving with him?"

"One hopes it does not come to that."

He raised his eyebrows. "My lady—"

"Keep your voice low," she said. They both fell silent as Cosimo's harried steward went hurrying by them with a distracted nod, into the hall, a long roll of parchment clutched in his hand, taking inventory.

"What is afoot, my lady?"

"Much. If you love your land, your shire, your king, you will not let Cosimo sail off this night."

D'Aumercy's face bunched into furrows of confusion.

From inside the hall, Cosimo's voice could be heard, shouting to one of the servants. "Where is Lady Mistral? By Christ, bring her to me."

She turned away from Noil and stepped into the hall.

"Ah, Lady Mistral," Cosimo said. "We have bread and ale and fruits to break our fast, and I have news."

"News, my lord?"

He turned her with a skillful sweep of his fingers and sat her down on a cushioned seat before the dais table, and servants hurried up with trays of morning food. "My shipment has been located. We have begun the transfer already; by Vespers it should be complete, and we will be ready to go."

"How pleasing," she said quietly.

He angled his head around. "My lady. Are you well?"

She touched her head briefly. "I confess, I feel somewhat unwell. I am not certain I ought accompany you on horseback." She smiled apologetically, glad for the weeks of practice at deceit, for she required every bit of it now to smile in an apologetic and faintly affectionate way. "Perhaps a litter could be sent back for me, once all is in readiness?"

He was all chivalric indulgence. "Of course, my lady. I shall travel out, oversee the loading, and come back myself with the litter."

"No, surely you ought to stay with the ships. And truly, knowing you are there . . . it is an easeful thing, to know I have someone, finally, to oversee it all."

He smiled at her like a hawk, hard and slanting. He was skimming over his prey now, and it was running very slowly indeed. "Very good, my lady."

"Perhaps I might lie down," she suggested, and he began helping her to her feet, calling for a servant.

Sophia heard a scuff of boots near the hall entrance but when she looked up, whomever it had been was gone. A moment later a servant hurried in, pale-faced. "Sir," he said quietly. "A moment, if you will."

Cosimo looked at the man's face, and then turned smoothly to Sophia. "If you will excuse me, my lady?" He gestured to the servant. "Escort Lady Mistral to her rooms."

He disappeared through the door. The servant took hold of her supposedly weakened arm, but in truth, Sophia felt strong, hot, prepared. It was as if a fever were about to break, a storm about to clear, if only she could hold on a little longer.

Cosimo stepped back into the hall. His boot steps echoed hard off the gray stone. "My lady?"

She looked up sharply, for no reason at all feeling suddenly afraid.

Then Remy stepped out from behind Cosimo, and her hot, prepared heart from a moment ago dropped like a sheet of ice, shaving off into the cold pit of Remy the Black's eyes.

"Yes, sir," he said. "That is Sophia Silk."

Sixty-one

Sophia's body shook once, then she stood absolutely still. Her first urge, to run, seemed unwise and unproductive.

"You have surprised me deeply, Sophia," Cosimo said in a strangely contemplative voice.

But then, Cosimo was a strange man, enamored of greatness and boldness, but the twisted sort, like a forged chain or a vine up a wall. His grip was a hard band of iron, and beneath the calmness of his words, she felt the shaking, barely contained wrath.

"I did not expect such depths from you, Sophia. But I should have. You have ever been a surprise. First, of course, I was surprised when you ran, and took the ledger with you." He gave another soft laugh. "That was most surprising. But nothing to worry over." He crossed his arms. "But then Richard disappeared too. Traitor. He and your father, trying to make off with *my* goods."

Sophia wanted to run, to bite, kick, claw, but she was frozen, unable to look away from his eyes.

Cosimo kept his gaze pinned on her, and ran a fingertip down her cheek. She gasped a small breath and closed her eyes.

"Oh, that will not help you now, Sophia. Neither the tears,

nor closing your eyes, as you have done for so many years." His calm, almost consoling voice was more terrifying than outright anger, as he outlined her litany of sins against his treachery. "You, all those years with the ledger, and Richard." He clucked his tongue. "That is too bad. Of course, we found Richard. Yes, Remy found him. But all we could learn was that the information we needed was in the ledger. So simple, was it not? A small silk merchant, half bankrupt, alone in the world. We simply take what we want. How could she resist, now that we knew where to find her?"

He bent and continued in a fetid murmur, directly beside her ear. "Ah, but you were a greater challenge than that, Sophia. You ran *again*." His hand closed around the vulnerable bend of her elbow as he yanked her closer against his side. "And now, this elaborate ruse?" He shook his head sadly, and ran the tip of his smooth, tapered finger down her cheek. She jerked away, and his hand became a claw as it closed around the back of her neck and yanked her forward.

"In this, though, you are in luck, Sophia," he hissed into her ear. "For while Sophia Silk is of no more use to me, Lady Mistral is." He smiled and pulled her face up to his. His lean body pressed against hers. "If you serve me well, I might even be convinced to let you live awhile longer."

Panic clawed at her. She tore free and started to run, but he reached out and grabbed hold of her skirts, dragging her back toward him as Noil came through the door.

His face fell when he saw Sophia, the back of her skirts in Cosimo's fist. He took in the whiteness of her face, the tangles of hair coming loose from the netting. And Remy, in the background, smiling.

"Good God, what is the meaning of this?" he demanded.

Cosimo tightened his hold and pulled Sophia to his side. "Step away, Noil. 'Tis no matter of yours."

Noil stood frozen.

"Return to your home and your cold English winters. Lady Mistral and I are going south."

"No!" she cried out, but Cosimo covered her mouth with a wide, pressing palm and threw her against the wall so hard her head hit stone. He pressed close, his breath fetid and cloying.

"Do you wish to live?" he whispered.

Darkness enveloped their corner of the hall, but Sophia felt the eyes of everyone watching. The servants, Remy, Noil. And no one was going to intervene, no one was going to stop him, no one but Kier, and Kier was not here. Sophia was alone, and if she wished to live, she must *think*.

"Aye," she managed to say through the fingers Cosimo had pressed to her mouth.

"Then, you will be silent, and do as I bid."

"Aye," she whispered.

"If you move in a way I do not expect, I will kill you."

She nodded, her eyes wide. Her body was cold.

"Do not think anyone here will stop me," he said. "They may complain, but that will be after the fact. After I am gone from England, after you are dead. Do you hear me?"

She nodded.

He watched her for a long moment, his eyes inches away, his palm pressed over her mouth, then he slowly lowered his hand. "I have a small errand to attend, during which you will wait here," he said in a low voice. "Then we will go to your ship."

She nodded again, trembling from her toes to her chin.

"Take her to her room," he ordered his guards. "And lock the door."

She was dragged up the stone stairwell. Slowly, as if in a dream, she listened to the scrape and tromp of boots and her slippers echoing off the stone walls. Dimly, behind her, she heard a messenger arriving, saying something about a wagon ready for loading. Faintly she heard Cosimo demanding to know why the wagon had come *here,* when he bid it go to the cliffs. Faintly she heard his steward murmuring, something about the tide, then Cosimo shouting about the necessity of leaving England *tonight.*

The guard tossed her inside the room with less care than he would give a sack of wheat. She listened to the key turn as she let herself be locked inside. Then the sound of boot heels, tromping away.

She stared at the door for a long time, trying just to breathe.

She put the heels of her hands against her temples to hold in the cold steel edge of terror that threatened to swallow her whole, leaving Kier out there to be ambushed.

Then she tugged down on her tunic and marched to the door and hammered with the side of her fist. "I demand to see Cosimo."

Nothing.

"He will wish to see me!"

Nothing.

"I have something for him."

Nothing.

There was absolutely nothing, not even the very particular silence of a man holding himself motionless.

For an hour she stood there, listening to the buzz of a bailey breaking down for a move, to the rusted chains that creaked as the gates were lifted, then the thunder when they slammed shut again.

Slowly, softly, she tugged a pin out of her hair and bent to the lock.

COSIMO raged like an animal unleashed. He swung his arm, smashing cups off the table, then spun and kicked out, hitting a chair and then a servant. Candles from the dais table flickered wildly, casting eerie shadows across the stone walls.

Oh, the irony of this. Sophia Silk had ever been the bane of his existence. Slowly, unwittingly, she had pulled out all the bricks of his carefully constructed empire.

First, Kier. Turning on Cosimo, betraying him, rejecting him and his plan for her, wanting to wed her, to save her from them, the fool. Kier, with all his potential, falling to the charm of a woman. What a *waste.*

Then Darnly himself, so worried for his daughter that he'd said he would not be part of importing the gunnes for Cosimo.

Not for Cosimo, no. But for himself, aye. Himself and Richard.

Cosimo seethed as he stared straight head, seeing nothing. He felt his hand squeezing something, heard people talking to him, but nothing penetrated the thick weave of hostility he felt for Sophia Silk.

She'd taken Darnly, Richard, and worst of all, Kier. Sitting in the shadows doing nothing of note, without effort, she'd taken from him the men most central to his schemes.

And then this mayhem, this ruse of Lady Mistral.

And now, goddamn her, *she had his gunnes on her ship.*

A voice finally penetrated. Noil, shaking him, wresting his hand off the arm of a servant he'd apparently been squeezing. She was screaming, and Noil tore her free, grabbed Cosimo, shook him.

"Jesus, man, what is wrong?"

"Her," Cosmio snarled as he jerked his head up. "I will destroy her."

Noil looked around in astonishment. "God's blood, man, I do not know what is afoot—"

"No, you do not," Cosimo hissed.

"But if you are speaking of Lady Mistral, we can simply go to her factor! Becalm yourself."

Cosimo went still. "What factor?"

Noil threw up his hands. "The Irish one."

Sixty-two

From the top of the stairs that led down to the cellars from which the servant had dragged himself, Sophia heard a bellow of such rage boom through the windows of the castle that it reverberated in the dark night air. Everyone in the bailey froze.

Sophia quietly pulled the trapdoor shut behind her, her lantern already lit.

Carefully she made her way down the knobbly earthen stairs, the lantern held low to see the step in front of her. Her body was shaking, her blood pounding in hard, unsteady beats, urging her to fly down the stairs, care and lantern be damned. She forced herself to step slowly, watching where she went, one hand on the damp stone walls.

It seemed as if she descended for hours. Surely it wasn't that long, but the close air, the pressing walls, knowing the earth was pressing in on all sides with no escape but to climb down farther—it all forced her to stave off panic with a repeated chant.

"I will trust Kier."

The air was cool, and slowly, the scent of salt water began tingeing it. And then she heard the faint, distant sound of water. Somewhere, in the distance, was the sea.

The stairs leveled out and a faint, ambient light illuminated the large space she found herself in, a large rock-hewn chamber. Small scuttlings of animals whispered off the walls, and she heard a faint trickle of water. A miniature stream, running through the center of the cave. A few tunnels parted off on either side, and in the distance, a wide gaping hole, with blackness beyond, and a few faint pricks of light. The night sky.

In gratitude, she sank to her knees and gave brief, heartfelt thanks to God. Then she rose and began feeling her way along the walls. She would wait, as she'd promised Kier, but she would not wait back *here,* in the sunken, echoing depths of the cave, where bats would no doubt be returning before morning.

Treading gingerly, she felt her way, her fingers slipping over the damp walls, her feet occasionally stepping into the little creek. Slowly her eyes adjusted, but she still stumbled as she went, bumping into small outcroppings or rocks underfoot, and once, a huge, soft bundle of something that lay right in her path.

She tripped and fell to her knees. Rising, she touched whatever had tripped her. It was a large sack, filled with something, but soft. She pushed at it with her foot. The contents inside slid about a little, tipping it over. She looked up and saw dozens of others, lying about, all tied about the neck with thick twine, ready for transport.

A cold chill ripped through her. She doused her lantern and dropped to her knees. Caves were the domain of smugglers.

Her swift breath, the near sound of a trickling creek, and the distant sound of waves were all she could hear. No one was here now.

She looked back at the sacks. What could they be smuggling in these small, fat sacks filled with something that shifted like grains of wheat?

She touched the sack again and what looked like sparkling

white sand began flowing out in a tight stream, a miniature pyramid of it, right beside her boot.

Sand? No. Not sand. Salt? They were smuggling *salt*?

Who would smuggle salt?

She turned and looked at the walls, then ran her hands across the almost glowing white limestone walls.

"Saltpeter," she whispered.

Cosimo was mining saltpeter from the caves, for use in igniting his terrible weapons.

Slowly she got to her feet, her hands running up the walls as high as she could reach. Towering twenty feet above her, and down miles of offshoot tunnels, the limestone walls wept the stuff.

"Oh, dear Lord," she said. "He cannot."

"Oh, but I can."

She spun. Cosimo stood there, a handful of burly men behind him. Her heart dropped into a cold, frozen abyss. She turned to run, but it was no use. She stumbled and tripped over the rutted ground. His men surrounded her in seconds and propelled her back to Cosimo, who took hold of her arm.

"Now, Sophia, *now* you have surprised me deeply," he said, his voice dropped so low it was like that of a lover. He pulled her to him.

Cold chills of horror swept across her body. She swung her head away, fighting tears. The stones behind her head bit into her skin as he dragged her face back around again. "Let us go find Kier, shall we?"

She lifted her chin and spat in his face.

He stared in astonishment as her spittle slid down his cheek. Then he wrenched her forward so hard she stumbled, and when her knees hit the floor, he dragged her back up again.

"Let us see how deeply I can surprise you, Sophia."

Sixty-three

They arrived at Tomas Moneychanger's apartments riding the fore edge of the storm.

Sophia did not know whether to be pleased or terrified that they were let in so swiftly. She'd already been recognized as Sophia Darnly; what more harm could Tomas Moneychanger, her father's old banker, do to her? But if there was harm to be done, Sophia knew it would be done by someone, somehow, very soon.

Trust in Kier, trust in Kier. Only the chant made her legs move, her heart beat.

They were shown into the darkened house by silent servants. Tomas greeted them in a tunic that had clearly been thrown on hastily, his hair in the sort of wispy disarray that comes from having a nightcap summarily dragged off.

Despite the late hour, the moneychanger calmly invited Cosimo into his inner office chamber, as almost anyone would do if one of the largest clients available in western England showed up at one's doorstep, no matter how late at night.

Cosimo propelled Sophia into the room before him.

"What can I do for you?" Tomas asked as he shut the door. He was a tall, older man in a long tunic with piercing brown eyes. His beard was a mingling of gray and black wiry strands, over a cragged face that had seen much.

No one would ever suspect, without touching it, how soft the wiry hair was. Not unless they had sat on his lap as a child and fallen asleep there, once, twice, too many times to count.

When Papa had not been there, Tomas Moneychanger had been.

Until he hadn't been anymore.

Hangings brought out the crowds, for certes, but they lost you all your friends.

Cosimo, hand on Sophia's back, said, "I require the money I sent you, monies for a payment to a Mistral's factor."

"It arrived a few hours ago."

"I require its return."

Tomas looked at him, saying nothing.

"We also require all papers on hand for Mistral Company. Do we not, my lady?" He was all but snarling.

"We do," she said softly.

"Tonight?" Tomas said mildly. He had not yet looked her way.

"Yes, tonight."

"That is unusual."

Cosimo's face tightened. "And imperative. As well as your duty, to release the monies entrusted to you."

"They were entrusted to me for a man named Kier," Tomas corrected, and sat down behind his table. "The papers, of course, can be produced. I merely express surprise."

"You will give me that money," he hissed.

"I am his banker, not yours. I will not."

At the doorway, Tomas's burly guards tensed off the wall. Cosimo glared at them, then whipped back to the old money-changer. "The papers, then. Lady Mistral and I have urgent business this night."

Tomas's brown eyes finally slid to her, distant as a cloud, floating over her. She held her breath. Then he rose and bowed and said formally, "I have not had the pleasure, my lady. Greetings of the . . . night. Tomas Moneychanger at your service."

She gave a whispered reply of greeting.

He turned back to Cosimo. "Is there aught else, or shall I have the papers brought?"

"The papers. And send word to the king's men," he said. "I am calling the hue and cry."

Sophia's heart skipped a beat.

Tomas's eyebrows went up. It was as close as anything had come to disrupting his equilibrium.

"And after all this," the moneychanger murmured, waving his hand over the papers just signed. He picked them up and turned to set them on a table behind him. "What is the crime?"

"An outlaw has been seen boarding one of Lady Mistral's ships," Cosimo explained. Glee made his voice high-pitched, almost like a girl's.

Sophia's heart felt as if it had been launched from a trebuchet. It went flying through the cold empty space of her chest.

"Who?" Tomas asked. His voice came from a distance.

"De Grey," Cosimo answered, also from a distance. "I do not know if you recall him. For certes, the king will. Edward will be exceedingly gratified to imprison this traitor. He has no special privileges, either; I suppose it will be drawing and quartering for him."

Sophia's body convulsed. Her mind stopped, time stopped. She had a fleeting image of herself murdering Cosimo, killing him, stabbing him in the heart. In her mind's eye, she saw herself reaching for the short, sharp blade that was sitting atop Tomas's table, used for sharpening quills.

But it was not in her mind. She truly *was* reaching for the blade.

Cosimo saw it too. His hand grabbed hers before her fingers could close around the hilt. She cried out as he gripped her so tight she thought her bones might crack. Closing his fist over hers, he brought their entwined hands to his chest, for all the world like a lover's embrace.

Tomas turned. His gaze fell to the hand Cosimo held to his chest.

"Southern tempers," Cosimo explained tightly. "Do not worry yourself, Moneychanger; we are to be wed. And for this untimely interruption, double your usual fee. No, triple it." His words were light, but his eyes were fixed on the old moneychanger.

"I will have the message sent," Tomas replied evenly. "Perhaps the lady would like to remain here, if there is an outlaw on board one of her ships?"

"I think the lady will come with me. She is a bold sort, not afraid of danger. Oft she has walked directly into it, have you not, my lady?"

His fingers squeezed tighter.

Sophia lifted her chin and looked at Tomas. Just behind were the burly guards Tomas retained. He seemed disposed to bring them into this matter, despite Cosimo's desire to significantly increase the weight of his pouch.

But that would save her, not Kier.

Cosimo would at best be distracted by the maneuver. Slowed. Perhaps he would even suspect a trap. And then, he would not go to the ships.

She needed him to go to the ships.

She needed to trust Kier.

It was the only way to save him.

She looked at Tomas. "My thanks, Moneychanger, but I shall go. Master Cosimo speaks true: I am not afraid of what lies ahead."

Cosimo all but dragged her to the quay as low thunder rumbled overhead.

Sixty-four

The boards of Mistral's ship creaked as it rolled gently. No breath of air moved tonight. It was warm and close. One would never know the boiling storm that lay overhead, like a dragon crouched above its hoard.

"Are you certain he is coming?" Dragus asked.

His voice sailed through the hull of the ship's belly and echoed back. It was a carrack, the largest sailing ship, a warship, in fact, and the cargo Cosimo's men had loaded onto it a few hours ago was pushed up against the walls, barely sufficient to perform as ballast.

"He will come," Kier said from behind him, his voice eerie as it came out of the deep shadows of the ship's belly.

Dragus grunted. Beside him, his men made small motions. The creak of damp wood and leather and the clink of steel were the only other sounds. He stared into the blackness. "I suppose you think to sic Cosimo and me on one another, whilst you sit back and collect the spoils."

"Is that what you suppose?"

Dragus gave another grunt. It belied the tension in his belly. It had been a long time since he had waited in the darkness to attack. "But then, you would not want to miss out on all the excitement, would you, Kier?"

"I am here, am I not?"

The quiet liturgical conversation was unnerving. Dragus shifted his legs, stretched out his knees.

"Be assured, Irish, I will take you down as well, if it comes to that."

"Then, you had best hope it does not," came the reply.

Dragus laughed suddenly. It ricocheted across the vast space. "What think you Cosimo will say when he steps on board and finds both the two of us here?"

"'*I shall kill them both*'?" Kier suggested.

Dragus laughed again, more quietly.

They heard voices outside the ship, muted but growing louder, then the flat slap of oars in the water. Dragus got to his feet. Around him, his men clambered up as well. Kier shifted the sword to his other hand, wiped his sword hand across his tunic, and transferred it back again.

"He comes," Dragus whispered.

"Yes, he does," Kier's eerie voice drifted out of the back of the ship. Then he gave a low laugh.

Curse the Irish. There was *fae* in their blood.

Dragus faced the hatch.

Sixty-five

Cosimo climbed on, pushing Sophia ahead of him. The king's men followed out of three additional wherries, climbing silently aboard. On deck, they drew their swords.

The moonlight was gone. A swift, thin flash of lightning coursed high through the clouds, then a low rumble of thunder vibrated the deck beneath their boots.

"Come, they will be belowdecks," Cosimo whispered. "Let him reveal himself, then you can apprehend him." He turned to Sophia. "Come, Dame Silk. I am sure Kier will want to see you one last time."

He went first. If Kier had wanted to kill him outright, he'd passed up ample opportunities. No, clearly Kier wanted to destroy him. Take his money, the shipment of arms. Mayhap he even had aspirations to take over as head of the *commenda* himself, usurp Cosimo entirely.

It almost made him smile. No, it *did* make him smile. Kier was good, but not that good. Cosimo was going to destroy him.

Again.

He went down slowly into the hull of the ship. Behind him came Remy, then Sophia, so Kier would not see her, not right away. Would not know that his plot had failed utterly.

"Greetings, Kier," he called out, lifting a lantern but keeping it low, so it lit only his knees, not his heart. A misshapen circle of light bounced and stretched across the dirty deck below.

He stepped out onto the plank floor. Stepped to the side as his men began leaping down, and braced his boots.

"Kier, I am here."

Someone stepped out of the shadows. "So am I."

He reeled away, but there was nowhere to go but into the knees of the next man coming down the ladder. Dragus stepped into the elongated circle of light.

"Jesus God," Cosimo whispered. "You bastard."

Dragus smiled. "Aren't I?"

Behind him, Cosimo could see masses of dark, glinting shapes moving forward, like wraiths with blades.

"Up, up, retreat, fly," he cried.

His men started scrambling backward up the ladder, Cosimo almost climbing over them. They made it above deck. Behind them, Dragus's men were pouring out like rats from the sewer gutters, shouting, hollering, waving their swords.

Then, by the light of swaying torches, Dragus and his men spotted the king's men, a score's worth, in livery, their swords drawn.

The gutter rats froze.

"Goddamn, Kier," Dragus hissed.

Cosimo laughed. "The soldiers are mine. I called the hue and cry."

Another rip of lightning shuddered behind the clouds. Thunder growled.

Cosimo, breathing swiftly, laughed as he lumbered across the rolling ship toward Dragus. He tapped his chest brazenly. "Kier has resurrected a great many people this night, but truth . . . you and he in league together? *That* I did not expect.

Does he know what you did to him? Does he know about you and the torch?"

"I do," said a voice from behind.

Dragus cursed.

Cosimo spun.

Kier stepped onto the deck.

Behind him, on the eastern horizon, clouds roiled like misshapen bubbles of steam. The rising moon glowed between and through their blue-black gauze, illuminating them with a peculiar light.

Cosimo lifted his blade. "I am sorry to disappoint you, Kier, but once again, you aimed too far, too fast, too high."

"Did I?"

"You did. The ship is mine," he called out triumphantly.

"You signed the papers?"

"I did."

"And filled the hold with your goods?"

This made Cosimo falter slightly. "Your flailings are for naught, Kier. You are doomed."

"Am I?"

Cosimo flung out his arm toward the rear of the deck, where the king's men stood. "I have brought the king's men."

And then Kier did something strange. He smiled.

"Funny. So have I."

Sixty-six

The moment he sent messages to Cosimo and Dragus, Kier had ridden like a demon for King Edward's chancellor, John Langton. On the cusp of war with France, the Lord Chancellor of England was a busy and oft moving man. But previous correspondence had shown Langton to be extremely interested in staying in touch with an outlaw, even when dealing with emergency council meetings concerning the king of Scotland and the war with France.

Kier swung off his horse, threw the reins to a stable boy, and strode inside without pausing.

"Tell him Kier is here to see him."

The warden stared at him. "But, sir, he is not taking audiences."

"Tell him."

Something about the look on his face, or something in his voice perhaps, or maybe the way Kier could feel he was forcibly restraining himself from running the man through for simply standing in his way, made the man turn and go up the stairs.

He came back down and to his apparent surprise, but not Kier's, showed him into the presence of the Lord Chancellor of England.

John Langton looked up from the papers strewn across the table and sat back with a low laugh.

"I could not believe my ears. Now, I cannot believe my eyes," he said in a quiet, amused voice. "Are you mad, coming here?"

"Of course." Kier drew up a bench opposite him and sat. He ignored the two armed men standing in the back of the room, now between Kier and the door. Sometimes, one had to take chances. "I have something for you."

Chancellor smiled, a mixture of incredulity and curiosity. "So your missives have said for some months now. Dare I inquire?"

"Dare."

Langton's smile turned to a grin. "Kier, I received your messages. And allegations. Against Cosimo Endolte. Are you mad? Wait, we've established that."

"He is up to some mischief."

Langton threw down a sheaf of papers he'd been holding. "Of course he is up to mischief. That has never been the issue. *Proof* is the issue. Can you prove it? Of course you cannot."

"I can."

The chancellor's gaze trailed down Kier, came back up. He leaned to the side and rested the length of his finger on his dark beard and rubbed it a few times. "Tell me."

"I'll do better. I'll show you."

Langton laughed outright. "Kier, I have always admired you, and think you were wrongly accused of many doings."

"Sadly, my lord Chancellor, for I feel the compliment deeply, I was not wrongly accused. Upon a time, I was a very bad man."

"And now, you are not."

"In the matter of Cosimo, I speak true. In fact, I have been thinking seriously of reforming *in toto*."

The cleric-turned-chancellor shook his head. "A woman. You have a woman."

Kier shrugged. "Are you coming with me?"

Langton sat forward. "Kier. Have you any notion what is afoot? What devilry lies on Edward's fronts, south and north and west?"

"France, Scotland, and the deep blue sea."

"France, Scotland, and *Wales*," Langton corrected. "They rumble even now. And we have just declared war on France. And now, Balliol balks at providing troops for the endeavor. So tell me, what do you think Edward needs most, just now?"

"Better councilors."

Langton laughed, then quickly sobered. "Without one such as you, he will have to limp along. What Edward needs is support. Support of his nobles, of the merchants."

"What he needs is money."

Langton nodded placidly. "Just so; is that not what I said? Now, Kier, tell me how you think all the rich merchants of England would respond to the matter of their sovereign taking under lock and key one of his very own merchants, one of his largest, most supportive merchants? One of the merchants upon whom he can—and has—relied heavily to help turn the others his way in talking sessions of parliament? Tell me, Kier, how do you think that would be received?"

"Not well?" he guessed.

Langton only smiled this time. "Do you truly expect me to counsel the king that he storm the home of one of his leading merchants on a rumor from an outlaw?"

Kier leaned forward, an elbow on the table. "This is all very interesting, my lord, but time a-wastes. Tell me: Are you coming with me, or am I going to need to convince you?"

Langton laughed, apparently eternally amused by Kier. "Convince me."

"There are weapons."

Langton grew quiet. "What did you say?"

"Cosimo has contraband, a cache of weapons he is attempting to sail from England this night."

"Then, I will summon soldiers," Langton said warily.

Kier could draw the trajectory of how things would proceed from here the way you could trace the flight of an arrow before it has been released.

Langton would send troops. Cosimo would see the troops. Cosimo would leave. Had he Sophia in hand, he would either leave with her, or, flinging her aside, she would be trampled to death, figuratively if not literally.

Then a cargo hold full of gunnes would be sitting on Kier's ships.

Inside Sophia's silks.

And Cosimo would get away. Again. Kier would be imprisoned, killed. Sophia—

His heart could not venture into those depths.

The chancellor seemed to realize Kier was planning something. He got to his feet, nodded to the two guards. They came forward. They did not lay a hand on Kier, but they flanked him on either side as he rose to his feet as well.

"I told you it was a fool's mission to come to me, Kier," the chancellor said sadly. "Months ago when you first made contact. I told you to stay out of England."

"Not the typical response for a chancellor, declining the opportunity to catch an outlaw."

Langton's face was sober. "As I said, Kier, I have always seen a thing in you that bears watching, a thing for the good. But that does not mean I am a fool. Neither that I do not abide by my duties as chancellor of this realm." He sounded almost sad. Or no, angry. "Did you truly think I was going to let you walk out of here? The one man on whom I *do* have proof?"

Kier sighed. Before anyone could make a move, he'd drawn his sword and spun to the guards. The nearest moved to take a step out of range, but not before Kier rammed his elbow up and knocked him like a hammer on the side of the head. His eyes rolled back in his head and he dropped like a rock.

Kier turned and kicked out with his boot, catching the other in his knee as he scrambled for his sword. A swift blow to his head and he went down senseless beside his companion. Then Kier turned and put his blade up to the chancellor's neck.

"And you did not think I'd come all this way to be taken prisoner, did you?" he asked softly.

Langton smiled grimly at Kier. The blade was steady on his throat. "Pirate lord," he ground out.

"I am no lord, my lord."

"Not anymore."

"There are many ways in which I am nothing like my father. Let me show you one. Please." Kier gestured with the blade. "After you."

"I will see you swing."

"That will be up to you and your king."

Sixty-seven

When they arrived at the ship, the storm was almost ready to unleash. The winds had picked up, and the ship rocked. Kier hung several lanterns belowdecks, and they swayed with wild shadows as the chancellor stared at the gunnes that lay beneath the canvas tarps and chests Kier had thrown open.

"God in Heaven," the chancellor said on an exhale.

"Aye."

Kier sat on one of the bundled goods, his arms hanging loosely over his knees. He still held his sword, but by habit. He simply hadn't thought to sheathe it again. He shoved back his hair with his free hand and gestured to the rest of the hull. "All along there. All the way to the back."

The chancellor made his way into the deeper shadows, every so often muttering or cursing. He came aft again, rolling with the motion of the ship. "And now?"

"They will be here soon."

Langton looked around. "The plan?"

"Extinguish the lanterns. Then we wait. Dragus will come first, should that please the Crown."

Langton settled himself on a canvas sack. "Have you invited anyone else thought long dead to the festivities? Cnut, perhaps?"

"Just we criminals."

He was suddenly terribly weary. All he wanted to do was hold Sophia. Have her sit in his lap, run his fingers through her hair, hear her laugh at his stories. Langton hadn't laughed for close to an hour.

"And if they somehow succeed and sail away with this ship?" the chancellor asked.

Kier shrugged. "They will sink. Somewhere about mid-channel."

Langton was silent a moment. "You've scuttled the ship."

Kier nodded.

"Your own ship."

He shrugged. "I have others." He tilted his head up. "Mayhap 'twill go toward the king's goodwill, a man sinking his own ships for the good of the Crown."

Langton nodded. "I can almost ensure it will. Have you the urge to live as a free man in England once again?"

"No. But my wife might."

"Wife?"

Kier gestured with the sword he still held in his hand; no point in putting it away now. "Place yourself in the back, my lord, behind the bulwark. Wouldn't do for you to be killed."

Langton made his way back into the shadowy depths, pinching out lanterns as he went. "I would feel distinctly more comfortable if the king's men were here, Kier."

"I should not worry overly much, my lord," Kier said, turning to the ladder; a sudden thunder of boot steps sounded above. "Cosimo will be bringing them himself."

Sixty-eight

And so they stood on the deck of the Mistral ship now, three small armies and Kier on a sinking ship, all with their swords out. Drops of rain started to fall.

Cosimo stared in amazement as the Lord Chancellor stepped up on the deck behind Kier. So did the king's men in the company he had brought. They jerked straight, stared in astonishment through the wet world.

Sophia had been shoved down to her knees behind Cosimo. Remy stood beside her, his sword out, his other hand gripping her shoulder. "Hush, if you know what's good for you," he snarled softly.

The sound of Kier's calm voice drew her head up. He stood, absolutely still, soaking in rain, his hair dripping, his sword out, backlit by eerie, blue-black clouds, somehow conjuring the Lord Chancellor of England to rise up out of the darkened hull behind him.

He was a wizard. A magician. Sorcerer.

Even from behind, Sophia could feel Cosimo's clever mind, figuring how to turn the situation to his advantage. And chances were he would.

"Stand down," the chancellor called from the other end of the deck. "All of you." He turned and aimed his finger at the men across the deck, mostly criminals, who would likely not stand down on the command of a king's man. "Stand down," he said in a low, commanding voice. And for the moment, everyone did.

Cosimo stepped forward, one of the few on board who was not a convicted criminal. "My lord, I am gratified to see you here. I do not know upon what lies you have been summoned, but I assure you, we are aligned in our desire to see the guilty men apprehended. I myself called the hue and cry on de Grey." He waved to the captain of the guard summoned at his behest.

"You have your duty, though, sir. The hue and cry was called; you must respond and apprehend. Start by arresting the known outlaws, would you not agree, my lord Chancellor? And we have two rather than one," Cosimo added, glancing at Dragus's wet face derisively. "How fortunate. The rest can be sorted out later."

The captain stared at him, then slid his gaze to the chancellor.

"Are the goods upon this ship yours, Cosimo Endolte?" Langton asked in a low, clear voice.

Cosimo stepped forward slightly. "My lord, why do we dither over merchant shipments when an outlaw stands before us?"

The chancellor didn't move.

Cosimo turned to the captain. "Did not Tomas Moneychanger himself send the message, a bulwark of propriety and trust? What more reliable source can be found? De Grey is an outlaw, and he is here before us. Well," he said impatiently, when no one moved. "What were your instructions, Captain? The message from Moneychanger?"

The captain's wary eyes traveled over the group, then he said, "The message read: *Cosimo Endolte calls the hue and cry on the outlaw de Grey.*" His gaze swept to Cosimo as he finished. "*'Ware the herald of this cry. Not all the wolves are gone from England.*"

It took a moment for it to sink in. Then Langton turned to Cosimo. "Do you think he means you?"

"Goddamned *moneylenders*," Cosimo snarled. He looked at the chancellor. "My lord, you must heed—"

"I ask you again, on your word, Cosimo Endolte, do the goods on this ship belong to you?" the chancellor interrupted loudly.

"And I say again, loudly, my lord: no."

"Yes," said Kier quietly.

Cosimo closed his hand over his sword hilt. *"No."*

Kier whipped out a length of parchment from his tunic and handed it to the chancellor. By a swinging torch, Langton bent his head and examined it, shielding the paper from the spitting raindrops with his hand. Then he looked up.

"This is your signature, Cosimo. Giving orders to load this shipment."

"What of it?"

The chancellor met his eye. "I have seen the shipment. 'Tis contraband. 'Tis treason."

Cosimo's face contorted. He gave a deep, almost anguished cry, *"No!"*

Everything moved at once into motion and yet very slowly. The chancellor started calling orders, the soldiers started moving forward, and the storm overhead finally unleashed. With a crack of thunder, the clouds burst apart and the rains came pouring down.

It was the unspoken signal to attack.

The deck exploded with the crash of swords and shouting men. Swords met overhead, knives slashed from below, and everywhere men stumbled into one another. Rain washed down over the violence as it did a field of wheat, disinterested in what humans did with their time. Gusts of wind rolled the ship as sharp waves slapped against its hull. Slippery with blood and rain, the deck was almost icy, and men went down hard on their backs and hips, as others tripped over them. It would be a bloodbath.

So I am a fucking pirate after all, Kier thought with grim humor, wielding his sword as he leaped down into the fray.

COSIMO'S men closed ranks around him, and behind this protective steely wall Sophia, forgotten in the melee, saw Cosimo turn to make his escape. He staggered for the rail.

All the king's men were out of reach, fighting their way through. Only Sophia was back here with Cosimo as he flung a leg over the side and prepared to drop into the sea below, dotted with little wherries and skiffs that could row him away, into the darkness.

Escaping again.

Still on her knees, she lunged forward, into the backs of Cosimo's knees, knocking him to the ground. The king's captain was moving toward them, fighting his way relentlessly through the blockade, coming closer yet.

Flat on the deck, Cosimo reached for her, grabbed her, and pulled her to him as he hauled her to her feet, extracting a blade from his waist that he held at her throat.

"I have her," he bellowed over the din. He backed her up to the side of the ship, her body in front of his. "I have her! Stay yourselves."

Almost no one knew what "her" meant, but it was a sufficiently menacing and generally arresting statement, and slowly the hand-to-hand battles stilled as everyone turned to him.

Her back was pressed to him, the knife pressed to the front of her throat.

"I have her now," he said again.

STANDING at the chancellor's side, Kier felt the air punched out of his lungs.

"And who is she?" the chancellor called out. He was surrounded by a thicket of steel, encircled by swordsmen of the king who'd moved in to protect him.

"Sophia Darnly," Cosimo said loudly. "Daughter of Judge Roger Darnly. And it is among her goods you found that shipment."

"He lies," Kier murmured. The chancellor glanced at him.

Cosimo called out. "I am here as you, my lord Chancellor, to apprehend criminals."

Silence met this.

It seemed to embolden him. He kicked his knee into the back of Sophia's, making her stumble as he pushed them forward a step. They took another step like this, then another, and another, coming out farther into the tenuous light of madly swinging lanterns and drenching rain.

In the strange, shifting, pale light, Sophia appeared some half-human, half-siren creature, drenched red gown pasted to her figure, masses of thick hair falling over her shoulders, deep brown with fiery, brassy highlights caught by the flashes of lantern light. Her face was pale amid the darkness, her chin up.

Cosimo moved them another step, to the side this time. He was making his way toward the ladders.

Someone stepped toward them and he hauled Sophia to a halt, pressing the blade against the skin of her throat. A trickle of blood appeared.

Kier's heart became flesh once again, no longer steel and impenetrable. It was a terrible thing.

"I said, *Stand down,*" the chancellor shouted in cold command.

Everyone stilled but Cosimo. He dragged Sophia another step toward the ladders.

"Let me kill him," Kier murmured to the chancellor.

"Let me handle this," the chancellor replied. "How do you expect to kill him from here?"

"I'll think of something."

"You will not. Do you want her alive?"

"I'm partial to that outcome."

"Then bestill yourself."

Cosimo called out again. "This *contraband* of which you speak, my lord Chancellor, 'twas among the silks stamped with the image of the *BDS Silks* seal, yes? Behold, that is Batten Down Silks. That is Sophia Darnly, reincarnate."

He pushed them another step toward their exit.

"I too have long sought to unravel this mystery, my lord Chancellor. See, even unto coming here tonight, calling the hue and cry, bringing the king's men to unmask this treason. And so I have done: I present to you Kier, once known as de Grey, and Sophia Darnly, daughter of a traitor."

The ship was as silent as a ship could be in the middle of a storm.

Then a figure came up from the ladder, followed by a voice.

"That is not Sophia Darnly, my lord Chancellor. That is Lady Mistral."

And Edgard d'Aumercy, Lord Noil, stepped on board. Behind him, a great many soldiers.

The chancellor thought dimly that one could only hope the French did not decide to stage a preemptive strike tonight, since half the king's men were here in Last Fells, upon this sinking ship.

IT was over then, swiftly. The soldiers climbing on board were close enough to grab Cosimo, stunned for a split moment too long by the appearance and swift betrayal of his longtime associate.

Sophia was released. Kier stepped away from the chancellor

and started toward her. She ran for him, through the forty armed men who stood between them.

He caught her in his arms, drenched and hot and tearful. "Are you hurt?"

"No, no, are you?" she replied, kissing him between words.

"Of course not. I thought you were going to run," he murmured into her hair.

"I had every intention of it. I did, in fact. Which is when I found the saltpeter."

He pushed her away from him, hands firm on her arms. "You what?"

"In the caves below the palace."

He shook his head slowly in astonishment, then pulled her back into his arms and kissed her hair. "Did he hurt you?"

She shook her head. "He had not a chance; you'd sent word. He needed this shipment, and he wanted you. He called the hue and cry."

"I took a guess he might try coming with king's men to finish the job he failed at so miserably last time."

"No," she said, looking up at him through the rain. "Truly, Kier, he has a great admiration for you. It wasn't until he learned that I was not Mistral but Sophia Silk—"

"What?"

"—and that you were my factor—"

"Ah, bollocks," he muttered.

"That he wanted to destroy you."

He ran his hands down her arms. "How?"

She swallowed. "Remy the Black."

Kier's face was grim.

"And Edgard d'Aumercy, Lord Noil, was the one who revealed you, Kier, albeit unintentionally."

They saw d'Aumercy's head bobbing amid the others, speaking to the soldiers and the chancellor. Kier looked at it a moment, then turned back to Sophia. "I suppose I can find some small charity in my heart for him, since he may have just saved your life."

She wrapped her arms around his waist and pressed her cheek to his chest. "Your mercy is great."

It was going to take hours to manage the affairs here. There were the arrests, then offloading the evidence to the king's storage. The statements, the reports. By then the ship would be under water. So, once all the criminals were offloaded, Kier began to lead Sophia off as well. The chancellor came pushing his way toward them.

Kier swung around, extended his arm with Sophia on the end of it. "My lord Chancellor, I am pleased to introduce you to Lady Mistral."

Langton stopped short, still a few steps shy. He paused for a long moment, closed his eyes, turned his face up to the sky, said what appeared to be a brief prayer, then sent Kier a dour look and her a smiling one.

"My lady Mistral," he murmured. "We have much to discuss."

"Much," she agreed gravely. "I should like to ask that my factor accompany us, if that is agreeable."

"Your . . . factor?"

Kier smiled and bowed. Langton shook his head, but said only, "Of course, my lady. Perhaps we can talk more in my chambers, on dry land, before your ship takes on yet more water?"

Kier was already turning her toward the ladder.

Langton followed behind. "As tonight has comprised one shocking revelation after another, I will take the precaution of planning ahead where I may. I shall find it needful to stop at Tomas Moneychanger's to take his statement on the night's activities." He looked between Sophia and Kier. "I should like to know now if that will become a problem for . . . anyone?"

Sophia smiled. "Not for myself."

Langton swung his gaze to Kier. "And you?"

Kier gave the chancellor a pitying look. "Why must you always look for problems, my lord Chancellor?"

Langton lifted his eyebrows. "Is that what I am doing?"

Kier held Sophia's hand in his as she turned to climb down to the wherry below. "Aye. You should look instead toward the opportunity."

"And that is?"

"Mistral Company and the services it can provide to your king."

Langton turned to Kier. "*My* king? Not yours?"

Kier looked down at the top of Sophia's head. "All things are contingent."

"On?"

Kier nodded toward Sophia. "If she wants England, then, aye, *my* king." He turned and met Langton's gaze. "If he'll have me."

"He'll have you," the chancellor assured him. "I'll see to it."

Sophia looked up from the ladder, and smiled. "Then we shall be indebted, my lord."

"Yes," he agreed dryly. "Although one could say that rivers run two ways."

Sophia glanced at Kier, who lifted his eyebrows. She lifted hers in return, very delicately, and turned to the chancellor. "The king may be interested to know that Mistral Company is willing to offer the Crown some very good terms indeed."

Kier smiled faintly as she went on, speaking to the chancellor but looking back at Kier with her shining green eyes.

"This is a partnership with untold promise, my lord. He will not wish to pass it up."

Epilogue

Sophia lay on the gently rocking ship, in the softly warm air, looking up at the stars, like tiny pinpricks pushed through a vast blue silk. Every so often, a sweep of light washed across their bed, golden and bright, not the ancient Pharos, but a newer one. Not as great, but still, the ruins of the old one were in place, and they'd spent the day combing over them, Kier as her guide.

"You were right, Kier. 'Twas a marvel that had to be seen," she whispered.

They lay in the luxurious captain's chambers of Mistral's flagship, a testament to the power and prestige of Mistral Company, whose fortunes were solid and growing. Sought after by wise men in all lands for transport of their most precious goods, from bankers' coins to noblemen's heiresses, Mistral Company had become synonymous with safe, steadfast transport through perilous waters. Its ships were highly armed, its captains were highly recompensed, and its owners were honored by kings and counts. There were rumors of a pirate past, and outlawry, but no one mentioned it when they met with Lord and Lady Mistral. And after those meetings, no one much cared.

Kier sat at the table, reading over a batch of missives they had picked up from the factor of Mistral Company at one of its regular ports. There were dozens of them, and at night, after the meals were done, after the meetings were concluded, after everyone who wanted something from Mistral had gone home, and only the lord and lady, who wanted each other, were left, then he read to her.

Sometimes manuscripts, ofttimes contracts, occasionally business proposals that had been presented, and these past few days, as the Mediterranean stars whirled overhead and the lighthouse of Alexandria burned, he read the news from England.

"Remy and Cosimo have both been charged with the murder or abduction of Sophia Darnly," he reported. "Remy was the last man to report seeing her, and she has, apparently, vanished. No one has seen her since she left hurriedly, following the arrival of a threatening note, found in her home, demanding she deliver her silks or suffer great harm. They are adding it to the rest of the charges." He looked up. "I hope this Sophia woman is safe."

She smiled. "I hope not. It was a terrible life for her, hiding so in fear and shame, too frightened to have friends, alone, without the man she loved. No, I am sure she has gone to a better place. Or would, if her husband would but come to bed."

He set down the papers and blew out the oil lamp. The room was plunged into darkness but for the stars and the golden lighthouse. He lay down beside her.

"Did I not once tell you that you would do anything to see the Pharos?" he asked, pulling her to him.

"Yes, you did," she whispered, lifting her knee and sliding it across his stomach. She sat up, straddling him. "You have such good ideas."

"Such as leaving your life behind?" he suggested, pushing his hands into the hair that fell down around her shoulders.

She nodded, her eyes bright in the night. "Yes, that. I left my life for you, and you gave me yours. This company."

"This company is not my life, Sophia. You are."

She smiled and took his hand, laid it on her chest. "You are here, in me." She put her palm atop his chest, just over his heart. "And I am there, in you."

He smiled and cupped the side of her face with his free hand. "Even though I am an outlaw?"

She smiled. "Even though I am the daughter of a traitor?"

He pulled her down to his lips. "We'll leave the past to its own sorrows, lass. We've a life to live."

"Yes," she whispered as she kissed him. "Our life."

He could never have seen this coming, not from a thousand miles away, that his heart could be broken and burned then hammered into steel only to be made to beat again, for Sophia.

So, it had come to this, after all.

Turn the page

for a sneak peek

at Kris Kennedy's first sexy romance

Defiant

Now available from Pocket Books

One

England, June 1215

At first, it appeared they both wanted the same cock.

But as Jamie watched, he realized the slender woman wasn't after the rooster at all. And neither, of course, was he.

He settled back in the shadows cast by the knobbly stone buildings along Cheap Street as clouds piled up in the twilight sky. He'd only noted the rooster because a priest had been studying it, and Jamie was on the hunt for a priest. But this was simply some poor vicar studying a fowl. Neither was his quarry.

Nor were they the woman's. Her gaze slid away with disinterest.

On opposite sides of the street, they were each tucked into dirt-packed alleyways, eyeing up the celebrations in the market square. The evening mists floated in flat ribbons around people's ankles as they rushed through the darkening streets. Jamie tilted his head to keep the woman in sight. Hood drawn forward over her head, lantern extinguished, an almost motionless stance, all bespoke hunting.

He should know.

Taking swift inventory of the busy, heedless market square, he slipped out of his alley, making for hers. Skirting the block, he came up behind her as the fair stalls closed up, leaving room for the more ferocious nighttime entertainments to come.

"Found it yet?" he murmured.

She jumped a foot in the air and tripped sideways. Quickly, with a graceful movement, she righted herself, her slim hand lightly touching the wall, fingertips trembling.

All he could see were the dark things about her. Her eyebrows slanted low in suspicion, little black ink swipes on a wide, pale forehead, framed by the dark hood.

"I beg your pardon?" she said in a cool voice. But her hand had slid beneath her cape.

She had a weapon. How . . . worthy of note.

He tipped his head in the direction of the crowd. "Have you found yours yet?"

She looked utterly nonplussed as she took a step back and hit the wall. "My what, sir?" But even in the midst of her confusion, she continued to appraise the crowd, swift, sweeping surveys of it and everyone within. Just as he did when he was on the hunt.

"Your quarry. Who are you after?"

She turned her full attention to him. "I am shopping."

He leaned his shoulder against the far wall, a state of repose. *I'm not dangerous,* it said. Because she might be. "The bargains are awful back here. You'd be better served to actually speak with a merchant."

Her eyes were dark grayish, but for all that, highly forceful. She watched him for a long moment, then seemed to come to some decision. Her hand slid out of her cape and she turned back to the crowd.

"Perhaps I am fleeing my husband and his terrible temper," she said. "You should leave now."

"How terrible would his temper be?"

She punched a small fist into the air. "This terrible."

He turned and surveyed the crowd with her. "Shall I kill him for you?"

She gave a low murmur of laughter. The dark hood she had drawn over her head swooped in small waves beside her pale face. Long black tendrils of hair drifted out around her collarbone. "How chivalrous. Would you so easily? But then, I did not say I *was* fleeing a husband. Simply that I might be."

"Ah. What else might you be doing?"

"Perhaps stealing roosters."

Ah. She was cognizant, then, that anyone watching her would have thought she was intent on the rooster. In which case, he oughtn't to be feeling the urge to smile whatsoever. A woman who knew she was being watched was a dangerous woman.

He turned and peered into the square where Father Peter was rumored to be coming for an evening meet with an old friend, a rabbi. Jamie had explicit instructions, which began with "grab the thick-skulled priest" and ended with "bring him to me." A ruthless royal summons to a skilled illuminator and agitator who had declined previous invitations. But then, a great many people declined invitations from King John these days, because so often, those who accepted were never heard from again.

Jamie scanned the market. The rooster in question was in a cage atop a cage atop a cage, all filled with bantams trying to strut. The topmost one, drawing all the attention, was a magnificent creature.

"Green tail feathers?"

She nodded. He nodded along with her, as if it were common to skulk in alleys and discuss animal thievery. "Pretty. Do you steal often?"

"Do you?"

"All the time."

She turned her pale face to him, her gray eyes cool and searching. "You lie."

"Perhaps. Much like you."

Why did he care? She was neither quarry nor obstacle,

therefore outside his realm of interest. But something about her bespoke the need to attend.

One of her graceful dark eyebrows arched up ever so slightly. "Were we to be honest with one another? I did not realize this."

"No, you would not," he rejoined, looking back to the crowd. Still no sign of the priest. "You don't often inhabit such warrens as this. I, on the other hand, regularly cavort with bandits, thieves, and the like, who inhabit such crevices of humanity as this alley, so I know such things."

From the corner of his eye, he saw one of her cheekbones rise. She was smiling. "Ah. How convenient for me. A tutor." She was quiet. "Cavort? Do thieves cavort?"

"You should see them around a fire."

She laughed, a small thing. He was vaguely surprised to find probing the intent of this stranger so enjoyable. He rarely . . . enjoyed.

They were silent for a moment, an oddly companionable condition.

In front of them passed a veritable river of humanity in the throes of madness. Or rather, jubilation, but of the mad sort. Civil war was imminent. On streets from Dorset to York, there was the feel of celebration in the air, a diffuse revelry that made men drunk. And reckless. Come midnight, it would turn to violence. It always did. The realm was like a fever, bright and hectic, flush with sickness.

"I am certain I ought to be frightened of you," she said quietly.

"You most certainly ought," he said grimly.

"Stab you with a blade, perhaps."

He shifted his shoulder against the wall and looked down at her. "We needn't go that far."

"I knew this, of course," she mused in a cool, graceful voice. "That you were dangerous. When I first saw you."

"When was that? When I crept up behind you in an alley?"

Again, the lift of her cheekbones, like alabaster curving. "When I espied you across the road." She tilted her head slightly, indicating the church on the other side of the square.

Ah. She had good eyesight. He had a way of blending in, being unseen. It was part of what made him so successful. That and the ruthlessness.

"Did you now?" he murmured. "What gave me away? The alley, the skulking?"

She glanced over. "Your eyes."

"Ah."

"Your clothes."

He looked down in surprise.

"The manner in which you move."

He looked up and crossed his arms in silence, inviting her to continue. She obliged him.

"Your smell."

His arms fell. "My smell—?"

"Your smile," she said, turning away.

"Well, that is about everything," he said, anything to keep her talking, for she was growing more intriguing with each word that fell from her lips, although he wasn't certain it was for the usual reasons. The vital ones, the sort that kept a man quick or made him dead.

"How do I smell, precisely? As if I am a hungry bear, or as if I am coated in the blood of my victims?"

"As if you get what you want."

She had a good nose as well, then. Smart and comely. And lying.

She looked back at the crowds rushing past down the streets. "And what of you, sir? Are you intent on a rooster?"

"No."

"A whore?"

He snorted.

"A head of garlic, perhaps?"

He paused, then, on impulse, told the truth. "A priest."

She started ever so slightly, a small, repressed ripple that shook the trailing black ends of her hair, which is when he had his first suspicion things were about to go downhill to such a degree he might never climb back up again.

The startle could simply have been surprise at his offhand and irreverent reference to a man of God. Or that they were speaking at all. Or that she hadn't been assaulted yet, huddled in an alley with only a blade for protection.

But Jamie had spent three-quarters of his life determining when people were hiding something, and she most certainly was.

She pushed away from the wall. "I must go retrieve my cock."

He grinned. "You will be missed."

She smiled over her shoulder, that cool, stunning smile, and he knew why he'd dallied with her. "You will not be lonely long. The Watch will come for you soon, I am sure."

He laughed. "Take care," he said, a caution that came from some heretofore unknown crevasse inside, for he hadn't seen it coming and didn't even recognize it as it emerged.

Again that little smile, which wasn't cold, he realized. It was covert. Clandestine. Beautiful.

She slipped from their narrow refuge and out into the moving tide of bodies, heading directly toward the green-feathered cock, her worn black cape swaying as she floated across the muck. Then, just before she reached the cages, she veered sharply to the left—and his downhill ride began.

By the time Jamie found the rabbi's home where the priest and his dangerous manuscripts were said to be staying, the rabbi was gone. The priest was gone. The documents were gone. And the gray-eyed woman was gone.

King John would not be pleased.

Jamie went after her.

Might I intrude?"

The softly spoken words hauled him up midstride as he barreled down the street. He snapped his gaze down. It was she, the dark-eyed elf who'd stolen his quarry.

He battled off the urge to shake her, seeing as she was about to talk without such inducements. Still, it barely lessened the urge. "What?" He spit the word out. "Where is the priest?"

"Some terrible and smelly men have taken him."

This brought him up short. It must have shown. She nodded sympathetically. "Yes, indeed. I was equally shocked."

"Perhaps not to the same degree."

"No, perhaps not, because you are with two shocks, and I have only the one. But still, it is a terrible shock, is it not?"

"Terrible," he agreed grimly. "Are you saying you did not take the priest?"

"Indeed, no. But I would use your help to recover him."

How did one respond to this? "Would you?"

She looked at him sharply. "Did you think they were *your* men who have run away with Father Peter? They did not look like your men, so do not worry that you have been successful in stealing my priest."

"I was not worried," he said drily. He did not use men, in

general, but for his single friend and boon companion Ry, who was at present saddling horses for a ride they might not be taking this evening with a thick-skulled priest in hand. "Why do you say the men weren't mine?"

"Come," she said, tugging on his sleeve. "They went this way."

He followed her down the narrow alley, his senses alert, allowing she could be trusted this far, to skulk down another alley together without having her turn and bash his skull in.

"I know they are not your men," she answered as they hurried through the twisting cobbled and dirt pathways, "because these men had tiny eyes and looked mean and brutish. Your men would look dirty and dangerous."

He eyed the back of her hooded figure as it swayed down the alley. "Are you wooing me?"

"Woo? None of this 'woo.' I am telling you, these offensive men have the *curé*. We must retrieve him, like a sack of wheat."

"Why?"

She stopped at the edge of the alley just before it crossed over the High Street. It was busy, people everywhere, hurrying home. It wasn't so much that it was dark, but the storm clouds had brought an early end to the evening. Lanterns were lit, people heading home or out into the dark, windswept night. Awnings of shops were being lowered and locked, while abovestairs, shuttered windows flared into flickering orange strips, glowing with candlelight as families and friends gathered in warmth for food and company.

Jamie scorned this time of night.

His companion turned to him, her curving dark eyebrows now flattened in reprimand. "'Why?' What does this mean, your question 'Why?'"

Over the top of her head, Jamie spotted two men dragging an insentient priest—now wearing a cap atop his tonsured head—between their arms. Three additional men in leather armor thudded behind. The five of them turned sharply down a street that led only one place: the docks.

He tugged on his new companion's arm, stopping her forward progress, drawing her eye.

In fact, he had no intention of allowing her to remain conscious for much longer. But if he knocked her out now, people would notice. And if he let her go now, he suspected she would run after those men and trip them or bite them or something equally attention-getting, anything to stop them from escaping with "her priest." And attention was the last thing he wanted.

Three different parties were now interested in Father Peter. A street full of drunk revelers seemed an unnecessary addition.

So he would bide his time. Those men might be headed to the docks, but the way they spread out and began approaching different vessels told him they had no boat of their own. They would not gain berth on so much as a fishing wherry at this hour, not without going into the tavern nearest to the quay, the Red Cock, where the captains, oarsmen, and other waterborne flotsam congregated.

The men with Father Peter had just bypassed it. Whereas Jamie was standing right in front of it.

Eventually they would figure it out. So he would wait and, betting that all *five* of them would not come into the tavern together, priest slumped between their arms, he would use their splitting up to bring down whichever unfortunates were sent in, once they came back out again.

It was a plan. That it was also improvised and risky mattered naught: he'd spent his entire life being just that.

And he decided, looking down, he would use his bided time to learn what he could from the dark-cloaked waif before he rendered her at best not a nuisance, at worst, bound and gagged.

He tugged her back into the shadows. "It means I want an answer. Why do you want the priest? Who sent you for him?"

"Me?" She turned, her pale face angry. "Why do *those men* want him, that is the question of better asking."

"I do not care 'of better asking.' I want an answer."

She plowed forward as if he were dirt beneath her anger. "These squinty-eyes are carting him away right now. You ought to care. Why do *you* want him? Mayhap we can start there, on our want of answers. Indeed, this is the sort of question I like better."

"He has something I want."

His swift, honest reply brought her up short. She blinked, long lashes sweeping down over her eyes. He followed her glance down. The tips of battered shoes poked out from beneath the hem of her skirts. She looked up.

"Does he now?" Her pale cheeks were flushed. "That is no answer. Of course he has something you desire; why else seek him? It is why I am after him as well. He has many things I want. I am desperate for these things."

"What sorts of things?"

"Baubles. A length of scarlet. Contracts he was witness to. Trunks of coin and relics from the Holy Land."

She'd mentioned many things, none of which were the things Father Peter was being hunted for. Which was interesting, seeing as she'd named just about everything else under the sun.

"Tell yourself whatever brings you comfort," she finished, turning back to the High, "and let us be about it. Please. Or they shall escape."

A rumble of thunder rolled through the sky. He folded his fingers around the underside of her arm, just above her elbow.

"Mistress, I do not tell myself things to bring comfort." He pulled her so close she had to crane her neck to peer into his eyes. "I care naught for comfort, or for you. You may not realize this, but I've shown great restraint thus far. You lie to me, yet tell me nothing at all. That is difficult to do. I am impressed. And aggravated." Her breath came out a little shorter and faster. "So why not try a good lie, and we can 'be about it.'"

"He is my uncle," she said swiftly.

"Peter of London is your uncle," he echoed, incredulous.

"As much as."

"Which means not at all. Do you know what your 'uncle' has done?"

"Angered your king."

"Mightily."

He saw her swallow. "Everyone angers your silly, stupid king. Silly, dangerous, killing king. Perhaps those men are from the king himself," she added ominously.

"Perhaps," he said almost regretfully. "But 'ware, woman, for I am made of worse."

Color receded from her face like a tide going out. She jerked on her arm and he opened his fingers. She stumbled backward, breathing hard. The thoughts tumbling through her mind might as well have been carved on the swinging tavern sign above her head: *Danger. Run.*

Yet she'd known he was about danger when she enlisted his help. She might not have realized he was from King John—"silly, dangerous, killing king" was a grave understatement—but she knew he wasn't there to save her "uncle." She'd taken a chance and trusted him.

A regrettable error in judgment.

He placed a gloved hand on the door, just above her head, and pushed it open.

"Inside. Now."